SPIDER TRAP

ALSO BY BARRY MAILAND

SPIDER TRAP

A Brock and Kolla Mystery

BARRY MAITLAND

ST. MARTIN'S MINOTAUR
NEW YORK

SPIDER TRAP. Copyright © 2006 by Barry Maitland. All rights reserved. Printed in the United States of America. For information, address St. Martin's Press, 175 Fifth Avenue, New York, N.Y. 10010.

www.minotaurbooks.com

Library of Congress Cataloging-in-Publication Data

Maitland, Barry.
    Spider trap : a Brock and Kolla mystery / Barry Maitland.—1st. St. Martin's Minotaur pbk. ed.
        p. cm.
    ISBN-13: 978-0-312-38528-6
    ISBN-10: 0-312-38528-5
    1. Brock, David (Fictitious character)—Fiction. 2. Kolla, Kathy (Fictitious character)—Fiction. 3. Police—England—London—Fiction. 4. London (England)—Fiction. 5. West Indians—England—Fiction. I. Title.

PR9619.3.M2635 S65 2007
823'.914—dc22

                                                                2007021780

First published in Australia by Allen & Unwin

10 9 8 7 6 5 4 3 2

Good stories need good sources. For inspiration, information and wise counsel I am indebted to many, including Pauline Edwards and her moving memoir of growing up in Jamaica, *Trench Town*, Dai Harvard MP, Dr. Tim Lyons, Andrew Harrison, Scott Farrow and the crew at Southwark OCU, Lyn and Kirsten Tranter, Annette Barlow, Christa Munns and Ali Lavau, and especially my wife Margaret.

ONE

SNOW BEGAN TO FALL over the city late on Thursday night, in mean little flakes at first, but then in plump silent gobbets. By dawn, when the security guard reached the school at the end of Cockpit Lane, the whole of London lay under a muffling blanket of white. As he checked the gates and fences he noticed what looked like a fresh trail leading through the snow beside the empty garage building next door, as if something had been dragged from its rear door. He was very much inclined to ignore it, but the garage was technically part of the school premises, and there had been a spate of fires recently. Investigating, he found the door slightly ajar. Inside, his flashlight picked out two figures curled up together on the bare concrete floor. He took them for children and might have said they were asleep, except that it was far too cold to be lying like that without blankets. They didn't respond to his challenge, and he noticed a spatter of dark stains all around them on the floor. When he moved closer he made out plastic tape binding their wrists, and then the shocking wounds in the backs of their heads.

THE MURDERS IN COCKPIT Lane might have passed without much public notice except that the victims were two young girls, only sixteen years old, both shot through the head. They had also died in the constituency of Michael Grant, member of Parliament for Lambeth North and a vigorous campaigner against crime in his inner South London community. The youngest black member of the House of Commons, Grant was a charismatic speaker whose compelling voice and handsome face were soon all over the media, describing the Cockpit Lane girls, Dana and Dee-Ann, as only the latest in a long series of tragic victims of, as he put it, an evil alliance of poverty, drugs, guns, and criminal business interests operating in the district.

The press immediately dubbed the shootings a 'Yardie' massacre, despite police reservations about the use of the term, which implied the involvement of Jamaican immigrants. To the press it was Yardie because it was violent, guns and drugs were involved (crack cocaine was found in the girls' pockets), and both the victims and just about everyone else in the neighbourhood were of West Indian origin.

By late afternoon, media interest in the tragedy had risen to such a pitch that Scotland Yard announced the formation of a Major Inquiry Team, led by Detective Chief Inspector David Brock and officers from Homicide Command, together with local detectives. They would be supported by members of the Operation Trident squad, which had been established some years earlier to combat gun crime in London's black communities.

BEYOND THE HISSING RADIATORS, through the tall windows of the upstairs classroom, Adam Nightingale could see over the back wall of the school playground to the dazzling white wasteland beyond, across which the thin black lines of the railway tracks traced a sweeping curve. On seeing the snow, his mother's first words that morning had been, 'That's it, Adam, we're goin' back to Jamaica.' They wouldn't, of course. She always said that when it snowed, but he thought it was magic.

The class was unsettled, whispering and passing notes. When

they'd arrived for school that morning they'd been met by the sight of ambulances and police cars blocking the Lane. They'd stood in huddled groups, lit by the strobing lights, straining to catch the squawk of the police radios. Gradually a little information had rippled through the excited mob, just enough to breed rumours and questions. Were the girls from Camberwell Secondary? Had they been raped? Throughout the morning, classes had been distracted by the sirens and the helicopters. When the bell rang for their lunchbreak, they'd rushed out into the street, hung around the police barrier and pestered the cops asking questions in the Cockpit Lane street market and searching the alleyways and backyards.

There were many empty seats when school started again in the afternoon, and the teachers struggled against the mood of distracted restlessness. Adam felt the horrible excitement more than anyone. It ate away at him and made him feel almost physically ill. He had his own ideas about what had really happened, but as usual no one was interested in what he had to say. It was the guns that fascinated them most and there had been much technical discussion about Uzis and Mach 10s, Brownings and Glocks, but the others only scoffed when he offered his opinions. He felt as if he might literally explode with frustration at the familiar sense of insignificance, of being excluded.

Mr Pemberton was oblivious to it all. He was drawing a graph on the board, a sweeping curve just like that of the rail line. A parabola, he said. Nobody paid any attention.

The train tracks formed one curving side of a triangle of railway land bordered by the school wall and by the back fences of the warehouses along Mafeking Road. The walls and fences were too high to climb, and so this inaccessible little bit of wilderness in the middle of crowded inner London had become an island of mystery to the kids of Camberwell Secondary. There were stories of valuable things buried there, of stolen goods thrown from trains, and of strange animals in hidden lairs. Adam's mind often turned to these stories when he lay alone in bed at night, imagining himself a hero, penetrating the mysterious triangle and making a stupendous discovery.

Now the coppers were on the railway land, searching with sticks and metal detectors along the border against the school and garage where the girls were found. They must be looking for the killer's gun, Adam thought, possibly thrown over the back wall. The sight of them filled him with anguish. Suppose those probing sticks, those powerful detectors, found something else, another prize, the great prize—his prize.

A train came rumbling around the bend from the Elephant and Castle direction, giving off vivid flashes of blue light where snow had drifted across the electric rail. In his nightly imaginings Adam had worked out a way of getting onto the triangle, in theory. In theory, because it would mean approaching from the other side of the tracks, and stepping over the high voltage electric rails that powered the trains. Adam shivered at the thought of that, imagining the treasure hunter turned to a cinder in a flash of blue.

Pemberton droned on, writing a formula with his squeaky marker, $y = ax^2 + b$, as if he could reduce the curve of the tracks, smooth and dangerous, to a few symbols on a board. From his desk by the window, Adam peered through his glasses at the undulating white landscape and was almost sure that he could make out the faint lines of fox trails converging on a darker patch, far beyond where the coppers were searching. He'd first spotted the foxes during a boring English lesson last year. This morning they'd have woken to find the entrance to their hide covered in snow, and if they'd dug themselves out and gone foraging they'd have left tracks that a hunter could follow back to their den, and to the trophies they might have hidden there, including, perhaps, the great prize. With a little glow he imagined the kudos, the respect, that would come to anyone who retrieved it. In his head he traced each stage of the journey he must make to reach it, replaying the various difficulties and the final triumph. He also imagined the awful possibility that the coppers would find it first. By the time the maths lesson came to an end, Adam had reached a decision. He couldn't put it off. This was a day of awesome events. This time he would really have to do it.

He considered asking Jerry, his only real friend, to come along as a witness. But Jerry was clumsy, with big awkward feet. If you could picture anyone tripping over the third rail and going up in a ball of blue flame, it would be Jerry. So Adam decided to go alone, that afternoon, as soon as the cops had left.

When school finished Adam ignored the crowd gathering at the police tapes and hurried away down Cockpit Lane towards the footbridge over the railway. From up there he could see the straggling line of coppers leaving for the night, making their way back to the opening they'd made in the back fence to the Mafeking Road warehouses. Worried about the fading light, he ran across the bridge and up the lane on the other side until he found the gap he'd spotted in the fence, hidden now by a drift of snow so deep that he almost had to dig a tunnel to get to the other side. Then he was through, in forbidden territory, at the top of the railway embankment. Plunging down, he was shocked by the depth of the soft snow, up to his hips in places. When he reached the bottom he crouched for a while behind a clump of bushes, out of sight of a group of kids crossing on the footbridge. His heart was pounding, his body steaming inside his parka, his legs and feet soaking.

He waited until the footbridge was deserted and there was no sound of trains, then stood up straight and advanced across the ballast, stepping cleanly over the rails, one after the other. He was across. Exhilarated, he hurried on to the corner of the mysterious triangle, reaching it just in time to crouch at the bottom of the school wall as a train roared past. Ahead of him he could make out the hillock of snow he had seen from Mr Pemberton's classroom, beyond which lay the fox trails. He made for it, falling flat as the snow collapsed into the mounds of dead bracken beneath. His glasses fell off and he groped blindly in panic until he found them and hauled himself upright and struggled on. There were the trails—paw prints—plain as anything, and the sweep of an animal's tail across the surface. He reached the dark patch where they converged, and at first he was disappointed, seeing the snow scraped away to reveal a few twigs half-buried in the hard ground. But when he looked more closely he felt a rush of blood to his face. It wasn't what he'd been looking for, but in its way it was a treasure even more fantastic. He grabbed hold of it, wrenched it from the ground, and stuffed it into his jacket pocket.

He wanted to go on, but the light was fading fast and he was trembling now with the cold. He had his prize, something that none of them could ignore, and it was enough. He turned and laboured back along the furrow he'd made towards the place where he'd crossed the railway tracks. There he paused to listen, his glasses misting up on his nose, then stepped carefully across the first steel rail, then the second. As he was about to cross the third, he was startled by a man's shout from the footbridge overhead. 'Oi!' He froze for a moment, and his foot wavered over the electric rail, raised up on its ceramic insulators. A wet fold of cloth brushed its surface, and a great blow slammed Adam to the ground.

TWO

DETECTIVE SERGEANT KATHY KOLLA found herself standing next to a grizzled middle-aged man who looked as if he'd been up all night. He turned and spoke, interrupting himself with a hacking cough. 'Morning. Bob McCulloch, DS, Lambeth CID.'

'Hello, Bob. Kathy Kolla, DS, Serious Crime.'

'Ah, you're with Brock's mob, are you?'

'Yes. Know him?' They both glanced down to the far end of the bare space where Brock was standing with a group, his cropped white hair and beard making him look out of place among the sharp haircuts and suits of the younger men.

'Not personally. My gaffer mentioned that Brock worked on this patch at one time.'

'Did he? I didn't know that.' There wasn't really a lot that she did know about Brock's early career apart from the names of some of his more famous murder cases.

'Long ago. Got out as soon as he could, I dare say. Three chief inspectors.' Detective Sergeant McCulloch nodded towards the group. 'Overkill, wouldn't you say?'

'Pressure?' Kathy replied.

'Politics. Three wise monkeys. And guess who'll be left to clear up . . . This is my boss now.'

He fell silent as the local DCI called for their attention and introduced DCI Brock as senior investigating officer, and DCI Keith

Savage from the Operation Trident team, a tough-looking character who glowered at them. It was over twenty-four hours since the two girls had been found here—their bodies had long since been removed for post-mortem examination and the scene of crime team finished with their examination of the place.

The DCI went on to describe the layout of the building and what had been discovered so far.

'They were found lying together just here . . . Cause of death was a single gunshot to the head of each girl, probably nine millimetre. The pathologist says the girls took a beating before they were shot—there was bruising to their bodies and faces. No sign of sexual interference.'

Kathy was thumbing through the crime scene photos that were being passed around. The girls had been wearing almost identical dark jeans and tops, and grey dust was visible on their knees, as if they'd been made to kneel. From some angles they appeared peacefully asleep, from others brutally violated.

'It looks as if the killers took some precautions to clean up after themselves. Two shots were fired but no cartridges have been found. Door handles were wiped clean and something, possibly a bit of cardboard, has been used to sweep footprints from the floor as well as from the snow outside. Judging by the state of the snow and the pathologist's estimate we believe the time of death was between one and three on Friday morning.

'We don't know how long they'd been squatting in here. None of the neighbours admits to having been aware of them, but from the state of the place we think several days at least. There were empty cans of food and a carton of sour milk in that corner, and they had a kind of nest over there, with a single sleeping bag. There was no heating and, as you can imagine, it was very cold in here.

'Both girls had extensive records of delinquency and crime—shoplifting, housebreaking, bag-snatching, joy-riding in stolen cars. They worked together, most recently in the robbery of a newsagent in Hendon. Their usual territory was North London, the Harlesden area, and we don't know what they were doing south of the river. They were known drug users and we found a small quantity of crack cocaine in their pockets, along with a pipe. And that's about as much as we have at present. We're currently continuing with house-to-house interviews, of course.'

'We won't get anywhere with that,' McCulloch murmured to Kathy. 'See and blind, hear and deaf—they still stick to the old rule around here. They're scared witless by the Yardie boys, and who can blame them?'

'Ballistics?' Brock asked.

'One bullet fragmented, the other intact but mangled. They say it's uncertain they'll be able to make a match.'

The DCI seemed pleased to be handing the case over to Brock, who talked about the next stages, in which his own and DS Mc-Culloch's teams would focus on the murders, while the Trident group worked on their intelligence sources and the wider pattern, especially the Harlesden connection.

As they emerged from the garage, a faint morning sun was try-ing to break through the heavy snow clouds. In one direction Cockpit Lane wound towards the distant spire of a church, the narrow commercial street blocked to traffic for most of its length by market stalls around which activity was beginning to stir. In the other direction, beyond the school and its deserted playground, uniformed police were standing by a van parked at a bend in the road.

'Yours?' Kathy asked McCulloch, who was pulling on his gloves.

'Yes, and transport police most likely. You heard about our other little drama last night? One of the kids from the school took it into his stupid head to cross the railway tracks to get onto the wasteland that lies behind here. We think he saw us searching for the murder weapon and decided to do his own investigation. Trou-ble was he touched the live rail on his way over. He was lucky there was someone on the railway footbridge who saw him and phoned for help. Rush hour train services out of Blackfriars were disrupted for hours.'

'Did he survive?'

'Last I heard he was in a coma. The weird thing was that when they got him to hospital they found something very strange in his pocket.'

'What was that?'

McCulloch paused—for effect, Kathy thought. 'A human jaw-bone,' he said.

'What?'

'Yes. We've no idea where it came from. We're checking where he went down there. Want to take a look?'

They walked over to the group, some of whom were pulling on rubber boots. McCulloch spoke to one of them, and together they set off along the laneway leading to the footbridge. From the middle of the bridge they had a clear view down over the scene of the previous evening's drama where the snow, lightly dusted by another fall during the night, was churned up all over the area where Adam Nightingale had made his crossing.

'We think he came down the embankment over there,' the officer pointed, 'and got partway onto the wasteland. That's what we're looking at now.'

They saw two dark figures stooping over an area of trampled snow. One of them looked up and waved. A moment later the officer's radio crackled. He listened for a moment then turned to McCulloch. 'They think they've found something, Skip. Maybe you should see for yourself. You'll need boots.'

They got them from the van, then followed the uniformed man through the hole that the rescue team had cut in the fence and climbed down to the side of the tracks. They tramped along the edge of the ballast, breath steaming in the cold air, then turned into the waste ground along a path trampled in the snow. The two men ahead looked up and moved to make space for them to see what they'd found. At first Kathy thought it was just a piece of smooth grey stone buried among the debris of frozen leaves and earth. Then she made out a pattern of dark lines wriggling across its surface, very like the suture lines on the dome of an old skull.

McCulloch squatted down and swept loose material away, then stopped and sat back on his haunches. Two eye sockets stared up at them from the frozen ground.

'Well,' he grunted and brushed off another lump of dirt, exposing a small neat hole punched through the forehead.

'Well, well.' He looked at Kathy and said, 'Your boss'll love this.'

ACTUALLY IT WAS HARD to make out what Brock's reaction was to the find. He came straightaway to see for himself, and dismissed McCulloch's suggestion that they might hand it over to someone else to deal with. Instead, he arranged for DI Bren Gurney to come down from Queen Anne's Gate to take charge of the site, and insisted that Dr Mehta, the forensic pathologist working on the two murdered girls, should also deal with this case. 'Keeps things simple,' he said. 'Don't want anyone else under our feet.'

Kathy, meanwhile, made her way back along Cockpit Lane to the local police station, where McCulloch had arranged facilities for the investigation. As she came to the area closed off to traffic for the markets, she heard a loud throbbing bass rhythm behind her and turned to see an electric-blue Peugeot convertible approaching. The front window slid down, ragga music booming out, and a beefy brown arm followed, draped with a large assortment of gold jewellery. The hand formed itself into the shape of a pistol, aimed at a young man tending the first of the stalls, who gave a quick flash of bright white teeth before the car roared away down a side street.

The goods on sale in the market were cheap and cheerful, the kind of things that a poor neighbourhood most needed—children's shoes and clothes, toiletries, parkas, CDs, plastic buckets, cutlery, gloves, small electrical appliances. Almost all the customers were West Indian, the traders too, rubbing their hands and stamping their feet to keep warm as they spruiked their goods. As Kathy threaded through the crowded stalls she felt people looking at her. She wondered if they knew she was police, or if it was just the physical difference, her pale skin and blonde hair, an ashen northerner in a snowbound Caribbean market.

She took the right fork where Cockpit Lane divided in front of the church of St Barnabas, and after a couple of blocks came to the police station, where she made some phone calls and picked up a car. An hour later she was in North London, at the offices of the Youth Justice Board with whom Dana and Dee-Ann had been registered.

She was met by a male senior manager and a younger woman, who was a Youth Offending Teams caseworker. The man wasn't familiar with the murdered girls and Kathy suspected he was primarily there to protect his department from fallout. He told her that Dana and Dee-Ann had shared the same designated YOT manager, who was currently on maternity leave. Their deputising manager was also absent, on stress leave. Mandy, by his side, on secondment to the YOT from the National Probation Service, looked barely older than the two victims but had worked with them in the past and was, the man assured Kathy, very conversant with their cases.

The two spoke to each other in a professional private language that Kathy didn't altogether follow, full of acronyms and special meanings, and she had to ask them to elaborate so that she could take notes. It seemed that between them, Dana and Dee-Ann had pretty well covered the full gamut of custodial and noncustodial sentences, community orders and programs available to the courts. They'd been ASROd and OSAPd, undergone Anger Replacement Training and Personal Reduction in Substance Misuse counselling, been curfewed, locked up and paroled. After the last breach, Mandy explained, the YOT had recommended electronic tagging, but the magistrate had instead put them on the Think First program, from which they'd promptly absconded. They had been missing now for three weeks and an arrest order had been issued.

Satisfied that Kathy seemed sufficiently baffled, the man told her apologetically that he had other business to attend to, but said that Mandy could fill in the details. He made Kathy promise that if there were any residual issues she would email him immediately. After the door closed behind him, Mandy was silent for a moment, then she said, 'I've never seen him in here on a Saturday before. Do you fancy a cup of coffee?'

'I'm dying for one,' Kathy said.

'There's nothing in here, but there's a decent caf across the street.'

The place was bustling with shoppers taking a break.

'Nothing worked,' Mandy said.

'What was their background?'

'Oh, you know—abusive families, dysfunctional peer groups, disadvantaged neighbourhoods. They first met when they were fourteen, and they would say it was the first good thing that ever happened to either of them. Apart they were desperate, together they became like two different people, a bonded pair, almost a single personality. I hadn't come across anything quite like that before. For a while they might be docile, completely absorbed in each other's company, whispering secrets, but then they'd wind each other up, get into a kind of hysteria, and do crazy, stupid, dangerous things together. So then we decided to separate them, keep them apart. Dana immediately became violent and aggressive, while Dee-Ann went into decline, self-harming and then attempting suicide. So we gave up and put them back together again.

'They were totally infuriating, destructive apart, manic together, uncontrollable either way. But when they were together they could also be full of fun and life, good with the other kids. They loved music and dancing. I'm really sad at what happened to them.'

'Yes. Do you have any idea what they were doing south of the river?'

'That was the first thing I wondered when I heard. I looked through their files. All I could find was the address of a cousin of Dee-Ann's. I checked it on the map. It's quite close to Cockpit Lane.'

'Right.' Kathy noted the details. 'Any thoughts about who could have got so mad at them, to kill them like that?'

'What, apart from the whole of our department? They could get anyone mad without trying. And there were the drugs, of course. They took terrible risks.'

'Anything specific?'

'They did get in trouble with the local bad boys around here, I know. One time they came looking for the girls in their hostel, and the police had to be called. I wasn't involved, but it'll all be on the police files.'

THE WOMAN'S FACE WAS young, pretty and fearful, peering around the door. 'What is it you want?' she whispered, barely audible over the insistent blare of the TV inside the flat. Reluctantly she let Kathy in. A small boy on the sofa barely gave them a glance before returning his attention to the screen. He gave a sudden chuckle at the sound of a cartoon animal shrieking in pain. 'Come through,' the woman said, and led her into a tiny kitchen barely big enough to contain them. She closed the door against the din.

'You know why I'm here, don't you, Rosie?'

The young woman reached for a box of tissues and wiped her eyes. She nodded her head.

'I can arrange for someone to call, to talk to you, if you like. Were you very fond of Dee-Ann?'

Rosie stopped sniffing at that. She frowned and shook her head abruptly. 'No. I hadn't seen her since she was little. At first I was glad to see her again. I said they could stay for a while.'

'Did she say why she wanted to come down here?'

'I guessed . . . She didn't spell it out, but I guessed she'd got into trouble in Harlesden and wanted to keep out of somebody's way.'

'Any idea who?'

Rosie shook her head. 'I really didn't want to know.'

'Okay. So what happened?'

'She came with her friend, Dana. It was a bit crowded, but we got on all right at first. They were nice to Jaryd, my little boy, and we had a bit of a laugh. I took them down the club and we had a good time.'

'When was this?'

'Maybe two weeks ago?'

'And which club was that?'

'The JOS.'

'J-O-S?'

'The Jamaica Omnibus Service. That's just its name, in Cove Street. Anyway, they stayed here for a few days. Then one afternoon I came back from work and found them in the room there, all doped up. I knew what it was from the smell, and there was this dirty glass pipe on the floor. My Jaryd was sitting next to them, watching telly like now. I went ballistic. I said, You're smoking crack in my flat and my little boy is breathing it in! They just giggled. I was really mad. I grabbed their stuff and threw it out the window, then I kicked them both out. I couldn't have them here after that.'

'Did you see them again?'

'The next Saturday night, at the JOS. But I looked away. I didn't want to have anything to do with them.'

'Were they with anyone there?'

Rosie blinked. Her mouth opened, then closed again. It was the look of someone who had realised that the path she'd been following had taken her to a place she didn't want to be.

'I don't know.'

'Come on, Rosie. Just a name.'

'No, sorry.'

'You'd best tell me. I don't want to make things difficult for you, but we'll have to go to the station and get you to give a proper statement.'

Rosie just looked at her. 'Who'd take care of Jaryd?'

'We'll get someone to look after him while we talk.'

'No, I mean later. Who'll take care of him when I'm dead?'

Kathy looked at her carefully and saw that she meant it. 'Well, Rosie, the thing is, I won't go away without a name. There must have been other people there. One of them might talk to us.'

Rosie took a deep breath. 'I think I saw them talking to one of the band, George Murray.'

'Where can I find him?'

'He lives on Cockpit Lane with Winnie Wellington—everyone knows her. But don't tell him . . .'

'I won't say a word. Thank you.'

From the other room there came the sound of something falling over, with the unmistakeable thump of real life, rather than TV babble. Rosie jumped to her feet and Kathy left her to it.

SHE RETURNED TO HER car and put a call through to Brock, telling him what she'd learned. She heard him discussing it with someone else, McCulloch perhaps, repeating the names, then he came back on.

'Come and pick me up, Kathy,' he said. 'We'll visit George Murray together.'

She drove through the winding streets, congested now with Saturday traffic, and spotted Brock waiting at the kerb outside the police station, a big man in a long black coat around whom pedestrians were making a wide detour. 'Where are we going?' she asked.

'The far end of Cockpit Lane. Winnie Wellington, eh? Who would have guessed she'd still be around . . .' He seemed lost in thought, staring out of the window.

'You know her?'

'Oh yes. The Tinker Queen of Cockpit Lane. A character.'

'Bob McCulloch was telling me that you used to work here once.'

'Did he? How did he know that, I wonder?'

'He said his DCI told him.'

'Really? Well, yes, I did, ages ago. It feels odd coming back. Like meeting an old friend again after a very long time, trying to square what you see with what you remember. The place doesn't seem to have changed much, though.'

'Bob thought you must have got out as soon as you could.'

'No, it wasn't really like that. I came a sergeant and left an inspector, so I suppose it couldn't have been that bad.'

Maybe it'll rub off on me then, Kathy thought.

She turned into the Lane opposite the school. Parking was difficult with so many visitors to the market and she stopped on a double yellow line behind the police van near the railway footbridge.

'Bren should be here by now,' Brock said, as they went out onto the bridge to watch the activity below. They made him out talking to a group of scene of crime officers, while uniformed men in boots stood waiting nearby, stamping their feet in the snow.

'What do you think it is?' Kathy asked. 'If it wasn't for the hole in the forehead I'd have said it was ancient.'

'We won't know until Sundeep Mehta's had a look.'

'But in any case, it's nothing to do with Dana and Dee-Ann, surely?'

'If their killer did throw the gun onto that land, I want to know about it. The boy's still in a coma, apparently. I'd like to talk to him, find out what he thought he was doing. Maybe he saw something.'

They turned back to Cockpit Lane and made their way past the school towards the market, in full swing now, people cramming into the narrow aisle between the stalls. Brock pointed to an elderly woman at the first stall, her brown face crowned by a halo of fine grey crinkled hair.

'That's Winnie. She's been selling pots and pans here for years. She seemed old when I was here. I'm amazed she's still at it—and firing on all cylinders too, by the look of her.'

They watched as she called to passersby in a high, piercing voice, then turned to scold the same young man Kathy had seen at the stall earlier, who stood with head bowed, unhappily kicking at the metal frame. When Brock stopped in front of them the old lady abruptly cut off the angry flow and smiled sweetly at him.

'What can I do for you, sir? A nice set of stainless-steel pots for dat wife of yours?' She snatched up a frying pan and brandished it at him. 'You won't see prices like this in Woolworths, I can tell you.'

'I'm sure you're right. Winnie Wellington, isn't it?'

She lowered the pan and squinted first at Brock, then at Kathy, with fierce probing eyes. 'Are you Witnesses? Because we're good Catholics here . . .'

Brock shook his head and showed her his warrant card.

'Coppers? I wouldn't have thought dat—it's the beard, I s'pose. Coppers don't usually have beards. Well, there was one I remember, long ago. I used to tell him, if you want to get on you'd best cut off the beard. Dey don' want no Rastas in Scotland Yard.' Her face split in a laugh.

'I think that was me, Winnie. Twenty-odd years ago.'

'Is dat right? Oh my! But your beard is white now, like my hair. Are you taking this young lady down memory lane? Maybe she's your daughter?'

'We work together.'

'Another copper? Well, there's been some improvements in twenty years, at least.' She winked at Kathy, then her face became serious. 'I don't suppose I need to ask what brings you back to Cockpit Lane. Those poor girls?'

'That's right. We'd like to talk to both of you, Winnie.'

The lad at her side frowned and eased back, and for a moment Kathy thought he might bolt.

'It's Saturday market!' Winnie complained. 'My busiest day.'

'And this is murder. Let's go into the shop. It won't take long.'

She shrugged and had a word to the stallholder next to her, then led them towards the door of the shop behind her stall. The sign over the front window read WELLINGTON'S UTENSILS EST. 1930. Seeing Kathy look up at it Winnie said, 'I'm not that old. My daddy started the business in Trench Town, in Kingston, and then brought it here, and I took it over from him.'

'You've been here a long time, have you, Winnie?'

'We came over in 1948 on the *Empire Windrush*, the first boat-load from Jamaica.'

The front shop had every imaginable metal container stacked on the bare wooden floorboards, shelves and counter—shiny saucepans, galvanised laundry tubs, zinc washboards, colanders, hip baths, watering cans. They stood surrounded by them, like grey ghosts, as Winnie closed the door and said, 'Well, how can we help you?'

Brock handed them photographs of the two murdered girls, taken from their police records. Kathy saw George's sulky indifference falter for a second.

'This is dem, is it?' Winnie said. 'So young. Ah haven't seen dem before. You, George?'

'Dunno. I may have seen 'em around.'

'Where exactly?'

'I can't remember.'

'You play in a group at the JOS, don't you, George?' Kathy asked. He blinked. 'Yeah, so what?'

'George?' Winnie was peering at his face suspiciously. 'What do you know about this?'

'Nothin'. I don't know nothin'.'

Brock turned to Winnie. 'Are you two related?'

'No, George works for me on the stall, and rents a room upstairs. He's a good boy, Mr Brock.' She put out a hand to touch George's arm but he flinched and pulled away.

'Are you from around here, George?'

'Kensal Green.'

'Not far from Harlesden, where these two girls came from. You do know them, don't you?'

'I've seen 'em down the club, that's all,' he protested, 'but I don't know nothin' about them.'

'They liked your music, didn't they?' Kathy said.

'Yeah, they liked good music.'

'So who else did they meet there? Who bought their drinks?'

'I don't know. I've no idea.'

'George, you tell the truth now!' Winnie sounded alarmed.

'It is the truth!'

'Oh no it's not. I know when you tell me lies. I can read it on your face.'

Still George refused to say any more, so Brock said, 'I'd like to have a look at your room, George. Would that be all right with you?'

'No!' George yelped. 'It's not all right with me.'

'We can sit here and wait for a search warrant, but it would be a lot better if you did it voluntarily.'

'George!' Winnie admonished, and his shoulders sagged. He shook his head resignedly and said, 'You do what you want.'

'Thanks,' Brock said. 'Will you lead the way, Winnie? I'd like you to be present too.'

'Don't you worry,' the little woman said fiercely, heading around the end of the counter towards a flight of stairs at the back of the shop.

They climbed past the next floor and up to the attic, where George led the way into his room beneath the slope of the roof. A dormer window was cracked open, despite the cold. Winnie switched on an overhead light and Kathy looked around, surprised at the neatness. She thought that anyone conducting a sudden search of her flat would find it a good deal more untidy than this. There was a keyboard and some CDs and sound equipment on a table near the window, and posters and notices stuck to the walls. Some were printed and others handmade with felt pens on coloured paper, like mock-ups for the printer. On one of these she read:

War amongs' the rebels,
Madness, madness, war.

George saw her studying it and, when she caught his eye, he said truculently, 'Linton Kwesi Johnson, yeah?'

She turned her attention to other posters with various versions of the name Black Troika. 'Is that your group?'

He nodded. 'Yeah.'

Brock, meanwhile, had slipped on latex gloves and was making a rapid search of the corners of the room. At one point he pulled a small pouch of marijuana from behind a pile of CDs, glanced over at George, then put it back again.

'All right,' he said at last. 'We'll be on our way.'

Winnie said, 'You see? He's not a bad boy.' She seemed to have collected her thoughts as she went up to Brock. 'You let him go, Mr Brock. It's Saturday, I need him to run my stall. I'll tell you who's behind any trouble around here. Everybody knows.' She formed a contemptuous curl of her lip. 'It's Mister Teddy Vexx, dat's who it is.'

'Winnie!' George said sharply. 'She don't know what she's talkin' about.'

'What's Mr Vexx up to, Winnie?' Brock asked.

'Anythin' and everythin' crooked. You want to know about drugs?'

'Winnie!' George cried again, sounding in pain.

'You want to know about guns?'

'I didn't mention his name, okay?' George said desperately. 'You can't say I did.'

'Dat's all I'm goin' to say.' Winnie folded her arms. 'You've got the wrong boy here, Mr Brock. Mr Teddy Vexx is the one you want to speak to.'

They made their way back out to the street, and Brock thanked them for their cooperation, which Winnie, at least, graciously acknowledged.

As they tramped back to the car, Kathy's phone rang. She put it to her ear and heard a familiar voice. 'Kathy? It's Tom, Tom Reeves.'

She was startled to hear from him again, and stopped and turned quickly away from Brock, who carried on walking.

'Tom?'

'Hi.' She sensed him registering the caution in her voice. 'Bad time?'

'I'm at work. You're back?' The banal words seemed absurd.

'Yes. I'd like to catch up.'

She couldn't think what to say. Or rather she could think of too many things to say and so said nothing.

'Can I buy you dinner tonight?'

'Sorry,' she said. 'Not tonight.'

'Ah . . . Another time?'

She saw Brock reach their car up ahead. 'All right. Give me your number and I'll call you.' She didn't think she would, but she wrote it down anyway. 'Got to go now.' She hung up and took a deep breath before hurrying on to let Brock into the car, feeling the burn in her cheeks, though he seemed oblivious.

As they drove slowly back through the crowded streets, Kathy gazed out at the drab little brick terraces sliding past and tried to decide how she felt about DI Tom Reeves. How long had it been? Seven weeks, she calculated, since he had disappeared. They had met the previous October when she and Brock were working on the abduction of a child from Northcote Square in an artists' quarter of the East End. Tom had been on protection duties at that time, escorting a judge whose life had been threatened and who came regularly to a studio in the square to have his portrait painted. Their paths had crossed, and when the case was over Kathy and Tom had gone out a few times together. He knew the detective boyfriend of Kathy's friend Nicole Palmer, and they had made a foursome to a concert, and gone to Nicole's birthday party together. Tom was good company, widely read and witty, but Kathy was also aware of how skilled he was at avoiding giving away information about himself, something she put down to his being in Special Branch. She knew he was thirty-six, and divorced, and assumed from his accent that he was a Londoner—and that was almost all.

He had mentioned that he had no plans for Christmas, and Kathy had caught herself actually looking forward to the break for a change. Then one December day she'd found a message on her answering machine. Something had come up and he had to go away for a while. After a couple of attempts to reach him she'd stopped trying, because she'd been down this road before, with another Special Branch officer who had vanished in the same way. In that case she'd discovered later that they'd changed his name, his address and his phone number, and she'd assumed something similar had happened to Tom. She'd told herself that she should have known better, and got on with her life.

She swung the car through the security gates at the back of the police station and switched off the engine.

THREE

'TEDDY VEXX IS KNOWN to us,' DCI Savage said. 'He and another local, Jay Crocker, have been in Trident's sights for some time. I was going to mention him as a possibility.'

They were seated at tables arranged in a square in the centre of the large room they'd been given in the local police station. A couple of computers and phone lines had been rigged on a bench along one wall, and on the opposite side a borough street map and crime scene photographs had been pinned up.

'You know them, Bob?' Brock turned to DS McCulloch.

'Oh yes, we know them.' McCulloch nodded. 'They're both bad boys with plenty of form. Vexx is the big shot. He's connected with the JOS club in some way—part owner, I think. He owns other businesses, too.'

Savage was interested. 'What sort of businesses?'

'A laundrette on Cove Street that his mother runs, and a tyre yard and repair shop in the lane behind. We've long suspected him of selling drugs through the laundrette and recycling stolen cars through the repair shop, maybe a crack laboratory somewhere too, but never been able to get the evidence. He scares people. Nobody wants to talk about Teddy Vexx.'

'Hm.' Savage tapped his pen on the table in front of him, thinking. 'Sounds like he needs stirring up. Of course, we could be barking up the wrong tree. It looks as if the girls were on the run from people back in Harlesden, and the odds are those people finally caught up with them down here. Maybe they got Vexx's help, maybe not. Funny thing is, it doesn't have the feel of a Yardie killing.'

'How do you mean?'

'Your classic Yardie murder has a spontaneous feel, all sudden violence in the heat of the moment, even when it's been pre-planned. A drive-by shooting, a shotgun blast through a car window, a burst of fire in a crowded nightclub . . . This seems more drawn out and deliberate.'

'Hell,' McCulloch protested, 'the crack, the guns . . .'

'Yeah, I know. Maybe they were trying to get something from the girls before they killed them. Anyway, people are upset, they want to see some response and soon, and if we can use the opportunity to put pressure on some local bad lads, so much the better.'

They were making an effort at team building, Brock knew, getting to know each other, but their interests were very different. McCulloch would be under pressure to put a blanket over the spotlight of publicity that had been turned on their patch, while Savage was more concerned with broader things, networks and connections beyond the borough. And what was his own interest? To get out of here as soon as possible? He had been less than open with Kathy about his feelings for this place. Cockpit Lane. He had been startled by the intensity of the memories it evoked, powerful feelings he'd long ago locked up tight.

The phone rang and McCulloch reached for it. 'What, now?' He grimaced and covered the mouthpiece as he turned to Brock. 'Chief, Michael Grant, local Member of Parliament; he's downstairs, wants to say hello.'

Savage groaned.

'All right,' Brock said. 'I'll be interested to meet him. Can they bring him up?'

'Time for a sermon,' Savage said.

'You know him, Keith?'

25

'Only too well. He's a member of our Independent Advisory Group. He tells us how to do our jobs.'

McCulloch hurriedly tidied away the remains of their sandwiches. There was a knock at the door and a woman officer showed in the MP. Kathy recognised him from TV, his face lively and intelligent, dressed casually in jeans and a padded jacket.

'Keith!' he cried, advancing on Savage with outstretched hand.

'Michael, great to see you. Let me introduce you to some of the key people in our team. DCI Brock from Special Operations is our SIO, and his colleague DS Kathy Kolla. You may have met Bob McCulloch from local area command, and some of my colleagues from Trident.'

Grant shook their hands warmly.

'I was just telling them that you're an invaluable member of our Trident IAG.'

'He means I'm a pain in the bum,' Grant said with a smile. He looked around the room and said, 'So, where are the battle plans? I expected great charts with arrows and pincer movements, like the Battle of Stalingrad.'

'Ah, it's all done on computers now, Michael. Anyway, this is just our local outpost.'

'But this is a local problem, Keith. This is where the people are dying.' He turned to Brock, the bantering tone gone from his voice. 'Not always in as dramatic a fashion as Dana and Dee-Ann, perhaps. Usually it's an overdose among the dustbins in the back lane, choking on their own vomit, but they're dying all the same, more quietly, more anonymously, without attracting the attention of Special Operations.'

Kathy wasn't sure if he was being hostile or just challenging.

Grant went on. 'That's why we have to strike while people are focused on this local problem.'

'We shall strike,' Brock assured him, 'when we have the evidence. That's what we're concentrating on at present, Mr Grant. Don't worry, we'll find it.'

'I admire your confidence.' Grant held his gaze for a moment, assessing him.

'We've been discussing that very point,' Savage broke in. 'Seizing the moment. And we're also mindful that the central problem here is the same, whether it's these two girls or the anonymous body in the alley. It's drugs.'

'Actually the central problem isn't drugs,' Grant said. 'The central problem is greed. The drugs are only the means to an end. This is about the exploitation of the weak by the strong, of the poor by the greedy. Don't you forget that, Keith.' He held up an admonishing finger. 'Don't you come to me at the end of the day with a few miserable black junkies locked up in gaol and tell me you've done your job.'

'Point taken, Michael.'

'Well, I won't hold you up. Maybe next time I'll get to see the battle plans. Glad to meet you all. Good hunting.'

After the door closed behind him, Savage let out a deep sigh and murmured, 'That's what I meant about the sermon. We get it all the time.'

McCulloch snorted.

'Could you interpret for us, Keith?' Brock asked.

'Michael Grant believes that the drug trade in this area is controlled not by the Yardies or the home-grown black gangs, but by white organised criminals who use the black locals as cannon fodder. It makes him feel better. It isn't blacks shamefully fouling their own nest, it's the old story of whites brutally exploiting helpless blacks for economic gain.'

'And he's wrong?'

'We have found absolutely no basis for his belief.'

'Does he say who these whites are?'

'He has made allegations, yes.'

'Mind telling me?'

'Principally a family called Roach. They used to operate out of Cockpit Lane in the old days, had a bit of a reputation for hard

27

dealing and long firm fraud. They moved out a long time ago and became respectable, but Grant is convinced they've still got their grip on the place. Right, Bob? He must have bent your DCI's ear.'

'So I'm told.'

'It makes no sense,' Savage went on. 'What would be in it for the Jamaicans? They've got their own network of mules bringing the cocaine in, their own crack factories to process it, and their own dealers. That's how it works.'

'I know of the Roach family,' Brock said. 'They were very active around here years ago, but I haven't heard anything recently. You, Bob?'

McCulloch shook his head.

'All right,' Brock went on, 'let's deal with immediate things. What were those girls doing around here for the past two or three weeks? They must have left tracks.'

'The JOS club?'

'Yes. And if they were there on two consecutive Saturdays then tonight is the best time to talk to its patrons.'

'And that's in Cove Street too?' Savage said.

McCulloch nodded. 'Just up the street from the laundrette.'

'Why don't Bob and I go and take a look?' Savage suggested. 'You can give me a tour of the neighbourhood, Bob.'

Brock nodded and watched them go, rubbing the side of his beard thoughtfully, and said to Kathy, 'Too many speculations, too few facts.' Then, as if in response, his mobile rang. It was Dr Mehta, the forensic pathologist. Brock listened, then got to his feet. 'Come on, Sundeep wants to see us.'

DR MEHTA WAS STANDING BESIDE the stainless-steel table where his assistant was working on Dee-Ann's corpse, swiftly sewing the flaps of skin together again. Behind him, Dana lay on another table.

'You don't look happy, Sundeep,' Brock said.

'I'll tell you, Brock, I have a bad feeling about this one.' He looked down at the girl's face as the technician eased it back into position over her skull. 'There are bruises all over her, and look at her knees . . .'

They looked, the skin grazed and torn.

'I noticed that the knees of their jeans were caked with dust,' Kathy said.

'That's right. It looks as if they were made to crawl around.'

Kathy had never seen Dr Mehta so agitated about one of his 'clients,' as he sometimes called them. She had never previously seen him show any distress at all.

'I noticed traces of adhesive around their mouths, and two balled-up pieces of tape were found near them, the same tape as was used to tie their wrists, so I assume they were gagged at first, then at some point the gags were ripped off.' He went over to a side bench.

'Adhering to one of the pieces of tape I found this . . .'

He held up a test tube in which lay a single coiled black hair.

'It's not theirs. I also found traces of semen on the tape. I've taken swabs of both of their mouths and faces, but I think only one of them was assaulted. This one . . .' He pointed at Dee-Ann. 'He forced her to perform oral sex on him before he killed her, Brock. That's what I'm concluding.'

There was silence for a moment, then Brock said, 'Make sure, Sundeep. I want his DNA. As soon as you can.'

'Is there someone we should be looking to match it to?'

'Possibly. We should have his profile on record. I'll get it sent to you.'

'Oh,' Mehta called after them as they made to leave. 'I'm told you're interested in this.' He pointed to another table on which lay an assortment of grubby bones.

'The schoolboy's find?'

'That's it. The jaw belongs with the skull, all right.'

'Can you tell us anything?'

'Adult victim, single shot to the head, probably nine millimetre too, like the girls, but long, long ago. Lots of tests to do, but I'd

29

guess it's been there at least ten years. They're finding bits all the time. Maybe tell you more on Monday.'

'Many thanks.'

THEY RETURNED TO LAMBETH police station to find Savage and McCulloch sticking photographs on the wall. Others had been pinning up maps and aerial photographs of the area around Cockpit Lane and Cove Street. When Savage spoke he seemed enthusiastic.

'The tyre yard looks abandoned—' he pointed to photos of an archway formed from old truck tyres and a faded sign, PART WORN TYRES '—but the building behind has had a lot of recent work: razor ribbon along the eaves . . . security cameras . . . heavy steel doors. Whatever they're doing in there is obviously worth a heap of protection. This is the laundrette, a unit in a row of shops with flats above. And this is the house, two streets away, where Vexx lives with his mother.'

McCulloch pointed to a photo of Vexx himself. 'A mean-looking bastard, six-two, eighteen stone, a serious bodybuilder with a taste for violence.'

The picture reminded Kathy of the thick brown arm at the window of the blue Peugeot she'd seen cruising past Winnie Wellington's stall.

'What I'm thinking,' Savage came in, 'is that we could use an information-gathering exercise at the JOS club, as Brock suggested, as a cover to put people in position for a raid on Vexx's properties in the early hours tonight.'

There was a surprised silence, then several people began speaking at once. The difficulties of mounting an effective operation at such short notice bothered some, especially Savage's own Trident team, who were accustomed to working with detailed intelligence and painstaking planning.

'Will we get a warrant?' one asked, and Savage replied grimly, 'Leave that to me.'

'We need to place Vexx in the vicinity of the murders on that night,' someone else suggested. 'We need to find witnesses.'

'And by the time we've done that he'll know we're onto him,' Savage countered. 'We've got to move fast, hit hard.'

Brock spoke. 'There is another possibility,' he said, and told them what the pathologist had discovered. 'Dr Mehta should be able to tell us if we have a match by Monday,' Brock said. 'We should wait till we have that before we move on Vexx.'

'You heard Michael Grant, Brock,' Savage snapped back. 'People want action and Saturday night is the best time. As you said yourself, that's when the girls visited the JOS.'

He read the doubt on Brock's face and added, 'If you prefer, we can mount this as a separate Trident operation.'

Kathy caught a small smile on McCulloch's mouth and remembered his comment when she first met him, about politics.

Brock said firmly, 'No, we won't split our forces. If we do it, we do it together. Let's take a closer look.'

They gathered round and began to see how it might be done, and gradually it did begin to seem not only possible but even necessary, to break the silence surrounding Vexx's activities and the deaths of the two girls. Then McCulloch took a call from one of his detectives. There were no CCTV cameras in Cockpit Lane itself, but a traffic camera on the main road two hundred yards away had recorded a Peugeot registered to Vexx at twelve forty-eight a.m. on Friday morning.

'Gotcha,' said Savage.

Once the decision was taken, things happened quickly and comparatively smoothly. More people were drafted in, the team broken down into task groups, detailed maps and photos assembled and observers sent out to watch and report on the various locations. By evening, enough had been achieved for most people to be sent home for a few hours' break. Kathy caught the tube to Finchley Central and walked back through the cold streets to her flat, where she ran a bath and defrosted a lasagne from the freezer. Later, she looked out from her twelfth-floor window at

31

the headlights on the streets below, people heading for a Saturday night out, and remembered Tom Reeves. She didn't call, but watched TV for a while, then pulled on her coat, feeling the knot of anticipation in her stomach.

SHE JOINED THE OTHERS arriving at the station just before midnight, greeting each other with croaky murmurs and wintry coughs. After she'd changed into overalls and boots and a protective vest, she took her place in the queue to be issued with her Glock pistol. With mugs of tea and chocolate bars they assembled for their final briefing from Brock and Savage, both of them precise, confident and apparently relaxed. There had been no sign of activity at the tyre yard or repair shop, the laundrette had now closed for the night, and Vexx's mother was said to have watched TV alone in the living room of her house until ten, when she'd gone to bed. Vexx had been seen at the JOS club, where he usually spent his Saturday nights, but had just been reported as having left and gone home, unaccompanied.

Then they were making their way down to the transport, clustering into their groups—the rooftop snipers, the dog-handlers, the paramedics, the cameramen, the heavy squads laden with battering rams and bolt-cutters.

Kathy had been assigned to the house. The van drove down Cove Street, past the club booming with sound and activity, then the darkened laundrette, and turned into the back streets. It drew to a halt at the end of a narrow lane and two of the men got out. There was a large dog in the backyard, they knew, as in most of the yards around here and Kathy was glad she was going in through the front. As the van continued around the corner into the street they saw Vexx's Peugeot 307 standing at the kerb.

A sharp crack and the front door slammed inward. Kathy and two others ran upstairs. They found Vexx's mother asleep in bed in the front room, the other two bedrooms empty. The two men continued up to the attic floor while Kathy waited, tense, on the landing, pistol gripped in both hands, straining for telltale sounds. But she didn't hear the bathroom door open behind her, and gave a spasmic jump when a deep voice at her ear murmured, 'Lookin' for me, darlin'?'

She turned to see Mr Teddy Vexx, all 252 naked pounds of him, towering inches away, wearing nothing but an assortment of gold chains around his neck.

'Christ!' She hopped back, bringing up the gun.

'Yeah,' he said softly. 'The little girls were impressed too.'

As they led him downstairs to the van, now dressed, the first reports started coming in over the radio from the other sites, of empty rooms and deserted buildings. Even the dogs had disappeared.

FOUR

THE RETURNING TEAMS MADE no attempt to hide their frustration, banging their equipment and kicking their boots. The adrenaline was still fizzing and it had nowhere to go. Tools and weapons were locked away again with a niggling sense of anticlimax. Vexx, too, was locked away, the sole arrest of the night. Only the drug sniffer dogs, snuffling in the corners of the deserted repair shop behind the tyre yard, gave grounds for hope, and forensic teams had moved in.

There was nothing for the rest of them to do and they began to drift away. Kathy finished her paperwork for Vexx's arrest and handed it in to the duty inspector, feeling raw and edgy. She returned home and went to bed, but found it impossible to sleep.

She felt lousy the next morning. Thinking fresh air might help, she tramped out through the snow to buy a paper, then ordered toast and coffee in an empty café. Her mind flicked back to Vexx, stark naked, and his jibe about the girls. He'd been trying to rile her, of course, and he'd succeeded, though he wouldn't be smiling if they made the DNA match.

On impulse she dug out the cheque stub on which she'd written Tom Reeves's number and dialled it.

His voice was a mumble, as if he'd just woken up, and for a horrible moment she thought she must have caught him in bed with someone. Then he apologised and said he'd had a mouthful of muesli.

'I just wondered if you were free for lunch?' she said.

He seemed keen, and they arranged to meet at a pub they'd visited together once before, in Camden Town.

Her doubts eased a little when she saw him come through the door, tall, confident, the dark hair swept back, the warm smile in his eyes as he spotted her. He came over and kissed her cheek and asked how she was. She'd already finished one glass of wine and he went to the bar to fetch a bottle, then sat opposite her and began to make small talk in that easy voice of his. The wine helped a little, but she still felt edgy and out of kilter. Eventually he asked her what was wrong and she told him about the previous night. He listened intently, then nodded and said, 'Oh, Kathy, I understand.' She looked up from the beer mat she'd been scouring with her nail and saw that he really did—he'd been through similar things so many times himself—and a weight lifted from her. He asked some questions and they talked it through some more and when he went to pick up the food she did feel much better. She told herself it was the wine.

When he returned he said, 'Interesting, the Jamaican thing. Have you ever been there?'

'To Jamaica? No. You?'

He nodded. 'Yeah, with the Branch. In fact, I had thought about trying to get onto the Trident team. I've met one or two of them.'

'You still want to get out of Special Branch?'

'Yeah. This last thing was the end. And I'm really sorry about how it must have seemed to you, disappearing without notice, without explanation. I don't want to live like that, Kathy. I want out.'

'Was it bad?'

'Actually it was fairly routine. I think I was being tested, to see if I could go back to undercover duties, but it didn't work, not for me anyway.'

He had referred before to some problem he'd had on undercover operations, and how he'd been transferred to the Branch's A Squad, providing protection for VIPs. He'd also spoken of being at odds with his immediate superiors, who seemed to be blocking his requests to move elsewhere.

'Are you back at work now?' Kathy asked.

He rolled his eyes. 'I'm protecting a colonel and his wife, a mass-murderer by all accounts, attending a peace conference in London for a couple of weeks.'

The conversation returned to the things that were troubling Kathy, to her doubts about the case against Vexx, and to all the things she didn't understand about the two teenage girls. 'They were children, Tom. What had they done to provoke such cold-blooded violence?' she asked.

'As to the violence, Kathy,' Tom replied, 'you know how it is with the Yardies. All about territory and respect. You step on the wrong guy's foot in the wrong dance hall and you're dead. It sounds like someone was making an example of those two. Where are you holding Vexx?'

When she told him he pulled the newspaper out of his jacket pocket and said, 'I was reading something else about Cockpit Lane . . . Yes, here you go.'

Kathy scanned the brief report on the discovery of human remains near the site of the railway accident involving schoolboy Adam Nightingale, reported to be still in a medically induced coma.

'You seem to be in the thick of the action,' Tom said. 'I'm envious.'

Just then Kathy's phone beeped with a message from Brock, asking if she could come in. She checked her watch. 'I have to get back, Tom. Thanks for lunch. It was good to catch up again.' It sounded as if she was saying goodbye, and she saw him hesitate, then smile and say, 'Yes, great.' He kissed her on the cheek and added, 'We didn't have much time together. Shall we do it again?'

'Fine,' she said, and made for the door. The words 'time together' stuck in her mind. She thought they sounded quite good.

SHE BUMPED INTO BROCK pacing down the corridor of the station.

'Kathy, right. We've got him. Sundeep's made the match to Vexx's DNA.' He looked reinvigorated, and relieved perhaps, as if a gamble he didn't really expect to win had paid off.

'That was quick.'

'Yes. Sundeep's pulled out all the stops on this one. He has a daughter Dee-Ann's age, did you know?'

'Ah. No, I didn't.'

'Yes. We've been doing extra tests and Savage is about to interview Vexx now. So far he's said nothing, just talked to his brief. That's another story.'

Kathy found it hard to read his expression. 'Oh? What's the problem?'

'Come and see.'

She followed him to the video monitoring room where they took seats in front of a screen. When she focused on the picture she felt a small jolt as she recognised Vexx's lawyer. 'Martin Connell,' she said. 'I see what you mean.'

In a way, she owed the fact that she worked for Brock to Martin Connell, with whom she was having an affair when Brock had first taken an interest in her. It was the reason he had. Connell represented the wealthiest, the most celebrated, the most notorious of criminal clients. With Martin Connell on your side you knew that no defence weapon, however dubious or unscrupulous, would be overlooked. You also knew that when you were found not guilty, few would believe it was true, although they would wonder who your friends were.

He had put on a few pounds, she thought, due no doubt to many excellent meals with his beautiful wife, Lynne, and her father, retired Judge Willoughby, and their four talented children, now at university she supposed. The sheer foolishness of the affair pressed in on Kathy as she studied him, but also the emotional force of it, even after all this time—because for her, at least, it had been very serious indeed. She wondered if he still made use of his friend's flat, the one with the sleazy bedroom with the mirror on the ceiling.

He was engaging in some initial skirmishing with Savage, points of clarification and procedure. Vexx sat beside him, massive arms crossed, eyes hooded, gold cargo glinting beneath the lights. Finally Savage began the questions.

'Do you know this girl?' he asked, showing Vexx a picture of Dee-Ann. Vexx barely dipped his eyes to look at it. He gave a grunt.

'Please answer the question, Mr Vexx.'

'Chief Inspector, a point of accuracy, if you please,' Connell intervened. 'My client's correct name is Mr Teddy Vexx, as a single appellation. To call him Mr Vexx is a bit like me referring to you as Inspector Savage, rather than Chief Inspector Savage.'

Savage stared at him for a moment with a look of loathing that registered vividly even on the small screen. 'Thank you, Mr Connell.' He turned back to Vexx. 'Do you know this girl?'

Vexx shrugged. 'I don' know. I don' remember.'

'I'm talking about within the last seventy-two hours, Mr Teddy Vexx. Have you seen this girl within the past seventy-two hours?'

'No, I don' think so.'

'Please think very carefully. She was found dead early on Friday morning. Did you see her during Thursday night or Friday morning?'

Vexx shrugged and shook his head.

'Is that a no?'

'Yes, it's a no.'

'Then I wonder if you can explain how your semen was found in her mouth.'

Martin Connell, who had been pretending an interest in his paperwork, looked up at that, a quizzical arch to one eyebrow. Vexx remained impassive.

'How can you explain that, Mr Teddy Vexx?' Savage repeated.

There was silence, then Connell began to say something, but

Vexx held up a massive hand and he fell silent. They waited a moment, then Vexx said, 'Maybe I did see her—'

Connell broke in, 'Don't answer, Teddy. I'd like a break to consult with my client.'

But Vexx went on, 'I picked up a woman, maybe one or two o'clock on Friday morning. But I don' remember her face.'

'Teddy,' Connell tried to insist, but Vexx ignored him.

'Where was this?'

'Camberwell, I don' know exactly.'

'What happened?'

'She waved down my car. She wanted money for sex. I gave her a few quid an' she gave me a blow job. I didn't look at her face. She got out an' I drove away.' He turned to Martin Connell and shrugged, as if to say, What else can one do?

Savage stared at him for a moment. Then he said, 'Were there any witnesses?'

'Yes, my business associate, Mr Jay Crocker.'

'Mr Jay Crocker witnessed this?'

'That's right.'

'Where was he?'

'Why, in the car. He'll tell you.'

'We'll want to examine your car.'

'What's to examine? She was in the car, man, for maybe two minutes.'

They saw Savage take a deep breath. 'I want a complete account of your recent movements. Let's start with the night of Thursday last, the third of February . . .' But they heard the fading confidence in his voice.

Ten minutes later Brock shook his head with disgust and got to his feet. Kathy followed him out the door. As they walked silently back to the incident room, Brock's phone rang. He listened for a while then turned to Kathy. 'It's Bren. They've found the remains of a second body on the railway land. Let's take a look.'

BREN GURNEY, DRESSED IN a thick coat and green boots and a beanie pulled down over his ears, was waiting on Mafeking Road to show them the way. The scene of crime people had taken over one of the empty warehouses behind the railway waste ground and had dismantled the rear fence to provide access onto the site. There were half a dozen vehicles parked in front of the building and as they tramped down its side they had to step back against the wall to let a truck, laden with snow, drive out.

'One and a half acres,' Bren said as they emerged onto the waste ground. 'Biggest crime scene I've ever been involved with. They're trying to get more people.'

The area that Kathy and McCulloch had reached from the other direction was now unrecognisable, scraped clear of snow and bracken and gridded with tapes. Two tents had been erected, and across the rest of the site figures were bent shovelling snow and working with survey instruments.

Bren, a big, soft-spoken Cornishman who had been a part of Brock's team from the beginning, led them towards one of the tents. 'They found it around lunchtime, about five yards from the first. Similar situation, shallow grave formed in a natural hollow. We're calling them Alpha and Bravo for the time being.'

He lifted the flap and they stepped inside. Two people were working beneath lights in a pit in the ground, a third watching from the edge. This man came over and Bren introduced him as the crime scene manager from Forensic Services.

'This one's in very much the same condition as the first,' he said. 'The remains have been disturbed, possibly by animals, and we weren't sure initially if this was part of the same corpse, until we found the skull.'

Brock raised an eyebrow and the man nodded, pointing a finger at his own forehead. 'Yes, exactly the same, like an execution. Back of the skull fractured by the exit. No bullets found as yet. Most of the clothing has rotted away, but we're finding bits—a belt buckle, buttons, remains of a shoe.' He squinted out through the door of the tent. 'It'll be dark soon, and more snow is forecast, but we'll keep going as long as we can. The press have been sniffing around, of course.'

'No more indication of age, gender, race?'

The man shook his head. 'You'll have to talk to the pathologist. We certainly haven't found any kind of identification.'

Brock thanked him and they returned to the warehouse, where material brought in from the site was being processed through wire-mesh sieve trays set up on trestle legs, then recorded and stored in labelled plastic boxes. A large map of the site was pinned to the wall, with a numbered grid drawn over it.

'Sundeep's going to have his work cut out,' Bren said. 'He was here earlier, with two of his assistants.'

'What do we know about the schoolboy?'

'Adam Nightingale? Only child, lives with his mother, no father. A bit of a nerd, we're told. Chess and computer geek, hopeless at sports, just one friend we could find.'

Brock said, 'Weren't you supposed to be taking your girls some-where today, Bren?'

'Tobogganing. We did a bit this morning, then I got the call about the second body. It's okay.'

'Well, go back to them now. I'd better see if I can arrange a press conference here for noon tomorrow. Meanwhile, you can put your feet up. You too, Kathy.'

Bren offered Kathy a lift to the tube station, and along the way she told him about the raid on Teddy Vexx and his interview. Bren swore softly. 'There's got to be some forensic evidence to put Vexx in the building with the girls, surely?'

'That's what we're banking on now,' she said. Suddenly she felt overwhelmingly tired. Bren's car was warm, and there was an in-definable smell of something she associated with childhood. What was it? Some kind of soap? Shampoo? With a sigh she closed her eyes and allowed herself to imagine, for just one self-indulgent moment, that she was a little girl again, like one of Bren's, in a warm safe world free of guns, drugs, oral rapists and Mr Teddy Vexx.

She woke with a start and saw a familiar row of shops rush past the window. 'Hang on,' she said. 'This is Finchley.'

'You were out for the count,' Bren said. 'Couldn't very well turf you out in the snow. You'll be home soon.'

'You didn't need to do that.'

'You looked all-in.'

'Christ, Bren, I'm not one of your little girls.'

He smiled. 'No, but we all need a ride home from time to time, Kathy. Even you.'

He pulled into the forecourt of her block. 'See you tomorrow.'

'Yeah, thanks. Give the girls my love. Tell them they're lucky to have such a nice dad.'

Bren waved her away, embarrassed, and put the car into gear.

EVERYONE AT THE STATION seemed fraught, Brock thought. He desperately wanted to soak in a bath with a big glass of whisky, but there were things to do first. Keith Savage was at his desk, and he didn't need to say anything for Brock to see that it had gone badly. 'No luck?' he asked.

'Forensics haven't come up with anything. I had to let him go.' Savage cupped his hands to his face and rubbed. 'Maybe the bastard's telling the truth.'

'I don't think so. He murdered those girls, all right.'

'Maybe. You think I pushed for the raids too soon?'

Brock shrugged. 'Wouldn't have made any difference. It could have been a brilliant success.'

'But it wasn't. I let our glamour Member of Parliament push me into it. We should have staked out Vexx and found out everything about him before we moved.'

'There's still plenty we can do—his associates, phone records, financial dealings . . .'

'Yeah, but you know, I think I was right the first time. I think the girls were killed because of something that happened back in Harlesden. Vexx may have lent a hand, some local muscle. And

42

you know what? I think he knew we were coming for him last night.'

'You think so?'

'Sure of it. I think he and his poncy lawyer put on a performance for us. They had it all worked out between them beforehand.'

'Any idea how?'

'This place . . .' Savage spread his hands. 'No security. Anyway, what's this I hear about another old corpse on the railway land?'

Brock told him about the discovery of the second body. Savage eased back in his chair and said, 'McCulloch told me you were interested in that, but I don't understand why. I mean, Mr Teddy Vexx would have been in nappies when those bodies were buried, yes?'

'Probably. I'm just curious. Anyway, I thought it would be better if we handled it ourselves rather than have another crew tripping over us.'

Savage studied him thoughtfully. 'McCulloch also told me you were in CID here some time ago. These wouldn't be skeletons in *your* closet, would they?'

Brock gave him an enigmatic smile. 'You never know. I thought I'd arrange a press conference on the site at noon tomorrow.'

'To be honest, I'm not interested. Last year we investigated over fifty shooting murders. The discovery of a couple of ancient skeletons with holes in their heads doesn't rate. But you go ahead. I'm going home for a drink and a hot meal. You want a lift anywhere?'

Brock thanked him but declined the offer. Instead, he phoned for a cab to take him across the river to his office in the Scotland Yard annexe in Queen Anne's Gate. The place was deserted and in darkness as he tapped in his security code at the door and made his way up to his room. He settled at his desk and switched on his computer, checked his emails, sent several of his own, then keyed in access to the Police National Computer database.

He'd had one of McCulloch's detectives checking incidents reported in Lambeth Borough during the previous three weeks for any that might have involved the two girls. He'd come up with a couple of housebreakings and a bag-snatch that were possibles, but they didn't suggest a motive for murder. He went through the Lambeth listings once again, finding nothing else. Then it occurred to him that Cockpit Lane wasn't far from the boundary with the neighbouring Borough of Southwark, and he tried that. It wasn't long before a name leapt off the screen at him. He stared at it, feeling a tightness in his chest, then tapped a key and read the report.

On the previous Monday, January the thirty-first, just four days before the girls died, a woman had had her car hijacked by a pair of black youths outside a house she was visiting in Camberwell. She had been thrown to the ground in the struggle and her injuries were sufficient for her to be taken to Maudsley Hospital, from which she was discharged later the same day. The woman's name was Adonia Roach.

Brock reached into the bottom drawer of his desk and took out a bottle of Scotch, from which he poured himself a sizeable measure, and read the entry again. Adonia, he thought, placing her: wife of Ivor Roach, accountant and Spider's second son.

He returned to the menu and entered the name Roach, selecting four names in turn: Edward, nickname 'Spider', now aged seventy-eight, and his three sons: Mark, fifty-four; Ivor, fifty-two; and Richard, fifty.

'So old,' he murmured to himself, remembering their youthful selves. Their criminal convictions were almost all familiar to him, petering out sixteen years ago with a substantial fine for tax fraud. Their old addresses near Cockpit Lane were listed, as well as new ones. They were still living close together it seemed, some eight miles to the east, in the suburb of Shooters Hill.

FIVE

THE FOLLOWING MORNING, KATHY picked up the constable she'd contacted at Peckham. Brock had been very specific in his instructions when he'd briefed her. This was to be an innocuous follow-up visit, the PC was to take the lead, and, above all, Brock's name was not to be mentioned.

The threatened bad weather hadn't materialised and sunlight glittered off the snow on Blackheath as they took the Dover road east. The constable was a cheerful young Asian woman called Mahreen, who chatted about her family and friends and seemed delighted by the change of routine. She had attended the original incident and thought Mrs Roach would remember her, although she'd been very shaken up. At least she'd sounded cooperative over the phone.

They turned off the main road at the sign for Shooters Hill and Mahreen map-read them through quiet suburban streets until they came to the entrance to a golf club. Beyond this the street became a private lane leading only to a set of tall wrought-iron gates and a sign announcing THE GLEBE.

Kathy drew to a stop. She took in the camera mounted on the high perimeter brick wall and the security panel on the buttress beside the gate.

'I'll have fries with mine,' Mahreen said with a laugh. Kathy pressed one of four buttons labelled 'Roach,' selecting 'I. Roach,' and said who they were. A tinny voice told them to drive to the second house on the left and the gates swung open.

The houses, in their mellow brick and dark timber, looked old at first glance, but only one, the first on the right, really was, Kathy guessed. It would originally have been the glebe house or parsonage belonging to the church whose spire they could see beyond the trees. The others, with their diamond-pane windows and classically columned porches, had the air of overblown reproductions. They sat around a large garden, brooding over the tennis court and tarpaulin-covered swimming pool laid out in the centre. Kathy followed the encircling drive, tyres crunching on the icy gravel, towards the woman who stood in the doorway of the far house, watching them approach.

'That's not her,' Mahreen said, and Kathy saw that it was a much younger woman waiting for them, in her twenties. She had large attractive dark eyes, thick black hair and a golden complexion, as if she'd just stepped off a hot Mediterranean beach.

She shook their hands, unsmiling. 'I'm Magdalen Roach.' She spoke rapidly. 'My mother's waiting for you inside. She tries to pretend that she's all right, but she isn't. The doctor's still very worried about her head and she's taking a lot of painkillers. It would be better if you didn't bother her.'

'Oh, we do understand, Magdalen,' Mahreen said, all calm concern. 'Don't you worry, we won't distress your mum. This is Kathy, she's a detective. A couple of minutes and we'll be on our way.'

Magdalen reluctantly led them into an expansive living room, dominated by an oversized gold and crystal chandelier, beneath which a fuller, middle-aged version of the daughter sat in a huge leather sofa. Adonia Roach had the thick black hair and dark good looks of her Greek family, and still carried the slightest trace of accent in her voice. She was carefully groomed, dressed in the finest cashmere, against which the heavy bruising on one side of her face and the bandage strapping her left hand and arm struck a discordant note.

'Please excuse me not getting up to welcome you,' she said. 'My hip is still quite painful. Will you have coffee?' She looked up at her daughter, who nodded and left. 'You really didn't need to come all this way just to see how I was.'

'It's part of our community outreach policy, Mrs Roach,' Mahreen explained enthusiastically. 'Support for victims of crime. And of course, there's always a chance that you might have remembered something else now that you've had a little time to recover from the initial shock.'

'Oh, I've done my best to put it out of my mind. Being thrown to the ground like that . . .' She gave a little start at the sound of a jarring crack of crockery from another room.

'Terrible.'

'Yes, the shock . . . It all happened so fast. I suppose they must have been waiting for me to come out to the car, but I didn't see them until they snatched the keys out of my hand. Then the other one grabbed my bag and it caught on my arm and they just swung me around and I fell . . . Well, you know.'

'You were visiting your mother, you said?'

'Yes, she's a widow, lived in Camberwell for years.'

'And do you visit her regularly?'

'Every week.'

'At the same time?'

'Usually Monday. It doesn't clash with her other activities. She keeps herself very busy.'

'And you said the two who attacked you were slightly built?'

'Yes, thin. One was a bit taller than me, the other about my height, but that was only an impression . . . I could be wrong, with the scarves over their faces and their hoods and baggy jeans, I don't know.'

'But definitely West Indian?'

'Yes, yes. Not . . .' She glanced cautiously at Mahreen. '. . . Asian.'

'We've got some photos for you to look at, Mrs Roach,' Mahreen purred, and Kathy handed her the sheaf of pictures she'd brought.

'Too thick-set . . . too . . . oh, I don't know.'

47

'Try covering the lower part of their faces.'

'Yes, but . . . This one's a girl, and this one. It wasn't a girl.'

'You're sure about that?'

'Well, I assumed . . .' She put her hand over the lower part of Dee-Ann's face. 'I just don't know. It could have been any of them.'

Magdalen came in with the coffee tray, which she placed on the table at her mother's side. While Adonia poured, her daughter picked up the photos and thumbed through them. She paused over the two girls, Kathy noticed. 'You recognise any of them, Magdalen?' she asked.

'Me? Why should I?'

'Maybe visiting your grandmother? If they come from around there.'

'No.' She tossed the photos back and took a pack of cigarettes from the mantelpiece.

'Not in here, darling. You know your father . . .'

Magdalen bit her lip and put them back. 'Yes, sorry.'

'It was the violence that really upset me. I mean they found the car the next day, undamaged. The other detective said that's often the case with joy-riders. And I didn't care about the money and credit cards. So why did they have to be so violent?'

Her daughter sat down beside her and put a protective arm around her shoulders.

'Oh . . .' Adonia put a tissue to her eyes. 'I'm sorry, I've gone soft in my old age.'

'I think you've been incredibly brave, Mrs Roach,' Mahreen said, and glanced at Kathy, who added, 'Yes. That sort of thing is always very hard to come to terms with, for you, and for your family. Your husband must have been very upset.'

'Yes . . .' She hesitated. 'Yes, of course.'

Kathy noticed that she was fingering a gold chain with a golden heart pendant at her throat. 'You said that they pulled the pendant from your throat. That must have been frightening too.'

'Oh yes!' Adonia looked wide-eyed, and her fingers froze.

'But you got it back?'

'Thank goodness. It was very personal—my husband gave it to me when Magdalen was born. I found it later under the floor mat in the car. They must have dropped it when they drove away.' Adonia took her daughter's hand. 'And the doctors say I'll make a full recovery. So really, I was lucky. But suppose it had been my mother instead of me. It could so easily have been. She wouldn't have survived.'

THE PRESS LIKED BROCK, Kathy could see that. They liked the slightly rumpled look, the way he scratched his white cropped beard meditatively as he considered a question, and the edge of dry humour that was never far away, even on such a case as this. It made a change from the close-shaved, close-mouthed men who usually briefed them.

With growing interest in the mysterious finds on the waste ground, Brock had invited them and their telephoto lenses down from their helicopters and their observation posts on the foot-bridge and the far embankment, down to the crime scene itself, now almost entirely stripped of snow and vegetation, gridded with bright pink tapes and dotted with three large tents.

'A third area was located this morning by Marlowe,' Brock said, and a black labrador was led forward by its handler. 'Marlowe is a cadaver dog, with specialist training in HHRD—Historical Human Remains Detection.' Brock waited while they wrote it down. 'He works with archaeologists as well as us. You could say he's got a PhD in old bones. He detected this morning's finds through two feet of frozen ground.'

The photographers formed a scrum around the dog, lights flashing. Marlowe accepted their interest with philosophical detachment, live humans apparently exciting him far less than dead ones.

'So far we've recovered a human fibula, a tibia, a pelvic bone and a bone from either a hand or a foot from that site.'

'Are you saying three separate corpses?'

'It's not possible to be sure at the moment. The remains have been extensively disturbed, most probably by animals.'

'Or schoolboys,' someone quipped. It was a notion that had been absorbing a lot of police attention, the possibility that Adam was only one of many visitors removing trophies from the place. Yet all of the interviews in the neighbourhood had met with the same response, that no one had ever heard of anyone getting onto the waste ground before, or known of the possibility of human remains being buried there.

'Could there be more? That Marlowe hasn't found yet?'

'It's possible. We'll be digging up the whole site, all one and a half acres of it, grid square by grid square, but that will take time.'

He waved an arm across the breadth of the area and, at the windows of the upper classrooms of Camberwell Secondary, dozens of grinning schoolkids waved back at him.

'What about the age of the remains? Any more information there?'

This was the crucial question; until they had some fix on that it was impossible to focus the investigation, and so far the pathologist had been frustratingly reluctant to commit himself.

'We've definitely ruled out an old burial ground or Blitz victims, as has been suggested. They are modern, probably between ten and forty years old. That's as close as we can get at present.'

'So you can confirm that they are murder victims?'

'That would seem to be the likely conclusion. We have evidence of what appear to be gunshot wounds.'

And two spent cartridge cases, Kathy knew. Just then she felt a hand touch her arm, and turned to see Tom Reeves at her side. She smiled and they moved away from the others so that they could talk.

'How's it going?' he asked.

'Fine. Aren't you guarding your mass-murderer?'

'I got an hour off and decided to come over. They told me you were here. I was worried about you. You were pretty stressed yesterday.'

'A good night's sleep helped. But thanks.'

'Maybe you should talk to somebody.'

'I did, over lunch yesterday.' She smiled at him and he grinned back.

'Look, if you're going to work around here you need to get some background. How do you fancy some Jamaican food tonight? I know an excellent chef.'

'That sounds interesting. All right.'

'Good. This is where I live . . .' He gave her a handwritten card. 'Can you come there? About seven?'

'Fine. I'll phone if I'm delayed.'

'I'd better get back. See you.'

She watched him stride away, amazed that he'd now divulged both his mobile number and his home address. Maybe he really was giving up the undercover life.

The press conference was breaking up and she waited until Brock was able to get away. They had heard that Adam Nightingale had recovered consciousness and might be fit enough to be interviewed. As she drove him up to Waterloo she described her visit to the Roach compound.

'Definitely promising. Adonia couldn't rule out the two girls as her attackers. She was badly shaken up by the attack, and the family has rallied around her, especially the daughter, Magdalen. She seemed very protective of her mother, but I got the impression that she doesn't get on so well with her father. He stops her smoking around the house and so on. Do we know why she's still living with them?'

'Pretty common these days, isn't it?'

'Yes. It's just that I had the impression she was used to her own space. She had to be reminded about the smoking, for instance. I might do some digging. Anyway, there was one definite flaw in their story. Adonia said they were particularly upset that the thieves snatched her necklace, a very personal gift from Ivor when Magdalen was born, but that she found it again under the floor mat of the car when it was returned. I checked with the forensic team that dealt with it, and they say that's impossible, they would have found it first.'

'Can we believe them?' Brock asked. 'People are under pressure, sometimes they cut corners.'

'He sounded pretty convincing to me. Apparently, at the stage they went over the car there was still doubt about how serious Adonia's injuries would turn out to be, and they treated it as a potential murder scene.'

'So you're thinking that Vexx recovered the necklace for Ivor, who slipped it into the car for Adonia to find later?'

'Something like that. It's plausible.'

'Ivor would have to have been pretty crazy to get involved personally in the murders. The Roaches are so-called respectable businessmen now, although they always did take personal affronts very hard.'

'We could look for indirect contact, then,' Kathy said. 'Phone records. If Ivor asked Vexx to track down the people who stole his wife's car, there'd be a phone call when he succeeded.'

'Certainly worth a look. And how has time dealt with Adonia? She was very attractive, I remember.'

'Not too bad, she's still very handsome, but pretty jittery underneath. I think the car-jacking shook her up more than she's realised.'

'Or maybe just being married to Ivor has.'

'Well, her daughter Magdalen's the glamorous one now.'

'I don't remember a daughter. Do you know what Adonia did?'

'No?'

'She was a beautician—for the dead. Her father Cyrus ran a funeral parlour, next to the Ship pub on Cockpit Lane. Young Adonia could make the most ravaged corpse look beautiful.'

They had reached the Albert Embankment. Across the river the finials of the Houses of Parliament bristled dark against the heavy sky, like a long rank of bayonets.

Kathy pondered. 'All the same, it's hard to believe the Roaches would have had two kids killed like that because they roughed up Adonia and stole her car.'

'Nothing would surprise me about the Roaches, Kathy.'

'Are you going to tell Keith Savage?'

'DCI Savage wants to shift the focus of his team's efforts to Harlesden. I think I'll leave him to it until we have something more definite. Were there any witnesses to the car-jacking, or fingerprints on the recovered car?'

'It seems not.'

MRS NIGHTINGALE WAS AT Adam's bedside, looking like a permanent fixture, and scowled at the arrival of the two detectives, as if they could only have come to make further trouble for her son. The boy seemed remarkably unscathed, peering through his thick glasses at an electronics magazine, trying to avoid eye contact with the visitors while his mother fussed.

They chatted for a while, about the burn on Adam's leg and his memory of what had happened. He told them that he had noticed fox tracks in the snow on the waste ground from the classroom window, and wanted to follow them to their hide before the snow melted and he lost the chance. His mother harangued him for his foolishness, but neither Brock nor Kathy was quite convinced by his explanation.

Finally Brock abandoned his questions and took a leather wallet out of the pocket of his coat. He offered it to Adam and said, 'I'm told you're a chess player, Adam. Have you seen one of these before?'

The boy opened it cautiously. Inside, the leather had been formed into a grid of tiny pockets, eight by eight, into which fitted slivers of black and white plastic, printed with the symbols of chess pieces.

'It's a travelling chess set,' Brock said. 'Have you got one?'

The boy shook his head, raising a sceptical eyebrow as he examined the little pieces.

'It's yours, if you want it,' Brock said. 'I haven't used it in ages.'

Adam looked at him dubiously, then at his mother.

'You can give me a game, if you like,' Brock added.

Mrs Nightingale's nose screwed up with suspicion. 'I expect you've got more important things to do with your time, sir.'

'I was up half the night,' Brock sighed, stretching his back. 'I don't mind a break for five minutes.'

'Good idea,' Kathy said. 'Why don't you and I get a cup of tea, Mrs Nightingale?' She took the woman's arm before she could refuse. Brock reached over to the little chessboard and took a black and a white piece, one in each hand, shuffled them behind his back and asked Adam to pick one. The boy pointed at the hand holding the white, and made the first move. The game developed routinely, Adam carefully studying each move, trying to work out how good his opponent was, until the detective suddenly pushed a bishop forward to attack. Adam moved a knight to counter-attack, and after considering this for a moment Brock seemed to lose interest in his attack and moved a pawn on the other side of the board. Adam saw a major mistake. He poked his glasses back on his nose and kept his face expressionless as he made sure. Yes, the copper had definitely screwed up. He moved his knight forward to take the bishop. Brock frowned briefly, then abruptly moved one of his own knights, right into the path of Adam's queen. Adam swiftly took that too, elated at what he would tell Jerry. This guy was supposed to be smart, he'd just seen him live on telly, and Adam was wiping the floor with him.

When Brock moved a third piece, his other bishop, into the line of fire, Adam took it with a small jag of regret; either Brock was humouring him or he'd forgotten everything he'd ever known about chess. But the sacrifice of three major pieces had cleared the board in front of Brock's queen, while shifting Adam's pieces to the sides. Brock now moved his queen straight up to Adam's back row, attacking his king.

'Checkmate, I'm afraid.'

Adam's mouth opened and closed. 'Oh . . .'

Brock picked up his three sacrificed pieces and laid them out, one by one. 'Did you know they were there, Adam?' he asked quietly. 'The bodies?'

'No, I swear.'

Brock pointed at the outline of the boy's leg in its frame beneath the blanket. 'Seven hundred and fifty volts direct current, enough power to push a train. You took an awful big risk blundering through the snow just to find a foxhole.'

The boy shrugged and pushed the chess set back to Brock. 'Thanks, I don't want this.'

'Suit yourself,' Brock said. 'You can give me another game, though.'

AT THE SANDWICH COUNTER, Kathy and Mrs Nightingale picked up their cups of tea and took them to a table.

'He's got an electronic thing he plays chess with,' Adam's mother said. 'I don't know what he'd want with that old wallet. What's your boss up to then?'

'Just trying to be friendly,' Kathy said. 'Do you believe Adam's story about the foxes?'

'I've brought him up to tell the truth.'

'But if it was something he thought you'd be angry about?'

Adam's mother looked uneasy. She stirred her tea, round and round.

'We need some help on this, Mrs Nightingale.'

The woman shot her a hostile glance and spoke in a low rush, not wanting anyone else to hear. 'That's easy for you to say. Who knows what you're diggin' up on that waste ground? And whoever put them there sure didn't want them disturbed, that's plain. And now my son's name and picture is in every newspaper. Yes, it's easy for you to say.'

'But surely he's in no danger if he didn't know the bodies were there, if he was looking for something else?'

Mrs Nightingale thought about that. 'Maybe, maybe not.' She

concentrated on her tea for a moment and then, as if changing the subject, said, 'Do you know what "brown bread" is?'

Kathy was puzzled. 'Well, yes. Bread made with wholemeal—'

'No, no, no, not that kind of brown bread. I mean, is it a name for something, a slang name? Like . . . drugs, maybe?'

Kathy saw the worry in Mrs Nightingale's eyes. 'You think Adam was looking for drugs?'

'No! I'm not saying that at all! You're putting words into my mouth.'

'Please.' Kathy gently put her hand over the other woman's. 'Tell me.'

'Oh . . . How do I know what's for the best? Just now, before you came, Adam's friend Jerry came to see him. I left them for a minute to go to the bathroom. When I came back they were talking. I stood on the outside of the curtain and listened to them. Jerry said like, "But why did you go over there?" and Adam said, "I was lookin' for brown bread."'

'Are you sure?'

'I thought I was mistaken the first time, but Jerry repeated it, see. "You were lookin' for brown bread? In the snow? You're crazy, Adam." And Adam said, "I thought the foxes had found it." When Jerry left I asked Adam what he was talkin' about, and he denied it, said I'd heard it all wrong, but I hadn't. He's a stubborn boy, but he's not big, and some of the other boys pick on him at school because he's good at his sums. I think he wanted to prove something, get some respect.' She shook her head angrily.

Kathy said, 'I'll ask around, see if I can find out what it means.'

'Yes, and you let me know, won't you? I mean, it couldn't be somethin' sexual, could it? Not in all that snow?'

Kathy saw that in her mind she had been going through all the possible ways in which a thirteen-year-old boy might transgress. 'I'll let you know.'

Later, in the car with Brock, she told him about the conversation.

He pondered. 'Brown bread? Well, it's cockney rhyming slang, meaning "dead." Could that be it? "The dead." Did they know all along that the bodies were there? I quizzed Adam again, but he denied it.'

'We could try Jerry.'

'Yes, let's do that.'

She drove straight to the school, where the afternoon classes had begun. The headmistress arranged for Jerry to be brought to her office, and Brock asked her to stay for the interview. When the boy was seated in front of them, Brock said sternly, 'I have just one question, Jerry: what do you know about brown bread?'

The boy gawped, swallowed, then shook his head. 'Nudin'. I don't know nudin' about that.' He kicked one foot awkwardly against the other.

The headmistress looked puzzled as Brock pressed him. Kathy thought he looked scared, refusing even to repeat the phrase, but he wouldn't change his story and in the end they let him go.

'What was that all about?' the teacher asked, and Brock explained. She said brown bread meant nothing special to her, and Brock asked her to keep it to herself.

They returned to Mafeking Road, and as they turned into it from Cockpit Lane they passed a crowded corner café called Stamp and Go, and for a brief moment they caught the rich smells of Jamaican food. Brock growled, 'Cheese sandwiches and a tea bag for us, I suppose.'

When they got back to the warehouse they found everyone crowded around one of the tables. Another set of arm and hand bones had been dug up, and one of the SOCOs was carefully scraping at the mud in which they were caked while another stood by with a camera. The reason for the excitement was a dark band around the wrist. As the spatula teased away at the dirt they caught a glint of glass and someone said, 'Yes, it's a watch, all right.'

THAT EVENING KATHY TOOK the tube from her place in Finchley down the Northern line to Kentish Town, then walked, guided
by her A–Z, to the address Tom had given her. It turned out to be
a basement flat halfway along a terrace, and she wondered if it
was significant that he, the undercover officer, lived below ground
level, while she perched on the twelfth floor of a tower block.

The door was opened by Tom, wearing a Hawaiian shirt, cream
trousers, a striped apron and oven gloves. His face seemed slightly
flushed but very cheerful, and he was backed up by a rich smell of
cooking coming from somewhere inside. He drew her in, kissed
her on the cheek and took her coat.

'Look, I hope this is all right, but on my way to see you today I
came across this café in Cockpit Lane called Stamp and Go. Have
you seen it? Have you smelled it?' He laughed. 'And next door
there was this grocer with Caribbean spices and vegetables and
bottles of sauce. And it took me back to Jamaica—only this was
Jamaica in the snow, so crazy. And I thought well, you should be
getting into this. I mean if you want to understand the people
you've got to understand what they eat.'

'You're right.' She sniffed. 'And you're the excellent chef you
mentioned?'

He beamed. 'Absolutely. I love cooking, when there's a point.'

'Well, after all this snow, a tropical evening sounds great.'

'That's what I thought, and I have the perfect thing to set the scene. One moment.' He raised a magician's finger and hurried away. The whole basement flat had been knocked into a single space from front to back, with a kitchen bay at the side, from which she heard the clink of ice cubes. She took in the cupboard of a fold-down bed against one wall, some new-looking leather furniture, and a flat screen TV and a laptop. Everything looked efficient and impersonal. But no books. That was what was wrong—no books.

Tom appeared with two tall glasses of what looked like a murky fruit salad, embellished with straws and little umbrellas.

'Cheers.'

'Mmm.' Kathy licked her lips, trying to identify the flavours, then felt the rum burn through. 'Wow.'

'Jamaican rum punch. One part sour, two parts sweet, three parts strong, four parts weak.'

'The rum being the strong, I suppose. I get the pineapple, but what else?'

'Guava juice, and limes.'

She sat down, feeling herself begin to defrost. The heating in the flat seemed to be on the highest setting, and she relaxed, letting the warmth seep through her from outside and in.

'Where are all your books, Tom? I expected masses of books.'

'In storage.' He shrugged. 'They take up so much room.'

'I know.' And they're heavy, she thought. Not good for a quick getaway. She had said the wrong thing, flattening his exuberant mood, but not for long. 'So you've been to Jamaica, have you?' she asked.

'Yes, great place.'

He began to tell her about the blinding white beaches of Negril, the hiking trails through the Blue Mountains, scuba diving in Montego Bay. Then some of the characters he'd met, ending up with a tale about a stay in a beach house and going to the toilet one morning with a hangover and hearing scratching noises from the bowl below and looking down to see the claws of a large crab waving up at him. It was a good story, well told, and by the end they were both laughing helplessly. Kathy guessed he'd been trying out the rum punch recipe before she arrived. It was certainly working on her.

'We haven't got crab tonight, have we?'

He shook his head and raised the magic finger again as he made off to the kitchen. After a while there was the ping of a microwave and he returned with a plate.

'I didn't make these. It's their signature dish, "stamp and go," the name for codfish fritters. Try one. I did make the sauce.'

They were crisp and spicy, the sauce sweet and sour.

'Really good!' She took another.

'You need more jungle juice.'

She followed him and watched as he put ice in their glasses and took a jug from the fridge.

'How are your bodies going?'

'Oh, we just keep finding more.'

'It's getting to you, isn't it? Taking your mind off Teddy Vexx and those two kids.'

Put that way it made her feel as if they were betraying Dana and Dee-Ann by letting this old case distract them. Yet something equally terrible had happened there, and nobody had known. The idea that those bodies had been waiting all this time for someone to find them and uncover their story *had* got to her. It had got to Brock too, right from the beginning.

'Are they male or female?'

'Looks like three young adult males, in their twenties, probably. Just to be original, we call them Alpha, Bravo and Charlie. At least two were shot in the head. But we have no idea who they were. We have no missing persons that seem to fit. No dentist in London has matched the dental records we've sent out. Yes, maybe I am getting a bit obsessed. Who were they, and why has no one missed them?'

'And you can't narrow the time frame?'

'Not on the forensic evidence of the remains, apparently. But we found a wristwatch on one of them today. It was digital.'

Tom spooned some chopped fruit into the punch. 'That would make it, what, post-1970 or so?'

'The first mass-produced digital watches came out in 1975. You had to press a button on the side to view the display. That's what this one looked like. They're checking now.'

Tom turned on the hotplate beneath a saucepan and gave it a stir, pondering. 'Were the victims black or white?'

'I don't know.'

'Wouldn't the DNA tell you?'

Kathy dipped another fritter in the sauce. 'Our forensic pathologist, Dr Mehta, gave us a little lecture on how race is only an adaptation to climate and we all have the same DNA.'

'Is that true? I mean, wouldn't those adapta . . .' His rum-anaesthetised tongue fumbled the word and Kathy chuckled, a little louder than she'd intended. He had another go. '. . . adaptations be there in the DNA, to determine skin colour, hair type, etcetera?'

'I don't know.'

'If they're black I'd bet after October 1980.'

'Why?'

'You wanna bet? A fiver.'

'Okay. But you have to tell me why.'

'That's when the Yardies came.' He handed her the glass, splashing in an extra hit of dark rum for good measure.

Sitting together companionably on the sofa, the few remaining fritters between them, Tom went on, 'Jamaica's the sort of place that makes you despair at how good people are at taking paradise and turning it into hell. We stuffed it, the English. Do you know how our high street banks got started? From the fortunes Mr Lloyd and Mr Barclay made from making Jamaica into a concentration camp for slaves to grow sugar. Then the world sugar price collapsed and we gave them independence and pissed off. Like walking out on this totally traumatised family you've been bashing up for several hundred years.'

It was the first time Kathy had heard Tom express anything like a political opinion, and it seemed to her that something personal lay beneath the surface.

'So, what did the Jamaicans do? Two cousins looked at their old masters and said, Yeah, we'll have two political parties like them—you have one, the JLP, and I'll have the other, the PNP. Now the people are starving and living in slums and their kids have to join gangs and steal to make a living, so what shall we do about that? Well, we'll give them jobs. We'll pay them to kick the supporters of the other party, and make sure they vote for us next time. And soon all the Rude Boys in the slums have got guns with the money we give them, and every neighbourhood and district is divided between our two sides, and the fields that used to grow sugar are now growing marijuana, at least until the Americans get fed up with us and come to burn the fields. So then the Rude Boys turn their hand to smuggling Colombian cocaine, which is more profitable still.'

Tom stretched his legs to kick off his shoes and took another slurp of his drink.

'And with every election the violence between the two sides gets worse and worse, with the political parties offering more and more bribes to the gangs to help them back into office. Until we get to the election of October 1980.

'That year, the violence gets so bad it almost amounts to civil war. The rudies are murdering parliamentary candidates, police officers, each other. The point is to terrorise the opposition, so the violence has to be really scary and graphic—families slaughtered in their beds, victims tortured, bodies bound up in wire . . . What's wrong?'

Kathy was staring at him. 'We've found traces of rust—wire— with the bodies. And one of the hands we found had each of its middle bones fractured, at or around the time of death, according to Mehta.'

'Interesting. Anyway, when the election is over the new government finally realises that things have gone too far, and they bring in the army and crack down on the gangs in a big way. An exodus of the rudies begins, heading north as "posses" to the States and Canada, and across the Atlantic as "Yardies" to the UK.'

Tom rose somewhat unsteadily to his feet. 'I've been talking too much. We should eat, don't you think? I'll put on some music.'

'Bob Marley?'

'Close. They shot him in the 1976 election, did you know that? Lucky to survive. No, this is his son, Ziggy.'

He put on a CD and gentle reggae filled the room. Kathy took a seat at the dining table as Tom brought two steaming bowls of dark soup, each with a pale dumpling floating in the centre.

'I didn't make this either, must confess. Takes too long to do it properly. Pepperpot soup. Try it. Isn't it great?'

Kathy agreed.

'But I am making the main course. Red Stripe pot roast. Trouble is, it won't be ready for a while.' He checked his watch. 'Mmm, quite a while. I wanted to do jerk, of course, but it's a barbecue thing really, and in this weather . . . I'll do it for you in the summer, okay? I do a great jerk sauce.'

'You really think that's what we've found, a Yardie graveyard?'

'Wouldn't be surprised. When they came they brought their guns and their cocaine, and also their old rivalries, the Shower Posse and the Spanglers, Jungle and the Chi Chi Boys. They were more lethal to each other than to anybody else.'

'You know a lot about this. Is that why you went to Jamaica?'

Tom nodded. 'In London we'd catch them and deport them and a few months later they'd be back with a new name, new passport. Genuine, too.'

'How'd they do that?'

'Easy. You have a customer, a UK citizen, dying for the crack you sell and more than willing to trade his birth certificate for an extra rock or two. So after a while we realised we needed some help from the cops over there, the Jamaica Constabulary Force.

We brought them here to identify who it was exactly that we'd got, and in return the JCF invited us back to Jamaica, to drink their rum and eat their jerk chicken. Seems reasonable, doesn't it?'

'Yes, absolutely.'

'But Brock will know all this, especially if he was working in Lambeth back then. Hasn't he talked about it?'

'Not really.'

'Keeps his cards close to his chest, old Brock, doesn't he?'

'He'll tell us when he's ready,' Kathy said, but she was thinking about Brock's instructions to keep the SOCOs within the bounds of the site, wanting to strictly control the information that got out. And there had been a deliberate vagueness at the press briefings about certain aspects of their finds, as if he already had suspicions that he wanted to keep to himself. Tom was absolutely right, she decided, with the clarity that a couple of large rum punches can bring—Brock was being secretive. Now she remembered another thing that had struck her as slightly odd. When they'd met Dr Mehta at the path lab that afternoon, he'd shown them a thighbone he'd cleaned up. This femur was dramatically curved, like a bow, and he'd explained that the owner had suffered from rickets, most probably due to a vitamin D or calcium deficiency in childhood. Kathy had been struck by the immobility of Brock's expression and his lack of questions.

'How's he going with his lady friend?'

Kathy was surprised. She couldn't remember mentioning this to Tom. 'She's still in Australia. I got a Christmas card from her, snorkelling on the Great Barrier Reef.'

'Why the hell doesn't he go out there after her? I would.'

Brock wasn't talking about that either, Kathy thought, but her thoughts were becoming increasingly blurry and euphoric, and it wasn't Brock's love-life she was interested in just now. 'You sounded very nostalgic about Jamaica. Was there someone special you met there?'

Now it was Tom who looked startled. 'Your glass is empty,' he said abruptly, getting to his feet. 'We should switch to Red Stripe.'

He made his way to the kitchen where he checked the oven, then returned with a couple of bottles. 'This is obligatory, I'm afraid. It's in the pot roast.' He sat down again. 'I did have some good friends there. Some who aren't around any more.'

'I'm sorry.'

'Oh well.' They clinked bottles and Tom began another funny story about tropical sanitation. As he rambled on, Kathy thought how intriguing it was, discovering someone else's life, but also how tricky. There were plenty of ghosts from her own past that she wouldn't want to share with him, not yet.

Much later, full of Red Stripe and pot roast, they collapsed on the sofa in an untidy heap. It had taken so long for the meal to reach what Tom felt was its full potential that it was now late in the night. He reached out a hand and stroked her hair.

'I love your hair,' he sighed exhaustedly.

It was straight, short and very pale blonde. 'Bit out of place in Jamaica,' she said, and then something she'd meant to ask earlier stumbled into her head. 'Have you ever heard of a phrase "brown bread"? Does it mean anything to you?'

'Mm?'

'Brown bread.'

'Why?'

'It's what the boy was looking for on the railway land, apparently, when he found the body.'

Tom mumbled something incoherent and Kathy closed her eyes, utterly relaxed. When she opened them again her phone was bleeping inside her shoulder bag on the floor at her feet. She blinked at her watch in disbelief, seeing seven-fifteen. Beside her, Tom lay sprawled in a contorted heap like The Body in the Bog. Swearing softly, she disentangled herself from his legs and groped for the phone. There was a message from Brock calling a case conference at Dr Mehta's laboratory at nine a.m.

SEVEN

ON HER WAY OUT she roused Tom from whichever tropical beach he was lazing on in his dreams. She rushed to the tube and sat on the northbound train in a daze, still half asleep. At home she rapidly showered, cleaned her teeth, and made some tea and toast. Feeling only a little less fragile, she returned to central London, this time to Embankment station, where she caught a cab to the hospital where Dr Mehta had his laboratory. She made it just in time.

She felt the tension as soon as she stepped into the room. Dr Mehta was with Brock over by the window, arguing fiercely. She'd never seen him angry before, and the others looked mildly embarrassed. It seemed the pathologist was scolding Brock for releasing Teddy Vexx after Mehta had provided the crucial forensic evidence against him. 'I pulled out every stop!' he protested angrily. 'I twisted people's arms, gave up my weekend, ruined my mother's eightieth birthday party! And what do you do? You mess it up! You let the animal go free!'

Brock said something placatory, but Mehta wasn't having any of it. 'Well, don't be surprised when I'm less than enthusiastic about going the extra yards the next time!' He turned away in a huff and started talking to someone else.

Brock, looking unperturbed, came over to Kathy and introduced her to a man from the Forensic Services Command Unit whom she hadn't met before. On the other side of the long table the three forensic experts were taking their seats. They represented, Brock murmured, 'flesh, bones and teeth'. Sundeep Mehta, 'flesh', the forensic pathologist, sat in the middle as nominal leader of the group. 'Teeth' sat on his left, in the person of Professor Lyons, forensic odontologist, a studious-looking elderly man in a white lab coat stained at the sleeves with something yellow. On Dr Mehta's right a black woman, Dr Prior, was 'bones', the team's forensic anthropologist. She looked to Kathy to be about her own age, early thirties, and was immersed in a document while Mehta worked out some of his anger in an energetic conversation with the odontologist about fees. Apparently, three bodies in a single incident would attract a separate case fee for each, whereas if they found any more, charges must be made at either a half daily rate or a reduced case rate, but whether this applied to all the bodies, or only the fourth and subsequent ones, was a matter for debate.

Brock cleared his throat and Mehta broke off and frowned at Kathy. 'Sergeant Kolla, how are you? Is this everyone, Brock?'

Brock said yes.

'No Inspector Gurney?'

'He's on site this morning.'

'Very well.'

Mehta sniffed at a scrap of paper. 'I have a message that Morris Munns has something he wants to show us. He should be along shortly. Now, this is really your meeting, Brock. We can only charge extra for police case conferences, not our own.' He gave Brock a grim look, inviting him to challenge him, but Brock said nothing. 'Anyway I thought we'd better speak to you, because we had another discussion last night and we seem to be approaching a preliminary consensus on your three skeletons.'

At that moment there was a tap on the door and a woman hurried in with a sheaf of papers which she handed to Mehta, who said, 'Perfect timing, Jenny.'

The documents were the combined forensic reports of the three specialists, fresh off the photocopier. Each person was given a set, and Mehta directed them to the final summary for the profile that had now emerged of the three victims, Alpha, Bravo and Charlie. It confirmed that they were all males, and provided rather specific estimates of their heights—167, 185 and 181 centimetres respectively—and ages—twenty-three, nineteen and twenty-eight. Both Alpha and Bravo were right-handed, whereas Charlie was left. Available teeth were generally in good condition, with no fillings or other signs of dental treatment. As children, Bravo had had rickets and Charlie had suffered multiple fractures to his left leg. Both Alpha and Bravo had probably died from single gunshot wounds to the head, whereas the cause of death of Charlie, whose skull had not yet been found, was unknown. The size of the entry wounds were consistent with the two nine-millimetre calibre cartridge cases found on the site.

All three skeletons showed evidence of fractures, which Dr Prior felt were probably sustained close to the time of death, although Dr Mehta wasn't so sure, emphasising how difficult perimortem trauma was to distinguish. There were sufficient traces of oxidised iron strands in the surrounding soil to support the conjecture that all three had been bound with wire to arms and legs at the time of burial. It was not possible to determine whether they had died together or on separate occasions, nor whether death had occurred on the railway site or at some other place, although the presence of spent cartridges might suggest the former. Fabric traces in the ground suggested that all three bodies had been clothed at the time of burial, but these traces weren't substantial enough to yield more specific information, apart from the remains of a shoe, a belt buckle, two zip fasteners and some buttons, which were being further investigated.

The condition of the remains indicated a date of death between ten and forty years previously. A Seiko digital wristwatch with plastic case and LED display had been found on the wrist of Charlie, indicating an earliest date for his death of 1978, when this model first came on the market. So far, the evidence did not warrant a closer estimate for date of death than the seventeen-year period from 1978 to 1995. Maternally inherited mitochondrial DNA had been obtained from the remains of all three victims.

'Sorry about the date, Brock,' Sundeep said, not sounding at all sorry. 'I suppose that's the thing you're most interested in, but we've tried everything—benzidine test, precipitin test, demonstrable fatty acids, nitrogen content. No go, I'm afraid. The only other time-related fact we have is that ballistics have matched the cartridge cases to a gun used in two other shootings in South London during the mid-eighties, but that doesn't really narrow your time frame, does it?'

'This bit about "indicators of non-Caucasian ancestry", Sundeep,' Brock queried. 'Can we be more specific?'

As they'd been reading the summary, Kathy had noticed Dr Prior shake her head several times. Now she answered Brock's question.

'They were black,' she said bluntly.

It was Dr Mehta's turn to shake his head. 'Dr Prior, I've been trying to emphasise to our colleagues here that such a term is arbitrary and meaningless in science. Racial categories have no biological reality.' He sounded testy.

Dr Prior gazed calmly back at him and said, 'That's nonsense, Dr Mehta. You've completely ignored my evidence in your summary. The morphological arguments are compelling and well established. Race is a biological fact, and the three victims were as black as I am. I think the police need to know that.'

'Nonsense!' Mehta almost shouted. 'I quote Sauer, I quote Brace:"There are no races, there are only clines." If we can't dispel this wicked misconception, who can?'

The odontologist, Dr Lyons, was peering over his glasses at his forensic colleagues. From what Kathy could make of his part of the report, the dental evidence had been disappointingly inconclusive, and throughout he'd had the air of someone rather bored and impatient to get back to his laboratory. But now he, the only white member of the trio, seemed intrigued by his colleagues' increasingly irate debate about race.

It was interrupted by the arrival of Morris Munns, who bustled in with a cheerful 'Morning all' and an ancient leather doctor's bag. The lenses in his glasses were so thick that Kathy was always worried that he would barge into something, which was ironic since he was perhaps the most skilful photographic specialist and enhancer of latent images available to the Met. Dr Mehta, some-what tight-lipped, invited him to speak, and from the bag he pro-duced a plastic evidence pouch containing an irregular lump of material.

'This is the remains of the shoe Sundeep gave me,' Morris said in his broad cockney. 'It was found with Bravo's body. And hidden beneath what was left of his leather instep, Sundeep was smart enough to notice something odd.'

Mehta's sulk relaxed a little, mollified by this compliment.

'Under examination, I found a fragment of what turned out to be rag paper. We 'ad a go with it on our new image detector equip-ment, digitally enhanced, and eventually came up with this.' He passed out copies of a photographic enlargement, twenty times life size, of an irregular area of grey. Across its surface was a blur of darker grey smudges. Kathy held the picture at arm's length, screwing up her eyes, until finally a pattern emerged.

'Kathy's got the idea,' Morris said, and handed round another image, in which the first had been overlaid by red symbols, corre-sponding roughly to the shapes beneath. The smudges now read:

Celia's Dream
8.22, 7/2, T4

'Brilliant, Morris,' Brock said, 'as always. What does it mean?'

'I reckon it's a betting slip, don't you? An old-fashioned one, handwritten. The horse is Celia's Dream, running at odds of seven to two.'

Horseracing was another acknowledged area of Morris's expertise, and Brock was impressed. 'What about the other numbers?'

'Dunno for sure. 8.22 can't be the time of the race—too early or too late and too odd. It could be the date, American style, month first—August twenty-second. Maybe Bravo was a Yank.'

'Or the bookie was,' Mehta suggested.

'All right, we'll see what we can find out,' Brock said. 'Many thanks. And thanks also to you and your colleagues for your report, Sundeep. Worth every penny, I'm sure. I realise what a rush it's been. Is there anything else?'

'Will you be wanting facial reconstructions?' Dr Prior asked.

'Definitely. Are the skulls in good enough condition?'

'Oh yes. Of course, there are big differences in the thicknesses of facial tissues for different races.' She paused with a slight smile on her lips, and Kathy realised she was needling Sundeep. 'But we have pretty accurate tables for both pure Negroid and mixed-race subjects. The South Africans have done a lot of work in this area.'

Dr Mehta winced at that, but he had obviously decided on a more dignified, patronising approach. 'Yes, well, as we know, the results of facial modelling are open to conjecture. But Dr Prior is a very artistic practitioner.'

Kathy gathered that 'artistic' was probably the most damning compliment that Mehta could find. As they got to their feet, Kathy made a point of speaking to the anthropologist. She introduced herself and they shook hands.

'What was that all about, with Dr Mehta?' she asked.

'Oh, it's an ongoing thing with us. Sundeep is a soft-tissue man, and they tend to see the way the responses of races to climate are evenly graded across populations, without clear breaks—the clines he mentioned. But deep inside you, in your bones, the opposite is true. There are sharp divisions between the races, and I can tell much more clearly what you are from your skull than from your skin. But of course, the reason Sundeep gets so heated isn't scientific. He thinks that exposing biological differences between the races encourages racism, so he wants to suppress them. I, on the other hand, believe the opposite. I think that if we don't explain exactly what science tells us, we encourage myths and stereotypes.'

When I was a student and my lecturer first explained the evolutionary basis of race I felt liberated. For the first time I understood why I was black.'

She paused, studying Kathy's face as if trying to make a decision, then added, 'And this case is about race, isn't it?'

'Is it?'

'Oh, I think so. I think these murders were racially motivated, don't you?'

'I don't think we know enough yet. They could be many things, gangland killings . . .'

'No, this isn't some crack-crazed Yardies taking pot shots at one another. And it wasn't done to intimidate the opposition—the bodies were hidden. This was deliberate, like a military execution, torturing them first, breaking their bones, then making them kneel, shooting them from above and in front, through the crown. This was cold hate. Race hate.' Dr Prior leaned closer to Kathy and whispered in her ear. 'Use your imagination, sister.' Then, as she was turning away, she added, 'And forget about Sundeep's jibe about facial reconstruction. I'll show you exactly what those two boys looked like.'

KATHY WAS SILENT IN the taxi back to Queen Anne's Gate with Brock, and finally he said, 'You're very quiet, Kathy.'

'Just thinking about what Dr Prior had to say.' She noticed mud on his trouser legs. The on-site teams were now working around the clock ahead of expected bad weather, and she wondered if Brock had spent the night out there. 'You've been pretty quiet yourself.'

Her remark sounded abrupt and he said nothing for a while, staring out of the taxi window at the dark figures hurrying along the cold streets. She wondered if she'd annoyed him. Then he turned and smiled. 'Yes, you're probably right. We should get together and talk about things. Soon.'

She wasn't sure if he meant about work or something else.

Then he added, 'But first I want to get a fix on when they died. From that, everything else will follow; without it we're helpless. What did you think of Morris's conjuring trick?'

'Pretty convincing.'

'Mm. Are you a punter?'

'Afraid not.'

'No, I didn't think so. Me neither. But I'd like you to make it your number-one priority.'

'You want me to track down Celia's Dream?'

'Yes. Drop everything else. I dare say it'll take time. Talk to experts, people in the industry, but don't mention where this came from. And don't tell anyone else about it.'

Kathy looked at him in surprise. 'The team?'

He shook his head. 'No one.' He hesitated, then said, 'I'll explain when we get a date. I may be quite wrong. I want you to go at this with a completely open mind.'

The cab had arrived at Queen Anne's Gate. Kathy made her way to the room where she had her workspace. The building seemed deserted, as if all the others were away doing something active and important. She made some strong coffee, sat down at her desk, switched on her computer and tried to get her brain working.

Celia's Dream could be many things—a book, a rose, a boat. Perhaps Bravo had arranged to pick something up from a boat at 8.22. She was puzzled by the particularity of the time, if it was a time. Or perhaps Morris was right and it was a date.

She got onto the Internet and began searching Google. Celia's Dream yielded 6,890 entries, most concerning a track of that name from an album by a UK band, Slowdive, released in September 1991. She couldn't find any reference to horses or boats. She tried horseracing websites, again without result, and then on one of the sites she noticed the word 'greyhounds' on the site map and she remembered a scene from long ago, her uncle Tom in Sheffield putting on his coat to go out and Aunt Mary telling her grimly that he was 'going to the dogs.' And the races must have been held in the evening as she remembered the streetlights on outside.

On greyhound-data.com she found 'Dog-Search,' and typed in the name. And suddenly, there it was:

Celia's Dream

color	WBD
sex	female
date of birth	MAY 1978
land of birth	IE Ireland
land of standing	IE Ireland
owner	Mrs Celia Frost

It gave the dog's pedigree through four generations and the percentage of Grand Champions in her bloodline over six genera-tions (10 per cent). It also gave her racing history. Kathy sat back and blessed the Internet.

She knocked on Brock's office door and went in. He was tilted back on his swivel chair, shoeless feet up on the desk and bright green boots on the floor nearby, as if he'd just come in from a spot of gardening. He was sipping from a mug of coffee, staring over his half-lens glasses at the opposite wall, which was covered with his own version of the crime scene information on the wall of the case room they'd established downstairs—a street map of the area around Cockpit Lane, a gridded map of the railway land, and dozens of photographs of what they'd dug up.

'Problems?' he asked.

'Answers, I think.' She handed him the printout of the dog's details.

He sat up sharply. 'That was quick.'

'And here's her racing history.' Kathy pointed to one line. 'On 11 April 1981 she won the 8.22 race at Catford from trap four with a starting price of seven to two.'

'Yes, of course! Catford dog track is just a couple of miles from Cockpit Lane.'

'That's right. Bravo was probably a regular punter there. Unfortunately the track closed down a couple of years ago, so I may have trouble tracing its records. I think I'll concentrate first on finding out about that date—what day of the week it was, what was going on then.'

For a moment Brock seemed mesmerised by the information on the page, then he slowly shook his head and waved her to sit down. There was no need to find out about the date; he already knew.

EIGHT

THE ELEVENTH OF APRIL 1981 was a Saturday, and warm for the time of year. Around midday Brock got a phone call at his desk at the station.

'Hello, Detective Inspector Brock.' The promotion was recent, and he still had to check himself from saying 'Sergeant.'

' 'Lo? I wan' fe talk to you.'

The voice was pitched low and he had difficulty at first understanding what the man was saying.

'Who is this?'

'Me name Joseph, seen? Paul gave me yo' number.'

Paul was a stallholder in the market and a useful informant, and Brock remembered being introduced to a tall, loose-limbed young black man. Joseph had cut a stylish figure in a white Kangol cap and black leather coat, and when he strolled away he almost seemed to be dancing on his markedly bowed legs.

'Fine. What do you want to talk about, Joseph?'

The caller hesitated, then said, 'Paul said seh you wan' fe put some bad bwoys ah goal, yeah?'

'Which bad boys do you have in mind?'

'Not on t'phone. Dem bwoys real bad, seen? You know dem. Is like dem cyan wait fe kill someone. I don't need fe talk to nobody, but I do need fe get money, seen?'

'Yes, I understand.'

'Tonight, six o'clock, the Ship in Cockpit Lane. Don' you be late.'

After he hung up Brock tried to find out if anyone else knew of this Joseph, but the station was in turmoil, uniforms rushing everywhere. There had been trouble on the streets the previous evening and more was expected. Brock decided not to hang around and headed out to catch a bus for home and lunch.

His felt the usual sag in his spirits as he approached the flat, a trendy shoebox. He hated the place, its miserable little rooms, low ceilings, windows looking out at blank walls. As he opened the front door he knew instantly that it was deserted. He felt the heavy silence, as if all the accumulated tensions had finally snapped like an overstretched elastic band. The kitchen was spotless, tidier than it had ever been since they'd moved in, three years before. A thousand days, a thousand nights. The lounge and bedroom were also immaculate, as if for a final inspection. Her drawers and wardrobe were empty.

There was no note, although in the bin beneath the kitchen sink he found two screwed-up attempts: 'Dear David, I can't' and 'David, I have to.'

He found a bottle of beer and a lump of cheese in the fridge, and sat for a long time at the kitchen table staring at them, trying to work out how he felt. Relief, on the whole, at the arrival of the inevitable. Perhaps in a week or two, when the repetitive cycle was broken, they might talk, he told himself, but found it hard to believe.

He left the house at five, the beer and cheese still untouched on the table. He felt light-headed, disengaged from the world, as if after a violent accident, and put the odd little dislocations he noticed around him down to this. The bus timetable seemed to have been disrupted, and it took longer than expected to reach Cockpit Lane. The street was unnaturally empty, and through front windows he could see the blue flicker of television sets. In the distance he heard the howl of an ambulance. He hadn't seen the news before he left, and he didn't have a police radio.

As he walked along the deserted street he thought how much

he liked this part of London. To those passing through on the commuter trains it might look like a scruffy mess of aging yellow-brick terraces, but to him they were dignified, sturdy, forgiving receptacles for the endlessly permutating human lives they'd sheltered for over a hundred years. These were the sorts of streets he'd grown up in, and the struggle of the West Indian immigrants today matched the earlier struggle of his own parents, fresh from the North. It was true, though, looking around with a critical eye, that these parts were going through a tough time now. Businesses were going bust, buildings falling vacant and being turned into squats, and a growing number of young unemployed men standing idle in the street. Always on the street. So where the hell were they now?

The Ship was a pokey little pub opposite the church at the end of Cockpit Lane. It had no room for gadgets like Space Invaders machines, jukeboxes or TV sets. Now it was deserted, the landlord leaning morosely on the bar studying form in the racing pages.

'Quiet tonight,' Brock said. He was five minutes late.

The publican grunted and shrugged. 'Something going on. What'll it be?'

'Half of bitter, please. Have one yourself.'

'Ta.'

'I'm supposed to be meeting someone here. Young black lad. Seen him?'

'Haven't seen nobody, mate. You're my first customer tonight.'

Brock glanced through the morning paper while he sipped at his beer. On page two he came across a report of the disturbance in Brixton the previous evening. Three police officers from Operation Swamp had been assaulted by a crowd after trying to assist a black youth who'd been stabbed. Bricks and bottles had been thrown, and six arrests made.

The time dragged on. He checked his watch again at six-forty and decided Joseph wasn't coming. Then the phone behind the bar rang. The publican had difficulty understanding what the caller wanted. Eventually he looked over and said, 'Your name Brack?'

'Brock. It's for me, is it?'

'Hard to say.' The man handed him the phone.

'Hello, Brock here. Is that you Joseph?'

'Yeah. Is you fe true, man?' He sounded out of breath, panicky, his voice pitched higher than before, no longer cool and husky.

'Of course it's me, Joseph. I'm waiting at the Ship, like we arranged. Where are you?'

'I cyan come dere now, seen? Dem try fe dus' me!' The voice rose almost to a shriek. Brock could hear thumping music and voices in the background.

'Who's trying to kill you?'

'You know who, supa. Dat big bad white bwoy.'

'White? You're talking about Spider Roach, is that right?'

Joseph gave a sob.

'Where are you now?'

'De Cat and Fiddle in Angell Town. Somebody ah follow me. Mek me laf yah, y'hear?'

'No, don't leave there, Joseph. I'll be with you in a couple of minutes. Just stay where you are!'

Brock was out of the door and running. It was a ten-minute walk, he reckoned, a five-minute run, a two-minute taxi ride. But there were no taxis. He reached the main road where the traffic was dense, not moving. A police car was stuck in the middle, lights flashing impotently. As he plunged across the road he heard the sound of a helicopter overhead, chop-chop-chop. He looked up and saw the word 'Police' on its fuselage. He'd read about the new Air Support Unit but it was the first time he'd seen such a thing over London. It was flying southwest, where he was going, towards a haze of smoke he now noticed in the sky, turning the late sun into a red disc.

He reached the pub at last, his chest heaving from the half-mile run. Sirens were braying everywhere around him now, although he still hadn't encountered the crisis, whatever it was. An excited crowd made up of both black and white youths was gathering in the street outside the pub. It was crowded inside and he struggled through, from bar to bar, without success. Joseph was nowhere to be seen. As he stood, panting, eyes roving, a soft voice murmured at his side. 'You wan' Joseph, sir?'

'Yes!' He swivelled, then dropped his eyes to face a tiny middle-aged woman staring up at him.

'You're his friend, sir?'

'I am. We were supposed to meet here. Have you seen him?'

'He phoned me too. I'm his aunty, Winnie Wellington's my name.' She offered a hand and he felt the skin hard and rough in his grasp.

'David Brock. I'm a policeman, Winnie. I've seen you in Cockpit Lane.'

'He needs yo' help. He's very scared, sir. He asked me to bring money for him. He said if I saw you to tell you he's gone to the Windsor Castle in Mayall Road. He feel safer dere among black folk, and he has a friend who can hide him. His name's Walter.'

'You saw Joseph here?'

'Only for a moment. He told me this, and then he saw somethin' dat scared the life out o' him, and he just ran for the door over there.'

'What did he see?'

'Two men came in the other door. Big men, hard men, in black leather jackets. White men.'

'Thank you, Winnie. I'll do what I can.'

She laid a hand on his arm. 'If you're goin' to Mayall Road you'd best take care, Mr Brock.'

He hurried out into the maze of streets heading south, turning eventually into Brixton Road. There he stopped dead, stunned by the spectacle of a circle of people dancing around a man on fire. His hair, his suit were ablaze with fierce orange flames, and it took Brock a moment to realise that it was a shop dummy. They were outside Burton's the tailors, whose glass windows had been smashed. Beyond them youths were lining both sides of the road, apparently waiting, although there was no traffic. Then a shout went up as a police car approached, heading down the street towards the centre of Brixton. As it reached the lines the people began hurling bricks at it. Swerving, siren blaring, it ran the gauntlet and sped on. Brock saw the pale face of one of the coppers inside staring back through the cracked rear window at the jeering crowd.

He hurried on past kids smashing shop windows. A white woman with long fair hair was wielding a broom at the window of an off-licence, sending glass shards flying. Outside a jeweller's shop, necklaces and watches were scattered across the pavement among the glass. A large crowd was milling outside the tube station. People were wide-eyed with excitement, some frightened, some laughing, exchanging stories. A line of uniforms was holding them back from entering Atlantic Road, where he wanted to go. He could see a police car down there in flames and the stench of burning petrol and rubber hung in the air. A fire engine stood by on this side of the police line, radio crackling, the crew waiting with arms folded. Familiar shop signs—COLLIERS, BOOTS, WH SMITH— seemed oddly out of place, as if they'd been transposed to another place and time, St Petersburg in 1917 perhaps.

Brock decided to move on and try to approach the pub from another direction. He ran past the town hall and turned into a residential side street. Ahead of him he saw a group of people clustered at a front gate. Several black youths with bricks in their hands had cornered an astonished white man, while his terrified wife and two small children looked on from a car parked at the kerb. Brock moved to help but several other black men appeared and pulled their friends away, leaving the man unhurt. Brock could hear distant shouts ahead and the incomprehensible braying of a megaphone. The sky was darker here, twilight compounded by a pall of smoke, lit from below by a flickering orange glow.

He turned a corner and stumbled into a squad of police. They were sitting on the kerb and against a wall, their shields and visored helmets on the ground beside them. One looked up at him and he recognised a young PC from his own station, dabbing at blood on his forehead.

'Hello, Stan,' he said. 'You all right?'

The constable didn't seem to recognise him. 'Got me with a fucking brick, didn't they? Bastards. They're chucking fucking petrol bombs at us now. Can you believe that? Molotov cocktails in the streets of London.'

He moved on, sensing the heart of the storm ahead from the noises of battle, the rhythmic beating of batons against shields, the crashes of destruction, angry cries. Then at last he emerged into Railton Road. The street was littered with upturned and burning vehicles, broken bricks and glass. A fire engine stood abandoned, black smoke pouring from its cabin. Brock found himself behind a double police line facing a chanting crowd. A flaring petrol bomb arced through the smoke and smashed directly onto an upturned shield, spraying fire over several cops. There was a whoop from the crowd as the police line broke, a shower of bricks, and then the mob surged forward into the flailing batons.

Brock ran across to the far side of the street and kept going through the crowd, barging his way down a side street and into Mayall Road. There he stopped, transfixed by the sight. Ahead of him the Windsor Castle was in flames. He could hear the crash of exploding spirit bottles, and felt the billow of scorching heat as the ground-floor windows blew out. He leaned back against the brick wall, catching his breath as he watched the silhouettes of dancing figures against the blaze.

NINE

'THE BRIXTON RIOTS,' KATHY said. 'I'd forgotten.'

'You'd be too young to remember.' Brock heaved himself to his feet and got them both another coffee from the pot he kept brewing.

'And you didn't find Joseph?'

'No. I never heard of him again. The following days and weeks were chaotic. I filed a report but didn't have a chance to follow up. The next time I saw Paul and Winnie at the markets I asked them if they knew what had happened to him, and they hadn't heard from him either. They guessed he'd gone back home to Jamaica. I thought that seemed likely.'

'And now you think we've found him.'

Brock nodded. 'The second body, Bravo, six foot two, age nineteen and bow-legged. Never collected on the race that Celia's Dream was winning for him at exactly the time that the Windsor Castle was burning to the ground.'

'Did you suspect this from the very beginning?'

'It was a possibility.'

'But I don't understand the secrecy. Why couldn't I tell anyone about Celia's Dream?'

'It gets more complicated, Kathy. Until I know exactly where we stand, I don't want any more information leaking out than I can help.'

She'd encountered this secretiveness in him often enough be-fore. It was a deeply ingrained instinct, formed by years of stalking dangerous people while working in an institution of ambitious gossips. And there was always a good reason for it.

'You think Spider Roach killed them,' she said.

He raised an eyebrow. 'Oh, I couldn't say that. But he's an obvi-ous candidate. We should go and talk to Winnie Wellington again. She was his aunt, and she was the last person to see Joseph that we know of.'

AS SHE DROVE THEM across Westminster Bridge, the sweep of the river sparkling in the crisp morning light, Kathy said, 'Winnie spoke of two white men following him.'

'Yes, although when Joseph first called me I assumed he was talking about being in trouble with some other Jamaicans, Yardies. You know about the Yardies?'

'I'm learning. Last night Tom Reeves told me something about them—he's been to Jamaica with Special Branch, did you know?'

'Really? No I didn't. When was that?'

'I'm not sure. He made a bet with me that if the three victims were black, then they were murdered after October 1980.'

'Smart lad. What else did he tell you?'

'About Jamaican food, mainly. And drink.'

'Aha.' Brock nodded sagely, as if that explained many things.

Kathy drove first to the warehouse in Mafeking Road, where they went inside to check on progress. Bren was there.

'Weather's holding up, and we've got something interesting, chief. Remains of a bullet.'

'Where did they find it?'

'That's the interesting part.' Bren led them over to the gridded site plan, now covered with numbered pins and scribbled annota-tions in a dozen different hands. 'C6.' He pointed to an empty grid square. 'We've just started excavating it. The bullet was on its own, embedded in the ground about six inches down. It's not in good shape. Probably won't help us match the gun. But it confirms what we assumed from the spent cases, that the victims were shot here on the site, not somewhere else and brought here for burial. This one presumably exited from either Alpha or Charlie and ended up a good ten or fifteen yards away.'

'And we've got something for you, Bren.' Brock told him about the betting slip and date. 'I'll be releasing some of this to the press this afternoon. In the meantime, Kathy and I are going to start talking to people who knew Joseph.'

'A photograph would be a help.'

'And a surname.'

They walked back down Mafeking Road to the junction with Cockpit Lane. The Ship public house stood on the corner, as scruffy and unwelcoming as when Brock had gone there to meet Joseph twenty-four years before. They turned into Cockpit Lane, threading through the market crowd until they reached the pots and pans on the final stall. Winnie was there, George at her side. She saw them and made a face.

'Oh no. What now. You want this boy again?'

'Not this time, Winnie. It's you we want to chat to. Nothing to worry about.'

'I've heard dat before. You want a cup of tea? Come inside.'

As she led them through the shop door there was a loud clatter from the street behind them and Winnie yelled back over her shoulder, 'Clumsy boy!' She shook her head with disgust. 'He wears those thick gloves, so he drops things. I tell him he's got to take the gloves off, but he complains, "Aw, Winnie, I'm so cold. I get frostbite." He's eighteen years old and he's a baby, dat boy.'

They settled in the small kitchen at the rear. A shed had been built in the backyard right up against the window, and they could see racks and cardboard boxes piled inside. Winnie put the kettle on and they sat around the kitchen table.

'You've heard that we've found some old human remains on the waste ground at the back here, beside the railway?' Brock asked.

'The whole street's talkin' about it. They say it's a Yardie burial ground. Is dat fer true?'

'We don't know, Winnie, but you've been here a long time, and I wanted to tap your memory. Back to 1981, the time of the Brixton riots, remember that?'

Winnie nodded. 'I remember.'

'I wanted to ask you about a nephew of yours—Joseph was his name. I used to see him in the Lane, all those years ago.'

'Joseph?' The old woman's lined forehead wrinkled as she thought. 'Yes, I remember Joseph. But . . .' She looked horrified. 'You don't think dat's him do you, lyin' out there in the waste ground all that time?'

'We've found a man who was tall, six foot two, and bowlegged from childhood rickets. He was about nineteen when he died, and he was black.'

Winnie put a hand to her mouth. 'Oh Lord above.' She crossed herself quickly and felt in the pocket of her quilted coat for her rosary beads. 'Was that 1981, when we met in dat pub in Angell Town?'

Brock nodded. 'You do remember. Did you ever hear of him again?'

'No, I never did. I just assumed he'd gone back to the yard—to Jamaica—but I never knew for sure.'

'The thing is, Winnie, there is a way we can be certain if it's him. If you're his aunt—his mother's sister—and you allow us to do a small test . . .' But Winnie was shaking her head.

'No, I'm not his real auntie. Dat was just a figure of speech. I really don't know who his baby mother was back there.'

'Oh. Well, perhaps you could give us some details about him— his full name, his age, anything you know.'

'But I don't really know anything. When he arrived I gave him a room upstairs and some work on the stall, like George out dere.

Just to get him started, you understand? I just always knew him as Joseph, dat's all.'

'The last time we saw him was the eleventh of April of that year. When did he arrive, exactly?'

She pondered. 'It was before Christmas, I think. Yes, I'm sure he was here for Christmas . . . Unless I'm mixing him up with Bobby. He was next, I think. Oh dear, I'm not sure.'

'So you think he was staying with you for four or five months? Something like that?'

'Yes, I'd say so. Somethin' like dat. I expect Father Maguire could tell you. He helped Joseph.'

'Father Maguire?'

'At St Barnabas, up the Lane, beyond the market. He's been here nearly as long as me.'

She got up to make the tea, bringing the pot and cups and saucers to the table. 'I'm afraid I can't be very hospitable. I don' have no cake. Maybe I can find some biscuits.'

'Tea will be just fine, Winnie. What else can you tell us about Joseph?' Brock coaxed. 'What about his friends?'

'Well, there was Paul, who sold shoes in the market. But he's long gone. I've no idea where he is.'

'You went to the Cat and Fiddle that night to give him money, do you remember? The message he asked you to pass on to me was that he was going to the Windsor Castle in Brixton to meet someone who could help him. His name was Walter. Did you know this Walter?'

Winnie seemed to draw her tough little body in upon itself, and not just from the effort of remembering, Kathy thought. She seemed troubled.

'He was always gettin' into hot water, dat Walter. He had a big mouth and never went to church. He came from a bad crowd in the Gardens.'

'Covent Garden?' Kathy asked, puzzled.

'Tivoli Gardens, in Kingston. Dat's where the Shower Posse hang out, you know? Walter and Joseph were both Garden boys.'

'They were rudies, were they?' Brock said. 'With the Shower Posse? Is that why they had to leave Jamaica?'

'Oh, dey weren't serious gangstas, Mr Brock. Dey was what dey call "fryers," at the bottom rank, but dey got in trouble with the police. When Joseph came here he tried to start a new life, but before too long Walter led him astray again. Dey called themselves the Tosh Posse, which was just stupid showing off to the girls at the club, and dey upset the Spangler boys across the railway line with their boasting about what big men dey'd been in the Gardens.'

'Were they selling drugs?'

She flared. 'I wouldn't have no drug dealers in my house! Joseph was a show-off and weak in the face of temptation, but he wasn't really bad. Father Maguire had faith in him. But Walter . . .'

'This Tosh Posse, who else was in it?'

'I only remember one other boy with them. He was older than them, nice-looking boy. Don't know the name.'

'How old was Walter?'

'He was a few years older than Joseph, I'd say. Dey made an odd pair, Joseph tall and so particular about his appearance, and Walter short and dirty.'

'How short?'

'Oh, shorter than her,' she nodded at Kathy, 'but not as short as me.'

'Was Joseph left- or right-handed?'

'How can I be expected—No, wait, he was right-handed. I remember watching him trying to write a Christmas card to someone back home. It was a struggle for him.'

'And you say they upset people across the railway—Spanglers?'

'Dat Shower and Spangler business was from the yard; it had no place here. But some of 'em brought it over with dem.'

'Any names?'

Winnie shook her head.

'When we met in that pub in Angell Town, you told me that Joseph had been frightened by two white men. They couldn't be Spanglers, could they?'

'Not if dey was white dey couldn't.'

'So who were they?'

Again, Winnie seemed to close in on herself.

'You'd seen them before, hadn't you? Come on, Winnie. Let's have it.'

'I wasn't sure. At first I thought dey might be coppers, but then I thought dey might have been Mr Roach's boys.'

'Yes,' Brock said quietly. He seemed to Kathy to relax, easing back in his chair as if finally satisfied. 'Did Joseph get on the wrong side of Mr Roach, do you know?'

'Not to my knowledge. Dey seemed to get on just fine. Too fine, if you wan' my opinion.'

'You've been very helpful, and the tea was just what we needed.' Brock got to his feet. 'Would you have a picture of Joseph or Walter?'

'No, I don't have no camera. I don't know if Father Maguire might.'

'We'll ask him. If he doesn't, I'd like you to help one of our computer people make a likeness of them and the third man. Would you do that for me?'

Winnie seemed quite taken with the idea as she bustled out with them to the street, where George was standing miserably stamping his feet.

TEN

THE SUN HAD DISAPPEARED behind dark clouds and the threatened rain or snow seemed imminent as they made their way between the market stalls towards the church. There were few
people around now, hoods and collars turned up against the sharp
wind. The church was locked, and they knocked on the door of
the presbytery next door. A housekeeper answered and told them
that Father Maguire was at the hospital and would be back in an
hour. Brock suggested they see if the Ship did lunches.

The pub had succumbed to TV, an absurdly large screen on one
wall showing a game of American football. Otherwise it seemed
little had changed. Lunch was limited to an assortment of greasy
sausage rolls and meat pies in a hot cabinet. Brock ordered a couple, and a beer and a tonic water, and took them to Kathy, who'd
found a small table as far as possible from the TV speakers. She
thanked him for the tonic and unbuttoned her coat.

'You need more than that,' Brock said.

'Had a big dinner last night.'

'Ah yes, with Tom Reeves. So how is he these days?'

'Fine.' She was going to leave it at that, then thought she should
say more, for the purposes of barter. 'He was called away over
Christmas, so we're just catching up again. Do you remember that
other Branch bloke we worked with a couple of years back, Wayne

O'Brien, who just disappeared one day? I thought the same had happened to Tom. They're difficult people to keep track of.'

'True enough. It's the nature of the job. Not easy.'

'He wants to transfer out. Anyway, he made a Jamaican dinner from stuff he bought here in the Lane—pot roast with Red Stripe beer. It was really good. You can get takeaway from the café, too.' She described the other dishes.

'I'll have to try that. It's ages since I tasted jerk.'

'He said that's next. Maybe we could do something together.'

Then, having prepared the ground, she said, 'How about you? Have you heard from Suzanne? I got a postcard from her from the Great Barrier Reef. Looked beautiful.'

He saw it coming, of course—but even so, the probe, gentle as it was, made him wince unexpectedly, like the slightest touch to an infected wound that doesn't want to heal. The trouble was that he hadn't been talking to anyone, so he hadn't developed the protective form of words. And there was the other thing too, which made it worse. In telling Kathy about 1981 he'd omitted the part about going home to the deserted house, but here he was back in Cockpit Lane again in much the same situation, twenty-four years later, locked into the same old patterns, as if nothing had progressed. He hadn't got a postcard from the Great Barrier Reef, but he had received a Christmas card from Suzanne's grandchildren in Hastings, back with their mother now, which had shaken him for a time.

'No, no. We haven't been in touch.'

'It's over then?' It sounded too abrupt and she sensed Brock flinch, but she was suddenly irritated by this cocoon of silence on the subject of Suzanne; Bren whispering, his wife phoning up to casually inquire about the boss's Christmas arrangements. She was also fairly certain that the old man wasn't talking to anyone else.

'I'm not sure, Kathy.'

'I mean, I'd be very sorry because I like her so much and I think she's great for you, but sometimes these things aren't meant to be . . . as I've discovered on numerous occasions.' She grinned and the sombre look on his face melted a little.

'Several times I've got as far as the travel agent's door,' he confessed, 'but I never made it inside.'

'Do you need a push? I'll take care of everything if you want.'

'Thanks. I know you would. We'll see. Now . . .' He addressed himself to the discouraging lump of pastry on his plate. '. . . what have we got here?'

'Are you going to tell me about the Roaches? You reacted to what Winnie said as if you'd been expecting it all along.'

He shot her a sideways glance as he chewed. 'You're annoyed I haven't been open with you?'

'Well . . . I've been getting the feeling that you've had these ideas from the start that you're not telling us about.'

'Mm, rubbish. This pie, I mean. No, you're right. From the beginning I've felt as if I were reliving the past with this one, which certainly suggested several possibilities, but I've been reluctant to . . .' The image that came to his mind was of stepping back into a tangled thicket. '. . . to jump to conclusions until I had a date for the murder, the race of the victims, and that comment from Winnie about who the two white men might have been.

'So, Spider Roach. Spider was one of the most vicious and most successful crooks in South London. He started out as a very smart operator in long firm fraud—setting up wholesale companies to buy goods on credit, then selling them fast and going bust or disappearing without paying their debts. He found he could double his profits by combining long firm fraud with arson and insurance scams, burning down the companies' premises and claiming for the goods, which had already been sold. Then, when he began to find it hard to get credit for his bogus companies, he discovered violence. He realised that he could persuade genuine companies, small family businesses usually, to act as the front for the fraud if only he could terrify their owners enough. The businesses were destroyed in the process, of course, and the owners usually ruined, but with sufficient violence—the threat of a brutal attack on the wife, perhaps, or on an elderly parent—they would keep quiet. He was a ruthless predator, and before long his violence escalated into murder. Spider was believed to be behind a number of particularly ugly unsolved killings in the seventies, but he was never arrested on any serious charge until 1980, when the supergrass Maxie Piggot named him for two murders. But by then juries and courts were getting wary of the evidence of supergrasses, and defence lawyers had had plenty of practice at discrediting them. The case against Spider collapsed.'

Brock pushed his plate away with a grimace of distaste and took a quick pull of his beer. 'Cockpit Lane was the heart of Spider's web. He and his family lived just behind the Lane. The shop next door to us here was a pawnshop he owned. What's now the cash and carry next to it was his funeral parlour.'

'Funerals? Adonia and her father?'

'That's right. He owned the premises and the Despinides operated the business. What better way to get rid of unwanted bodies? We suspected that's what they were doing, but we couldn't catch them. After two unsuccessful exhumations the magistrates became reluctant to go on giving us permission to dig up the Despinides' customers.'

Kathy thought of Adonia, in her cashmere and gold jewellery. 'My God.'

'Anyway, Spider flourished. I should say the Spider clan, because he had three sons who all followed him into the business. He got on well with the West Indians coming into the neighbourhood, and his long firm frauds were aimed at them, offloading the kind of things they wanted and would buy up quickly—cheap booze, bedding, thermal underwear, confectionery, toys, you name it.

'When the Jamaican bad boys started arriving in '80 and '81, with their cocaine and their crack and their fancy guns, some of the established London gangs got a bit shirty, but not Spider. He had discovered drugs years before when he'd pressed a chemist into one of his scams, and he'd developed a local clientele in a small way, but now he saw a huge new opportunity. The drug gangs in Jamaica were making the island a staging post for Colombian cocaine on its way north, and Spider saw the chance to tap into that golden stream. He welcomed the former Garden boys and Spanglers and all the rest, and they became his partners.'

Brock stared morosely at the slimy sausage roll lying untouched on his plate. 'I'm still hungry. I missed my dinner last night, and breakfast this morning.' He picked it up and bit it.

Kathy watched, feeling queasy, as if Tom's rum punch might still lurch up in her throat. She wondered whether she should try to pacify it with a hair of the dog. 'So you were involved in trying to catch Roach?'

'Actually it's not as bad as it looks.' Brock took another bite. 'Yes, very much so. This was my patch. We knew each other well. I'd bump into him and his sons in the market, in court, in here. He always had a leery smile for me. Sometimes I even suspected he felt a little sorry for me, getting nowhere. And I knew his victims, or the people they left behind, every one. Spider Roach was my big failure, Kathy. We all have them. He was mine.'

Kathy did feel sick. She got to her feet and said, 'Can I get you another beer?'

'Shouldn't really. Oh, what the hell.'

He handed her his empty glass and she went to the bar and ordered a rum and Coke for herself. When she returned he glanced at it and said, 'Switched to Coke now? Not much nutrition in that either.'

'Oh, you'd be surprised. So, are you ready to share your theory?'

He sipped, wiped his beard and nodded. 'Whatever Joseph planned to tell me when he first asked to see me, he couldn't have realised it implicated Spider. If he had, he'd never have suggested meeting here, right on Spider's doorstep. But then he must have realised. He was no longer safe in the Lane. He headed into the heart of Brixton to be among black folk, as Winnie told me. But Spider's boys tracked him down.'

Kathy thought. 'If they were Spider's boys. Winnie's first thought was that they were cops. Is that possible?'

'I've wondered about that too. It was the time of the riots, maybe a time of settling old scores . . . But no. I've thought back over the people I knew then, and I'm sure there was nobody . . .'

'Was Bob McCulloch here then?'

'I don't think so.'

'And Spider's still alive?'

'I believe so. He'd be in his late-seventies now. The last time our paths crossed was over ten years ago. I was investigating a murder in Epping. The victim turned out to be a drug dealer and the Drugs Desk got involved. Then the trail turned up a drug-smuggling route and Customs and Excise got in on the act, followed by the Fraud Squad and Special Branch. Before long we realised that Spider Roach was at the centre of it all, and a joint operation was mounted. It was a fiasco—too many cooks, all trying to outdo each other. The whole thing was so badly bungled that it led to a major review of joint operations. Several senior officers took early retirement. And once again Spider's teflon magic had worked. By the end he was better off than ever—nobody wanted to know about him.'

'I see. This is why you've been so cautious?'

Brock nodded. 'If we pursue him now we've got to be very sure of our ground, and we've got to keep it very quiet until we're ready. In the meantime we'll continue checking every detail of what Dana and Dee-Ann did when they came south of the river and who they met. I'm meeting DS McCulloch later this afternoon to work out how his team will help.'

He checked his watch. 'Come on, time we met the priest.'

FATHER MAGUIRE OFFERED THEM coffee in front of a gas fire in the sitting room of the presbytery.

'The warmest room in the house,' he said. 'It's far too large this place, impossible to heat, but there you are. I bumped into Winnie on the way back just now, and she told me something of what you're after.'

A vigorous elderly Irishman with rosy cheeks and given to explosive gestures with his hands to punctuate his words, he wasn't much taller than Winnie. Kathy could picture the two of them together, a formidable pair.

'Those poor souls. So you're still trying to identify them?'

'We think they may have been buried in April 1981,' Brock explained. 'You were here then, is that right?'

'Yes, I arrived in '76. Winnie mentioned the name Joseph. I couldn't immediately remember.' He tapped his head. 'Getting to the stage where if a new name comes in an old one drops out to make room. Ha! Anyway, fortunately I keep a diary of parish matters.' He went to a bookcase behind his desk and ran his fingers across the spines. 'Yes, here we go, 1981.'

'We might need 1980 as well, if he arrived that year.'

'True.' The priest brought both volumes.

'Winnie thought some time before Christmas.'

They waited while he thumbed back through the 1980 diary, clicking his tongue, until finally his finger shot into the air. 'Got you! Thursday September eighteenth, "08.55 Gatwick, BA 2262, Joseph Kidd 19 & Michael Grant 15. JK to WW, MG to AL." Well, well, he came over with young Michael then. I do remember that morning. A fine pair of likely lads.'

Kathy was making notes. 'What does that last bit mean?'

' "JK to WW" means Joseph went to stay with Winnie Wellington, as you know, and young Michael was taken in by Abigail Lavender, just down the street here.'

'Is that Michael Grant the MP?'

'Oh indeed! The star of Father Guzowski's boys, you could say.'

'Father Guzowski?'

'I'm sorry, I'm not explaining myself very well. Father Guzowski is a saint, or at least he will be, I've no doubt of it. He was an American priest, from New York, and he went down to Jamaica to run a mission in the slums of Kingston, with the poorest and most desperate. He worked miracles in the worst of circumstances. He saved lives and brought hope to thousands. And one of the things he did was to help lift young people out of the pit and offer them a new start, a new life, overseas. They were Father Guzowski's boys, and in New York, in Toronto, and elsewhere in London, there are people like me who met them off the planes and helped to get them a job and a place to stay.

'It didn't always work out, of course. They came from violent backgrounds, some of them, and found it difficult to shake that off.'

He stared at the diary entry again. 'You know, I'd forgotten that they came over together. I suppose you could say they represent both ends of the spectrum of Father Guzowski's boys. We worked hard on Joseph, as I recall, especially Winnie, but he was only interested in fast money and girls. It wouldn't surprise me if he'd been dealing drugs. And now, it seems he died a violent death. Michael, on the other hand, was younger and more malleable, receptive to Abigail's encouragement, and very bright. From the most rudimentary education in one of Father Guzowski's schools, he developed remarkably fast. By his early twenties he was studying at university, and a few years later he was a union official with UCATT, back here in our area. Soon he came to the attention of the local politicians, and was adopted as our parliamentary candidate. Michael Grant MP is now the member for Lambeth North.'

He said the final words with a flourish of his arm, as if proudly presenting not only Michael's but his own triumph over life's many obstacles, the draughty old presbytery, the recalcitrant youths, the shortage of funds. 'You might talk to Michael about Joseph, you know.'

'Yes, good idea,' Brock said.

'His constituency office is in the shop next door to the Ship.'

'Where Spider Roach had his pawnshop? You'll remember Spider Roach, of course.'

'Oh indeed.' Father Maguire seemed suddenly wary.

'He must have been a thorn in your side. He certainly was in mine.'

'He was a powerful figure around these parts, all right, and a baleful influence on many lives. But I hear he's a changed man now, a great giver of charity. In point of fact . . .' Kathy thought she detected some embarrassment here. '. . . he paid for the repairs to the church spire last year, and donated computers to the school. A sinner's repentance is a wonderful thing.'

He met Brock's stony gaze.

'Does he still come down here then?'

'No. I haven't seen him in years.'

'What about his sons?'

'Nor them. I heard they all moved out to Shooters Hill.'

'Do you have anything else that might help us then, Father? Any particular friends of Joseph? Or any recollections of that night, Saturday the eleventh of April 1981? It was the time of the riots in Brixton.'

The priest thumbed through the second diary but found nothing. He couldn't remember the surname of Joseph's friend Walter, or anything about a third member of the group. Abigail Lavender's husband had died and she'd moved away, but he wasn't sure where to.

'Maybe you could ponder on it and let us know if anything comes to mind. Would you have a photograph of Joseph?'

'Well now, that is possible. I used to make a habit of taking a picture of the boys when they arrived, to send back to Father Guzowski. Let's see, let's see. We've been making an effort to get my papers in order.'

He bustled across to a couple of old wooden filing cabinets in a corner of the room and began searching through the drawers. 'Here we are. It would be with these, if it's anywhere.'

He laid a sheaf of photos on his desk and turned them over until one caught his eye. 'This would be them, I think. Yes.' He showed a picture of two young men grinning at the camera, one tall and skinny and bow-legged with his arm around the shoulders of the other, more guarded and boyishly handsome.

'Thank you, Father.' Brock took the picture. 'You've been a great help.'

'I'd like it back, if that's all right. I've had it in my mind for some time to write a little memoir of Father Guzowski's boys. Somebody should.'

The path from the front door of the presbytery to the street wound around an ancient black yew tree, and as they emerged from its shelter they noticed a blue Peugeot convertible parked at the opposite kerb, emitting the usual heavy thumping bass. The side windows were tinted dark so they couldn't see who was inside. Just then, with perfect timing, a police patrol car swung around the corner and pulled in behind the Peugeot. Two young uniformed cops got out, a man and a woman, and approached it. The woman tapped on the driver's window and the door swung open, filling the quiet street with booming hip hop, and Mr Teddy Vexx heaved himself out. The policewoman said something to him and he reached back inside the car and turned the music off, then straightened again. She stood close in front of him, a good foot shorter, and delivered a short lecture, pointing to the no-parking sign, the double yellow line and the distance to the corner. All the time he stood there impassively, huge arms folded across the gold chains draped over his chest, staring across the road at Kathy and Brock. He was wearing a black bandana around his head and dark glasses. The constable asked for something and he reached to his hip pocket and produced a wallet, handing her his driver's licence. While she walked away, talking into her radio, her partner was peering into the car. The rules prevented him from searching it without due cause, something suspicious he could actually see or smell, and he looked slightly comic bent to the opening, nose twitching, straining for an excuse. Vexx said something and the cop straightened sharply and said, 'What's that, sir? Speak English, please.'

Kathy and Brock walked away.

ELEVEN

'I OWE YOU A fiver.'

He chuckled. 'You've established a date?'

'April 1981.'

'Interesting. How about buying me a pizza tonight? You can tell me all about it.'

'Suits me.'

'Can I pick you up at seven?' he asked.

'Fine.'

'And I may have something interesting for you.'

'Great, as long as it's not rum punch.'

'Aw, I thought you liked my rum punch.'

'I did, but it refuses to let go.'

'I know what you mean. I've got this strange limp today.'

'Strange limp what?'

'Now, now.'

That afternoon Bren had returned to Queen Anne's Gate to set up the case room for a new phase of the investigation, while Kathy got to work on Joseph Kidd. She established that he had entered the country on the eighteenth of September 1980, but there were no further records of him either leaving or returning. He had been allocated a National Insurance number the following month, but there were no records of any social security, national health or income tax transactions on that number. He had had no driver's licence, bank accounts, police record or traffic offences. As far as the record was concerned, sometime during 1981 Joseph Kidd had simply ceased to exist, although no one had ever reported him missing. Kathy looked at the copy of Father Maguire's photo of the two boys pinned to the wall, feeling the poignancy of that brief moment of elation at the arrivals gate at Gatwick. One boy had gone on to success in his new country, the other had disappeared into the void. She began to assemble the material that would be sent to the JCF in Kingston and to Interpol.

Brock, meanwhile, had got through to Michael Grant in his office at the Houses of Parliament. The MP had already heard from Father Maguire, and said he'd been intending to contact Brock. He said he'd come over immediately, Queen Anne's Gate being only a short walk away, and ten minutes later Brock met him at the front door. Seeing him again he recognised the handsome boy of the photograph, but the caution in his look had been replaced, or masked, by that air of open energy and confidence.

'I've been wanting to get in touch again ever since the rumours started about finding bodies on the railway land. Is this where you're running that investigation from? No chance of seeing the operations centre, I suppose?'

'Of course. This way.' Brock led him along the corridor to the main case room, once a merchant's drawing room with tall sash windows to both the street and the small courtyard at the rear. There he introduced him to Bren and Kathy, whom he remembered, and gave him a tour of the material on the walls—the gridded site map, the photographs of retrieved items and, most recently, the enlarged photograph of Joseph and himself.

'Oh my goodness.' Grant stared for a long moment at the picture. 'Father Maguire said he'd found a photo. I never knew it existed. Is there any chance, do you think, of getting a copy?'

'Certainly.' Brock had a word to Kathy, who nodded and went to her computer. 'Let's sit down and see what you can tell us, shall we? Tea or coffee?'

'Tea would be good.'

'Yes, always the safer bet.' Brock led the way to a conference table by the window overlooking the rear courtyard.

'So you think Joseph is one of your victims?'

'It looks very likely, Mr Grant. We're trying to contact his family in Jamaica to make a DNA match, but we're having trouble tracing them. Can you help us with that?'

'I don't think I can. You see, I didn't know Joseph before we came out together. Father Guzowski introduced us for the first time at Kingston airport.'

'Didn't Joseph talk about his background? Mrs Wellington thinks he was from Tivoli Gardens.'

'Actually, that does ring a bell. I'm sure we must have chatted about things like that on the flight over, but I don't remember. He was a few years older than me, and I can recall feeling a bit intimidated. To tell the truth, I was pretty overwhelmed by the whole experience. It was my first trip out of Kingston, my first flight. And I didn't come from Tivoli Gardens.' He gave a wry smile. 'The Gardens was a rough district, but we used to think of it as a step up from where we lived. I came from Riverton City, on the edge of town. Riverton City was the Soweto of Kingston, grown up around the Dungle, the Kingston City rubbish dump, which was pretty much the only resource the people there had to live off. It's all been cleared away now, transformed into what they call Riverton Meadows.'

Kathy arrived with his copy of the photograph and mugs of tea.

'You would have kept in touch with Joseph when you arrived here, I take it?' Brock asked.

'No. Oh, I saw him around, but I wasn't in his circle. The whole point of Father Guzowski sending me here, as he drummed into me again and again, was to get an education. He believed in me, said I could do it and mustn't let him down. I worshipped the man. With the help of Father Maguire and Abigail Lavender I just buried myself in schoolwork—I was so far behind the English kids, you see. I don't know what Joseph was up to, but it certainly wasn't studying.'

'What about his friends, someone called Walter and another, older man? They called themselves the . . .' Brock checked his notes. '. . . the Tosh Posse.'

'Oh, after Peter Tosh, yes?'

Brock looked puzzled.

'He was one of the three original Wailers, with Bob Marley in Trench Town. But no, I didn't know Joseph's friends. You think they could be the other bodies?'

'It's possible.' Brock described the physical characteristics they'd been able to establish, and for a moment he thought that something registered with Grant, then faded.

'No, I'm afraid I can't be of much help with Joseph or his friends. I'm sorry. And what about the murders of the two girls? Has there been any progress there?'

'DCI Savage believes they were killed because of something that happened in Harlesden, where they came from. He's quite optimistic about some leads he's following up there.'

'I see.' Grant looked carefully at Brock. 'You don't sound entirely convinced.'

'I'm keeping an open mind. We're still trying to trace their movements after they arrived in Cockpit Lane, and find the people they made contact with. It's a slow business, but it usually brings results in the end.'

'Good.' Grant paused, looked back over his shoulder at the people working, then leaned towards Brock and spoke more softly. 'Father Maguire mentioned to me that you were asking about Spider Roach. Can I ask, do you think he was involved with the bodies on the railway land?'

Brock hesitated. 'What would your interest be in that?'

Still in the same quiet voice, but stabbing the table with a finger to emphasise his points, the MP said, 'When I arrived in Cockpit Lane I thought it was paradise compared to where I'd come from. But I quickly learned that there was a nasty serpent in paradise. Spider Roach and his gang had an iron grip on that part of the city, and everyone was terrified of him. I saw what he did to people. Abigail Lavender's husband had both legs broken because he threatened to go to the police with something he'd seen. They told him the next time they'd take the hammer to Abigail.'

Brock nodded. 'I was a detective in the area then. I remember Mr Lavender. The hospital reported his injuries, but he wouldn't say a word.'

'Then you know what I'm talking about. But do you know that Spider Roach is still there, still sucking the life out of those people like a predatory leech?'

'Still there? I thought he'd moved away?'

'Oh, you won't see him on the streets any more, or his sons, but they're still operating there, through their agents, behind the scenes, intimidating, destroying our young people with drugs.'

Brock looked sceptical. 'Do you have any evidence of this?'

'I have evidence enough to know I'm right, but not enough to interest the police. Perhaps you know of the reluctance in some quarters to pursue Spider Roach. But if you have some new evidence against him, it may be that I can help you. I have a strong constituency network, including people who were around in 1981.'

Still Brock hesitated, weighing the risks. In the end it was the strong impression that Michael Grant had made on him, his passion and conviction, that persuaded him to open up.

'Joseph Kidd disappeared on the night of April the eleventh, 1981, the night of the Brixton riots. He told a witness that he was going to the Windsor Castle, which was burnt down that night. He appeared to be in fear of his life, and was apparently being pursued by two white men. A witness thought they might be Roach's men. I'd be very interested to know if Joseph and his friends had upset Roach in some way, if they did jobs for him, or were ever seen in the company of Roach and his sons. I'd also be interested in finding anyone who was in the Cat and Fiddle in Angell Town that night, or between there and the Windsor Castle, and who may have seen Joseph or the two men.'

'I'll see what I can do.'

'But very discreetly, please, Mr Grant. As you say, plenty of people around here never want to hear Roach's name mentioned again.'

'I understand. Thank you for being so open with me, Chief Inspector.' He glanced at his watch. 'Now, I must dash. I have a committee meeting. Home Affairs Committee, you know it?'

Brock caught the gleam in Grant's eye. 'I don't think so.'

'You should. It's a Departmental Select Committee, charged with scrutinising the operations of the Home Office, the Attorney General's Office, the Crown Prosecution Service and the Serious Fraud Office. You lot, in other words.'

He grinned and got to his feet, shaking Brock's hand.

When he returned to his office Brock put a call through to Keith Savage. The Trident detective spoke with a renewed confidence. Things were going well, he said, and arrests were expected shortly. Several sources had confirmed that Dana and Dee-Ann had stolen drugs from a powerful underworld figure in Harlesden, and Savage hoped their murders would provide the opportunity to close him and his operations down for good. And this time the team was going to do the job properly, at their own pace. Brock told him what they'd learned about the bodies on the railway land and asked if the Trident records might throw any light on them.

'They don't go much further back than 1998,' Savage said, 'when we were formed. There were earlier operations, of course, going back to the "Yardie Squad," Operation Lucy, in 1988. Before that you're talking ancient history, I'm afraid. Things have changed a lot since those days. For a start, most of our villains today aren't Yardies at all—they were born here.'

'While other things never change,' Brock said. 'The guns and the crack are still concentrated in the poorest boroughs.'

'True enough.'

'So you don't think you can help us identify our three victims?'

'Sorry, it's all too long ago. Ancient history.'

'Right. Incidentally, I came across a little quirk of ancient history that may intrigue you. That name that Michael Grant gave you—Roach.'

'Yes?' Savage was cautious. 'What about it?'

'It seems that Mrs Ivor Roach was hurt one day last week in a robbery.'

'Oh yes?'

'Her car was stolen as she was getting into it, by two unidentified black kids. I'm wondering if there could be a connection.'

Savage was silent for a moment, then said, 'Million to one, I'd say.'

'Yes, you're probably right.'

KATHY'S PHONE RANG PRECISELY on seven. Icy rain was battering the window.

'Hi, I'm downstairs.'

'I'm ready, be down in a minute.'

'I'll meet you at the door. I've got a brolly. By the way, I, er . . . I have someone else with me.' He sounded uncharacteristically hesitant.

'Okay, fine,' she said, slipped on her coat and grabbed her bag. She took the lift down to the lobby and saw his car parked directly outside under the lights. In the rear window she could make out the pale face of a small figure.

Tom wrestled his umbrella open. 'Hi.' He offered her a smile and an arm, but no kiss. 'What a night!'

Kathy smiled back. 'Hello. Who's your passenger?'

'It's my daughter, Amy. I'm sorry, I'd forgotten that I'm supposed to feed her before I take her back to her mother's.' He looked acutely embarrassed.

'That's fine,' she said, sounding more enthusiastic than she felt. 'I'd like to meet her. How old is she?'

'Nine.'

They scurried across to the car together and Kathy slid into the passenger seat and turned around to meet the eyes of the young girl staring at her from the back.

'Hello, I'm Kathy.'

'I'm Amy.' Her expression was grave, and Kathy couldn't quite shake off her first impression of a little old lady.

'We've been out together, Kathy,' Tom said. 'Tell Kathy where we've been, Amy.'

'The London Dungeon,' the girl said, still inspecting Kathy carefully.

'Oh yes? Any good?'

'Yes.' Amy turned away as they moved off, wipers beating against the storm. 'It was all right.'

'It was horrible,' Tom said. 'I felt sick.'

Amy said flatly, 'He didn't like the blood when they cut off the queen's head.'

'Too right. Not a good evening to be out on your site, Kathy.'

'No, they were expecting this. It'll be flooded.'

'Is that the murder site?' Amy asked. 'Can we go there?'

'Not tonight, sweetheart,' Tom said.

He dropped them at the door of the pizza restaurant while he tried to find a parking space, and Kathy and Amy hurried inside together. The place was bright, warm and busy, and they found a table and took off their coats. Looking around Kathy saw young women in studded belts, stretch jeans and pointy black boots, looking like refugees from the eighties. On the wall were framed posters for The Cure and Depeche Mode. It seemed that Brock wasn't the only one having an eighties revival.

She noticed that Amy had been clutching a fat paperback under her raincoat.

'You're a reader, like your dad.'

'Yes,' Amy said, settling herself. 'We're very alike.' She glanced around at the other tables. 'I shouldn't really be here. I'm on the Atkins diet.'

Kathy looked at her in surprise. 'Are you?'

'Yes.' She screwed her nose up at the menu. 'The most dangerous food additive on the planet is sugar, in all its forms.'

'Is it?'

'Yes. How many bodies have you found so far?'

'Three.'

'Yuk, doughnuts, twenty-seven carbs. Were they all together?'

'No, they were spaced apart.'

The precocious manner sat uncomfortably on the little girl and Kathy suspected that it was her form of protest at having to share her father with her.

'Can you draw a plan?'

Kathy smiled at the girl's serious expression, as if they were discussing a professional problem of great mutual concern. She took a pen from her bag and drew a diagram on a paper napkin with three crosses. 'We call them Alpha, Bravo and Charlie.'

'Hm . . . Doesn't that mean they were shot separately? If they were shot at the same time you'd dig one big hole, not three little ones, wouldn't you?'

'Sounds reasonable.'

'How did the murderers get onto the land?'

'We think from here, a derelict warehouse.'

'So this would have been the first grave . . .' Amy pointed to Bravo. '. . . followed by Alpha, then Charlie.'

'How do you work that out?'

'Bravo is the closest to where they got in, right in the middle of the site, halfway to the railway. The next time they went past that spot to here, and the third time further again, to here. I bet you I'm right, fifty p.'

'Okay, you're on. You're pretty smart. Do you want a Coke?'

'I'm going to be a forensic pathologist. Forty-one carbs, no thanks. I'll have a Diet Pepsi, zero carbs.'

'You should meet our forensic anthropologist, Dr Prior. You'd like her. She worked out just about everything we know from their bones.'

'Cool. If you're going to have pizza, I'd advise the thin 'n crispy, and definitely not the Hawaiian.'

'All right.'

Tom arrived, shaking off rainwater. 'How are you doing?'

'Fine. Amy and I have just made our first bet. And here's the fiver I owe you.'

They ordered, three thin 'n crispies, and chatted happily for an hour until Tom said he had to get Amy back to her mother's. As she sat in the car, watching Tom and his daughter running to the front door beneath the umbrella, Kathy felt as if she'd been given another little glimpse into Tom's life, and wondered if it had been as accidental as he'd made out. Afterwards they went for a drink, and he told her a little more about his ex-wife, divorced now for six years.

'Amy seems very bright,' Kathy said.

'She's like a sponge, soaks it all up.'

'Isn't she a bit young to be on a diet?'

He laughed. 'Is that what she told you?'

'Yes, she's very serious about it, telling me exactly how many carbs there were in everything on the menu.'

'She was having you on, Kathy. That's her mother, she's obsessed by all that stuff. This afternoon Amy had, let's see, one chocolate milkshake, two hot dogs, one sticky doughnut, two Cokes and a bowl of chips. All the stuff her mum tells her she can't have.'

'I see.'

'What's your bet about?'

'She told me the order in which the bodies were buried, for fifty pence.'

'Aha.'

Kathy saw the grin on Tom's face. 'What's the joke?'

'Nothing. She's smart all right.'

They both felt like an early night and Tom drove her home. They reached the forecourt of her building, the rain still pounding, and ran with the umbrella to the front door. Beneath its black canopy he kissed her cheek, then mouth.

'You didn't mind too much, me taking you out with Amy, did you?'

'No, of course not. I was really pleased to meet her. It was fun.'

'Good. Oh, look, I forgot about that thing I've got for you.' He patted his pocket. 'We really need some light.'

'Want to come up to the flat?'

'Maybe I should.'

As they went up in the lift Kathy realised that this was the first time she'd brought a man up to her flat since Leon had lived there with her. She felt a little itch of disquiet, sharing her lift, her front door, her living room, with a man again.

'Take your jacket off,' she said. 'It's wet. Want a glass of wine?'

'Thanks. So are my trousers.'

'Feel free,' she laughed, but he kept them on. In fact, he seemed to sense her reserve about having him there, and sat quietly on the sofa.

She got a bottle of verdelho from the fridge and poured two glasses, giving him one. In return he handed her the envelope he'd taken from his jacket pocket. Inside she found a single sheet of paper with a short paragraph of print. She sipped her wine and read.

The Browning 9mm Hi-Power automatic pistol remains the weapon of choice among Yardie gang members. These guns are often difficult to trace as they are sold, exchanged and passed around between different users. On the other hand, tracking the use of the same weapon in various locations can be employed to reveal previously unknown connections between different groups (see ATF case study US/1/84). Sometimes individual guns acquire a reputation and a nickname, often playing on the Browning label, as in 'Brown Maggie', 'Big Brownie' and 'Brown Bread.' The last, never traced, is believed to have been used in at least six separate shootings across South London in the 1980s.

She stared at it, surprised that he'd remembered. 'Hell. Why didn't we find this?'

'It's one of a series of Special Branch internal intelligence memos. I tracked it down this morning. I couldn't find any other reference to the six shootings, but you're bound to have that gun somewhere on your files, probably from the days before records were computerised.'

'Yes, thank you, Tom. That's terrific. Brock'll be delighted.'

'As long as you are.' He hesitated, then said, 'If he needs more, just let me know. I can maybe do some digging.'

'Okay. He's interested in your having been to Jamaica.'

'Oh yes? Well, this should earn you a few Brownie points.'

She laughed. 'That's right, and I got a few this morning when I worked out the date of the shooting.'

'Yes, tell me about that.'

So she told him about her day, and then he told her about his, escorting the sinister colonel's wife around Harrods while her husband was negotiating at the peace conference.

He put his arm around her. 'I blew it last night, didn't I? Too much rum punch and Red Stripe. Sorry about that.'

'I enjoyed it. Anyway, there's plenty of time.'

'That was the first time I'd invited a woman to my flat in years, you know. I got a bit carried away.'

She stroked a slick of rain-damp hair from his brow, feeling a growing warmth inside her, but also an unease that wasn't just to do with having a man in her private space. Perhaps it was the lack of preparation for meeting his little girl, or more likely the sighting of Teddy Vexx again that afternoon.

'What's wrong?'

'Nothing. I'm just tired.'

'Sure.' He smiled and shrugged on his jacket, still wet. 'Thanks for the pizza. And thanks for being so nice to Amy.'

'And thank you for the stuff on Brown Bread. I'll speak to Brock first thing. He'll want to see this as soon as possible.'

TWELVE

THE NEXT MORNING KATHY met Brock on his way into the office. She showed him Tom's information on Brown Bread and he raised an eyebrow.

'Could be something in it, I suppose. You could speak to the boy again. He might say more without me around. Tom Reeves seems to be taking quite an interest in the case.' Brock gave her a little smile.

'Yes, well . . . the Jamaican connection, you know.'

She returned to her computer and tried to find references to the six Brown Bread shootings, but without success. Neither of the records of the two shootings that ballistics had linked to the cartridge cases found on the railway land carried any references to 'Brown Bread.' Finally she rang up her friend Nicole Palmer in Criminal Records at the National Identification Service, to ask for her help.

'And how's the boyfriend?' Nicole asked. 'I hear he's back.'

'Nothing gets past Palmer of the NIS, does it?'

'The real question is why you kept it a secret, Kathy. I had to rely on Lloyd bumping into him. He said that you were going out again.'

'Bit early to say.'

'Oh, come on, Kathy. Get in there. He's perfect.'

'Apart from the odd prolonged disappearance.'

'That's his work. And according to Lloyd he's getting out of Special Branch as soon as he can. We need to talk about this. I'm worried about your attitude.'

Kathy laughed. Nicole was perfect for the NIS, she thought. She just loved information, the more human and intimate the better.

'If you can get me anything on Brown Bread by lunchtime I'll buy you a sandwich.'

'Done.'

THE HEADMISTRESS AT CAMBERWELL Secondary seemed pleased to see Kathy again. 'I can't pretend we don't find all this pretty exciting. It's a struggle to keep the kids' attention in the classes on the upper floor, from where they can see your people working, and it's the only topic in the staff room. Have you found out what brown bread means?'

'It's possible that it's the name of a pistol,' Kathy said, and watched the enthusiasm drain from the other woman's face.

'Oh no. Not guns again.'

'Has that been a problem here?'

'Not inside the school, so far, which is a miracle I suppose, given what goes on right outside the gates these days. The shooting of the two girls next door wasn't the only one. Somebody shot the newsagent round the corner last month, just for a packet of cigarettes. I've dreaded becoming one of those places with guards and metal detectors at the front gates.' She shook her head in frustration. 'I'd never have thought it of Adam Nightingale, but none of them are immune, are they? Not when there are so many terrible role models out there.'

'I'd like to talk to him again. It may not be what we think.'

The boy appeared, sullen and withdrawn, and was told to sit facing Kathy while the headmistress took her seat behind her desk. Kathy waited for a moment, saying nothing, staring at Adam long enough for him to shift with discomfort, then she reached into her shoulder bag and took out something wrapped in black plastic, about the size of a hand. She put it down on the edge of the desk between her and the boy, hard enough for him to hear the clunk of metal against wood.

He gave a sharp gasp, staring at it. 'You found it,' he whispered. 'It was there.'

'IT WAS LIKE A quest,' Kathy said later at the team meeting. 'The story had been circulating among the boys in the school for years, an urban myth, passed on from generation to generation, of a gun called Brown Bread belonging to a notorious gangsta murderer being thrown from a passing train onto the waste ground and never found. By the time it percolated down to Adam's year it had almost faded away. Nobody really believed it except him. He was obsessed by it. The gun became a kind of talisman that would give him some respect around the place and stop him being bullied. When he saw McCulloch's people searching the railway land he panicked and decided to get in there first. Afterwards he couldn't admit what he'd been after without being seen as an even bigger nerd, and the bullying would've got worse. I let him think we found it.'

'But it isn't there?' Brock asked Bren.

'Not a chance, chief. We've now covered every inch of our site and along both railway banks to north and south for a distance of fifty yards with metal detectors and ground-penetrating radar. There won't be any more surprises.'

Bren went on to report progress at the site. More fragments of bones and clothing had been found, but neither a third cartridge nor Charlie's skull. Someone asked about the foxes and Bren pointed out on the plan where two dens had been found. That was normal, he said, as foxes liked to have an alternative hiding place for emergencies. This being the breeding season, they'd found three dead pups in one of the dens, together with some small gnawed human and animal bones. The foxes themselves hadn't been seen.

He then came to the final part of his report and, although Bren rarely showed much excitement, it was obvious from his animation that he thought this was good. It was a line of reasoning that he had been developing with the forensic team, to understand the sequence and timing of the three murders. On a map of the railway land he pointed out their locations and the probable routes taken by the victims and their killers, and put forward an argument for the order of events that was almost exactly the same as Amy had suggested to Kathy in the café the previous evening.

Brock was impressed. 'Makes sense,' he growled, as if edging closer to some hidden truth. 'So Bravo—Joseph Kidd—was the first of a series of three separate murders and burials that began, presumably, on the eleventh of April. How long did it last?'

'Can't say for sure, chief, but Dr Prior says the skeletal remains are indistinguishable in terms of aging. She doesn't think they were too far apart.'

When they broke up Kathy spoke to Bren. 'That was a neat bit of deduction. When did you work it out?'

'Yesterday. It was Dr Prior's idea mainly.'

'You didn't happen to mention it to Tom Reeves yesterday, did you?'

'Yes, I did actually. He called in to the site. Said he was just passing. He seems very interested in this case. Aren't they keeping him busy enough in Special Branch?'

'He's on some escort duty, pretty boring I think.'

'Do you reckon he's looking for a transfer over here?'

'Over here?' Kathy was startled. 'I don't think so. There wouldn't be a vacancy anyway, would there?'

'S'pose not.'

As she went back to her desk, Kathy turned this over in her mind. She was finding herself thinking about Tom more and more these days, but the idea of him moving into Brock's team made her feel distinctly uncomfortable. Experience had taught her to keep her private life separate from her work, but there was also the matter of her rank and position in the team. As detective sergeant, Kathy had already passed the exams for inspector, but her promotion was on hold because it would mean moving to another unit, which she refused to do. If there was any possibility of an inspector position becoming available at Queen Anne's Gate, she was determined it was going to be hers.

She met Nicole for a quick lunch as arranged, but she too had been unable to find any references to Brown Bread. It seemed it existed only as an old piece of intelligence buried in the internal files of Special Branch. After some probing interrogation and advice from her friend, Kathy paid for the lunch and returned to the office, where she rang Tom's mobile.

'Hi, can you talk?' she asked.

'They're halfway through a hugely expensive lunch at the Connaught, no doubt at British taxpayers' expense.'

'Lucky you.'

'Not me. I'm sitting outside drinking a cup of coffee. How are you?'

'Okay. What were you doing on the site at Mafeking Road yesterday?'

'Looking for you, of course. Had to make do with Bren Gurney.'

'And he told you about his theory of how the murders were committed, which you then told Amy.'

'Ah. It's a fair cop. Are you mad at us?'

'Not really. I should have worked it out.'

'Amy was nervous about meeting you, but she told me later that she liked you.'

'Well, it looks like I owe her fifty pence. Now I wonder if I can ask a favour?'

'Sure, go ahead.'

She told him about her difficulty in tracing the Brown Bread shootings, and he said he'd make some calls. He got back to her half an hour later with one name, Johnny Mulroy, a thief and police informant who had been murdered by Brown Bread in 1985. Tom said it would involve a lot more research to track down the other five shootings, but for Kathy that one was enough. She knew of the Johnny Mulroy case, because it was one of the two shootings that ballistics had tied to the cartridges on the railway land.

'That's great, Tom. Thank you. I owe you.'

'How about a drink after work tonight?' He mentioned a bar and she agreed, then went to see Brock and told him what she had.

He was very interested in Brown Bread now. 'We need those other five cases, Kathy. If we can tie the Roaches to any one of them, then we can tie them to our three corpses.'

'It'll mean a trawl through Special Branch files.'

He nodded. 'I'll speak to them.'

SHE WAS THE FIRST to arrive at the bar that evening. She sat watching the door, and felt a warm buzz of pleasure when he appeared. Nicole was right, she decided, he was exactly what she needed.

He kissed her cheek, his face cool from the night air. 'Hi,' he said, then stood back a moment and stared at her.

'What's wrong?'

'Nothing,' he said. 'I came through the door there and saw the most beautiful girl in London sitting at the bar, and she was waiting for me.'

She laughed, pleased by his flattery. 'I'm a cop, Tom, highly trained to detect bullshit.'

'But I mean it.' He ordered a drink and sat beside her. 'How was your day?'

'Good. Brock was very impressed with what you gave me. He said he'd speak to your people about searching out the other cases.'

'Yes, he did it. I thought I was in trouble when my boss called me in and asked me how come I'd been giving information to Brock. But he seemed happy enough when I explained. He's keen on interdepartmental cooperation. I think it's in our mission statement somewhere. Anyway, it seems the colonel and his wife are heading back to Africa and no longer need me, thank goodness, so the boss offered my services to Brock to follow up on the Brown Bread cases. Good, eh? I'll get to work with you.'

'Oh . . . yes. That's great, Tom.'

'Yeah. I'm to report to Queen Anne's Gate tomorrow at eight-thirty to brief Brock on what's involved.' He took a deep pull at his lager. 'I must admit, it feels good to get involved with some real detective work again.'

THIRTEEN

THE NEXT MORNING, KATHY met Tom in the front lobby of the Queen Anne's Gate offices and took him up through the labyrinth of corridors and staircases that had been knocked together from the original houses that made up the terrace.

When they reached the top floor she introduced him to Brock's secretary Dot, and said, 'Look in on me when you're finished. I'll be in the case room on the ground floor, down the corridor from the entrance.'

'I think I'll need Ariadne's thread to find my way out again.'

'Dot'll show you the way, or she can give me a ring to come and get you.'

Kathy returned to the case room, where she settled at a computer and got back to trying to find references to a possible missing person called Walter. Around her other team members dribbled in, starting the day with cups of coffee and yawning accounts of what they'd done the previous night.

Tom appeared after half an hour, looking bouncy and cheerful. He said hello to Bren and the others, then Kathy walked with him to the front door. 'How did it go?'

'Good, especially after I recognised the picture of Spider Roach on his wall. You didn't mention that you were interested in him.'

'No, I didn't. How do you know him?'

'We did a little bit of work on him, some time ago. We helped put a couple of his business buddies away. You should have mentioned it.'

'I didn't know we were working together then.'

'He's asked me to report back later this afternoon with whatever I've found, so maybe I'll see you then.' He waved goodbye, and Kathy returned to her search.

It was frustrating work, and there were continual interruptions, so that she felt she'd achieved nothing by the time Tom returned. He, on the other hand, seemed to have done well. He was carrying a box of files and papers, and she showed him to a meeting room for his briefing, where they were joined by Brock and Bren.

He had been able to identify all six of the shootings referred to in the Special Branch memo. They comprised four murders, one attempted murder and one drive-by shooting. They included the two shootings that ballistics had linked to the railway land cartridges, and they had all occurred between 1981 and 1987. Tom had marked the pattern of their locations across a map of South London, like a cluster of hits on a target.

'Interesting,' Brock said, unfolding his half-lens glasses and peering at the map intently, as if he might decipher some hidden message. 'You've pretty well exactly defined Spider Roach's territory during the 1980s. It's like the map of some lethal dog pissing on lampposts.' He stuck a finger at Cockpit Lane at the centre. 'And that was his kennel.'

He sat back down with a look of satisfaction.

Tom went on to summarise what he knew about the victims. Apart from their own three corpses, there had been two West Indian, one South Asian and three white victims, all male. Two of them had criminal records—Johnny Mulroy, and a well-known Jamaican disc jockey whose charges of drug trafficking were pending at the time of his death. Three other men were local businessmen and the sixth appeared to be a chance victim caught up in a car theft.

'Indiscriminate and non-racial,' Brock said. 'That's Spider.'

Kathy noticed Tom give a grudging nod of agreement, his theory of feuding Yardie gangsters apparently demolished.

'What now?' Brock asked.

'We should reopen the files on the six cases. There may be witness statements describing the gunmen, maybe facial composites, fingerprints even.'

'But all of these cases were unsolved, yes? And the matching gun was never found?'

'That's right. In most of the cases the ballistic evidence isn't very helpful, which is why you didn't get a match straightaway. The name "Brown Bread" came from undercover sources. Apparently it was widely believed among young Jamaicans at the time that the disc jockey had been shot by a gun of that name, and that the gun had been used in a number of other shootings, which were narrowed down to those six.'

'We should get ballistics to review all the evidence,' Bren suggested. 'They've got better equipment now.'

They discussed the individual cases for a while, Brock listening in silence, then he sat up and told them what they would do. There were three urgent lines of inquiry, he said. The first, to be investigated by a team led by Bren, would reopen the six Brown Bread cases that Tom had discovered; a second team would scour the dozens of possible sources of film and still photographs taken in Brixton on the night of the riots; and the third, led by Kathy, would work the area from Cockpit Lane down to the centre of Brixton looking for eyewitnesses from that night, starting with whatever sources Michael Grant had promised to find.

'Tom,' he added, 'you've been a great help with this, and I'm sure there's more about Brown Bread and the Roach family tucked away in Branch files. Are you interested in spending a bit more time helping us?'

'Yes, absolutely.'

'Then, if you're agreeable, I might ask your boss if you could be spared to work over here with us for, say, a couple of weeks. What do you think?'

'I think he'll probably be delighted.' Tom grinned.

He was right, apparently, and the next morning he arrived with several boxes of files, as well as a carrier bag containing assorted bits and pieces, including his coffee mug, as if he were moving in for the duration. Bren gave him a desk next to his own, and they settled down to work on the old case files. When Kathy later went to see what they were up to, she was surprised to find the two of them in the basement, in the Bride of Denmark, the curious little private snug bar which the previous owners, a publishing firm, had lovingly constructed out of bits retrieved from bombed and demolished London pubs. Bren and Tom were leaning on the ancient bar, beer bottles in hand, heads together as if they were old mates at their local. The Bride was, to say the least, an anachronism in a Scotland Yard office building, studiously overlooked by Admin, and only Brock had ever invited outsiders down there. Kathy had never seen any of the team take a drink except at Brock's invitation. Bren knew this, of course, and there was an awkward moment as he saw Kathy stoop through the low vault to come in.

'Kathy, hi. I was just showing Tom around. Would you, er, care for one?'

'No thanks.'

'Isn't this just the most amazing place?' Tom said. He waved the hand holding the bottle, almost empty. 'The stuffed lion, the salmon, the mahogany. I mean, who would believe it?'

'Well, just don't go telling any of your mates at the Branch,' Kathy said. 'If head office hears we're down here boozing all day they'll have the wreckers over in no time.'

'Relax, Kathy,' Tom said expansively. 'I'm not likely to let them in on this now, am I?' As if he were no longer one of them. 'And you know you're partial to a drop now and again. I was telling Bren about Red Stripe. Maybe I'll buy a case for the Bride next time I'm down Cockpit Lane.'

Kathy frowned at Bren, who winced with embarrassment. 'I just came down to see how you're going with the case files.'

'It's coming along,' Bren said. 'Tom dug up a lot of useful stuff. How about you?'

'Yes, making some progress. I'm going over to see the MP soon, to see what he's come up with. Well, see you.'

'Yes.' Bren hurriedly finished his bottle and began gathering up the bottle tops as if cleaning up a crime scene.

Tom followed Kathy out. 'Hey, you okay? You sound fed up.'

'I'm fine.'

'Um, I'm going out with some of the blokes tonight to play squash, otherwise . . . You free tomorrow evening?'

'No, I'm going to see some friends this weekend.' It wasn't quite true, but she suddenly felt she wanted a bit of time to herself.

'Are you sure you're not mad at me over something? Is it Amy, me springing her on you like that?'

'No. I liked Amy.'

'I'm glad. She's been talking a lot about you. She had some idea you were taking her to a path lab, but I told her that wasn't possible.'

Kathy didn't remember actually saying she'd take the girl to Dr Prior, but she said, 'I may have mentioned something along those lines. Yes, I will try. When would she be free?'

'Oh well, if you're sure . . . any afternoon after school, I suppose.'

'I'll see what I can do, Tom. No promises.'

She got on the phone when she returned to her desk. Dr Prior was cooperative.

'Yes, no problem, but could you make it tonight? I'm off to a conference in Germany on Monday and I won't be back for a while.'

Kathy phoned Tom, who phoned Amy's school (a small domestic emergency, he explained) to speak to Amy, and within twenty minutes it was arranged.

Tom gave Kathy a lift to Michael Grant's constituency office in Cockpit Lane in his Subaru, saying he would pick up his daughter while she was busy.

'I really appreciate you doing this for Amy,' he said. 'She's beside herself.'

'It's a pleasure.' Kathy felt she'd maybe been too defensive about Tom moving into Queen Anne's Gate. Perhaps things would be all right. 'What do you think about Brock's idea that the Roaches are behind all the killings?' she asked.

'I didn't like it at first, though I could be convinced. But really, all we've got is a possible sighting of two white guys in a crowded pub, twenty-odd years ago. The witness could have got it completely wrong, you know how these things are. Maybe the two guys weren't white, or maybe they had nothing to do with whatever was scaring Joseph.'

'I know.'

'You don't think Brock's got himself a mission, do you, putting the past to rights? That's worrying you, isn't it?'

'Yes, but you've doubted him before, don't forget, on the Tracy Rudd case, and he was right then. I trust his instincts.'

'Yeah,' Tom said, as if to himself. 'Loyal Kathy. I like that.'

Tom turned into Cockpit Lane and pulled over to the kerb. 'Half an hour?'

'Fine. See you.' Kathy watched the grin form in his mouth and around his eyes, and realised how much it was growing on her.

A chill east wind buffeted her as she hurried forward. More snow was promised and the wind tasted of it. She noticed a slight, dark figure standing at a shop window filled with PlayStations and digital gear. The face was covered by the hood of a parka and she was almost past before she recognised the glint of Adam Nightingale's glasses.

'Hello, Adam. How are you?'

He shrugged, pushing his glasses back up his nose. 'Saw them packing up from the school window. Leaving are they?'

'Yes.'

He looked forlorn, as if a moment of meaning or excitement in his life was coming to an end, and she felt sorry for him. 'You're interested in that forensic stuff, are you?'

He nodded.

'Actually I'm on my way over to the laboratories where they're working on the skeletons, reconstructing their faces.'

'Wow. Cool. I wish . . .' His sentence trailed off into inarticulate silence.

'Well, I could probably arrange for you to come, but we'd have to get your mother's permission.'

'She's at work.' He whipped a mobile phone out of his jacket pocket and offered it to her. Kathy watched him press the keys, then she took the phone and spoke to his mother, who was delighted that someone was willing to take Adam off the streets for an hour or two.

'Okay,' Kathy said to the boy. 'I've got some business to do. Be here in half an hour.'

The shopfront next to the pub was plastered with pictures of the MP's handsomely smiling face alongside public service posters reading, 'Stop the Guns,' 'Crack Kills,' 'Let's Work Together.' She pushed open the door and stepped into a fug of heat and clamour, Magic FM competing with clattering keyboards, a whistling kettle and a group of women arguing loudly over the messages on a noticeboard. An electrician stood on top of a stepladder fixing a light, and in the middle of it all, oblivious to the turmoil, Michael Grant posed for a photograph being taken by a reporter from the local paper. Grant was wearing jeans and a T-shirt with the slogan OUR STRUGGLE and a clenched black fist.

He caught sight of Kathy and clapped the reporter on the shoulder and swung over to her. 'Hi! DS Kolla, right?'

She shook his hand, unable to resist the dazzle of his smile. It wasn't just the mouth; his whole face seemed animated by it, and as they spoke he focused on her as if nothing else in the world interested him. A politician's trick perhaps, she thought, but he did it brilliantly.

'Come through and meet Kerrie, my office manager.' They manoeuvred around the stepladder and approached a young black woman sitting behind a desk, arguing with someone on the other end of the phone, smacking the file in front of her to emphasise her point. She put the phone down and nodded at Grant.

'He'll see you at noon tomorrow. I'll line up the media.'

'Well done, Kerrie! Didn't think you'd do it. This is DS Kolla from Scotland Yard.'

'Kathy.'

'Hello. Yes, we've got one or two leads for you.' She handed Grant a sheet of paper. 'I'd better get on with organising things for tomorrow, Michael.'

'You go ahead. I'll take care of Kathy.' He waved her through to a seat in a quieter area at the back of the shop and poured them both cups of coffee from a percolator.

'It may not look like it, Kathy, but this is a war room. We're involved in a life and death struggle, literally.' He tapped the slogan on his chest. 'This isn't idle rhetoric. We have a three-pronged youth crisis here—unemployment, drugs and crime. My job is to motivate my community to action, to break the vicious circle. We're on the same side, Kathy, and we'll do anything we can to help you take the drug kings, the crime bosses, out of the picture.'

'Right, I appreciate that, sir.'

'Michael, please.' He glanced at the sheet of paper. 'These are people we've found who can remember Joseph. They've all expressed a willingness to help. To save you having to traipse all over the district, one of the girls on the front desk can set up times when they can come in here to talk with you, if that suits. I think they'd feel more comfortable here than at the police station.'

Kathy scanned the list, half a dozen names and addresses. 'That's great. You're doing my job for me.'

'It's a start.'

'We're making up posters of the three victims on the railway land. This is what we've got so far.' Kathy handed him photographs of Dr Prior's reconstructions. 'Joseph Kidd and the one we believe was called Walter.'

Grant gasped as he took in the lifelike images. 'How on earth did you get these?'

Kathy explained. 'Do you recognise them?'

'Yes . . . Well, Joseph, certainly. It's very close. The other one looks familiar, but I'm not sure.'

Kathy handed him the third image, based on Winnie's sketchy memory of the other member of the Tosh Posse. 'This is the one we have the least information about—no name and no skull to make a reconstruction from.'

Grant stared for a moment, then shook his head. 'No. This means nothing to me. But once you have the posters we can put them in the front window here, and I'm sure we can persuade shopkeepers in the area to do the same.'

'You're being very helpful, Michael. Thank you.'

They arranged for Grant's office to set up interviews on the following Monday, and Kathy left. Adam was waiting outside.

The Subaru drew up a few minutes later and Tom got out and spoke to Kathy and Adam while Amy waited in the car, watching. Kathy led the boy over to introduce him.

'Adam, this is Inspector Reeves's daughter Amy, who wants to be a forensic pathologist. Amy, this is Adam, who is helping us with our inquiries.' She paused while Amy's face froze at the form of words. 'He's coming with us.'

'Coming with us?' she whispered. 'In our car?'

'Yes, that's all right, isn't it?' Then she added casually, 'Adam was the one who found the skeletons.'

'Oh! It was you? You got the electric shock? Everyone's been talking about you at school.'

Adam ducked his head, embarrassed and pleased. They all got into the car, Adam in the back with Amy, and drove off.

DR PRIOR WAS AN EXCELLENT guide, explaining everything clearly and treating their questions seriously. The youngsters were captivated by the microscopes, the chemicals and the bones, but the high point was the computer imaging of Alpha and Bravo. The precise profiles of their skulls had been scanned, and then data for average Negroid soft tissue thicknesses all over the head had been applied to flesh them out. The resulting images could be rotated and viewed from any angle and with different hair and beard styles. The result for Bravo was startlingly similar to the photograph of Joseph that Father Maguire had provided, while the other was a reasonable match to the representation of Walter that Winnie had arrived at with the computer artist.

While the other three played with the computer, experimenting with dreadlocks, glasses and various Rasta beards, the anthropologist had a quiet word with Kathy.

'How's the investigation going? Any suspects?'

'Nothing definite, but we are looking at some possible white suspects.'

'What did I tell you? A race crime.'

'But we're not clear about motive. It could simply have been a dispute over drugs or punishing an informer.'

Dr Prior shook her head. 'Look.' She drew Kathy over to Bravo's skull, mounted on a stand on the bench. Her finger traced around the bullet hole in the upper forehead. 'This is a close-range shot.' She pointed to diagrams and hard copies of computer images on the wall, tracing the probable angle of the bullet into the skull.

'Get down on your knees,' Dr Prior said.

'What?'

'Go on, I want to show you how it was.'

Kathy's smile faded as she saw how serious the other woman was. She knelt.

'You're Joseph Kidd—Bravo, right? Imagine it. Apart from soft tissue damage, we've just broken your right leg in the middle of the shin and crushed two of your fingers. We hit you on the left side of your head with maybe a hammer or a pickaxe handle, so hard that your skull is cracked. You've been unconscious for a time and you're in deep shock. Now you find yourself on wasteland in the dark, your arms and legs are trussed with wire, you're on your knees, there's blood in your eyes and mouth. Imagine it.'

Dr Prior reached for a test tube from a rack on the bench, and pressed the end hard against Kathy's forehead. 'This is a Browning automatic and now you're going to die. We're not doing this to make an example of you, because nobody will ever learn what happened to you. This isn't business. We're doing this because we want to. Understand? We've gone to a lot of trouble, hurting you, bringing you here, and now you will disappear. Die, you black bastard.'

There was a deathly hush in the laboratory. Kathy blinked and for a moment she saw herself, not as Joseph, but as Dee-Ann kneeling on the hard concrete floor of the garage. Then the test tube was withdrawn and she realised the other three children were staring at her.

'Right,' she said, getting to her feet. 'Very convincing.'

AT THE END OF the tour they thanked Dr Prior and returned Adam to his home behind Cockpit Lane. All the way back he and Amy were immersed in a hushed conversation, punctuated by little whistles and gasps. When the car pulled in to the kerb, Adam and Kathy got out. He thanked her awkwardly. 'That was . . . really cool,' he said, then, 'I'm not the only one who's been watching you, d'you know that?'

'How do you mean?'

'There's a guy who's been spying on you from behind the fences on the other side of the railway. I've seen him from the school window on the top floor.'

'Probably a reporter.'

'No, he doesn't have a camera, just binoculars. Big ones with red lenses. He's loosened some of the wooden palings of the fence so he can push them apart. You can't see him, only the binoculars. He's been there a lot, for whole days at a time. Must have warm clothes.'

As they drove Amy to her mother's home, the girl also seemed subdued by their trip. She thanked Kathy without any of the boldness of their previous meeting. Kathy put out her hand to shake, and when Amy did likewise the girl felt the fifty pence coin pressed into her palm.

Kathy winked. 'Don't spend it all on chips.'

She was silent as Tom drove her home. The odd little performance in the laboratory weighed on her. It wasn't that it had told her anything new, but that replaying the actions had given them a physical presence in her mind that hadn't been there before. That had been Dr Prior's point, of course.

Tom broke into her thoughts. 'Tired?'

'Just thinking.'

'You take work too seriously, you know that?'

'Do I?'

'Yes. I bought you a book to take your mind off things.' He reached across to the glovebox and handed her a paper bag. 'I think you'll like it. It draws you in, makes you forget everything else. But a bit heavy for tonight, perhaps. You need something buoyant. A movie? Maybe an old favourite? What's the best movie you'd like to see again?'

She thought. 'The Blues Brothers.'

'Yes!' He tapped the steering wheel. 'Brilliant. And appropriate, too—1980.'

'It's not as old as that, is it?'

'Want to bet?'

She laughed. 'I'm not making any more bets with you or your immediate family. Are you sure?'

'Yep. I can remember seeing it on my first blind date. I was twelve. I had to borrow some money from my mum afterwards to buy the sunglasses. What do you say we get takeaway and The Blues Brothers.'

'I thought you were playing squash tonight?'

'I cancelled.'

'Well, that sounds good, if I can fit in a bath somewhere.'

And so it was. As she lay in her bath, aware of his presence in the room outside, she realised that she hadn't felt so awkward about having him in her flat this time. He seemed to fit into the small space without intrusion, opening a bottle and following her instructions for a salad. It was a talent, she felt, for sympathetic manners, adjusting his dimensions (for he was actually quite a big bloke) to the available psychological space. Or maybe it was just part of Special Branch training, melting in, lulling the mark.

The meal wasn't bad, the film great. When it was finished they stayed sitting on the sofa together and she was acutely aware of his physical presence so close beside her, like a source of warmth and life. He told her how much he'd enjoyed being with her over the previous days, and when he got up to leave they kissed, and it seemed natural and inevitable. She even felt a small tug of regret as he disappeared into the lift.

THE FOLLOWING MORNING SHE drove back down to Cockpit Lane, where the Saturday morning market was in full swing. The wind had died down, the dark clouds dispersed and, although it was still cold, sunshine lit up the colourful striped awnings of the stalls. She drove down Mafeking Road to the warehouse. A single car stood in the yard, and when she went inside she found one of the SOCOs making a final inspection.

'Lucky to catch me,' he said. 'Just about to lock up and give back the keys.'

'Give me two minutes.'

She went through to the rear boundary, now reinstated and sealing off access to the railway land. She scanned the fences at the top of the embankment on the far side of the rail tracks. Most were brick or metal panels but among them she made out a section of wooden palings, almost opposite where the school stood. She left the warehouse and made her way back around Cockpit Lane to the footbridge across the railway beyond the school. From there she was able to see the wooden fence again, and estimate how far away it was.

She turned into the street running behind the railway embankment and paced the distance to the start of a row of small brick houses. She knocked at the first front door and, when there was no reply, walked down the narrow side passage to the backyard.

There was the wooden fence, with no sign of disturbance. She tried the next house, again with no reply at the front door, but with a huge Rottweiler in the back, hurling itself against the gate as she tried to look over.

A young man, yawning and scratching his crotch, answered the third door. Kathy showed her identification and said she was investigating reports of a prowler in the street. The man shrugged and said he'd heard nothing, but she was welcome to look around the yard. There, in a corner hidden from sight of the house by a small shed, she found an area of ground cleared of snow, in front of a section of fencing in which the nails had been removed to allow the boards to be slid apart. From this sheltered hide she had a perfect panorama of the whole of the crime scene site. She searched the place thoroughly but could find no traces that might interest the SOCOs—no footprints, no cigarette butts or sweet wrappers, no threads caught on the rough wooden boards, which would probably yield no fingerprints. Whoever it was had been careful. She was turning to leave when her eye caught a tiny flake of white in the trampled ground. Using a key she flicked away dirt until she could see more of a scrap of paper, which eventually revealed itself as the remains of a hand-rolled cigarette end, crumpled, shrivelled and stamped into the earth.

BROCK, TOO, WAS PROWLING—in his case at Queen Anne's Gate, restlessly roaming the empty offices. From long experience he sensed that both murder inquiries in Cockpit Lane might be approaching some sort of turning point, in which, for good or ill, evidence would begin to swing their random searches into more deliberate directions. For his own reasons he had been more preoccupied with the older murders, but in the other case they had now accumulated a considerable list of people who had seen the two girls during their stay in the area, and the interviews were beginning to reveal distinctive patterns.

He came to Bren's desk and noticed an unopened priority

delivery pouch from Forensic Services. Opening it, he discovered the report of the review that he had ordered of the available ballistics evidence from the Brown Bread shootings. All of the surviving bullets and cartridge cases had been reexamined in the laboratories to confirm their common source. In one case, the murder of Johnny Mulroy, both cartridges and viable bullets had been recovered from the crime scene, and it was this that made it possible to tie all of the others, in which one or the other was missing, to a single source, Brown Bread.

Brock read the report carefully until he came to an addendum sheet at the end, which stopped him short. He scanned it again, unable to believe what he was reading, and when he reached for a phone he realised that he had been holding his breath. According to the report, the single intact bullet found at the scene of Dana and Dee-Ann's murder had also been fired by Brown Bread.

He got through to Forensic Services, but the person he wanted wasn't at work this Saturday morning, and it took some insistence to get a contact number for the author of the report. When he eventually reached him, the man confirmed the result. Both of the multiple murders in Cockpit Lane, committed twenty-four years apart, had been carried out using the same weapon. The scientist who had made the connection had recently worked on the Dee-Ann case and had recognised the markings straightaway on the Johnny Mulroy bullet. The result had been confirmed by a second examiner.

Brock sat back, stunned. Was it really possible that one of the Roaches, after all this time, should return to the same old haunt and repeat his actions in almost the same place with the same gun? And if it were true, how must he now be feeling, reading the newspaper reports, realising that his latest handiwork had led, through the misadventures of a schoolboy, to the discovery of his old crimes?

He tucked the report back into its pouch and picked up the phone again.

HE WANTED A LINK, he told them after they'd broken off their weekend shopping, sport and family excursions and reassembled at Queen Anne's Gate, a link between Shooters Hill and Cockpit Lane in the early morning hours of Friday the fourth of February. More specifically, between Mark, Ivor or Ricky Roach on the one hand, and Teddy Vexx, Dana and Dee-Ann on the other, at that critical period of time.

Failing eyewitnesses and forensic traces they turned their attention to telephones and Rainbow. There had already been an attempt to trace Vexx's phone calls on that night, frustrated by the discovery that he appeared to have access to a number of stolen phones and SIM cards. A check of phones registered to the Roach brothers yielded nothing promising. That left Rainbow.

The London metropolitan area, the largest in Europe, sprawls blindly across some six thousand square miles of southeast England—blind, but not unseen. Its fourteen million inhabitants are observed as they move about its streets by tens of thousands of camera eyes. The eyes cluster along its major highways, its rail and underground stations, around the perimeter of the Central London congestion zone, the City of London's 'Ring of Steel,' the Docklands and the airports, and they spread out in a fine pattern wherever people transact business, cross each other's paths and commit crimes. They are not uniformly intelligent, these eyes; some merely record what they see, others can read vehicle number plates, and some, the smartest of all, are said to recognise faces. Together they comprise the creature known as 'Rainbow,' watched over by police Rainbow Coordinators in the borough commands.

The team began contacting the coordinators, armed with numbers and descriptions of all the vehicles registered to the occupants of The Glebe.

By Sunday evening Brock was forced to accept that they had found nothing.

FOURTEEN

KERRIE, WITH HER FASHIONABLE shoes and hair pulled severely back, was a very efficient organiser, and when Kathy arrived at Cockpit Lane on Monday morning the first of her appointments was already waiting, sitting chatting to the women volunteers who always seemed to be present in Michael Grant's office. Kerrie introduced Kathy to Mrs Parker and showed them to a quiet table at the back of the shop.

'I remember when this was the pawnshop,' the woman laughed. 'I had to use it once or twice, I've got to admit.'

Middle-aged and smartly dressed, it didn't look as if she had much need of pawnshops now. She must have caught Kathy looking at her large and expensive rings, because she fingered them and said, 'I had cold feet about coming back to the old neighbourhood. You read these stories in the papers. But then I was curious, too. It's years since I was here.'

'Have you come far?'

'Croydon. But I keep in touch with Michael, Christmas cards and that. Wonderful man.'

'Well, I do appreciate you coming in.'

'Oh, I was fascinated. Is it really Joseph you've found?'

'Looks like it.' Kathy showed her the three pictures.

'That's Joseph all right, and that's Walter. But I don't know who that is.'

'How did you know them?'

'We all used to go to Studio One, up on Maxfield Street. Oh, it was a terrible dive, a hellhole really.' She smiled at the memory. 'A dance and drinking club, a shebeen, down in the basement, always packed out on a Saturday night. We knew the DJs. And that music! The Pioneers, The Roots Radics, Rankin' Dread— you remember "Hey Fatty Boom Boom"?' She laughed. 'No, course you don't. Anyway, for a time there Joseph and me were, well, close.'

'You went out with him?'

'Yeah. I was really soft on him, but it was no use. All the girls went for Joseph, and he loved us all, young and old, black and white, but especially white, so I didn't have much chance.'

Kathy saw the wistful look in her eyes. 'You still think of him, eh?'

'Sometimes, I must admit.'

'When did you go out?'

'I was trying to remember that. He hadn't been here long and he spoke with a really broad Jamaican accent. The weather was cool, not as cold as now, but I remember him complaining about how grey and cold it was.'

'He came over towards the end of September.'

'Yes, that would be right. I saw him around a few times, like in the market, then we got together one night at Studio One and bang, that was that. His mate Walter had a room in this squat and we hardly left it for a week. My mum and dad went spare. It was before Christmas, I think—yes, definitely before Christmas, because by then he'd moved on to other girls and I was sobbing into the mince pies.'

'He was a bastard, was he?'

'No! He was lovely, funny, sweet. He just couldn't say no to girls. He loved it over here, said he was going to be rich, some hopes. There wasn't a nasty bone in his body. Not like Walter. He could be very mean.'

'Do you remember Walter's surname?'

'Yes, it came to me on the way over here. Isaacs, I think that was it, Walter Isaacs.'

'Good. Did you see much of them after you broke up with Joseph?'

'I stopped going to Studio One for a while after he dumped me, but it was hard not to catch sight of them, or hear from someone who'd seen him there with his latest flame.'

'What about April of the next year, 1981, the time of the Brixton riots, do you remember that?'

'Not in connection with Joseph. Was he involved in that?'

'We think he was murdered that night, April the eleventh. He was seen at a pub in Angell Town, and said he was going to Brixton. He seemed to be running away from someone. Do you have any idea who that might have been?'

'Not specifically. I mean, I wouldn't be surprised if he'd upset people. He would do things without thinking. Like I remember him telling me how he'd made the moves on this girl right after he arrived, and she was the girlfriend of one of the Spangler boys across the tracks. He was lucky to talk his way out of a knifing.'

'Apart from girls, what else was he into?'

Mrs Parker lowered her eyes, then nodded. 'Yes, they were into drugs. I don't just mean ganja. When I was with him in Walter's place I woke up one morning and the room was stinking of that horrible bitter smell of crack, the two of them smoking their first pipes before breakfast. It was Walter, I'm sure, got him into it. He was older and he'd been over here longer.'

'And they dealt as well?'

'Yes, I'm sure they did. Joseph brought some cocaine with him when he came over, and Walter had some girls he called his "yard ants," smuggling for him.'

'Did they work with anyone else?'

'There was a third guy they were friendly with, but he didn't look like this picture here. Didn't have a beard for a start.'

'Can you describe him?'

'Older than the other two, tougher, more serious. Made Joseph look like a little boy.'

'How tall?'

'Not quite as tall as Joseph; maybe six foot? Fit looking. He wore a black Kangol flat cap and plenty of gold cargo, oh and he had a gold tooth, too.' She tapped one of her front teeth. 'The three of them would greet each other that way, you know, like the ghetto kids, touching closed fists and saying "Hit me, star!" or some such.'

'Did he have a name?'

Mrs Parker pondered. 'Robert? Bobby? Robbie? Yes, that's it, Robbie.'

'Surname?'

'No, sorry.'

'Did Joseph tell you anything else about himself that might help us? Any plans he had, or people he knew?'

The woman shrugged vaguely, and Kathy had the feeling that her store of memories—apart, perhaps, from some fondly remembered intimacies—was pretty much exhausted.

'You mentioned the pawnbrokers that were here. I believe they were owned by a local family called Roach. Do you remember them at all?'

She hesitated as if some faint memory stirred, but then shook her head. 'Sorry, no.'

'Well, you've been very helpful, Mrs Parker. There is one more thing. I'd really appreciate it if you'd sit down with our computer artist to make a picture of this Robbie. Would you do that?'

'Ooh, that sounds like fun, though I don't know if I can do it after all this time.'

Kathy got on the phone. When she'd made the arrangements she asked Mrs Parker one last question. 'Did they have guns, those boys?'

The woman nodded sadly. 'Oh yes. Look, when I think back it's no wonder my parents were mad with worry about me. The things you do, eh, when you're young and foolish? Joseph's gun looked shiny and new. He was always stroking and cleaning it, like it was his pet. He even called it a name, Brown Bread. Is that stupid or what?'

THE NEXT THREE WOMEN to see Kathy were all in their fifties and had some memory of Joseph. Two had worked in the market and could remember his good-natured cheek, and one had been a barmaid in the Ship and recalled Joseph drinking amicably with the Roach boys. The fourth visitor, also a woman, was older and had a far grimmer memory. Joseph had befriended her son, who used to walk through the market on his way home from school, and had given him his first taste of crack. Within six months of Joseph's death the boy, too, was dead, thrown from the window of his home on the tenth floor of a council block by Yardies from whom he'd tried to steal drugs.

None of the women were able to add anything concrete to Kathy's search, and none remembered 'Robbie,' although one thought that a girl called Rhonda may have gone out with someone of that name.

The last person on the list was the only man and, according to Kerrie, the only white person, and he didn't show up. Kerrie said he'd left a phone message that he couldn't leave work at a building site about a mile away, where he was site manager, but that Kathy was welcome to call there for a quick chat. She thanked Kerrie and the other women and drove to the place, an extension to the rear of a supermarket. She parked nearby and made her way down a narrow back street, squeezing past two concrete trucks waiting outside the wire gates, where the site hut was pointed out to her. Inside she found the manager, Wayne Ferguson.

'Sorry I couldn't get over,' he said. 'We decided to take a chance with the weather this morning and go ahead with the main concrete pour, and I had to be here. So, Michael said I might be able to help you.' His attention shifted to the window, through which they could see men hosing concrete like porridge over a bed of steel mesh.

'You knew Joseph, did you?'

'Who?'

'Joseph Kidd, in 1981.'

Ferguson looked blank and Kathy pushed the pictures in front of him, making him turn away from the window.

'All the usual suspects, eh? No, don't recall them.'

'Well, I—'

'I was on the bar at the Cat and Fiddle on the night of the riots. Part-time job.'

'Ah. But you don't remember seeing this one?'

'No. It was packed out that night. The only ones I remembered— I told Michael—were the two Roach lads, the oldest one and one of the others. I knew them 'cause I'd seen all three of them come onto the site I was working on in my day job. I was an apprentice then. They were looking for somebody, and there was a bit of a barney with the boss, almost a fight. He told me afterwards who they were and to steer clear of them. When I saw those two come into the pub I thought there might be trouble.'

'And was there?'

'Not as far as I know. I lost sight of them after that. Don't know what happened to them. Not a lot of use, is it? Sorry. I told Michael, but he said you might be interested anyway.'

'Yes, I am. Thanks.'

'Great feller, Michael.'

'How do you know him?'

'He used to be a union man, UCATT. That's how he started to get noticed. He helped us sort out a few problems. His heart's in the right place. There should be more like him in Parliament.'

Kathy thanked him and made her way back to her car, wondering how she was going to get the muck off her shoes. As she sat sideways in the driver's seat, wiping her feet with tissues, she caught sight of a blue car sliding out of view at the end of the street.

FOR THE REST OF that week, Kathy and three other detectives worked across the Borough of Lambeth, following up leads to people who might have been in the right place in 1981. Most were cooperative and interested, happy to nudge their memories back in their own ways. 'Ricky Villa's magic goal against Manchester City, remember that?' 'Sheena Easton, right? "My baby gets the morning train." Loved that one.' 'I do remember hearing the news, that someone had shot the Pope.' '*Chariots of Fire*, that was my favourite.' But it was too long ago. If any of them had ever known anything useful, it had faded and gone.

The other two teams were luckier. The search of old TV footage and newspaper archives had yielded two unpublished photos of the early stages of the fire at the Windsor Castle, before Brock had arrived. They clearly showed two white men in black jackets, frozen in the action of running towards a black man who was staring at the flicker of flames visible through the pub window. When enhanced, the faces made a convincing match with those of Mark and Ivor Roach, and Joseph Kidd.

Bren and Tom's team, meanwhile, going back through the Brown Bread shootings, had reinterviewed the Asian witness, Mr Singh, to the car theft outside his shop in 1986.

'It was a beautiful car,' he said, 'a red Porsche 911, just like I used to dream about. A young blonde lady parked it right outside the shop. She was a looker too, no mistake. She saw me standing in the shop doorway and gave me a lovely smile, then took off across the road to the hair salon over the way. Dad was in the back storeroom and he called out to me and I was about to go in when suddenly, quick as greased lightning, these two men appeared out of nowhere and went to the Porsche. One bent over the lock in the driver's door and in two seconds he'd got it open. I was amazed, I just stood there with my mouth hanging open. He got in, opened the passenger door, against the kerb, and the other man went to get in. I stepped forward and I said, quite politely, "Excuse me, sir. Is that your car?" The man was as close to me as you are, face plain as day, one foot still on the pavement. He looked at me for a moment, then at the shop behind me, then up and down the street, all very calm and deliberate, see? Then he took a gun out of his jacket pocket and pointed it at me, just like that . . .' The man pointed his finger at Bren's stomach. 'I thought, I can't believe this, it's just like a film. Then he pressed the trigger. I didn't feel the bullet go through me. I just passed out.'

The man's recollection was so fluent that Bren was sceptical. 'You seem to have a very clear memory of this, Mr Singh. It happened a long time ago.'

'Have you ever been shot, Inspector? It was the biggest thing that ever happened to me. I had to go over it again and again, for the police, for my friends, for the newspapers, and then, afterwards, in my head and in my dreams, again and again.'

'And you helped the police make an image of the man.' Bren showed him the drawing of a scowling face that could have been anyone.

'Yes. The other one's face was a blank, but this one was vivid in my mind—it still is.'

'Still, nearly twenty years later?'

'Oh yes. You see, I saw him again, about eight years ago.'

'I don't have a record of that.'

'No.' The man looked sheepish. 'I never reported it. My dad decided he wanted to get himself a new Volvo, so I went with him around the showrooms. We'd just walked into this one when I saw him, sitting there at the manager's desk in a smart suit and tie. It hit me like a blow. I managed to turn and run, and when I got outside I was sick, sick as a dog, in the gutter. My dad had to take me home. I couldn't get out of bed for days. I couldn't tell the coppers about it. This is the first time I've talked to anyone, apart from Mum and Dad.'

'Where was this showroom?'

'Eltham. Roach Motors.'

Bren showed him a picture of Ricky Roach, son number three. 'Oh my God. That's him.'

FIFTEEN

COMMANDER SHARPE WAS NOT comfortable. He twisted in his seat, twitched his narrow pointed nose, rubbed his long pianist's fingers fretfully before he set Brock's report back on the desk with care, as if it might draw blood.

'You're aware of the history of our dealings with Mr Roach, of course.'

'Of course.' Brock felt curiously free. The ship was now launched and others would want to have a hand in steering it. There was still much detective work to do, but others would have their say in that, too.

'Looks fairly damning. Pretty obvious, I suppose, the Roaches. Cutthroat mob back then. Different story now, mind you. Penny bought her sports car at that showroom, dammit. Nearly had a fit when I saw the name on the invoice. Several of her smart friends buy their cars there, apparently. Action?'

'We have no choice in the matter of Ricky Roach. A credible witness, a clear body of circumstantial evidence, a previous record.'

'Mm.'

'The same can be said of Mark and Ivor. We can place them in pursuit of Joseph Kidd on the night he was murdered. They have to be questioned.'

'All a matter of identification, though, isn't it? You say Mr Singh is credible?'

'Credible but nervous. I've offered him protection, but he's worried about his parents and his business. I've persuaded him that none of them will be safe until he helps us put Roach behind bars.'

'And Ferguson?'

'Solid.'

'So the first step is identification parades, yes? Conducted by uniformed branch, of course.' Sharpe took a breath, as if relieved that at least that would be out of his hands. 'Who do you suggest? Eltham?'

'The offences took place in Lambeth.'

'Of course, yes. You've heard of KCG Resources? They have mines, Canada and South America. Their shares are hot at the moment. Resources boom. The DCC told me to buy some. Safe bet, he said. The Roaches are major shareholders. Where do you buy your wine? Paramounts? They'll have an off-licence down your way. One of the Roaches' companies.'

'I know it won't be easy.'

'And you seriously think that they were physically involved in the murder of those two kids recently? Wealthy, respectable men like they now are? It beggars belief.'

'I think when faced with something personal they reverted to type. But I can only connect them to those murders through the gun that was used. We have to go for the old cases.'

'But something else worries me.'

'What's that?'

'You, Brock. You're not happy, are you?'

'I know I'm right about the Roaches.'

'But?'

'But I know how slippery they are in a corner. I'm reluctant to show our hand until we've got a watertight case. The trouble is, we're not going to get one without getting close to them and stirring them up. It's all just too long ago. The evidence isn't out there any more.'

'Let's get the question of identification sewn up, then we'll talk again.'

THREE DAYS LATER BROCK was summoned back to his boss's office. This time Sharpe had a third person on hand, Virginia Ashe, prosecutor from the Crown Prosecution Service. She grinned and barked a greeting.

'Brock! Good to see you again. How's tricks?'

'Fine, Virginia. Congratulations, I saw you on the news last week.'

'Oh, that. But you've been beating me on airtime lately. Everybody loves a grizzly corpse; three old skeletons and two young girls is unbeatable. Absolutely royal flush.'

Sharpe broke in. 'Sit down, please. I've asked Virginia to assist us with our discussion, Brock. You've heard the results of the lineups? Three clear identifications. Fine, so we consider the next steps. Interview Mark and Ivor, I take it, warrants if necessary, and a warrant for the arrest of Ricky? You've read the summaries, Virginia. You agree?'

'Ye-es, but we are on thin ice with the first two, don't you think? I mean Brock has done brilliantly constructing a chain of evidence of their movements on that night, twenty-four years ago. Amazing really, but it doesn't actually prove anything, does it? If they don't want to cooperate, there's not enough for a case to be brought for murder. Unless you could prove they still have the gun, say. Where is the gun, by the way? Does anybody know?'

'No,' Brock said. 'I think we have to assume that it's well and truly disposed of by now. But we certainly need to search their compound at Shooters Hill. Virginia's right. Let's concentrate on Ricky. We have a witness who saw him use that gun in 1986. He's the one to start with.'

'Mm.' Sharpe stared at the ceiling. 'The way my thoughts are going is this. Given the publicity surrounding the case, it would make sense for criminal proceedings to be instituted by the DPP, would it not?'

'By us?' Virginia looked sharply at him. 'Rather than the police? By laying an information?'

'Yes. With our full resources behind you, of course.'

Brock saw that Sharpe had been doing some homework and probably taking advice. If 'an information,' as the case for an arrest warrant was called, was laid by the police, it would be done not in the name of the police force as a body, but in the name of an individual officer, a chief constable or someone designated by him. Commander Sharpe didn't want his name on that document.

'Well,' Virginia said. 'I'll take it to the boss, shall I?' She shot Brock a deadpan look as vivid as a wink.

'Yes, why don't you do that, Virginia,' Sharpe said, getting to his feet. 'Excellent idea.'

RICKY ROACH SAT FACING Bren Gurney and another detective across the table. He was much plumper and sleeker than in the old photographs, with more scalp showing through the well-groomed hair, but with the same contemptuous curl to his mouth. Beside him sat Martin Connell.

Brock, not wanting at this point to disclose that they had made the link of Brown Bread between the Cockpit Lane murders and the shooting of Mr Singh, had decided not to carry out the interview himself and was sitting at Kathy's side. Virginia Ashe was also there, keenly watching the screen.

Bren opened the proceedings with the standard preliminaries, then said, 'We're investigating a series of thefts of luxury cars during the 1980s.'

Roach looked at him in disbelief. 'Oh yeah? The 1980s? Are you serious?'

'Perfectly. You were in the car business at that time, I believe. You had a sales yard and workshop in Lewisham, yes?'

'I don't believe this.' Roach turned to look at his lawyer. 'The 1980s?'

'I thought the charge was attempted murder,' Connell said.

'We'll come to that. The matters are related. We want to examine your business records for the period 1979 to the present.'

Roach laughed. 'No way.'

'They don't seem very worried, do they?' Virginia said.

Bren was laying three documents on the table in front of Roach and Connell. 'These are copies of warrants to search your business premises at Eltham, your accountant's offices in the City, and your home at Shooters Hill. Officers are executing these warrants as we speak.'

Roach picked up one of the sheets. 'You're searching Ivor's office? He won't like that.' He smirked.

Connell had picked up another of the warrants and had turned away from the camera, pulling out his mobile phone. After a short conversation he snapped it shut and turned back to face Bren.

'My client's wife is asleep.'

Bren looked mystified. 'What?'

'Don't you know the rules? "In determining when to make a search, the officer in charge must always give regard to the time of day at which the occupier is likely to be present, and should not search at a time when the occupier or any other person on the premises is likely to be asleep." I quote. My client's wife is recuperating from recent surgery and is currently at home asleep. I have advised her sister, who is with her, not to permit entry to her home. Then there is Mrs Adonia Roach, my client's sister-in-law, also resident at The Glebe, who is recovering from a street robbery in which she was seriously hurt. I suggest you advise your officers to withdraw.'

There was a moment's silence, then Kathy said flatly, 'They knew. They were expecting this.'

Brock's phone rang. He listened, then turned to the others. 'The team at Shooters Hill. They're being refused entry to The Glebe. It seems the construction of the perimeter gates and wall is more problematic than they anticipated. They're going to have to bring in heavier gear.'

Virginia Ashe stared at him. 'He's right, you can't break in. It's our warrant, Brock. Tell them to back off.'

For a moment it looked as if Brock wouldn't agree.

'Please,' she said.

Brock nodded and spoke into his phone.

On the screen Bren was questioning Roach about his movements and operations in the mid-eighties. To every question Ricky replied, 'Don't remember.' This went on for some time, the same reply given again and again until Bren's exasperation began to show. Then Connell broke in.

'This isn't getting us anywhere. Can we cut to the quick? These warrants mention the evidence of a witness as grounds for a search. Who is this witness?'

'We're not prepared to disclose their identity at this stage.'

Connell sat back, fingers laced across his belly. 'I think we're wasting our time here, don't you?'

BROCK HAD PERSUADED MR SINGH and his wife to take a holiday with cousins in Birmingham. The witness had become increasingly anxious after his first conversation with Bren, and was on a variety of medications against panic attacks and hypertension. Brock had noticed the way he unconsciously fingered his side where Roach's bullet had hit. When the couple finally agreed to leave London, Brock made arrangements with the police in Birmingham to keep watch on the cousins' home.

On the day of Ricky Roach's arrest, the patrol car parked across the road watched a white Volvo registered to Mr Singh's father draw up outside the cousins' house. This was expected, as the police had monitored a phone call that morning from the older man to his son saying that they would drive up from London to pay him a visit. The elderly couple got out of the car and entered the house. An hour later a second patrol saw two people return to their car and drive off.

When Brock phoned later that day to speak to Mr Singh, his cousin answered and said that wouldn't be possible, as he was lying down with a severe migraine. When Brock asked to speak to his wife, that also was refused on the grounds that she was in the bath. There was something about the conversation that made Brock uneasy and he called the Birmingham police. When officers called at the house they found the cousins and the elderly parents, but no sign of the Singhs.

Brock got a fast patrol car up the motorway with lights and siren going. When he arrived at the suburban house there were already three police cars there, and West Midlands detectives were questioning the four occupants of the house. Brock chose the elder Mr Singh, who had so far refused to say a word.

'Are they safe, Mr Singh? That's our first priority. You must tell us that.'

The old man, back straight, very dignified in his black turban, blinked at the clock on the mantelpiece and murmured, 'I believe they are, sir, yes. But I can say no more.'

At that moment a detective hurried into the room and glared at the Indian. 'They took a flight to Paris, sir, five hours ago. We've just heard. We found the Volvo at the airport.'

It was another hour before it was established that in Paris the Singhs had transferred to an Air India flight to Mumbai.

'It was too much to ask, sir,' Mr Singh said sadly to Brock. 'You don't know what it was doing to him. Couldn't eat, couldn't sleep. He lost eight pounds in a week.'

'He didn't receive any direct threats though, did he?'

'No, he didn't.'

'What about you? Did they threaten you, Mr Singh?'

'As to that, sir, I cannot say.'

Brock regarded him carefully. It was as if the man couldn't bring himself to tell an outright lie.

'I understand. But it would help me to know when this unspoken event took place. We arrested the man who shot your son at nine this morning, and you and your wife must have left for Birmingham at, what, nine-thirty? Not much time for a visitor this morning.'

'There were no visitors this morning.'

'We can trace telephone calls, discover when tickets were purchased . . .'

'There's no need to trouble yourself, sir. There have been no strange telephone calls. I myself purchased plane tickets for my son and his wife last night, on the Internet.'

'So you had a visitor last night.'

'As to that, sir, I cannot say.'

'Thank you, Mr Singh. How long does your son intend to stay in India?'

'Hard to say. There are many relatives. It may be a long trip.'

LATER THAT EVENING, ON the insistence of Virginia Ashe, the charges against Ricky Roach were dropped and he was released from custody. At about the same time, Kathy took a call from the builder, Wayne Ferguson. He just thought he should let her know that, although he was absolutely clear in his identification of the two Roach brothers at the lineup, because of course he had seen them before, he was less sure now about whether it was actually that particular night that he'd seen them in the Cat and Fiddle. It was such a long time ago, and if he were put under cross-examination he couldn't honestly swear that it couldn't have been some other night.

'Has somebody been talking to you, Mr Ferguson?' Kathy asked.

'No!' He sounded offended. 'Certainly not, no way,' he protested, too much.

She called Brock, on his way back down the motorway. He sounded tired and flat, as they all did.

WHEN HE GOT BACK to London, Brock spent a couple of hours in his office dealing with urgent paperwork. A note from Dot told him that a meeting with Commander Sharpe had been scheduled for first thing the following morning. He put a sheaf of signed documents on her desk and left the building. It was a cold but dry night, and he walked the length of Whitehall to Charing Cross station, stopping on the way for a glass of whisky at the Red Lion, a stone's throw from Big Ben. He caught his train home and walked from his station to the high street, where an archway gave access into the cobbled courtyard that led to the lane in which his house stood. In the far corner, at the beginning of the lane, stood a large horse chestnut tree, its black skeleton silhouetted against the dim clouds. A man was standing motionless beneath its branches, watching him approach. Brock looked around and was able to make out a second figure in the darkness against the wall of the old warehouse.

Brock walked on. The man under the tree had both hands in the pockets of a long coat, a scarf around his neck, face hidden in the shadow of the brim of a hat, and it wasn't until he cleared his throat with a spittly grunt that Brock realised, with a surge of heat to his face, who it was.

'Mr Brock.'

'Spider Roach.'

'You remember me, then? Course you do. Thought we should talk.'

The voice was weaker, hoarser, but still with something of its old menace. And as the man moved Brock recognised, even muffled by the winter clothing, the angular frame, all elbows and knees, with its stealthy stretching and sudden pouncing gestures, that was the source of his nickname.

'That business today, with Ricky, what was the point of it?'

'Solving crimes is what I'm paid to do.'

'Settling old scores, more like. Your recent visits to Cockpit Lane must have stirred up old memories, eh? Put you in mind of old times. But it's a mistake to look back, Mr Brock. That way you trip over what's bang in front of you.'

'You're bang in front of me, Spider.'

'Times have changed. Me and my sons are respectable business-men. You'll find that out if you do your homework properly. You and I are very different people now, older and wiser, I hope. I have ten grandchildren, four great-grandchildren, imagine that. What about yourself? That attractive wife of yours still around?'

'She found someone better a long time ago.'

'Too bad. And no new wife waiting for you at home, no children, no grandchildren . . .' It wasn't a question, Brock realised. Spider Roach had always been careful to keep himself well informed about the opposition. 'Pity, they put things in perspective. Without a family to give him a sense of proportion, a man can get obsessive about things that don't really matter. Still, there must be other attachments, people you care for. Everyone has those.'

'It's cold out here, Spider. Too cold to listen to the ramblings of an old man. What do you want?'

'What I want . . .' The voice was suddenly hard. '. . . is to never hear of you again. Make an effort to see that happens, eh? Make an old man happy.'

Spider Roach strode past him towards the archway, the other shadow falling in behind. Brock followed them, watching them get into a black Mercedes four-wheel drive. The interior light showed him the face of Mark Roach, the eldest son, getting in behind the wheel. As they drove away, Brock turned and walked home, thinking over Spider's words. Inside he went from room to room, but found no signs that they had been there. He poured himself a whisky and sat down. The conversation had brought back two distinctive things about the way Spider used to work. He always took a lot of trouble to gather information about his victims, so that by the time he pounced he would know all about their family and business networks. Brock had no doubt that Spider had brought himself up-to-date on his situation. The other distinctive thing about Spider was the way he exerted pressure, by threatening someone close to the target, leaving them no choice. He pondered on that, and the throwaway comment about 'other attachments, people you care for,' and the more he turned the phrase over in his mind, the more uneasy he became.

He made a list of people he cared enough about to interest

Spider. It was very short, mostly connected with work. He began by phoning Kathy, then continued through the names. No one had heard from the Roaches. Finally, there was just one name left.

He hesitated, poured another drink, thumbed through his address book and dialled a long number.

'Hello?'

'Hello, is that Doug?'

'Speaking.'

'This is David Brock, Doug, in London. Suzanne's friend.' Was that the best choice of words?

'Oh . . . well, well. Hello, David. What can I do for you?'

'Is Suzanne there?'

'No, I'm afraid she's not with us any more.'

'What?' Brock gripped the phone more tightly. 'What happened?'

'We put her on a plane last night. Ironic, isn't it? After all this time, and you miss her by a few hours. She's on her way home.'

'Oh . . .' He let out his suspended breath. 'Is she all right?'

'Yes, fine. She's having a couple of day's stopover in Tokyo on the way back. Do you want to know when she gets in to Heathrow? I've got it here somewhere.'

Brock waited, feeling his heart rate subside. Doug came back on the line with the information. 'Better make it a big one, mate,' he added.

'What?'

'The bunch of roses. You're not exactly flavour of the month.'

'No, I can imagine. Thanks.' He hung up and sipped at the Scotch.

Even if Roach's words had been meant as a threat, there was no possibility, surely, that he would have known of Brock's friendship with Suzanne. Coming upon him like that, the silent figure waiting in the dark, the familiar features, the toneless voice, Brock had been abruptly transported back two decades, and the experience had unsettled him more than he'd have thought possible. He remembered another winter's night, long ago, when he had gone to see a snout who provided regular low-level gossip and rumour about the gangs.

As usual, they were to meet beneath a spreading plane tree on the edge of a local park. As he approached, Brock could see the man standing there, moonlight casting shadow stripes across his pale anorak, but there was something odd about his posture, the tilt of his head. Closer still and he made out the taut vertical of a rope connecting the man's throat to the heavy branch above. Brock's foot crunched on gravel and the figure twitched and gave a hoarse cry.

'Help me!'

They had made him stand on tiptoe on a brick set on its edge, and had pulled the rope so tight that if he'd lost his footing he'd have been finished. When Brock found him he'd been standing there for twenty minutes and was on the point of passing out. He refused to say who'd done it, but the style was obvious to Brock— the grim joke, choking off the talker, and the indifference as to whether he lived or died. The man never spoke to the police again.

Brock recalled that the last bit of information the man had given Brock at their previous meeting was that the Roaches employed children to take down the numbers of cars driving in and out of the secure yards of local police stations, and now had a comprehensive list of unmarked police cars operating in the area. Spider's intelligence had always been depressingly good. And still was, obviously. They had known about Singh and Ferguson before Brock had made his move. Did they have a friend at the local station who had told them who had attended the identity parades? Or had they been shadowing Kathy and Bren, himself too, perhaps, as they made their way around the neighbourhood, asking questions? He recalled the blue Peugeot waiting across the street when they'd left Father Maguire's presbytery.

He had been disturbed by Spider Roach's unexpected appearance, but Roach had also been unsettled. The case had already collapsed, yet he had felt the need to warn Brock to back off. Something fragile, important, needed to be protected from blundering coppers. Brock wondered what it was.

SIXTEEN

COMMANDER SHARPE WAS PHILOSOPHICAL about the Roach case. It was unusual to see him in his office on a Saturday morning, and it was clear from the way he fingered his shirt cuff and the file set out ready on his desk that he had more important things on his mind. 'Good try, Brock, but the odds were stacked against us. Look at it another way, the three unsolved murders go into the 1981 results, not this year's. So they make the current dismal figures look marginally better, by comparison.'

'All the same, I'll keep one or two people working on it for a day or two, tidying up loose ends.'

'Mm.' Sharpe's attention had returned to the cover sheet on his file. 'You'll let me have a one-page summary, will you? The OCLG want it on record.'

Brock frowned, puzzled. The Organised Crime Liaison Group was a subcommittee of the Joint Intelligence Committee, the central body for interdepartmental intelligence, reporting directly to the Prime Minister's office. 'Is the OCLG interested?'

'Apparently there's a standing brief on friend Roach. I've warned Penny that she'll have to go elsewhere for her next motor, but it'll be hard to avoid Paramounts. Have you seen their latest prices for Côte de Beaune?'

'I didn't know they had a file on Roach.'

'Nothing that would have been useful to us. You know what

their research office is like, Brock—hoarders of inconsequential trifles, stamp collectors.' Then, as if changing the subject completely, Sharpe added, 'You mentioned that MP in your earlier report, Michael Grant. Has he been in touch again?'

'He gave us some help in tracking down possible witnesses. Useful.'

'Mm. Admirable fellow by all accounts. Very supportive of Trident, strong antidrugs and anticrime stance in his constituency and in the House. Bit of a fanatic, though, I'm told. Cuts corners, ruffles feathers. All right for him, of course, he's protected by parliamentary privilege. For the rest of us, it's best to be wary.'

Dismissed, Brock descended to the street and began to walk back to his office in Queen Anne's Gate. There was a deceptively spring-like lift to the morning, pale sunlight sparkling off wet pavements, a feeling that heavy coats might soon be discarded. He picked up a cappuccino along the way and continued past the end of his street and across Birdcage Walk into St James's Park, where he crossed the grass to an empty bench in the sun. A military band was playing in the distance, some children chasing along the edge of the lake towards Duck Island, groups of tourists drifting towards the palace. As he sipped at his coffee his phone burbled in his pocket.

'Chief Inspector Brock? It's Michael Grant here. How are you? Were my contacts any help?'

'I was just thinking of you, Mr Grant. They were very useful, helped us put together good likenesses as well as personal information for all three bodies on the railway land.'

'Yes, I've seen the posters. What about the killers?'

'I'm afraid we haven't been so successful in that area. Not yet, anyway.'

'There's talk in Cockpit Lane that one of Spider Roach's sons has been charged. Is that not true?'

'He was arrested yesterday morning, but released later for lack of evidence.'

'Ah.' Silence for a moment, then, 'I can't honestly say I'm surprised. Are you very busy today?'

'I'm currently sitting on a bench in St James's Park contemplating the ducks and envying their simple life.'

Grant chuckled. 'How do you fancy lunch at my factory? I think I can offer you something better than stale bread.'

'Sounds interesting.'

'Do you know the Red Lion pub on Parliament Street? Behind it in Cannon Row there's an entrance to Portcullis House. I'll meet you there at twelve-thirty, okay?'

Brock made his way there at the appointed time and found the MP chatting to the security staff at the rear entrance to his 'factory,' the Houses of Parliament. Farther down the lane loomed the striped brickwork of the old Norman Shaw building in which the Metropolitan Police had once had their headquarters, and Brock recalled old photographs of his predecessors in that place, waistcoated, moustached and bowler-hatted men like Chief Inspector Walter Drew, snapped digging with his team in Dr Crippen's garden in Hilldrop Crescent. A hundred years later, he thought, and we're still digging.

'You don't need to worry about this one, Artie,' Grant said. 'He's a copper.'

'Seen you on telly, haven't I, sir? *Britain's Most Wanted*, was it?' He chuckled. 'See you later, sir.'

Grant led the way down a corridor that came out into the glazed-roofed atrium forming the centre of Portcullis House, the modern annexe of Parliament across the street from Big Ben. The court was busy with people, groups talking at tables, individuals hurrying to appointments. Brock recognised famous faces among them, one of them stopping to say hello to Grant.

'Charles, let me introduce you to Detective Chief Inspector Brock.'

'Ah yes.' The home secretary beamed at Brock, shaking his hand. 'My wife's a great admirer of yours, I assume because we both have beards. I hope Michael's not wasting police time press-ganging you onto his committee, is he?'

Grant laughed. 'It's not my committee, Charles.'

'No, just feels like that sometimes.' He clapped Grant on the shoulder and they moved on.

'All chums together,' Grant murmured as they reached the far side of the atrium and entered the corridor leading under Bridge Street to the Houses of Parliament proper. They emerged briefly into the watery sunlight to see a long queue of women in hats moving slowly across New Palace Yard.

'Widows of war heroes,' Grant said. 'The Queen's holding a reception for them in Westminster Hall. Have you been here before?'

Brock hadn't.

'I'll give you a quick tour, if you like.'

He led the way again, through the Victorian Gothic splendours of the Palace of Westminster, its corridors and lobbies, chambers, libraries and committee rooms, pointing out its treasures with a kind of hushed glee that reminded Brock of a small boy taking a friend into the forbidden haunts of his father's den.

'*The Death of Nelson*, see? Never mind the quality, feel the width—all forty-five feet of it. Look at the ceiling above . . . Can't show you the only really old bit, unfortunately, Westminster Hall. Can't crash Liz's party.' He chuckled.

They finally arrived at the Strangers' Dining Room, where they took a table by the window against the terrace overlooking the Thames.

'This view is very important, very symbolic,' Grant said. 'Over there is the real world.' He nodded at the bulk of St Thomas's Hospital across the river. 'That's where they took the boy who found the bodies, wasn't it? And beyond that, a short ambulance ride, is Lambeth and Brixton and Cockpit Lane. The river is like the Styx, separating the living world from the beyond. Monet captured it perfectly. He sat over there on the south bank and painted the towers of Westminster across the river, glowing through the fog like the city of heaven. Over there people die violent deaths; over here we are immortal. Did you know that?' He grinned. 'Truly.'

'How do you mean?'

'It's a tradition. Nobody dies in the Palace of Westminster. If one of us has a fatal heart attack or stroke, we remain, be we stiff as a board, technically alive until the ambulance crosses the river to St Thomas', where we are pronounced dead. Whereas on the other side, the boy was found dead on the railway tracks and brought back to life in St Thomas's. A nice symmetry.'

Grant leaned forward, lowering the volume of his voice a little, though not its intensity. 'I'm not playing with words, David. This distinction is a living thing for me. It is what motivates everything I do. My mother and father met briefly in Kingston docks. She was a whore and he was possibly an American sailor, though she was necessarily vague about that. They exchanged infections—she gave him the clap and he gave her me, which was worse for her. As soon as I was born she did what she'd done with my brother before me and gave me to our grandmother, who made some kind of an honest living from the Dungle in Riverton City, which I think I mentioned to you. I grew up on a rubbish dump, literally. It sounds like some Victorian fable, doesn't it? But it's true. So when I look at myself sitting here, when I show a visitor around my palace, when the home secretary jokes with me in the corridor, I am in a state of suspended disbelief, and it is very important that I should remain so.'

Their lunches arrived, fish and chips and a bottle of Paramounts' white burgundy.

'Old parliamentary joke,' Grant said. 'The Lord Chancellor hired a new research assistant called Neil. He told him to report for work in the Central Lobby—remember it? The one with the statue of Gladstone and the golden chandelier. Seeing him there the next morning, the noble Lord, resplendent in wig and scarlet gown, cried, "Neil!" And all the tourists did.'

Grant grinned, pouring the wine. 'You see my point? For a while I've joined the immortals, and while I'm here I have to do what I can for those people on the other side, in the world where people kneel to get a bullet in the head.'

'Father Guzowski must be very proud of you.'

'I like to think he would be. He died several years before I got into Parliament, gunned down by a young kid stoned on crack. But I still feel him here, at my shoulder. When I get too big for my boots I feel him turning my head back, across the river.'

'I'm told you have a reputation for cutting corners.'

'That depends on where you stand. If you come from a comfortable background and believe the world is basically on track, give or take some minor adjustments, then yes, I take outrageous liberties. But if you grew up on a rubbish dump and know that most people are doomed to spend their whole lives in some version of the Dungle unless somebody does something about it, then no, my methods are painfully law-abiding and slow. And I do abide by the rules. When we arrive here, freshly elected and full of ambition, along with our security pass and our Parliamentary Intranet access, they give us a book, the Members' Handbook, which tells us the rules of their gentlemanly game. I studied that book very closely, believe me.'

They ate for a while in silence, finishing their fish. 'Pudding?' Grant offered. 'Treacle pudding and custard for a cold February day? It's extremely good.'

'That sounds hard to refuse. I don't know how you keep so lean, Mr Grant.'

'Michael, please. I use the gym in the old police buildings across the road, and I don't usually eat lunch.'

'Then why am I so honoured?'

Grant laughed. 'Down to business, eh?'

'You said you weren't surprised that we hadn't been able to press charges against the Roach brothers.'

'Let me guess—obstructive tactics by the best lawyers money can buy, intimidation of witnesses, fabricated alibis, inside information on police moves . . . . Am I right?'

Brock nodded.

'It's all happened before. So what do you do now? Are you giving up?'

'As things stand, I have no hard evidence that any of the Roach clan were involved in the murder of those three men on the railway ground. But the case is open; I'm still looking.'

'Another symmetry—three Roach sons and three victims. One side lives and flourishes, the other dies. But maybe there's another way to even the score.'

'You think so?'

'Oh yes. I'm a very low form of life in this great institution, David. There are 659 MPs and I'm one of the youngest and most junior of them, but even so, I have important resources available to me. I have my own research staff and access to a remarkable range of information sources through the House of Commons Library. I am also a member of committees, in particular the Home Affairs Committee, which I mentioned to you when we last met. It is one of eighteen committees set up by Parliament to scrutinise the work of government departments, in our case the Home Office, and we're broadly interested in anything to do with public order, including organised crime and its impact on the community. We don't investigate crimes, of course, but we can affect the climate in which they are investigated. We have the power to call witnesses and have them give evidence under oath. We can broadcast their evidence on live webcast and through transcripts, and we can do all this under the cover of parliamentary privilege—you know what that means?'

'They can't sue you.'

'Exactly. Of course privilege mustn't be abused, but what is permissible is open to interpretation. The chair of our committee is Margaret Hart.'

Brock knew of the veteran socialist politician and union activist, famous for her frankness.

'Margaret gives me plenty of leeway, much to the disgust of the more conservative members, and I've had a few successes that have made people sit up. I don't need the hard chain of evidence that you do in order to pursue Roach, but I do need solid information to persuade my committee that it's in the public interest that his affairs should be brought out into the bright light of public scrutiny.

That's my primary interest. Not what Roach and his people may or may not have done twenty-odd years in the past, but what they're doing to our community today.'

'You said that before, but I thought the Yardies controlled the drug market in your area?'

'They're his partners. That's the point. To begin with, they supplied him, but now it's the other way around. The days of the Yardie mules and swallowers, the women coming over on free plane tickets with a few ounces of coke in their stomachs, they're finished, David. Now it comes over by the hundredweight in containers, through legitimate import companies like those owned by Spider Roach. Roach sells it on to the Yardies, who turn it into crack and peddle it on the streets. I've been collecting material on this for some time, but I need more.'

'I don't think I have any information that would help you, Michael.'

'You have access to the police files.'

'As I say, I haven't seen anything that would help you. The Trident people don't seem to have anything on Roach.'

Grant looked disappointed and unconvinced. 'What about the JIC files?' He saw the sudden attention in Brock's eyes and went on, 'The Joint Intelligence Committee gives us briefings from time to time, but they're a cagey lot.'

'What makes you think they have a file on the Roaches?'

'I know that Special Branch, Customs and Excise, and MI5 have all taken an interest in them at one time or another. It seems inconceivable that they haven't pooled their information, don't you think?'

'Even if it exists and I could access it, I couldn't possibly pass on confidential JIC material to you, Michael. Can't you approach them through your committee, or through the Prime Minister's Office?'

'I've tried that, but they've had their fingers burnt by Roach before. They say they have nothing of relevance to the Home Affairs Committee. Look, I'm not asking you to break any confidences, just to compare notes informally, give each other pointers. I'm willing to share what I know with you, and in the light of what you may know from JIC sources or wherever, you may be able to provide a critique, help me focus my arguments. We're very much on the same side, David, approaching the same problem from different directions.'

Brock wasn't sure about the consistency of that last sentence. 'There is another difficulty. If you use police evidence on your committee, there's a risk, isn't there, that you could compromise a future criminal trial?'

'Our guidelines cover that. The key phrase is "matters currently before a court of law." At the rate the police have been going, how long will it be before that happens?'

Brock nodded. 'Point taken.'

'But I appreciate the sensitivities, and in view of that I'd like to suggest that we don't communicate directly on this. How about you nominate a member of your team to chat from time to time with my research officer, Andrea? Keep things at arm's length.'

It seemed innocuous enough, and Brock agreed.

On the way out they passed through the Central Lobby again, midway between the House of Commons and the House of Lords, and Grant stopped suddenly, staring at a line of people waiting at an information counter.

'Kerrie?'

The only black woman in the queue turned, looked embarrassed for a moment, then broke into a big smile. 'Michael!'

Grant introduced her to Brock. 'Kerrie's the manager of my constituency office in Cockpit Lane.'

'Yes, hello. I've been helping Sergeant Kolla contact people.'

'But what are you doing here, Kerrie?'

'I'm doing the PDVN course.'

Grant looked blank.

'The Parliamentary Data and Video Network course, Michael. We talked about it, remember? Andrea set it up for me.'

'Oh yes, sorry. There's this big divide between the staff in the

House and staff out in the constituencies,' he explained to Brock. 'It's very important for people like Kerrie to come over and get brought up to speed.'

'Apart from which I can move your constituency office broadband and email onto the central system and save you money.'

'And access the intranet, yes. So what's the problem?'

'I can't find the room.' She showed Grant the memo.

'That's Norman Shaw South,' he said. 'Come on, I'll show you.'

He led the way down the steps to the lobby in front of the entrance to Westminster Hall, now screened by a temporary partition, beyond which they could hear an excited hum of conversation.

'Sounds like the widows are having fun,' he said, and continued on through St Stephen's porch into the sunlight of Parliament Square, where he shook Brock's hand and said goodbye.

THAT EVENING TOM REEVES took Kathy to a screening of Jean-Luc Godard's 1960 film *Breathless* at a New Wave movie festival that was running at the National Film Theatre. She hadn't seen it before, and Tom promised that she would find it interesting. She did, both for itself and for what it told her about Tom. At first it had seemed paradoxical, to say the least, that a cop should be so enthusiastic about the Jean-Paul Belmondo character, Michel, a crook who murders a cop. But then she began to notice subtle reflections of Tom in him—witty but also moody, and with a laconic smile that seemed to suggest unshakeable scepticism about the world and all its works. Even their looks found an echo, vaguely roguish and battered, though no one could look quite like Belmondo, with his concave boxer's nose and thick Gallic lips.

'At the end of shooting,' Tom explained, 'the American girl, Jean Seberg, was so disgusted by the whole thing that she said she didn't want her name attached to it, and Belmondo, too, was appalled by the amateurishness of Godard's production. Then the film came out and everyone went crazy about it, and they both realised that it was the most important thing they'd ever done.

That's genius, you see. The masterstroke that no one recognises until it's been pulled off.'

The way he said it, it didn't sound so much like a bit of film criticism as a statement about life. Kathy wondered if Michel would have put it like that.

Tom had another quote about Belmondo. 'He said that women over thirty are at their best, but men over thirty are too old to recognise it.'

She wasn't quite sure what to make of that, but took it as a compliment, and as he drove her home she found herself warming to the thought of him coming up to her flat. She even got as far as trying to remember if she had any eggs to give him for breakfast, but when they reached her door he kissed her tenderly for a long moment, then said he couldn't stay.

SEVENTEEN

ON MONDAY MORNING BROCK reassigned his team to other cases. No one referred to the Roach episode, as if it was over and best forgotten. But by the end of the briefing Kathy and Tom hadn't been mentioned. Brock nodded to them as the meeting broke up and they followed him up to his office.

They noticed that he hadn't removed his own copies of the Brown Bread material from the big wall facing his desk. Kathy was struck by the symmetry between the pictures of the Roach family on one side and of the Brown Bread victims on the other, like the lineup for opposing soccer teams.

'Despite what I said downstairs,' Brock said, pouring coffee, 'I still believe that discovering the truth behind the events of twenty-four years ago will be the key to finding Dee-Ann and Dana's murderers. So . . . your boss says you can stay with us for a while longer, Tom.'

'Glad to be rid of me, is he, Chief?'

'He didn't say that exactly. It was my request. You all right with that?'

'Yes, certainly.'

Brock smiled benignly, passing the cups around, but Kathy wasn't fooled. He was watching their body language, the way they chose seats and leaned in together for the milk, trying to work out what was going on between them. Or maybe she was just being hypersensitive, the three of them together like that in his room.

'Good. I didn't mention it downstairs, but I'd like you two to stick with Brown Bread for a while longer, tie up some loose ends. Tom, you're our Roach expert now. Commander Sharpe has asked for a summary of our investigation to put on file for the Organised Crime Liaison Group. Did you ever come across an OCLG or JIC file on Roach?'

'Don't recall one.'

'You might use your Branch contacts to see if there is such a thing—informal approach, nothing official.'

'Okay.'

'Did you meet the MP, Michael Grant? His office in Cockpit Lane helped Kathy track down the identity of our victims. Grant is also interested in Roach. He's a bit of a crusader against drugs and crime in his community, and he's convinced the Roaches are still operating, in partnership with the local black gangs.'

'Really?' Tom looked doubtful. 'News to me. The Trident people didn't think it likely, did they?'

'No, but still, Grant claims to have information that he's willing to share with us. I want you to talk to his research officer, Andrea.' He handed Tom her card. 'See what you think. They'll want some quid pro quo, I daresay, but don't give them anything without talking to me first.'

'Haven't really got much to give, have we?'

'True. Kathy . . .' He put his hands flat on the desk, as if at a loss. 'What do you think?'

'Loose ends? Well, who pressured the Singhs and Ferguson?'

'Yes. Anything else?'

'Neighbours? Rainbow?'

'Ah, Rainbow, of course. How did we manage without it?'

'I'll have a look, shall I?'

'Please . . . By the way, did Michael Grant put you in touch with Mrs Lavender among his contacts, by any chance?'

'No, he didn't.'

'Mm, she may have passed away by now. All right. Let's meet again tomorrow afternoon, see how we're doing.'

On the stairs, as they turned a tight corner, Tom slid an arm around Kathy's waist and gave a squeeze. 'Did we pass scrutiny?'

'You felt it too, did you?'

'We must have a talk sometime, about your relationship with the old man.'

KATHY ARRANGED TO VISIT the Rainbow coordinator at the area command that covered the elder Singhs' home in Streatham. There they identified the cameras operating in the immediate area. There were none in the Singhs' street, but a local council camera covered its junction with a shopping street at one end, the most likely direction of approach. As she talked to the coordinator, Kathy began to appreciate the difficulties. What exactly was she looking for? She had a list of cars registered to members of the Roach family, but Ricky was a car dealer and could presumably lay his hands on any number of other vehicles. Then there were the unknown associates and employees who may have been sent to give the Singhs the message. In the end, the coordinator agreed to try to provide a list of all the vehicles that had passed through the junction over a four-hour period on that night.

'You realise that'll probably be a couple of thousand? Who's going to authorise the request?'

Kathy gave Brock's name and returned to her office, where she found two phone messages, one from forensic services and the other from a Mr Connell. She stared at the name, feeling a slight flush in her face, then rang the first number.

The man at forensic services began by apologising for the delay. 'We've had a rush of work and you did say it wasn't top priority.'

Kathy didn't at first recall the job, and the man had to remind her about the cigarette end she'd found behind the fence over-looking the railway site.

'That spliff you sent us. Interesting smoking mixture, must try it some time—tobacco and marijuana, half and half, with a garnish of cocaine. Prime sensimillia ganja too, nothing cheap. Mr Murray has the right connections.'

'Murray?'

'The smoker. We've got his DNA on file. George Murray. Done for possession in a raid on a South London nightclub eight months ago. Charges dropped due to processing irregularities. We should have wiped the record. Oops.'

'Do you have an address?'

'Eighteen Cockpit Lane, SW9. Know it?'

Kathy did. She could picture the sign over the window, WELLINGTON'S UTENSILS EST. 1930.

She thanked him and then, more cautious this time, pressed the numbers for the second call, a mobile.

'Martin Connell, hello?'

The voice still had that sonorous tone, which could be so skilfully adjusted to each occasion: a TV news soundbite, a judge, a former lover. Kathy waited a beat before revealing which one it was.

'Hello, Martin.'

'Kathy! It's so good to hear your voice again. Seeing Bren Gurney the other day made me think of you. How are you?'

'Fine. You?'

'Yes, great. You know what I was thinking, while Gurney was going through all that nonsense?' He said it as if he knew perfectly well that she'd been watching. 'I was thinking how really good it would be to see you again, have lunch, catch up.'

'I don't think so.'

'I know, you're frantically busy and we're just old history. But we were important to each other once, and I think it's wrong to lose contact completely with people who have been important in your life, don't you? Christ, there aren't that many of them when it comes right down to it. I don't suppose you heard about Daniel?'

It took a second for Kathy to remember. 'Your brother?'

'That's right. We buried him last month. His heart packed in, just like that. It was a hell of a shock—makes you stop and think, Kathy.'

'I'm very sorry.' She'd never met Daniel, but she remembered the tone Martin's voice took on whenever he spoke of his elder brother, a mixture of admiration, envy and intense frustration.

'Well, anyway, maybe you're a little curious, eh? To catch up?'

She laughed. He'd perfected that inveigling pitch at an early age, she'd once decided, to get whatever he fancied—his brother's cricket bat or his mother's undivided attention—and it still worked a treat with juries and impressionable younger women.

'What do you really want, Martin?'

'Just to buy you lunch, and talk to an old friend, and maybe pass on a little gossip for our mutual entertainment. How about tomorrow?'

She agreed. The key words were 'pass on.' Martin was a messenger. And he was right, she was curious.

WITHIN AN HOUR THE weather had turned bitterly cold again, dark clouds looming overhead. Kathy parked her car in a side street, pulled a woollen beanie down over her ears, turned up her coat collar and paced briskly towards Cockpit Lane. The market was deserted, the stalls stripped back to metal frames, cardboard boxes stacked ready for collection. There was a light showing in Winnie's shop window and Kathy pushed open the door. The old woman heard the buzzer and emerged from the back, wiping her hands on a towel.

'Hello, dear,' cautiously. 'What can I do for you?'

'Hello, Winnie. I wondered if George was around. There's something I need to ask him.'

Winnie's face fell. 'He's not here. Maybe I can help you?'

'I'd really like to speak to him. Any idea where I can find him?'

The woman's brow creased like an old glove as she shook her head. 'He's gone, he don't work for me no more and I haven't seen him in over a week.'

'Oh?'

'We had a row, a week ago last Saturday it was. I wanted him up early to get things ready for the market, but he was out till four or five o'clock the night before, doing goodness knows what. He said some wicked things and walked out. I haven't seen him since. What is it you want to ask him? Is he in trouble?'

'I don't know. We got some reports that someone was watching us when we were digging up the railway bank, from across the other side, in one of the gardens. Whoever it was was smoking drugs, and now we've learned that it was George.'

Winnie nodded resignedly. 'Dat don't surprise me. The drugs, I mean. He wasn't even tryin' to hide it from me no more. And it's true, for over a month now he's been disappearing for hours at a time, just when I need him.'

'Why would he spy on us? There wasn't much to see.'

'Once, when I asked him where he'd been, he said I wasn't the only one prepared to pay for his services.'

'Any idea who he'd be working for?'

The old lady shrugged as if to suggest the worst. 'All I can tell you is that one of my friends in the market said the other day that she'd seen him with some girl. Maybe he's staying there. I don't know. She lives over the laundrette in Cove Street, back of the tyre place, you know?'

Kathy knew very well from their abortive raids on Mr Teddy Vexx. She hurried back to her car and drove to Cove Street, then turned into the laneway that led past the tyre yard. From there she could see the back of the block of shops and laundrette. Stairs led to an open access gallery to the flats above. There were lights on in one and Kathy was about to get out when its front door opened and a young woman, heavily wrapped against the cold, manoeuvred a child's pushchair out onto the deck. She reached back into the flat to turn the light off, then carefully locked the front door with three separate keys before pushing the chair towards the stairs. Kathy guessed that there was no one left in the flat, and stayed where she was as the girl struggled down the stairs. Kathy realised why it was such an effort when she emerged into the lane and Kathy saw that the pushchair was a double one, with a pair of little pink hats visible under the hood. Kathy locked her car and followed.

After a couple of blocks the woman slowed at a shopfront beside a bus stop. There was another struggle as someone on the inside opened both doors and helped lift the pushchair's front wheels over the threshold. The sign stencilled on the front window read CAMBERWELL GUM CLINIC. Kathy continued walking towards it as the woman disappeared inside, and as she reached the front door it opened again and she saw into a room crowded with women. A smaller sign on the other window said GENITOURINARY MEDICINE.

Kathy guessed the woman was going to be there for a while, and picked up a paper at the corner shop before crossing to a café over the road, where she bought a mug of tea and a toasted sandwich.

An hour and a half later the girl reemerged. As soon as she was out on the footpath she lit a cigarette and blew a great puff of relief into the frosty air, then headed off again along the street, turning eventually into a grim little park where she released the tiny twins to totter around on the soggy ground while she sat on a bench and lit another cigarette. Kathy checked the name of the place, Tallow Square, then followed the narrow road around the edge, convinced now that she was wasting her time. The sky was growing darker and more threatening by the minute, and she was on the point of turning back when she noticed parked ahead of her a car that she recognised, an electric-blue Peugeot convertible. It looked remarkably pristine and sleek among the battered dustbins and graffiti-covered walls on this more derelict side of the park, as did the glossy red BMW sports car behind it. At that moment a man stepped from the mouth of a lane midway between Kathy and the cars.

Kathy stopped dead, recognising George. The tree trunks behind her were as black as her coat, otherwise he would surely have noticed her. Instead, his attention was caught by the figures in the park. He gave a shout and trotted towards them, and at that moment the sky overhead flickered with light, followed almost immediately by a massive bang of thunder. Kathy came abreast of the lane from which George had appeared and caught an image of battered fences topped by barbed wire and a faded sign, REILLY'S USED CARS. She heard the savage howl of a dog, then the first heavy raindrops hit the ground.

She hadn't noticed cameras, but she kept her head down, shoulders hunched, and continued past the cars, noting the number of the BMW and of several other cars further up the street. The rain turned into a torrent and she broke into a run.

WHEN SHE GOT BACK to Queen Anne's Gate she phoned DS McCulloch to see if he knew anything about George Murray, who didn't have a police record. He said he'd check and get back to her. Then she decided to see how Tom was doing. She found him in a room in the basement where he had taken all the material they had accumulated on the Roach family. Cold and vaulted like a crypt, he called it The Roach Room, and had covered its walls with photos and diagrams.

'Take a seat,' he offered. 'Your hair's wet. Did you get caught in that downpour?'

'Yes,' she sniffed. 'I think I'm getting a cold.'

He plugged in the electric heater he'd brought down there and she moved closer to it, looking around at the images on the walls. 'Why are they all dressed in black?'

'The most recent pictures were taken at a funeral four years ago, when the whole family turned out to farewell Cyrus Despinides, who happened to be a friend of someone else Special Branch was interested in. Cyrus Despinides was an old business partner of Spider, and his daughter Adonia is married to Ivor Roach, the second son, the accountant.' Tom pointed to a family tree diagram.

'Yes, I've met Adonia, and her daughter Magdalen.'

'How come?'

Kathy explained.

'So you've actually been inside the family compound, The Glebe?' There was a plan and an aerial photograph among the pictures on the wall.

'Yes, strange place, like a fortified village trying to pretend it's just an ordinary bit of posh suburbia. But I suppose that's what they mean by a gated community.'

'It is a bit odd. They had it purpose-built for themselves. I mean, you'd have to think there was something a bit pathological about a family wanting to stick so close together. Imagine being one of the women, marrying into a deal like that. And they do stick together. Neither Spider nor any of the boys have divorced.'

'The only other member of the family I've seen is the youngest son, Ricky, when we interviewed him.'

'Right.' Tom pointed to the pictures of the brothers. 'They're all in their fifties now. Mark, the eldest, the big-shot businessman, travels a lot, owns a lavish holiday villa on the north coast of Jamaica and an apartment in Hong Kong. He's married with five children and three grandchildren. Ivor, the second son, is an accountant in his own practice, which is effectively dedicated to the Roach business operations. Ricky, number three, has the luxury car dealership in Eltham, wife and four kids.

'And then there's the old man, Edward "Spider" Roach. He was widowed eight years ago and had a brush with cancer shortly after. Since then rarely seen in public except as a regular church-goer, but known to be a generous donor to a variety of charitable and political organisations, including the Catholic Church, Save the Children and the Conservative Party.'

'So what are we looking for?' Kathy asked.

'Points of weakness,' Tom said. 'I'm meeting Michael Grant's researcher, Andrea, tomorrow. We'll see what they've come up with.'

THAT EVENING KATHY SPOKE to her friend Nicole, who mentioned that they'd received a request from Brock that day, to unearth old files relating to a surveillance operation back in the early eighties.

'What kind of operation?' Kathy asked, curious.

'A funeral parlour,' Nicole said, laughing. 'Maybe he's writing his memoirs. Anyway, how's it going with Tom?'

'All right. I'm just getting used to having him around the office all the time.'

'Mm, but apart from that? You're not seeing him tonight?'

'No. It's fine.'

'He's not being a bit slow, is he?'

Kathy changed the subject, and they agreed to try to get together the coming weekend.

EIGHTEEN

THERE WERE TWO REPORTS waiting for Kathy the following morning. One had arrived by fax during the night from the police in Kingston, Jamaica, regarding her inquiry about the three victims, Walter Isaacs, Joseph Kidd and Robbie X. From the details taken from their passports when they entered the UK, the JCF had been able to identify the first two. It seemed that both had died, Isaacs in 1970 and Kidd in 1976, long before they arrived in London.

The second report was on her computer, a long string of vehicle numbers from the Rainbow coordinator in Streatham. She poured a cup of coffee, pondered, and decided to begin with a shortlist of those that appeared more than once, on the basis that anyone visiting the Singhs would have first come, then gone. She set about comparing these with the list of numbers they'd compiled of cars known to belong to the Roach family.

Towards noon, when Brock came by, she'd found no matches. She told him what she was doing and the result from Jamaica, and he just nodded, preoccupied.

After he'd gone it occurred to her that the big point of all this wasn't so much to prove that the Singhs had been intimidated by the Roaches—that probably wasn't going to be possible. Rather, it was to prove that there was a continuing connection between the Roaches and the black gangsters of Cockpit Lane. She opened her notebook to the rain-wrinkled page where she'd written the numbers of the cars at the park the previous day and started comparing them with the Streatham list. Disappointingly, neither Teddy Vexx's Peugeot nor the red BMW came up, but then, just as she was checking her watch and deciding it was time to go, one of the other numbers on her screen showed a match. It was that of a Ford Mondeo parked farther up the street. A minute later she had the name, Jay Crocker, known to them as an associate of Teddy Vexx. She reached for the phone to tell Brock but found that he had left the office.

MARTIN CONNELL ROSE TO his feet as she approached his table. The monitor hadn't lied about the extra pounds, and there were other subtle signs of time passing about the corners of his eyes and mouth. She saw that he was making a similar appraisal of her. Ten years had put their mark on both of them. She hoped his success hadn't made him pompous. Whatever else he'd been, he'd never been that.

'Great view.' She looked out at the sweep of water.

'I hope it wasn't too far.'

'No.' She'd been glad that the place he'd suggested was some way upriver from the office. 'I've heard of this place, of course. But I've never been here.' Not at these prices, she thought.

'I'm very glad you've come. Really, I didn't think you would.'

The smile of course, racy and ironic like . . . well, Belmondo perhaps, or even Tom a little. She made a mental note to work that one out later. 'I'm not sure why I did. I mean, we're not interested in each other's private lives, are we? And we can't talk about work. Doesn't leave much to fill in the odd hour.'

He laughed. 'We never had any trouble filling in the odd hour, Kathy. I did mean what I said on the phone. Since Daniel . . . Okay, you're not interested, but I got to thinking, if it had been me instead of him, what would I look back to, most of all? And what came into my mind was you—no, don't look at me like that, it's true. You were very important to me. And I thought how sad it would be if we never had another chance to sit together at a fine white tablecloth with a glass of wine, and talk.'

As he spoke, using that persuasive voice, Kathy realised that the differences she'd noticed in him had disappeared and he now seemed the same as he'd always been. Or perhaps he was a little more mellow, a little less obvious in making known what he wanted. He had no difficulty in finding funny, neutral things to amuse her with. The river was a cue for a story of an evening with fellow lawyers (no mention of wives) on an evening cruise, being serenaded by a famous operatic soprano, whose improvised stage at the stern had buckled under her considerable weight, almost tipping her into the river. The theme of punctured human dignity led on to a courtroom story from his early days, and then to a convoluted account of a meal with a senior Tory member of Parliament (wives included this time), whose well-known habit of ending a good story with a flourish of his pocket handkerchief had come unstuck when the handkerchief, like a magician's prop, had been followed by a pair of ladies' black silk knickers—not, so his wife calmly observed, her own.

The food was excellent too—French new wave, he said, as if he'd read her mind about Belmondo. An hour passed in no time, then another, before he looked regretfully at his watch and called for the bill.

'You mentioned gossip on the phone,' Kathy said.

'Did I? Oh yes, there was something . . . But you were right, no shop. There is one thing I will say, though. It's absolutely ridiculous that you're still at the same rank as when we . . . as before. I mean, it just makes me angry, Brock keeping you tucked under his wing at DS when everybody knows you're the best thing he's got, far better than Gurney. I mean, he won't be there forever, Kathy, and when he goes . . . It could be sooner than you think, they'll move someone in, maybe already have . . .'

'What do you mean?'

'It's the way big organisations work, Kathy. I know. You've got to look out for number one.'

'You didn't buy me lunch to give me a lecture on ambition, Martin. What is this all about, really?'

'I told you what it was. I realised I was mortal, and couldn't stand the thought of not seeing you one more time.'

He gave her a lift back to the West End and left her, mystified. Altruism wasn't Martin's style, and though he'd always been generous, there was always a motive.

BROCK CHOSE A SPOT towards the back of the waiting crowd and to one side, where he could see the arrivals without making himself obvious. One by one, then in a steady stream, they came around the corner, bent to their laden trolleys, eyes expectantly scanning the confusion of bobbing faces. Then she appeared.

If he'd intended it as a test of his own feelings, it would have rated as a complete success. The sight of the familiar face, the intelligent searching eyes, the determined chin, instantly dispelled all the doubts that had haunted him these last months and sent a warm surge of blind relief and affection through him. He saw with concern the fatigue in the shadows around her eyes, and began to push towards the end of the railings so that he could wrap his arms around her and tell her that it was good, so very good, that she was home at last.

Only she wasn't pushing a trolley, and then he saw her face light up, not at him, but at someone on the far side of the crowd. Then he saw two children break out of the crush and run forward into her arms. Suzanne's grandchildren, he realised, followed by a smiling woman he didn't recognise. He watched Suzanne embrace her too, then turn to make a gesture of introduction to the man pushing the trolley behind her. He shook hands all round, grinning broadly; a tall man, tanned and good-looking, fitter and younger than Brock. The crowd shifted and surged and Brock lost sight of them, then he saw them off to the side, talking together in an excited cluster before moving together towards the exit doors, the woman explaining with hand signs where her car was parked.

He stood for a while, a fixed point in the swirling mass, letting the bitter sick feeling subside, then he followed them out into the chilly afternoon.

KATHY MADE HER WAY to the office of the Streatham Rainbow coordinator, who set her up in front of a monitor to watch the tapes of the junction at the end of the Singhs' street. There was a gap of half an hour between the two appearances of the Mondeo, the second timed just a few minutes after the elder Singh had made the online plane bookings for his son and daughter-in-law. In both clips it was apparent that there were two occupants in the vehicle, bulky men who seemed to fill the car's interior.

On the way back to Queen Anne's Gate, Kathy got a phone call from Tom. He sounded rushed and there was a lot of background noise, as if he was in a train station.

'How's it going, Kathy?'

'Fine, I'm just heading back. I found one or two—'

'Great, me too. Look, I've only got a minute . . . Oh, got to go. See you later.'

'Where—?' But he was gone.

Back at the office, Kathy tapped on Brock's door. He was at his desk, bent over a file, one of a stack of faded buff folders of a type she hadn't seen in years.

She sat down and told him what she'd learned and he listened in silence.

'So Michael Grant is right,' she said. 'We can show a connection between Roach and suspected drug dealers in Cockpit Lane. Should we tell Trident?'

'Not yet,' Brock murmured. He seemed still absorbed in whatever he'd been reading. 'What other checks can you make on Vexx and his crew?'

'Phone records, and I could speak to the lad, George Murray, try to find out why he was spying on us.'

Brock nodded. 'Yes, do that.'

'What's Tom up to, do you know?'

'He's been spending time with Grant's research officer. Apparently they've got quite a lot of stuff—press cuttings, company information, things like that. But he's not sure if any of it will help us.'

She turned and left, thinking how tired and preoccupied he looked.

THERE WAS A PILE of material on Kathy's desk relating to two other cases she'd put on hold. Now they needed urgent attention, a file report and preparation for a court appearance at the impending trial for another murder case, and several phone calls and a briefing document to the CPS in relation to a serial rapist. She sat down and worked through till almost nine before she headed home, picking up some Chinese on the way.

She was sitting on her sofa in front of the TV when she jerked upright, conscious of having fallen asleep. The empty plate was on the coffee table in front of her, a subtitled movie playing on the screen. Then a rap on the door. She assumed that was what had woken her. She got up stiffly and looked through the spy hole to see Tom's face grinning back at her.

'Saw your light on from the street,' he said, bringing a gust of cold outdoors and other smells in with him. There was a bottle in his hand and his voice sounded loud and cheerful. He gave her a kiss. 'Someone let me through the front door.'

'Oh . . . I fell asleep in front of the box. What time is it?'

'"'Round Midnight." You know that one? Thelonious Monk. Classic.' He was searching for glasses, humming to himself.

She checked her watch. It was just after three. 'You sound happy. Where have you been?'

'Working, working. We never sleep.' That seemed to be the cue for another melody while he worked on the cork, filled the glasses and collapsed on the sofa.

'Phew, I'm bushed. Cheers.'

She joined him. She hadn't seen the shirt before, purple silk with a dark pattern of some kind. Not a work shirt. He smelled of cigarette smoke, and something else.

'Cheers. Did you drive here?'

He looked penitent. ' 'Fraid so. Shouldn't have. Won't be able to drive home after this. Can I stay here?'

'Of course.'

'Wonderful.' He put his glass down with a bump that splashed wine across the table, then laid his head back on the sofa and closed his eyes. 'You are wonderful, you know that, don't you?'

Kathy got up to wipe the spilled wine. 'What was that all about this afternoon, your phone call?' she asked, but there was no reply and when she turned back he was asleep. She looked down at him for a moment, at the self-absorbed concentration on his sleeping face, and wondered if she really knew him at all. She spread a spare blanket over him and went to bed.

When she got up in the morning he was still there, curled up beneath the blanket. He woke to the sounds of her making coffee and toast, and sat up with a groan, rubbing his face. She handed him an orange juice and he said he was sorry.

'What happened?' she asked. 'Where had you been?'

'Oh . . . I met somebody, had a few drinks. Sorry. Was it very late? Did I wake you up?'

'Don't worry. How's your head?'

'Nothing a shower won't fix. Thanks, Kathy.' He checked his watch with bleary eyes and jumped to his feet. 'Hell, I'd better move.'

He had a fast shower, pulled his old clothes back on again, kissed her and ran out the door while she was still making breakfast. As she sat at the window munching her toast she contemplated the smell on his jacket. Cigarette smoke, curry and something else, something familiar. She got up and shook out the crumpled blanket on the sofa and a small white handkerchief fell to the floor. It didn't look like a man's handkerchief. She picked it up and was aware of that scent again . . . J'Adore, that was it. J'Adore perfume, she was almost sure. She wondered what perfume Michael Grant's research officer—what was her name? Andrea—wore.

She went to the window and looked down at the car park. Tom's Subaru was parked at an odd angle in the corner. She watched him get in, reverse and head for the street, and as he accelerated away she noticed a dark green car take off after him. She reached for the phone and dialled his number.

'Yes?'

'Tom . . .' She looked down at the handkerchief in her hand, then tossed it aside. 'Is there a green Mondeo on your tail?'

'What? Hang on . . . No, Kathy, don't think so.'

'All right. See you later.'

NINETEEN

THE FOLLOWING DAY KATHY was caught up in one of her other cases, her court appearance scheduled and rescheduled in a frustrating series of delays. While she waited she thought about Brown Bread. Her Rainbow success, identifying the Mondeo, had been a small victory, but it didn't seem to lead anywhere. The whole business of Rainbow surveillance had previously seemed rather dumb and unsavoury policing, but now she could appreciate its possibilities. Before long the net would be so extensive that they would probably be able to say where any given vehicle was at any particular time and, with the new facial recognition technology, any given person, too. She smiled grimly to herself at the thought of giving the coordinator Tom's car number and asking where it was at one o'clock the previous night. What was he playing at? Come to that, what was Brock up to? The whole investigation felt directionless and remote.

When the Crown solicitor finally told her in the afternoon that she wouldn't be called until the following day, she decided to take the long way back to the office. She made her way down to the Old Kent Road, across Blackheath and onto the Dover road, noticing several cameras along the busy route, but not at the point where she turned off to Shooters Hill. When she reached the golf club she turned into the car park and switched off the engine. There had been a spate of car thefts in recent months as well as two burglaries of the clubhouse bar, and Kathy was interested to see cameras covering the building, the car park and, of greatest interest, the entrance gates.

She got out of the car and walked around the clubhouse, seeing no one. The paraphernalia of golf carts and little flags and greens and fairways brought back the memory of an illicit weekend in Norfolk with Martin Connell, long ago. She'd forgotten about the game of golf they'd played, his instructions and guiding hand. The recollection was intense and bittersweet.

The course was deserted, the open ground enfolded by dark woods. She walked up the first fairway and then cut through a belt of dripping trees to emerge on the edge of the returning eighteenth. On its far side she could see the roofs and windows of The Glebe above its encircling wall. Some of the upper rooms had large picture windows, glinting in the reflected light of the low red sun, and balconies, so that their occupants could enjoy views out over the parkland and woods and the stream that had been turned into a picturesque water hazard across the final fairway.

Her phone trembled in her pocket and she turned back into the trees to answer it. It was Tom.

'Hi, where are you?'

'Playing golf.'

'Don't be sarcastic, Kathy, it's not you. Look, I owe you a huge apology for last night.'

'It's all right. You can crash at my place whenever you want.'

'I'd like to make it up to you. Can I buy you dinner tonight?'

'Fine. How's it going with Andrea?'

'Oh great, we've had a good day. She's given me one or two interesting things to think about.'

'I'll bet. Smart is she?'

'Very. They all are, working over here, but she particularly. Oxford degree, you know. I'll have to get her to show you around.'

'Good idea. Damn.'

'What's the matter?'

'Sorry, I trod in something. My feet are soaking wet.'

'Where are you, really?'

'I'll tell you tonight. And you can tell me about Andrea.'

HE TOOK HER TO L'Odeon in Regent Street, which Kathy had to admit made it a handsome apology. When he gave her a hug she found herself sniffing his collar like a jealous lover. No trace of J'Adore. Maybe she'd been mistaken, what with the curry and the cigarette smoke. But then she remembered the handkerchief. What had she done with it? On balance she decided not to bring it up.

She told him about her day and he laughed.

'You really were on that golf course? Alone? In the dark?'

'It wasn't quite dark. But I felt I needed to get to grips somehow with the reality of the Roaches.'

'I know what you mean. And did it help?'

'Not really. I couldn't see much. I didn't even want to ask the professional if they played there, in case he got suspicious.'

'They do play there, the three sons and their wives, and some of their children. They're all members.'

'How do you know?'

'Article and picture in the *Plumstead Gazette*, a family golf competition day last year. The whole clan in their snappy golf gear, the women with dazzling smiles, the men and kids scowling. I feel I know everything about them, and nothing. Like you say, it's all on paper.'

'Andrea had their picture from the *Plumstead Gazette*? Why?'

'That's a good question. She's got passport records of every overseas trip they've ever made—how did she get those? She just laughed when I asked her. And she's got graphs tracking the share prices of their companies against the FT Index. Michael Grant sounds rational enough, but I think he's obsessed. He's convinced the Roaches are behind half the drugs trade south of the river, and he's got Andrea dredging for anything that might fit into an incriminating pattern.'

'How does she feel about it?'

'She believes him. He's very convincing, very impassioned. She thinks he's wonderful.'

'What's she like?'

'You can meet her. Grant's daughter is giving a concert on Saturday evening to raise money for one of her father's good causes. We're invited, Brock too. Will you come? Apparently she's very good.'

'Oh, well . . . Nicole and Lloyd suggested we go out with them on Saturday.'

'They could come along, then we could get a meal together afterwards.'

'All right, I'll ask her.'

'You're right, you know, about the case,' Tom said. 'We're doing it all wrong, not being aggressive enough. What's Brock doing, do you know?'

'He seems to be immersed in old police files.'

Tom shook his head. 'More paper. It's like he's becoming bogged down in the past. Either we should have a go at the Roaches or we should forget about them and get on with something useful.'

'What could we be doing?'

'I've got one or two ideas.'

'Like what?'

'Not now.' He looked at her. 'There are more important things to think about, like what we're going to eat. The steamed sea bass is supposed to be a speciality of the house, so I'm told.'

Later she caught him looking at her with an oddly sad expression. 'What's wrong?'

'I've been neglecting you,' he said.

'We've both been a bit preoccupied with work.'

'I'll make it up to you, soon. Maybe we could go away somewhere, take a trip, get out of London.'

'Where do you fancy, Jamaica?' She smiled, but he just looked nonplussed, as if he couldn't see that it was meant as a joke.

Later, he drove her home. She asked him up for a nightcap but he refused, saying he needed to get a few things prepared for the morning.

KATHY WASN'T REQUIRED IN court until ten that day, and decided to pay another visit to the flat above the laundrette in Cove Street. She guessed that George, if he was living there, was probably not an early riser. As she pulled into the kerb outside the tyre yard she saw the woman step out of the flat onto the access deck, this time unencumbered by her twins. Kathy waited while she hurried down the stairs and ran towards the street, then she went up to the front door. There was a light visible through the frosted window. She knocked, waited, then knocked again. Finally the door opened.

'Yeah, yeah, yeah . . .' George grumbled, wiping his hands on a cloth. 'Wha—'

He stared at Kathy and his mouth stayed open as he recognised her.

'Morning,' she said. 'Can I come in?'

He recovered himself, sticking his head out of the door and darting his eyes up and down the deck and over the street below. 'What you want?'

'A few words, George.' From somewhere inside a baby began to cry, then another, their wails rising to a coordinated shriek. 'Won't take a minute.'

He looked harassed. 'All right then.'

She followed the sounds of distress as he closed the door behind her and found the source on the floor of a cramped living room, two shiny brown sets of limbs thrashing on newspaper.

'Oh, phew.' A pair of soiled, freshly opened nappies lay next to their bottoms.

'Yeah, 'orrible, innit?'

'Got fresh nappies? I'll give you a hand, if you like.'

She squatted down and they took one each.

'You're better at this than me,' Kathy muttered, trying not to breathe. 'Are they yours?'

He shook his head, mouth turned down with disgust. 'No way. Where you parked?'

'Outside the tyre yard.'

'Anybody see you come up here?'

'I don't think so, why?'

'The landlord don't like coppers. He'd get really pissed off if he knew you were here.'

'Teddy Vexx, eh?'

'Teddy, yeah. How do you know that? What you want anyway?'

'Winnie's worried about you, George. Why did you leave?'

'She got on my nerves, nagging all the time, wouldn't stop telling me what to do. I couldn't take it no more. Carole said I could move in here as long as I helped out with the twins.'

From the look on his face as he stared down at them he wasn't sure he'd made the right choice. Kathy noticed a keyboard and some sophisticated-looking electronic gear on the table, mixed up with the jumble of breakfast things. 'You working, George?'

'Off and on.'

'Where did you nick that stuff?'

'Give over, that's all mine. That's the other reason I had to leave Winnie—she couldn't stand me practising.'

'Is your group playing at the moment?'

'Yeah, at the JOS. It's the place, man. We just started there. It's our big break.' For a moment he grew a little stiffer with pride, then he sagged again. 'What do you want, anyway?'

'Where are the binoculars?'

George looked startled. 'What binoculars?'

'I want to know why you spied on us when we were digging up those bodies on the railway land.'

Now he was acting offended. 'I never did! Who told you that?'

'Don't lie to me. We found a spliff you were smoking over there. Pretty potent. You want me to arrest you and talk to you on tape?'

'Oh . . .' He slumped into a chair, shaking his head in disbelief. 'This is so unfair. All the stuff that's goin' on and you pick on the little people like me.'

'Stop moaning, George, and tell me what you were doing.'

'I don't know. They paid me, that's all that mattered to me, but I don't know what was the point. I sat up there freezing day after day and I said, What's the point? They've cleared the snow, they've put up tents, I can't see anything. And he just said, How many tents? Where are they? He wanted a daily report.'

'Who did?'

'Teddy. But it was for somebody else. He was doing a favour for somebody who was interested, I don't know who.'

'You must have some idea. How did Teddy contact him? Did they meet? Did you ever see Teddy talking to him?'

But George was too afraid of Teddy Vexx, and knew he'd already said too much. 'You've no idea, no idea at all, what he can do. Just leave me alone. I don't know nuffing.'

'You should get away from Teddy and his friends, George. Concentrate on your music.'

'I don't have no money, do I? And he got us the gig at the JOS.'

'Good luck.'

George darted ahead of her to the door and looked cautiously around outside before letting her go. Behind them the twins started bawling again.

When she got to court she found herself on hold once again, and she took the opportunity to make a couple of phone calls. She started with the Rainbow coordinator at Greenwich Borough. When she got through she told him about the camera at the gates of the golf club, and he promised to check and get back to her. Then she rang Nicole and told her about the invitation to the concert on Saturday night.

'What sort of music is it?' Nicole asked.

'I don't know. Classical, I think. It's for a good cause, not sure what.'

'Oh well, we'll give it a go.' She made a note of the arrangements, then added, 'What's got into your boss these days, Kathy? He's driving us mad with his demands for old files, buried in the deepest recesses. Is he writing a history book or something?'

TWENTY

ON SATURDAY MORNING BROCK sat at his desk surrounded by columns of stacked files that looked as if they'd been unearthed from some ancient crypt. Dot had attempted to rearrange them, he saw, perhaps to make an easier route to the door, but she hadn't made much impression. From her withering looks the previous day he understood that she no longer considered the situation tenable. He sympathised, of course, but he couldn't stop now, not having come this far. The problem was that the material evoked so many memories, so many side trails, that it was easy to get distracted. To focus his researches he had pinned a large sheet of detail paper over the top of the Brown Bread wall, and it was now covered with a hand-drawn timeline and incident record chart decipherable only to himself. Maybe today, maybe tomorrow, something would emerge out of the mist. He knew he couldn't go on much longer.

Then the phone rang, his mobile not the office one. 'Hello?'

The caller said nothing for a moment. He heard an intake of breath, and repeated, 'Hello? Brock here.'

'Hello, David.'

It was his turn to be silent, giving the buzzing in his ears a chance to subside. 'Suzanne,' he said at last.

'Was that you at the airport on Tuesday?'

'Yes . . . yes it was. I got cold feet when I saw the children.'

'I'm coming up to town this morning. Do you want to meet?'

'Yes,' he said. 'I'd like that.'

KATHY ALSO HAD A surprise in store that Saturday morning. Tom picked her up at nine for what he described as a mystery trip. He was wearing a warm jacket, and she noticed the strap of a camera hanging from its pocket. They headed north and east on roads she didn't know, and after a while she began to see signs for the Lee Valley Regional Park, Waltham Abbey and Epping Forest. They drove through woodland on narrow lanes over rising ground, and eventually emerged on a hilltop, where Tom pulled over in front of a panoramic view back across the city. It was a fresh, blustery morning, with sunlight piercing the gaps in high cloud to pick out parts of the Thames basin in pools of brightness. Suddenly the sound of birdsong and the hum of distant traffic were punctuated by the sharp staccato rattle of gunfire.

'Now do you know where we are?'

Kathy shook her head.

'Lippitts Hill? You haven't been to the firing range here?'

'Oh, yes, but I must have come a different way. Have you brought me for a morning's shooting then?'

'Not quite. Something more fun, I think.' He pointed up at the sky, and after squinting at the cloud for a moment Kathy was able to make out a tiny object dropping fast towards them. A little later and the growing dot was accompanied by a thumping noise that became a deafening clatter as the helicopter passed overhead and dropped behind a copse of trees. Tom restarted the car and drove after it to a set of gates beside a notice for the Metropolitan Police Air Support Unit.

'I thought we might hitch a ride,' Tom said. 'Okay?'

He was friends with the inspector who ran the police staff on the base, a former Special Branch man, who introduced them to the pilot. They had a cup of coffee together while the Twin Squirrel was being refuelled, and he pointed out the aircraft's special features: the Nitesun searchlight, the Skyshout loudspeaker system, and the gyro-stabilised, thermal-imaging video camera.

Tom was trying to impress her, Kathy realised, and doing quite a good job, though she'd have been more impressed if he'd volunteered what he'd been doing the night before.

They climbed in, fastened seatbelts, and rose into the blustery air. Below them the canopy of Epping Forest spread away to the north. Spiralling higher, the full extent of the city became clearer, sprawling away to the distant horizons, east, south and west. They headed down the Lee Valley, following the chain of reservoirs, marshes and waterways towards the great silver snake of the Thames, crossing it near the Isle of Dogs and losing altitude over the ant-line of cars on the Dover road across Blackheath.

Now Kathy realised what Tom had in mind. Soon she could see the pattern of tees, greens and bunkers on the golf course like a neat abstract painting, and recognised the belt of trees from where she had looked across the eighteenth fairway to The Glebe. Then it was laid out below them, an irregular octagon of roofs around the central space in which she could make out someone washing a car and two others on the tennis court. The tennis players paused in their game as the shadow of the chopper passed over them.

Tom was taking pictures and gestured for her to look at something to do with the stream across the golf course, but she couldn't work out what he was saying. The helicopter banked into a wide sweep to the south before returning across Shooters Hill and heading back over the river towards base.

'It was a great trip,' she said to the pilot as they stepped out onto solid ground again, and she meant it, for the noise, the buffeting wind, the vibration, the exhilaration of height had energised her and she felt her face tingling with life. They thanked Tom's friend, who said he couldn't join them for lunch, but recommended a nearby pub, the Owl, which had its own pet owl in a cage in the garden.

Over pies and beer, Tom said, 'Did you get the point about the stream?' He, too, seemed charged by their flight.

She said she hadn't, so he got out his camera and replayed his pictures on the monitor screen.

'You can see the route of it back here, beyond the old church, where there's a winding line of willows. It curls around the church towards the original glebe house, then disappears.' He clicked on through the frames. 'Then we come to the Roaches' compound, and on the other side the stream emerges again to form that hazard across the golf course, becomes the small lake near the club-house, and continues north to run into the Thames somewhere around Woolwich.' He sat back with a quizzical smile, waiting for her conclusions.

'So it's been culverted where it runs around the Roaches' place?'

'Not around, under. To put together a big enough site for his family compound on the edge of the golf course, Spider had to build The Glebe across the stream. It runs in a culvert right under the development. And for maintenance purposes, there are two manhole access points into the central courtyard.'

As he made this revelation, Tom had a look of breezy elation on his face that made Kathy think of Biggles or the Famous Five, and she wondered if their aerial adventure had made him slightly drunk.

'How do you know this?'

'Because I've seen the plans lodged with the local authority. Planning approval was conditional on providing adequate means of access for council engineers.'

'Andrea?'

He gave a smug little smile. 'Actually, no. I dug this up myself.'

'You're not seriously suggesting . . .'

Tom's eyes lit up with mischief as he followed what was going through her mind, daring her to say it.

'. . . posing as a council engineer?'

'Not exactly that, perhaps. But let's face it, the only conclusive evidence we're likely to get against Roach will be inside The Glebe, yes?'

'You want to break and enter?'

' "Covert entry" sounds so much better than "break and enter," don't you think? Sounds almost legitimate. Like nobody need know a thing about it.'

'Tom . . .'

'A moonless night,' he mused, turning away to contemplate the owl in its cage outside the window. 'The new moon is next Thursday . . .'

Kathy began to protest at how ridiculous the idea was, how impractical and potentially disastrous, until she saw his shoulders shake and realised he was having her on.

'Tom!' She punched his arm.

He turned back, laughing, and she joined in.

'All right, you got me going.'

And yet, the reason she had fallen for it was that she had seen a quality in him that made it seem all too plausible. You might call it impatience with due process, or reckless courage, or the Nelson touch. She admired it, but also mistrusted it. Maybe she recognised a shade of it in herself.

'I called in on Brock yesterday,' Tom said later, as they were finishing their lunch. 'Have you seen his office lately? Like a paper recycling dump. We have to do something, Kathy, bring him back to the real world.'

THEY HAD ARRANGED TO meet at a small restaurant in Chelsea, a favourite haunt from years ago when Suzanne had lived in nearby Belgravia before she had moved down to the coast to open her antiques shop in Battle. Brock wasn't sure what to make of her choice of venue, whether it was meant to resurrect the feelings they had shared when they first met, or to demonstrate how different things were now. He felt both sensations tugging at him as he stepped across the familiar threshold. Nothing had changed, not the decor, the layout of tables, or even the management. He was the first to arrive, and took his seat at a secluded table at the rear, ordered a dry martini because that was what they had done in those days, and sat watching the door with a trepidation he hadn't felt in a long time.

She'd had her hair cut he realised as he rose to his feet, remembering the travel-worn figure he'd seen at Heathrow. The thick, shoulder-length dark hair had been trimmed back to her jawline in a new style he liked. He smiled to himself, for he too had visited the barber on his way over here. For a moment, as she approached, he wasn't sure what to expect. Then her face broke into that warm generous smile of hers and she was holding out her hands to him.

'David!'

He took the offered hands, then pulled her closer and wrapped his arms around her. 'Suzanne,' he murmured, with enormous relief. The maître d' beamed approvingly and eased out her chair and they sat.

'Oh, dry martini! Yes, please.'

For a moment they said nothing, hands laid on the white tablecloth with fingertips just touching in mute contact. She looked reinvigorated, he thought, charged with new life.

'Thank you for ringing,' he said, 'for suggesting this.'

'I wasn't sure if it was a mistake, until I saw you just now. How have you been?'

'The same. You look marvellous. The trip has done you good.'

'Yes, I feel refreshed . . . in different ways.'

But he detected a shadow behind her words, and had the sudden awful suspicion that the purpose of this meeting was to make a final break.

'A new perspective?'

'Yes . . .'

He sensed some hard thing about to emerge, but then she veered away and spoke about the things she had done: riding horses on a cattle station, scuba diving on a reef, hiking through a rainforest.

Her martini arrived and he raised his glass to hers. 'Welcome home.'

She lowered her eyes. 'Did you miss me?'

'Every day. Three months is a long time.'

She was about to reply to that when the waiter came for their order, and when he left she instead turned the conversation to the restaurant and its memories. Did he remember the old couple that always sat at that table over there, and how they'd invented their story from small clues—his taste in shoes, her silver-tipped walking stick, the tiny appointment diaries they would compare? And how they would get tired of that, or discover a new clue, and invent a completely new story for them?

'I had this idea that I could change our story too,' she went on. 'I used to think you were suffering from a malignant condition that I called Brock's Paradox, a belief that you could only keep a relationship alive by not allowing it to reach its full potential.' She gave a little smile. 'I thought if I could get you away for long enough I could show you that it needn't apply, so I planned a long trip for us, overseas, but at the last minute you backed out. Work, you said.'

She propped her chin on a hand and looked at him quizzically. 'Where did Brock's Paradox come from, do you think? Was it your wife leaving you? Or does it go further back? Something to do with your mother?'

Brock was recalling that it was on the tenth anniversary of his divorce that he'd first seen Suzanne, been immediately struck by the woman getting out of the red sports car and going into the small antiques shop she ran just off Sloane Square. He had followed her inside and got her to tell him all about her cabinet of eighteenth-century English glassware.

'So things didn't quite work out as I'd planned. Quite the opposite, in fact. The thing was that, even though I'd put thousands of miles between us, every time I saw something interesting— green shoots coming out of the ground after a bushfire, an electric storm out to sea, a flock of pink-chested parrots filling a tree—I mentally turned to you to compare notes. I thought I could change you, and there I was, unable to change myself. You were still inside my head, and I decided I didn't want to let you go.'

'I'm glad,' he said, and was.

'But that wasn't why I came home.'

The waiter appeared with oysters and a bottle of white wine.

'Last week I got a panicky phone call from Ginny, who's been running the shop.'

Brock stiffened. Had Roach made a move against her after all? It would be ironic if he'd been the cause of bringing her back.

'Stewart had been in touch with her. He said that he and Miranda had been living on their own for the past two weeks, without anyone knowing—doing their own shopping and cooking, getting themselves off to school—but now they'd run out of money, and didn't know what to do. He was quite apologetic. He had no idea where their mother was.'

Suzanne's grandchildren would now be ten and eight, Brock reckoned, and it was their return to the care of their mother, after Suzanne had looked after them for a number of years in her absence, that had precipitated Suzanne's plans for an overseas trip.

'Ginny called the police, who traced Amber to the psychiatric hospital in Hastings. Apparently, she'd been found lying on a headland outside the town after taking an overdose. She had no identification.'

'Oh no. I'm sorry.'

'You know what she was like, always erratic in her moods. After she came back from living with that man in Greece she went through a black period, very depressed. Her doctor referred her to a psychiatrist who diagnosed her as suffering from Bipolar I Disorder. That did make sense. It's a long-term illness, and it seemed to explain a pattern of extreme mood swings over the years. Also it's heritable, and her father had similar symptoms—and you know he killed himself. The thing is that it's treatable, with drugs and psychotherapy, and when she went on the medication she improved so much that I was tremendously relieved. When she said she wanted to look after the children again, I was really confident that she could do it. She was doing fine when I left . . .'

Neither of them had touched their oysters, and Suzanne's voice had dropped to a flat murmur. Brock tasted his wine and she followed suit.

'I'm sorry,' he said. 'I should have kept in touch with them. I never thought.'

'No, you couldn't, not after the way we parted. It seems the hospital disagrees with the diagnosis. They think she's suffering from Borderline Personality Disorder, which has similar symptoms but is less amenable to treatment. Also, when the social services went to the house to see the children, they found drugs—cannabis and methamphetamine. It seems Amber had never really given them up. I didn't know. I should have been more careful. When I got home I discovered she'd taken things from my house, little things she could sell, and Ginny told me she'd discovered things missing from the shop.'

He watched the distress building in her, and reached out to put his hand over hers. 'You don't deserve this. It isn't your fault.'

She took a deep breath, reining her feelings in. 'Anyway, I wanted you to know; that's why I've come home.' She picked up her fork and stabbed it at a grey mollusc.

They ate in silence, then she said, with a forced attempt to change the subject, 'So, and what are you doing at the moment?'

He told her about Dee-Ann and Dana, and despite her preoccupation, she gradually became drawn into the story.

'Michael Grant, yes, I've seen him on TV. I thought he was very impressive. I wish there were more like that at Westminster. So the other three victims were his contemporaries. I suppose he could have been one of them, if things had been different.'

'Exactly. This is why he's taking such a personal interest in the case, that and his suspicions about Roach.'

'But if he has evidence against him he should give it to you, surely?'

'He's giving us access to his files, but I don't know if he's holding something back. So far we've seen nothing we can act on. We're looking for a pattern of incrimination, you could say. My lot are beginning to think I'm obsessed.'

'What, you?' She laughed. 'Don't they know you by now?'

'When your hair turns grey people start to look for signs of a similar deterioration inside your head. Kind of applied metonymy. Even Dot's giving me funny looks.'

'And how's Kathy?'

'Okay, I think. She's going out with a bloke who's working with us at the moment, on secondment from Special Branch. I'm keeping a close eye on him.'

'I'm sure she'll be glad about that. Why don't you just let her get on with it?'

'I don't interfere!' he protested. 'I'm just not sure about her taste for Special Branch officers. Why can't she meet a nice lawyer or something? Someone with a safe desk job. Anyway, you can catch up with her yourself this evening, if you feel like it, and Michael Grant too.' He explained about the concert. 'And maybe afterwards . . .'

'I have to get back this afternoon, David,' she said quickly. 'I've got a note of the train times. Thanks.'

'Of course.' He stiffened, mentally cursing himself for spoiling everything. 'They're staying with you now are they, the children?'

'Yes, back to the old routine. I must say they seem happy about it. I wonder what went on, what they saw.'

The main course came, and suddenly they both discovered that they were very hungry. Later, over a shared dessert, Brock casually came out with the question that had been haunting him all week. It seemed that the tall, tanned man pushing Suzanne's trolley at the airport was an acquaintance of her sister's from Sydney, who just happened to be on the same flight.

TWENTY-ONE

THE CONCERT WAS TO be held in a new library and community centre in Michael Grant's constituency. The radical-looking structure, a prismatic blue oblong supported along one side by oddly angled columns, looked as if it had been dropped in, by helicopter perhaps, among the jumble of scruffy buildings cowering beneath the streetlights and drizzle along the high street. As she and Tom made their way towards it, Kathy could see other people, some in suits with umbrellas and others in anoraks and jeans, heading under the raking columns towards the entrance. They waited in the shelter of the overhang until they saw Nicole and Lloyd running towards them, hugged and shook hands and made their way inside, where a stairway took them up into the belly of a curving pod, within which they found themselves in the foyer of the community hall.

Michael Grant was there, welcoming visitors. He shook their hands warmly, showing where they could leave their coats and find a glass of orange juice or wine, and said to Tom, 'You must introduce your friends to Andrea. There she is, over there.'

He gestured towards a very attractive young woman who was talking animatedly with another couple. As they approached, however, the group broke up and the young woman turned away to speak to someone else. Tom led Kathy and the other two past her to a small, erect, grey-haired woman whose glass was being refilled.

'Andrea!' he cried, and bent to kiss her on the cheek.

'Tom!' The elderly woman's eyes twinkled with delight. 'And is this Kathy? At last, I've heard so much about you.' She took Kathy's hand and squeezed it hard.

Andrea, Kathy later discovered, had been the CEO of a merchant bank in the City and then the head of a large charity before retiring, becoming very bored, and joining Grant's office. As she talked, pointing out people who were present, it was clear that her mind and her wit were razor sharp. It transpired that the attractive young woman they had seen was Michael Grant's daughter Elizabeth, who would be performing for them that evening with three of her friends from the Guildhall School of Music and Drama.

'She's extremely talented,' Andrea whispered, 'and very beautiful. Isn't that the most perfect complexion? Creamy butterscotch. One day, when the mixing pot has done its work, we'll all have skin like that, the ultimate human colouring. Too late for a wrinkled old mouse like me.'

She pointed out Grant's wife too, an elegant, rather calm-looking woman alongside her husband's restless vitality, in conversation with a couple who looked as if they'd dressed for the opera at Covent Garden, and whose stiff expressions suggested they wished they were there instead.

'Nigel Hadden-Vane and his wife,' Andrea explained. She pronounced his name with an exaggerated posh accent that made it sound like 'hard and vain.' 'Tory MP, on Michael's HAC—sorry, Home Affairs Committee. The enemy,' she added, 'or one of them. Margaret Hart does her best to keep him in line.' She pointed out a woman wearing a dramatic deep-red cloak. 'She's the chair of the committee. Great fun. She tells people exactly what she thinks of them. You can watch them live on webcast. There's another round of sittings coming up. But of course you've got better things to do.

'Talking about the enemy, the person I'd really like to have invited here is Edward Roach—I've never met him in the flesh. Have you? No. But your Mr Brock has, hasn't he? Is he coming tonight?'

'He was invited, Andrea,' Tom said. 'Though he seems to have a lot on his mind at the moment.'

But at that moment Kathy spotted him arriving at the top of the stairs, making his way towards Michael Grant, who greeted him enthusiastically. She watched them talking together and was struck by how different Brock looked from when she'd last seen him in his office, weary and preoccupied. Now he had a smart haircut and seemed ten years younger and as animated as Grant. The MP led him over to meet his wife and daughter, and it was apparent from the way they were responding that he was being amusing and charming.

There were other faces there that Kathy recognised—Father Maguire, Winnie Wellington and, to her surprise, George Murray, trying to keep out of Winnie's line of sight. He looked anxious when he saw Kathy watching him, and she smiled and gave him a little wave. As they took their seats, Lloyd made some comment about classical music and what to do if he started snoring too loudly. It occurred to Kathy that Lloyd had insulated himself with a few drinks before coming. 'The tragedy is he means it,' Nicole said, as Michael Grant appeared on the stage and silence fell.

Grant welcomed them and gave an outline of the youth programs their money would support, then introduced his daughter and her companions. Elizabeth took the microphone and explained that they called their ensemble 'Doctor Breeze,' taking the name of the warm trade wind that soothes the beaches of Jamaica. They had selected a variety of pieces of music, she said, to reflect the diversity of the audience and the community they represented. She was a flautist, holding her flute as she spoke, and she introduced a classical guitarist, a cellist, and a young man at the piano, but behind them the audience could see other more esoteric instruments laid out on a table—a lute, a viola da gamba and others.

They began with Telemann, and Kathy heard Lloyd groan softly and saw him close his eyes. From Baroque Europe they then moved to twentieth-century South America with a piece by Villa-Lobos, then further south to Argentina and Astor Piazzolla, for whom Elizabeth exchanged her flute for an accordion-like bandoneon, to capture the poignant spirit of the Tango Nuevo. As the group moved from classical to jazz to world music, exchanging instruments, centuries and countries, the audience seemed to fall under a spell, both stimulated and lulled by every unexpected twist in the journey. They finished with a Vietnamese piece by an American composer, Monica Houghton, 'We Rise Above Our Little Quarrels,' and by the end the listeners really did seem transformed. The applause was spontaneous, a single roar of sound, to which the group responded modestly. An encore was demanded, and they ended by returning to the eighteenth century from which they had begun, this time with Marin Marais. Lloyd had fallen asleep, and mumbled his objections as Nicole dug him in the ribs and they got to their feet.

Kathy wondered if she should say hello to Brock before they left, but he was deep in conversation with Jennifer Grant and the others were keen to leave, so they joined the crowd milling around the cloakroom. Kathy found herself standing next to Kerrie, the manager of Grant's office in Cockpit Lane, and they were chatting about the concert when the imposing figure of Hadden-Vane swept by. Stopped momentarily by the congestion, he half turned to them. Noticing the flounce of a blue silk handkerchief in his top pocket to match his tie, Kathy thought of Martin Connell's story about the MP and the knickers. She smiled, then abruptly suppressed it as Hadden-Vane turned and looked straight at her. His eyes connected, then passed on to Kerrie and lit up. He leaned towards her in a little bow and said softly, 'Hello, Kerrie. Enjoy the show?'

She smiled back and he continued on his way. Seeing Kathy's look of surprise, Kerrie, still smiling to herself, said, 'He's an MP. Full of himself. Reckon they all are over there, don't you?'

Their coats arrived and Kathy said goodbye and joined the others. They headed down the street for a curry at a place nearby that Lloyd recommended. They took their seats and while they waited for their drinks to arrive they talked about the concert. Lloyd queried the fact that they'd played so many different instruments. He seemed to think this was a bit flashy and disreputable until Tom suggested it was like being a pentathlete. Then Lloyd caught the look on Nicole's face and changed the subject. 'Your boss didn't show up then, Kathy?'

'Yes, he did eventually. He was talking to Grant's wife when we left, otherwise I'd have introduced you.'

'Pity, I'd have liked to have met the great man before he quits.'

Kathy was used to Lloyd playing the joker, and she assumed from his exaggeratedly innocent expression and the flicker of exasperation on Nicole's face that he was having her on. Still, she took the bait and said, 'Quits?'

'Sure, any day now is what I hear. Hasn't Tom told you that he's taking over?'

Now it was Tom rolling his eyes, as if this was an old joke that had outlived its use-by date.

'No, I don't think he mentioned that.'

'Really?' Lloyd frowned with puzzlement and concern. 'Well, he's told us all about it, hasn't he, Nic?'

'Shut up, Lloyd,' Nicole answered, but Kathy noticed she didn't actually deny it. Tom was looking uncomfortable.

'Oh God, yes, all kinds of plans to streamline . . .'

There was an awkward pause while the Indian waiter brought their lagers.

'No, well,' Lloyd went on, 'I'm probably jumping ahead. I'm sure he'll consult with everybody before he puts the more draconian measures into practice.' He leaned forward conspiratorially. 'It's the timing that's so perfect, Kathy. Cheers.'

'Shut up, Lloyd,' Tom growled, 'for Christ's sake. You're not funny.'

'What do you mean, about the timing?' Kathy asked.

'Well, he can't go back to Branch now, can he? Not now.'

Tom made to say something, but Kathy cut in. 'Why not?'

'Hasn't he told you about that, either?' Lloyd's face was a picture of innocent bafflement. He turned to Tom, then to Nicole, one of whom had apparently kicked him under the table. 'What?'

'Why?' Kathy said, trying with difficulty to make her voice sound light and amused. 'Why can't he go back to Special Branch?'

Lloyd shrugged, looking as if he suddenly realised he'd gone too far. 'Personality clash, Kathy. Tom's boss is an old woman.' He frowned, realising that wasn't the right thing to say either. 'A geriatric desk-jockey at forty. Sad case. Resents like hell the fact that this guy has balls. Well, you'd know all about that . . .'

'Oh please.' Nicole finally stepped in. 'That's enough. He's been drinking this afternoon, Kathy. Take no notice of him. I know we all work for the Met, but do we have to talk shop?'

'Hear hear,' Tom said. 'It's slightly shop, but Kathy and I got a flight with Air Support this afternoon.'

'Oh really! Where did you go?'

It was a good try, but it would have taken a better actor than either of them to make it sound convincing. Lloyd gave Kathy a sheepish look and muttered, 'Yeah, they're right, take no notice of me. I'm pissed. Had a bad week. Almost killed a guy . . .'

And so the conversation veered off, but Kathy hardly heard it.

NOT HALF A MILE away, Brock also was seated at a restaurant table, but in much more relaxed company. The Grants had insisted he join them and the musicians for a meal and now the conversation flowed easily around the table in the mood of post-performance euphoria. They were all so likeable, he thought, modest and talented and full of youthful optimism, talking excitedly about their plans for when they finished at the Guildhall later in the year. Elizabeth had been accepted for the Artist Diploma program at the Juilliard in New York, and her mother was proud but anxious about her move away from them.

At the end of the meal Brock made his good nights and set off home, stopping along the way to phone Suzanne. She sounded pleased to hear from him, and they agreed that it had been good to see each other, and they would do it again soon. They were both careful in what they said, but warm, definitely warm. The atmosphere of the restaurant still clung to Brock and he hummed a snatch of Tango Nuevo as he went on.

THE ATMOSPHERE OF THE restaurant clung to Kathy too, as Tom drove them away. She waited for him to say something, but when he remained silent she started.

'So what was that all about, you not being able to go back to Branch?'

'I told you I'd been having problems there lately.'

'Not really. You haven't really told me anything about what's been happening.'

'Like Lloyd said, it's a personality clash. It happens all the time.'

'And what about your plans?'

'I'm just playing it by ear.'

'That's not what Lloyd said. He and Nicole seemed to know all about them.'

This was the nub, of course, that her friend Nicole, who'd never met Tom until she'd introduced them, seemed to know more about what was going on inside his head than she did.

'Oh, it's nothing. I bumped into them one lunchtime and was shooting off my mouth about stuff, that's all.'

Kathy bridled. Tom didn't shoot his mouth off to strangers. He was secretive and highly selective in what he said. 'Stuff you haven't told me.'

'Look, it's difficult sometimes to discuss certain things with you. You're involved, with me, with Brock . . .'

'Brock? What about him?'

'You've been with him a long time. You're very loyal to him, understandably so.'

'And I would see your thoughts as disloyal?'

'I'm just saying that it's difficult sometimes to air ideas freely without feeling they may be taken the wrong way.'

'Whereas with someone who's practically a total stranger, like Nicole, you can feel free to shoot your mouth off? That's bullshit.'

She felt the knot tightening in her stomach. What also irked her was the way in which he hadn't discussed where they were now going, but had simply driven north towards Finchley on the assumption, presumably, that he would be inviting himself in. They were almost there now, and she was just preparing some line to challenge him when he pulled over and said, 'I'm sorry, Kathy, we got off on the wrong foot tonight. It was Lloyd's fault. Let's leave it for now. We'll catch up tomorrow or Monday and talk about it. Okay?'

Stung, she unfastened her seatbelt and got out of the car, and then, looking back in through the window, she caught a glimpse of him checking his watch impatiently before he waved and took off. She stared after him and thought she saw a familiar shadow draw out behind him as he crossed the junction down the street, but this time she didn't phone him.

TWENTY-TWO

SUNDAY, A DARK OVERCAST morning, and Kathy woke after a disturbed sleep. The knot of tension in her stomach was still there, and she found she couldn't swallow the coffee she made. There was only one cure she knew of, and that was work, so she took an empty tube train into the city and walked to Queen Anne's Gate. The offices, too, were deserted and she felt like an intruder in the silent building.

Loose ends, Brock had said. She went back over her case notes and identified a few. They still hadn't been able to contact the owner of the red BMW sports car she'd seen in Tallow Square, a Mrs Coretta Wilkins with an address in Chigwell, and Kathy tried the phone number again without success. They had no record for Mrs Wilkins, whose car hadn't been reported stolen, and it seemed that her improbable presence there must be coincidental. Then there was Mrs Lavender, whom Father Maguire and Brock had mentioned from the old days in Cockpit Lane, but hadn't been on Michael Grant's list. She could try to track down people who worked at the old Studio One club on Maxfield Street where the three victims used to go, or trace 'Rhonda,' who had possibly had a boyfriend called Robbie, perhaps the third and most elusive victim. Or she might find out more about Teddy Vexx and Jay Crocker, and their dodgy laundrette.

She worked for five hours with little success, finding nothing that stirred any real interest in her, until the silence began to get her down. She switched off her computer and left, walking across St James's Park to Trafalgar Square and on past Leicester Square to Gerrard Street where she had a quiet meal in a tiny Chinese restaurant she knew. Afterwards she went to a movie, feeling as if her life were on hold, waiting for something significant to happen.

The following day she was called to a meeting with the Crown prosecutors, and it wasn't until the early afternoon that she returned to her desk, determined to draw up a report for Brock, along with a request to be taken off Brown Bread. There was one new bit of information waiting for her on her computer, a list of car numbers courtesy of the Greenwich Rainbow coordinator, taken from the golf club camera in Shooters Hill. Comparing them with her list of numbers of interest was what her old schoolteacher would have called busywork, but there was a kind of mindless entertainment in it, like playing a poker machine, hoping for a random match. When she had eliminated all the numbers known to belong to Roach family members, she had a list of their visitors' cars for the past six days. Unfortunately this didn't cover the night of the Singhs' intimidation, for the camera tape had been reused since then, but in any case, there was no sign of Vexx's Peugeot or Crocker's Mondeo on the list. She began to run checks on the unknown numbers and soon came to one that made her sit up—Mrs Wilkins' red BMW had been a frequent visitor to The Glebe. Kathy checked the times. Not just any visitor, but an overnight visitor no less, on three of the last six nights.

Encouraged, Kathy continued to check numbers. Several were innocent enough—a plumber, a messenger service, guests for Sunday lunch who lived nearby. Then Kathy hit another jackpot, and this time she felt that little dizzying adrenaline shock that people describe as heart-stopping. She checked the number again. It occurred four times, twice coming and twice going, both late at night, after midnight, in the early hours of Sunday and before that on the previous Wednesday. A Subaru, registered to Tom Reeves.

She took a deep breath, then got on the phone to Greenwich,

requesting digital copies of the camera images for a number of the times recorded. They said it would take a couple of hours if it was top priority and she told them it was, giving DCI Brock's name. Kathy waited, heart thumping, then rang down to the front desk to see if Tom had signed in that day and was told that he'd been there since noon. She forced herself to complete her check of the car numbers, then saved the file with a new password and began her report for Brock, no more than a list of key facts, the way he liked it.

The file of requested images finally arrived on her computer and she opened the first, for the early hours of Wednesday morning, when he'd turned up exhausted at her flat. And there he was, no mistake, his face caught behind the windscreen by the street-light opposite the golf club entrance, and beside him, smiling prettily, Miss J'Adore. Then she checked the most recent image, just the other night, after the concert and their quarrel—same again, with the same dark-haired girl. In each case there was a second image taken less than an hour after the first, showing the Subaru emerging from the lane leading to The Glebe, the driver now alone in the car. And then she realised who Miss J'Adore was.

Kathy moved on to the other images she'd requested, of Mrs Wilkins' BMW, and there was the girl again, behind the wheel this time. She should have thought of it, she told herself—wasn't Coretta a Greek name? Coretta Wilkins was probably an aunt or cousin of Magdalen Roach, Miss J'Adore herself, who'd been borrowing her car.

'You bastard,' Kathy whispered, staring again at the image of Tom and Magdalen in his Subaru. 'You stupid bastard.' She pressed the key for a print.

SHE FOUND HIM IN the basement 'Roach Room.' He was sitting tilted back in his chair, feet up, hands behind his head, contemplating the photos on the wall when she opened the door, and he reacted with a jump, swinging himself upright.

'Oh, hi, Kathy. How are you?'

She closed the door behind her. 'A bit clearer now, Tom. Here, I've got another picture for your rogues' gallery.'

He reached for it with a smile. 'Oh, thank—' He froze as he took in what it was. 'Fuck.'

'Is that what you do with her?'

He stared at her, mouth open.

'An eloquent answer. I'm going to see Brock. Want to come?'

'No!' He leapt to his feet.

'What, this is all a terrible mistake, this is not what it seems? Don't insult me, Tom. There are other pictures.'

'My God. How . . . Who?'

'Never mind.' Kathy reached for the print and turned away. 'I think I'll see him myself first.'

Tom rushed towards her, and for a moment she thought he was going to grab her, but instead he threw himself between her and the door. 'Kathy, listen, don't do anything until you've heard what I've got to say. Please.'

She considered a moment, then said, 'All right, but it had better be good. One false note and I'm off.'

He took a deep breath. 'Sit down, please.' He went back around the table and took his own seat. 'I'm not going to stop you leaving, but it's very important that you hear me out. It wasn't my idea to target Magdalen.'

'Target? Is that what you call it in the Branch?'

Tom held up his hand. 'Just listen. What I told you about wanting to get out of Special Branch was true—I can't get on with my boss, and he's been making things difficult. So when he offered to loan me to Brock for the Brown Bread investigation I was very happy. Then when Brock made it plain that he was going after the Roaches, I had a quiet word with one of my mates in the Branch. He said he'd heard something about another operation against them.'

'What operation? We haven't heard about this.'

'I don't know, it's probably in the past. My friend had the

impression it might have originated outside the Met. MI5 maybe, or the JIC. Anyway, he felt it could be useful my being here, in Brock's team, in terms of my career.'

'As a spy.'

'No, no. I've had no contact with these other people, if they exist, and I haven't been talking about Brock's investigation. It isn't like that, Kathy. I may be able to help him, and us too.'

'By screwing—sorry, targeting—sweet Magdalen?'

Tom took another deep breath. 'I asked my friend to keep his ears open, and he came back with a hint about one of Roach's grandchildren being rebellious and a possible source of inside information on the clan. I took a good long look at them all and came to the conclusion that it had to be Magdalen. She's been a bit wild, recently divorced, reputation for partying. Four months ago she was picked up for drink driving, with traces of coke in the glove box, and when local CID interviewed her she said one or two odd things about her relatives that the detective thought significant enough to pass on to the Central Crime Squad. She had her driver's licence suspended. The drugs matter wasn't pursued.

'So I decided to find out more about her, where she goes, who her friends are. I arranged to bump into her a couple of times at clubs, and gradually got talking to her. She let me take her home, because she shouldn't be driving, although in fact she does use a car belonging to a relative who's overseas. Since her divorce she's been living in her parents' house in The Glebe, but she's pretty hostile about some members of the family, especially her father, Ivor. She's really vitriolic about him and the way he treats her mother. That was the main reason she went to stay with them, she said, to keep an eye on her mother. They seem to be very close. She's told me things we didn't know, like the fact that her grandpa has a trophy cabinet, with guns.'

He let that sink in, watching Kathy's mind working. 'Brown Bread?' she asked.

'It's possible. That's one of the things I'd like to find out. We joke about her being like Rapunzel, living in a castle, and how I'd like to see inside. That would be impossible, of course, with her parents there, only they went to New York at the weekend for a few days, and most of the rest of the clan are travelling up north today for a family function. I'm seeing Magdalen at the club tonight, and she's promised to take me home and show me around.'

'Bren knows about all this, does he?'

Tom shook his head. 'Nobody does, until now.'

Kathy gaped at him. 'Nobody? You've carried out your own private operation on the Roaches and you haven't told anyone? And tonight you're planning to walk into The Glebe without backup, without letting anyone know?'

'I've put everything down on file. It's in the cabinet over there, everything I've done and learned, and when the time comes I'll go to Brock with it. But not yet.'

She made to protest, but he leaned urgently across the table. 'Kathy, you know that Michael Grant was right about the connection between the Roaches and the Yardies, but we're getting nowhere. We're like a ship without a rudder. This is what I do— undercover work. If I find something, I'll take it to Brock. If not, no harm done.'

'You've got to tell Brock before tonight, Tom.'

'And if I do, what will he say? My guess is that he's been told to back off. If so, he can't afford to let me go in.'

'Try him.'

'Kathy, it's better he doesn't know.'

She thought about that. It dawned on her just how badly Tom wanted a coup, something spectacular to recharge his career or wipe out whatever had gone wrong for him in Special Branch. His secretiveness was breathtaking, but then that was the way he'd been trained to be, and maybe only he could pull off the stunt he was planning. She also remembered Lloyd's niggling joke about Tom wanting Brock's job.

'But I know.'

'No you don't. This conversation never happened.'

'Of course it did. I'm involved now. If we don't tell Brock, then I'm as responsible as you are. So I've got to be part of it.'

'No way.'

'She won't see me, but I'll be there, your backup. You'll keep in touch by texting me, and if you're not out of The Glebe by a set time I'll call in the troops.'

'No. Having you in the background will only increase the risk to me, Kathy.'

'Tough.'

'You don't trust me, do you?'

'I wonder why?'

He sighed, and reluctantly began to negotiate their working arrangements for the evening.

TOM HAD ARRANGED TO meet Magdalen at a pub in Eltham, a short taxi ride from her home, and drive her from there to the club where they planned to spend the evening. It was the same one, the JOS, part-owned by Teddy Vexx, where George Murray had told Kathy that he and his group were appearing, and she found the coincidence alarming, especially when Tom confirmed that Vexx and Jay Crocker knew and were friendly with Magdalen, who apparently had a taste for Jamaican music.

For this reason, Kathy didn't go into the JOS, but waited in her little Renault in the street opposite. She saw Vexx and Crocker arrive in the throbbing Peugeot, and later Tom and Magdalen in his Subaru. While she waited she watched the customers coming and going, listened to the muffled thump of the music and studied the band posters covering the outside walls, Black Troika among them. She wondered if George Murray was any good.

Shortly before midnight her phone signalled a text message from Tom: 'WAKE UP ON OUR WAY.' They appeared soon after, Tom having to support Magdalen down the front steps. Her long legs looked as unsteady as a newborn pony's or the rubbery hand she flapped at another couple leaving in the other direction. They laughed and waved back, and Tom gave them a rueful grin that Kathy felt was probably meant for her before he turned to steer his partner away down the street.

He drove at a sedate pace across South London, Kathy on his tail. It was twelve-forty when they reached the golf club gates at Shooters Hill, where Kathy pulled onto the verge beneath a low tree and watched Tom, parked farther up the lane leading to The Glebe, ease Magdalen out of his car and help her walk towards the gates. They fumbled with the keypad for a while and then they were inside and everything was still.

The agreed deadline for Tom's return was two, but at one-fifty Kathy received another message: 'WORKING L8 MAKE IT 3.' The minutes crept by, getting closer and closer to the hour, until Kathy had her phone out, pressing the numbers for help—and then he was there, letting himself out of the gate and hurrying towards his car, head down, arms wrapped around his chest as if against the cold. His footing seemed unsteady, and at one point he stumbled and almost fell. Then he was in his car and turning, coming fast back up the lane. He hurtled past as Kathy made her turn and she watched his taillights disappear into the distance.

He was waiting for her at the junction with the main road, turning onto it as she appeared, and for a couple of miles she followed him towards central London. His driving seemed erratic, the Subaru weaving in and out of its lane and at one point almost colliding with a turning truck, and Kathy became alarmed, worried that something was wrong. Finally he signalled a turn into a quiet suburban street and drew in to the kerb. Kathy parked behind him, jumped out and pulled open his door.

'Are you all right?'

'Yeah, yeah. Just not fit to drive. Take me home, will you? I'll leave the car here.'

He hauled himself out and stumbled to her car, still clutching his leather jacket as before, and sank into the seat with a sigh.

'Are you sure you're all right?'

He nodded, eyes closed. 'God, she took a bloody age to pass out.'

'So, how did it go?'

'Okay, I think.'

'Did you find anything? Brown Bread?'

'Not that, but maybe something better.' He looked up at her with a Belmondo grin, took hold of the zip on his jacket and slid it slowly down, revealing a fat yellow envelope. 'Let's go home and see what we've got.' He closed his eyes again and fell asleep.

As she turned her car back to the main road Kathy felt a surge of relief. At least it hadn't been a total disaster.

Tom woke as she drew to a stop outside his flat. 'Thanks,' he mumbled. 'I don't think I'd have made it.'

He let them in. 'I'm having coffee,' he said. 'Want a drink?'

'Coffee's fine. So tell me about it. What happened?'

'Oh, she got pretty legless at the club, more than normal, but at least she was willing to leave earlier than usual. Not for me,' he added quickly. 'With her parents away there was another attraction. When we got to the house she said her father kept dope in his office safe and she wanted my help to get into it. She had the key and a combination for the lock, but she couldn't get it to work.'

'Why did she think you could do it?'

'I've told her I work as a security consultant. So she took me into her dad's office and I had a look. It took me ten minutes to figure out what he'd done—you had to subtract one from each of the digits he'd written down to get the true entry code. Inside there were half a dozen sachets of cocaine, some of Magdalen's mother's jewellery, a pile of papers and a file. Magdalen removed one of the packets of coke and we went out to the living room.' He shrugged. 'Like I said, it took forever for her to fall asleep. She got all wild and lively again, wanting to dance, and then finally flaked out, just before the time I was supposed to leave. So I sent you the message and went back into the office and had another look. The papers seemed innocuous—birth certificates, company registration documents, stuff like that—but the file was odd. It was labelled "Dragon Stout," and seemed to be concerned with a consignment of Jamaican beer for the Paramounts off-licence chain. I thought it was strange having just one business file in among that other stuff, and I had a closer look. Most of it was straightforward letters and documents about suppliers' contracts, container layouts, shipping arrangements, customs forms, things like that, but then I came across this sheet ! . .'

Tom opened the yellow envelope and emptied its contents onto the coffee table. He thumbed through them for a moment, then lifted a single sheet with the letterhead of the head office of Paramounts Beers, Wines and Spirits, Importers and Retailers. It was dated the previous year and took the form of a handwritten list of points, like a summary for a presentation or a report, and ran as follows:

TERMS:

- *standard 20' container holds 1120 cases of 2 doz bottles of DS*
- *300 (25%) cases of 'special' = 7200 bottles*
- *@ 80 gm/bottle = 576 kg FGBC*
- *@ £20,000/kg = £11.52m*

'DS is Dragon Stout?' Kathy said.

Tom nodded.

'What's FGBC?'

'Could be first-grade base cocaine. Twenty thousand a kilo is about right for wholesale Colombian, uncut.'

'You think they're bringing it over in bottles of beer?'

'That's how it looks.'

'This isn't the original, is it?'

'No. There was a photocopier in the room, and I copied as much as I could of the file until I ran out of time. I haven't really examined the rest. I know there are letters to the bottling plant in Jamaica and the names of distributors in the UK.'

Kathy frowned, worried. 'Isn't this a bit too easy? I mean, are they really going to put this sort of stuff down on paper?'

'It's a business, like any other, Kathy. They have to keep records of what's been agreed, what's been paid. Look at the initials at the bottom: I.R., Ivor Roach. He's the accountant, he has to know. It's his file, in his private safe, in his home. Where else would it be?'

'When is this going to happen?'

'It already has. According to the dates there were four container loads delivered last year. That's forty-six million pounds worth of cocaine wholesale, say a hundred million on the street as crack or coke.'

'Well.' Kathy felt incapable of judgement. It was four in the morning and she wanted sleep and time to step back and digest this. She felt she barely recognised the man beside her. His face was flushed, his pupils contracted and his nose running. 'No wonder they've all got better cars than me,' she said.

'Yeah.' He sniffed and wiped his nose. 'And no wonder they've got plenty of friends. You look tired.'

'Yes, I'll be on my way.'

'Kip here. Then you can run me back to my car in the morning.'

She was too weary to argue, and they tumbled onto opposite sides of his bed and fell into a troubled sleep.

TWENTY-THREE

IT WAS ONE OF the more difficult interviews of her life. Tom managed it as well as he could have, speaking with conviction, taking full personal responsibility and painting her role in the most favourable light. But still, she felt rotten. Brock didn't rant or scold, that wasn't his way. His silence was far more eloquent. He just sat there behind his desk, expressionless, his eyes fixed on Tom as he told his story, occasionally appearing to focus on some detail of his appearance, his puffy eyes, his inflamed nostrils. He didn't look at Kathy at all, and she felt his disregard like a weight on her chest. Then, when the story was finished, he bowed his head over the papers and read them carefully, line by line, making notes on a pad in his deliberate script.

Finally he said, 'You haven't corroborated any of this? The shipping movements, the customs details, the contractors' companies?' This to Tom.

'No, we thought we'd better talk to you first.'

'Check what you can, without arousing suspicion. Come back at noon.'

'Right.' Tom began to draw back his chair.

'And bring a written report of your operation, as brief and succinct as possible. Leave Kathy out of it.'

'Fine.' Tom was on his feet.

'How did she get hold of the key?' Brock asked suddenly.

'The key?'

'To her father's safe. You said she had the combination and the key.'

'Oh, yes. There was a false bottom in one of the drawers of his desk. The key and the note of the combination were kept there, along with other keys. She'd seen him access it.'

'Hm.' Brock turned away and they left.

THEY WORKED AT ADJOINING desks, Tom tracking the movement of the containers and their consignments of Jamaican Dragon Stout through a friend in Customs and Excise, while Kathy checked the details of companies whose names appeared in the record using Companies House and a contact in the Fraud Squad. By noon they had compiled a fairly comprehensive background to the story outlined in Tom's photocopied material. He had also written a highly abridged account of how he had come by it, with the help, so he said, of an unnamed member of the Roach family.

'So there certainly were those orders and those shipments last year, Chief,' Tom said as Brock finished reading their report.

'What about this plastics business?' Brock pointed to one of the names on Kathy's schedule of companies involved in the transactions. 'Are you sure it existed?'

The order to PC Plastics in Solihull was one of the most incriminating items in the Dragon Stout file, involving the supply of 50,000 brown plastic sleeves, described as 'wine sample containers.' These would presumably have been used to hold the cocaine inside the 'special' bottles of beer, hidden in the middle of each container load. However, the company had gone out of business the previous year and Kathy hadn't been able to contact its directors.

'It certainly existed,' she said, the first time she'd spoken. 'I got details from Companies House, and I rang the local chamber of commerce, who knew of it. They also know of the managing director, name of Steven Bryce. He has other companies that are still functioning. I tried one of them and was told he's overseas at present, on a business trip.'

A hurried breakfast and several cups of strong coffee had restored her confidence to some extent. They hadn't been able to find anything in the papers that didn't have some form of corroboration, and Kathy was beginning to be infected by Tom's obvious excitement. Brock, though, betrayed no particular enthusiasm.

'All right,' he said eventually. 'Leave it with me.' He reached for the phone and they left.

'I'll buy you lunch,' Tom said as they made their way downstairs. 'He might show a little interest. What does he want, signed confessions?'

Kathy turned down lunch. She didn't want to listen to Tom building up his hopes. She wanted to think.

Later that afternoon she drove into South London and parked in the lane outside PART WORN TYRES. Which part? she wondered. The light was on in the window of the girl's flat above the laundrette. She silently climbed the stairs to the access deck and listened at the door. She thought she heard the sound of soft music, but not of babies. She knocked.

The door opened on George's face then began to swing shut again. Kathy stuck her foot in the gap.

'Go away,' he complained. 'Go away.'

'On your own, George? Don't keep me standing out here, there's a good lad. Someone might see me.'

George gave a moan and let her in. 'Carole'll be back soon.'

'Won't take long. Just need a bit of help. Nothing heavy. How did you enjoy the concert on Saturday?'

'All right.'

'I was watching you. You seemed really taken with it.'

He shrugged, scuffed his shoe on the worn carpet tile. 'It was cool.'

'They were raising money for people like you, George, for scholarships—music scholarships, for example. You could apply.'

'Nah. I don't do classical stuff.'

'Not just classical, any kind of music. I know Michael Grant, the bloke who organised it. Would you like me to ask him for you?'

George met her eye with a kind of pained anxiety, as if he knew this was a trap but couldn't help responding. 'Maybe.'

'All right, I will. I passed the JOS last night and saw your posters. Were you playing?'

He nodded.

'Teddy Vexx and Jay Crocker were there too, yes? I saw their car.'

Another nod, more wary.

'Do you know a girl called Magdalen, friend of theirs?'

'Yeah . . .'

Something about the way he said it made Kathy ask, 'Fancy her, do you?'

'Nah.' He looked down at the floor again, embarrassed.

'She is very pretty though, isn't she? You'd have to notice her. Was she with Teddy and Jay at the club last night?'

'Nah, some other bloke.'

'Ah. Has she split up with Teddy then?'

'Not as far as I know.'

'Didn't Teddy mind her being with this other bloke?'

George suddenly recognised danger. 'Did something happen to him? Look, I didn't see nothing. There wasn't no trouble at the club. Magdalen and the bloke left about midnight, but Teddy and Jay stayed on till three or four—I swear, I saw them.'

'That's okay, George. There was no trouble. Look, between ourselves, Magdalen's family are worried about her drugs and the company she keeps, that's all.'

'Ah.' He looked relieved. 'The other bloke looked okay. White guy. I've seen him around. I was surprised, though, that Teddy didn't seem bothered.'

'Did he know Teddy?'

'Don't think so. I didn't see them speak.'

'All right, that's all I wanted, George, thanks. And I will look into that other thing for you . . .'

At that moment they heard the clatter of feet on the deck outside and the impatient rattle of a key in the door.

'Oh fuck.' George panicked. 'She'll see you here. She'll tell
Teddy . . .'

'What's her name?' Kathy said quickly.

'What?'

'What's Carole's other name?'

'Marshall, why . . .?'

The door swung open and Carole marched in. 'Those bleedin'—'
She glared in surprise at Kathy.

'Ms Marshall?' Kathy said. 'Hello, I'm from the clinic. There's
been a mix-up over medications. They asked me to come down in
person to check you've got the right ones. Sorry about this. Can I
just see your bottles?'

'Eh? Clinic?'

'GUM, dear,' Kathy murmured tactfully and shot a coy smile at
George, who looked blank. 'Are they in the bathroom?'

'Oh . . . no, they're here.' Carole, flustered by Kathy's imitation
of a caring health professional, rummaged in her bag and produced a plastic bottle of pills.

Kathy examined the label. 'Oh, that's fine. Not you then. Marvellous. I'll be on my way. Bye.'

She walked out.

BROCK WAS CALLED TO his second meeting with Commander
Sharpe the following morning. The first briefing, to acquaint his
boss with Tom's report, had been met with a frosty bewilderment,
as if Sharpe really didn't want to know what had possessed Brock
to ignore his earlier advice, and was embarrassed at having to do
something about it. By the second meeting, he had regained his
usual confidence and precision, and was unambiguous in his
instructions.

'We drop it.'

'You don't think it's evidence of a serious crime?'

'Absolutely not. I'm advised that it's flawed, unattributable and potentially scandalous. You will not pursue this, Brock, and you will make sure that your errant team member doesn't either.'

'Hm. May I ask if you're aware of any other ongoing investigation into the affairs of the Roach family, sir?'

'There is no such thing.'

'Are you sure? Not even at OCLG level? Five, perhaps?'

Brock noticed a small flush of colour tinge Sharpe's cheeks as he leaned forward to say, in a lower but even more insistent voice, 'I am sure, Brock, because your half-baked fantasy went all the way up to JIC, where it was treated with the contempt it deserved. Get Roach out of your head and get on with something else. Do I make myself absolutely plain?'

TOM AND KATHY REPORTED to Brock's room in the early afternoon. The old files had been stacked neatly in a corner, they noticed, as if ready to be returned, and the pin board facing Brock's desk was bare. Brock himself was eating a sandwich. He popped the last bit into his mouth, smacked his hands together, wiped them on a paper napkin and threw it into the bin.

'Come in. Sit down.'

There was no sign of their report on his desk.

'Your little operation has gone through channels,' he said. 'There will be no further action.'

There was a moment's silence, then Tom said, 'What? Why not?'

'The evidence had no provenance, Tom, no search warrant, no witnesses, no credible means of access. CPS won't touch it. And the story it told was suggestive at best, open to interpretation. You know that's true.'

'Yes, but—'

'It was taken seriously, it went well up the chain, but the decision was no. We're bound by that. I expect you to be bound by that. No further action. Sorry. I appreciate your initiative, but that's it.'

'I can't accept that.' Tom rose to his feet, holding himself rigid, face pale with anger. 'I put myself on the line to gather legitimate, damning evidence—evidence that couldn't be obtained in any other way. It provides conclusive information about a crime of massive proportions. So what is this? A cover-up or a cop-out? Are you all too bloody weak—'

'That's enough, Tom,' Brock growled.

Kathy couldn't quite make Brock out. His words were his, but he sounded as if he had something stuck in his gullet. It was hurting him to do this to Tom, and she wished Tom would stop, but he couldn't.

'Do you realise what two tonnes of crack on the streets means?' he yelled, his voice incredulous. 'Do you have any idea what devastation—'

'There's another way of looking at this, Tom.' Brock's voice was suddenly hard. 'If you'd come to me before you went in last night, if we'd set it up another way, things could have turned out differently. As it is, the whole case is closed down. Whatever leeway we had has been taken from us.' He gestured as if to take in the whole office, the empty pin board, the stacked files.

Tom glared at the faded files in disbelief and shook his head, unable to find the words. Then he turned and stormed out of the room.

Brock put his head in his hands for a moment, then looked across at Kathy. 'Couldn't you have stopped him, Kathy? Couldn't you have let me know?'

TWENTY-FOUR

TOM WASN'T AT HIS desk when Kathy returned downstairs. Bren was standing nearby, and he gave her an odd look.

'Hi, Kathy. Everything okay? Tom—'

'Where is he?'

'He just charged in here, grabbed his stuff and ran. Didn't say a word.'

Kathy hurried to the front lobby, but Tom had apparently left. There was no sign of him outside in the street. She returned to the office and told Bren what had happened. When she finished he shook his head and said, 'The old man wouldn't be happy about that.'

'He wasn't.'

'Maybe I'll go up and have a word.'

While she waited for him to return, Kathy tried Tom's mobile number and got his answering service. She didn't leave a message, deciding it would be best to let him cool off.

When Bren reappeared he gave Kathy a wink. 'He'll come round. How do you fancy a spot of rape? Sad Simon's made another hit.'

She groaned. 'Oh, not again.'

'Yeah. All hands to the pumps. Brock wants you to work with me. Keep you out of mischief. Come on, there's a briefing out in Barnet in half an hour.'

Kathy grabbed her coat and bag and followed Bren out to the car. It was the best thing, of course, a new case, a fresh start.

Over the following days she tried a number of times to make contact with Tom, but without success. He wasn't answering his phones and there was no sign of him at his flat. She rang Nicole and asked if Lloyd had heard from him, but he hadn't. As time passed without contact she was more and more haunted by an image that George had conjured up, of Tom at the JOS with Magdalen, flirting, dancing, drinking, and of Teddy Vexx watching them, apparently unmoved.

By Friday she was sufficiently worried to talk to Bren about raising the alarm. He was inclined to let it lie for a while. 'It's only been a couple of days. He's got you in enough trouble, Kathy. Raising a false alarm will just make things worse. He's probably gone away for a while till the dust settles. Did you check with personnel if he's asked for leave?'

'Would they tell me?'

'Hm. I'll get Dot to give them a ring. And admin over at Special Branch too, see if he's contacted them.'

She thanked him. Bren's calm, imperturbable solidity reassured her a little, and she waited while he went upstairs to speak to Brock's secretary. As she sat there, staring at the blank screen on her desk, her phone rang and she was surprised to recognise the voice of Andrea, Michael Grant's research officer.

'Kathy? So glad I caught you. How are you? I hear you've been getting into trouble.' She chuckled.

'Andrea? Have you seen Tom?'

'Oh yes. He's standing here beside me as a matter of fact. That's why I'm calling.'

'Where are you?'

'We're waiting outside a committee room.'

'Where?'

'Parliament. Michael's Home Affairs Committee has just reconvened. They're in private session at the moment, and we're waiting for them to open the meeting up so we can go in and watch. Tom thought I should tell you. He thinks you and your boss will be interested in the proceedings this morning. Michael's planning to cause a bit of a stir. You can watch on live webcast on your computer—www.parliamentlive.tv.'

'Oh no . . .' Kathy groaned softly to herself. 'Andrea, will you put Tom on, please?'

'Sorry, they're opening the doors. I'll have to turn my phone off now. Tom sends his love and apologises for the short notice.'

The line went dead.

Kathy immediately dialled Brock's number. Dot answered, telling her that Brock was in a meeting.

'You'd better put me through, Dot. He needs to hear this now.'

She did so, and a couple of minutes later Brock came into the office to join Kathy in front of her computer. Kathy had warned Bren, the word had spread and the other detectives were also clustered in front of screens around the room.

The picture showed a horseshoe-shaped table with the chair, Margaret Hart, in the centre. Michael Grant, further round to her left, was conspicuous as the only black member, and Kathy also recognised Nigel Hadden-Vane facing him across the central space. Margaret Hart was deep in conversation with an aide at her shoulder, querying something, nodding, and then speaking briskly into her microphone.

'That's confirmed then, all of next week's meetings will be held in this room. The schedule of witnesses has been confirmed. Now, let's get down to business. Mr Grant, you have something you want to raise?'

'Yes, Madam Chair. I have a matter of such great relevance and urgency that I would beg your and the committee's indulgence and request that I be allowed to introduce it immediately.'

'How long will this take, Michael?'

'No more than an hour.'

Hart looked around the table. 'How does the committee feel? Can we suspend our agenda for an hour for Mr Grant?'

There was a murmur of conversation and several heads on the Chair's right turned to Hadden-Vane for a lead. He drew himself up and said, 'We've become quite used to the distractions offered by the Honourable Member for Lambeth North. I'm sure we can spare the time to be entertained by him once again.'

Several people chuckled. Margaret Hart nodded at Grant. 'Very well. As quick as you can, please. You know I like to stick to our timetable.'

'Thank you.' Grant opened the file in front of him and paused for a moment, as if the contents were so significant that he had difficulty finding words to begin. Then, into the expectant silence he said, 'I am indebted to my colleague for his invitation to entertain the committee, but I can assure you that what I have to say will only shock and horrify you. As you know, the subject of our current inquiry is the involvement of organised crime in legitimate commercial activity in the UK. Well I have here evidence of a carefully planned and implemented conspiracy between apparently legitimate British businesses—household names on our high streets—and organised criminal gangs both here and abroad, to carry out criminal activity on an industrial scale and for enormous profit.'

There was a ripple of interest around the committee, but it was clear from some of their expressions—amused, sceptical—that they were used to hyperbole from Michael Grant and were waiting for something tangible. He proceeded to give it to them.

'I will table evidence that the well-known off-licence chain Paramounts Beers, Wines and Spirits, wholly owned by members of the Roach family in London, has been used, with their knowledge and active participation, to import Class A controlled drugs into the UK under cover of innocent international trade.'

Now the room erupted in noise. Some members showed outrage or shock—no doubt, like Commander Sharpe, they were regular customers of Paramounts—while others were gesticulating to each other as if to say that Grant had finally gone mad. Only two figures were still—Grant himself, sitting with head bowed while the comments fizzed around him, and Margaret Hart, who was gazing at him with a worried frown. In the background, Kathy heard Bren's muttered 'Blimey.'

Hart allowed the turmoil to continue for a few moments before calling the meeting to order. 'Mr Grant, you have just made an allegation of the greatest seriousness. I have to warn you of the limits of parliamentary privilege.'

'Hear hear!' Hadden-Vane rumbled. 'Madam Chair, may I comment? Some of our committee will recall that this is not the first time that Mr Grant has slandered this family under cover of privilege. They will recall his description of them as "slum landlords" and other scurrilous terms during earlier inquiries. The fact is that Mr Grant has a pathological hatred of this family, who have extensive business interests in his constituency. This committee is no place for a private vendetta of this kind.'

'That is true,' Hart replied, 'but I was going to point to another limitation on privilege. If, as you say, you have evidence of specific criminal acts, which presumably could become the subject of a police investigation, then you are bound not to reveal information that might prejudice a later trial.'

Grant nodded and said, 'I have consulted with the clerk of the Committee on this, and understand that I must not comment on matters currently before a court of law or where court proceedings are imminent. But that is not the case here. In fact, this brings us to a crucial issue and the reason why this committee must listen to what I have to say and must act upon it. The fact is that the irrefutable documentary evidence I have here was provided to me by sources close to the Roach family. When confronted by this evidence these sources rightly took it to the police, who declined to act upon it. Only then did they bring it to me, and one of the most serious questions that this committee must ask is why the authorities have refused to investigate. We are the last bastion of the truth, Madam Chair. We must not shirk our duty.'

More turmoil, Hadden-Vane shaking his gleaming pink head in disgust.

'I think,' Margaret Hart said loudly, 'that we will move to private session to discuss the implications of this.'

'Personally,' Hadden-Vane came in again, 'I would favour hearing Mr Grant's so-called evidence in open session. We've had enough of his outlandish and irresponsible behaviour. Let him have his say and live by the consequences.'

'All the same, I'm calling a ten-minute recess to consider this. Will all those who are not members of the committee please leave the room.'

After a moment the image on the screen was replaced by a blank background behind the words COMMITTEE IN PRIVATE SESSION.

Everyone in the office swivelled round to stare at Brock. He rubbed the side of his chin. 'Hm. I'd better tell one or two other people to watch this. Are we recording it by the way?' He got to his feet and ambled out.

THEY HAD ARMED THEMSELVES with mugs of coffee by the time the image flicked back to the live picture from the committee room. They leaned forward together in the attentive way that screens carrying breaking news command. Margaret Hart briskly announced that they would hear Grant's submission in open session, a decision that provoked a murmur of excitement from the committee room and clicks of disapproval from around the office. Brock watched impassively.

Grant reached for a bag beside his chair and produced copies of a document for each of the eleven members of the committee. As he began to lead them through it, Kathy realised that they had repackaged Tom's material as a dramatic narrative, a blockbuster thriller. With the help of photographs, diagrams and maps, the MP introduced them to the route taken by cocaine smugglers from Colombia to Jamaica, showed them the Dragon Stout brewery in Kingston, a bottle of the malty beer, twenty-foot containers stacked at the Kingston Container Terminal, the container ship

Merchant Prince, which had brought the first consignment across the Atlantic, a Paramounts store in South London with cases of Dragon Stout on special offer and, finally, a chilling picture of blank-eyed crack-smokers in a derelict squat.

Grant also gave them copies of key documents supporting his accusations. His presentation was measured and unemotional until he came to the conclusion, a summary of the likely impact of the drugs on the people of South London.

Despite herself, Kathy was impressed, and so was the committee. When Hart called for discussion, Hadden-Vane's attempt to find fault sounded like empty bluster. When he demanded that Grant reveal his sources, Grant neatly turned it into a further attack on the Roaches. He would not name his sources, he said, because they would be at serious personal risk, and to support this he would provide members of the committee with a list of criminal convictions of various members of the Roach family. Hadden-Vane seemed to realise that he was being outmanoeuvred, and after some heated debate around the table he proposed that discussion be suspended so that members could have time to study and digest Grant's material over the weekend. Grant concurred, adding that he intended to bring to the committee at its next sitting, on the following Monday, a list of witnesses that he would ask the committee to call for interview under oath, including members of the Roach family.

As the committee moved back to their scheduled agenda, Dot appeared at the door. Her usual poise seemed ruffled. 'Brock,' she said, 'Commander Sharpe on the phone.'

Brock got to his feet. 'I'd like a transcript,' he said. 'But our priority is catching Sad Simon. Let's concentrate on that.'

LATER THAT AFTERNOON KATHY got a call from Dot to say that Brock wanted to see her. He waved her to a seat.

'Damage control. They're going to keep mum to the press and

try to nobble the committee chair, Margaret Hart, behind the scenes. I don't fancy their chances. How far do you think Tom will go with this, Kathy? You know him better than I do.'

The coldness in Brock's voice confronted her: Tom was the enemy now, the threat. She'd sensed that in the others' murmured comments all morning, but coming from Brock she realised how absolute Tom's betrayal had been.

'I'm not sure. He was very angry after our meeting on Wednesday, and I haven't seen him since. I've been trying to contact him but he won't answer my calls.'

'I don't like to ask you to betray confidences, Kathy.' He spoke slowly, eyes on a heavily marked-up copy of the webcast transcript lying on the table in front of him. 'But I need to understand what he's doing. Is this some kind of elaborate professional suicide, or does he really think he can prove a point and come back to us covered in glory?'

All morning Kathy had been asking herself the same question. 'I've had the impression, right from the beginning, that Tom felt he had to prove himself in some way. I mean in a personal, individual way, not just as part of the team. I didn't realise it at first, but he wasn't being open with me, not about what he was really thinking. He didn't tell me about what he was planning with Magdalen until I came across a surveillance picture with the two of them together, and then he had to tell me. But he was desperate that nobody else should know until he'd pulled it off, and in the end I agreed, on condition I could go along as backup. That was a big mistake, I know. I'm sorry. I really am, Brock. This is my fault.'

'Divided loyalties,' he murmured, putting a reassuring hand on her shoulder. 'It does for us all.'

'I think it goes back to a problem at Special Branch. He had some kind of personality clash there.'

'It was a bit more than that. He didn't tell you?'

Kathy shook her head, puzzled.

'A couple of years ago there was an IRA group operating in the UK, responsible for a series of big robberies up north. It was believed they were based in a neighbourhood in Liverpool. Tom had had some earlier experience on the IRA desk and it was decided to plant him and another officer, a woman, in the area, as a couple moving in as new teachers at the local school, he for PE, she for maths. They settled in, got to know their neighbours through their children. They'd worked together before, Tom and this woman, and they made a convincing couple. The trouble was that it became a little too real. After a time they announced that they were going to get married, and they did, inviting their neighbours to the party. Branch disapproved, but didn't do anything. Then things went wrong. A new gang member came over from Ireland and recognised Tom. They did nothing at first, then one night they paid Tom and his wife a visit. Only Tom was away from home, reporting to his people in Manchester. When he got back he found his wife battered to death.'

'Oh God.'

'The Branch brought Tom back to London and moved him into their A Squad, protecting VIPs. He never really settled into it. There may well have been personality clashes as he told you— I've only heard his boss's side of the story. Anyway, I was happy to give him a berth here for a while.'

'He never mentioned any of this to me,' Kathy said. 'I didn't even know he'd been married twice.' The story was a jarring revelation, throwing everything she thought she knew about Tom into a new context, every word, every action open to fresh interpretation. 'You said he'd worked with the other officer, the woman, before. Was that in Jamaica?'

'I believe it was, yes.'

Kathy remembered the evening of Jamaican cooking, the stories, funny and wistful. I have been a surrogate, she thought, no more than a channel to old memories, a Band-Aid for old wounds.

'I think he'll go all the way with this,' she said sadly. 'Maybe the real question is, how far will Michael Grant let him go?'

KATHY'S PHONE RANG AS she was getting ready to leave the office for home. She recognised his voice, and sank back into her chair. 'Tom. I've been trying to reach you.'

'Yes, I know. I've been very busy. There's been so much to do.' He sounded elated, speaking fast. 'Did you see it?'

'Yes, we all did.'

'What did you think?'

'I think you're going about it the wrong way.'

'Why?'

'You're a serving police officer.'

'There are higher loyalties than that. To the truth, for instance. This is the only way. They left me no choice.'

There was a pause, then Kathy said, 'Brock told me about your second wife.'

'Did he? I didn't think he knew . . . I'm sorry, I almost told you several times, but then I held back. It didn't seem relevant to us.'

'Wasn't it? Isn't it what this is all about?'

'Is that what Brock's saying? Listen, Kathy—' he was angry now—'what I'm doing is getting at the truth, the only way I can, the only way they've left me. I'm sorry you can't be with me on that.'

'Tom, you—' But the line was dead.

TWENTY-FIVE

THE MEDIA WERE FULL of the story over the weekend, their appetite for scandal only sharpened by the refusal of any of the players to speak to them. For the moment they didn't identify the Roaches by name, but there were clear hints that as soon as witnesses were called before the committee, their names would be published and the whole story brought out into the open. There was a great deal about Michael Grant, his background and his history of campaigning for the underprivileged.

On Monday morning the TV channels were carrying pictures of scenes outside the Houses of Parliament as reporters tried to get access to the committee meeting and to catch participants for comment. It seemed that some agreement had been reached to broadcast the session live on TV, and one of the channels was promising coverage during its morning news show. The picture was clearer than on the webcast, and in Queen Anne's Gate, just a couple of hundred yards away, someone had fixed up a TV in the main office, around which people were clustering.

As the committee members took their seats Kathy had the impression that the mood was different from that on Friday, less informal and congenial. When Margaret Hart opened the session she sounded sombre. She reminded them of the duties and powers of the committee, and called upon them to use these responsibly.

'Mr Hadden-Vane has asked to address the meeting.'

The MP acknowledged her with a nod, and when he spoke his voice was harsh and forceful, with none of the empty bluster of before.

'On Friday we were confronted by an unprecedented accusation against a British company, and evidence of criminal activity on a huge scale. Since then I, like all of my colleagues, have been trying to form a dispassionate assessment of this shocking evidence. In the short time that's been available to me, I have been able to discover several witnesses who can throw further light on it. It is crucial that the committee hear what they have to say, and I beg leave to call these witnesses immediately.'

The room was very still.

'They are here?' Hart asked.

'Yes.'

'You know the normal procedure for calling witnesses, Mr Hadden-Vane,' the chair frowned. 'The committee will need notice . . .'

'When he interrupted our agenda on Friday, Mr Grant claimed that what he had to say was of such importance that the committee should suspend its normal procedures and we agreed. I claim the same latitude. People's reputations are at stake here. Mr Grant has made this a matter of extreme urgency.'

Hart looked around the room, taking in nodding heads. 'Very well.'

'Thank you. The first witness is Mr Steven Bryce.'

Kathy stiffened and turned to Brock. 'The boss of the plastics company that went bust. The one that was overseas.'

Hadden-Vane turned to speak to the clerk and handed him a sheet of paper. While they waited for him to bring in the witness, the MP went on, 'Madam Chair, I propose that my witnesses give their evidence on oath. I know this is unusual, but Mr Grant proposed that his witnesses should do this and I don't want mine to be seen as any less credible.'

'This is not a competition, Mr Hadden-Vane,' Margaret Hart snapped. 'And they are the committee's witnesses, not yours or Mr Grant's. However, under the circumstances, it may be advisable.'

A slight, rather anxious-looking man came into the picture, and was shown by the clerk to the witness table across the end of the horseshoe, facing the chair.

'Mr Bryce,' Margaret Hart said, leaning forward and smiling warmly at him. 'I understand you're willing to assist this committee with your testimony, is that correct?'

The man cleared his throat and said yes.

'It has been proposed that you give your evidence under oath. If you do so, you will be liable to the laws of perjury. Do you have any objection to this?'

'No, that's been explained to me. I don't mind.' The man's flat Midlands accent was distinct.

The clerk stepped forward and Bryce took the oath, then Hadden-Vane spoke.

'I'd like to place on record our appreciation to Mr Bryce for attending today. He was overseas when we were finally able to contact him yesterday, and he came back immediately when he understood the seriousness of the situation. Mr Bryce, were you the managing director of PC Plastics of Solihull?'

'That's right.'

'Your company ceased trading last December, is that correct? Would you describe what it did before that.'

'We were a small company, manufacturing a variety of plastic components for customers, mainly retail outlets.'

'Was the Paramounts off-licence chain one of your customers?'

'We did several jobs for them, yes.'

'Now I'm showing Mr Bryce the order for 50,000 brown plastic sheaths that was included in the documents Mr Grant provided on Friday. Do you recognise this, Mr Bryce?'

'You showed it to me last night, when I got back from Poland.'

'Will you tell us your reaction, please?'

'I'd never seen it before.'

'You're quite certain? Would you have seen every order that came into your company?'

'Absolutely. We never received this order.'

There was a stir of consternation in the room. Michael Grant was staring at the witness, a frown on his face.

'Have you any other comment on the document?' Hadden-Vane went on.

'Well, that's certainly our name and address at the top, but the rest looks pretty odd to me. In the first place, I don't think we'd have been capable of carrying out such an order. We did fibreglass mouldings, some vacuum forming, generally small-scale, short runs—shop signs, display stands, promotional material, that sort of thing. I'd say this job would have needed a large injection moulding machine. We've never had one of them.'

'I see. Anything else?'

'Well, the letterhead is Paramounts' London head office, but we never had correspondence with them before. We always dealt with their regional office in Birmingham.'

'Right. What about the signature at the bottom of the order, that of Mr Ivor Roach?'

'I've heard of Mr Roach, but I've never had any dealings with him. I wouldn't know if that's his signature or not.'

Hadden-Vane beamed. 'Thank you. That's all I wanted to ask, Mr Bryce.'

Margaret Hart asked if anyone had further questions, and all heads turned to Michael Grant. He seemed stunned and didn't re-act for a moment, then said, 'Your company went out of business in December, you said?'

'Yes, that's right.'

'You're in financial trouble, are you?'

Hadden-Vale exploded. 'That's irrelevant and insulting!'

'It's all right,' Bryce said mildly. He smiled at Grant. 'I'm not down on my uppers, if that's what you're suggesting. I own eight other companies that are doing very nicely, thanks. I just decided to get out of plastics. It's an overcrowded field.'

'Thank you very much, Mr Bryce,' the chair said hurriedly, raising her eyebrows at Grant. 'I don't think we have any other questions. We're most grateful.'

Hadden-Vane's next witness was a document expert. His credentials were impeccable—formerly head of documents section in the Police Forensic Science Laboratory, now in private practice and well known to Brock and several of the other detectives in the office. His evidence was brief and decisive. He had examined the signatures on the order to PC Plastics and the handwriting on the summary sheet, and had compared them with dozens of samples of Ivor Roach's signature and handwriting taken from other documents, and declared Michael Grant's material to be forgeries. When the rumpus that this provoked had died down, he added the dryly amused comment that it seemed a little odd that the Paramounts letterhead used on these forgeries was obviously old stock, since the telephone and fax numbers listed in small print at the bottom of the pages predated the change in the London codes.

'From your long experience, could you make any general observations on these forgeries?' Hadden-Vane invited.

'Well, I'd say the forger was either incompetent or in a big hurry.'

Michael Grant didn't ask any questions.

A third witness, an office manager from Paramounts' London head office, confirmed that the letterhead design in Grant's documents hadn't been used for at least four years. She had been unable to trace any record of the order to PC Plastics.

By now a new mood had settled over the committee members. They no longer shook their heads in astonishment at each new revelation from Hadden-Vane's witnesses, but instead focused more and more openly on Grant to see how he was reacting. It seemed to Kathy that the spaces on either side of his seat had widened.

'I've had less than seventy-two hours to demolish Mr Grant's so-called evidence against Paramounts and the Roach family,' Hadden-Vane said. 'Given more time and resources and expertise than I possess, I've no doubt that much more could be uncovered. But I think we've heard enough.' There were murmurs of agreement around the table. 'I believe I've established the "What" —a number of forged papers have been added to a file of real documents relating to a legitimate consignment of beer from Jamaica to the UK to give the appearance of a criminal act. Our colleague was then persuaded to put this rather crude deception before us and broadcast it in the public domain under cover of parliamentary privilege. But that's only part of the story. We must also discover the "How"and the "Why." I now call on the member for Lambeth North to explain to the committee exactly how and from whom he obtained the documents in his report.'

There was a long silence while the two men held each other's eyes, Michael Grant with a look of loathing apparent even on the small screen. Then he turned to Margaret Hart and said, 'I'm sorry, I can't do that.'

A murmur of disapproval grew steadily louder.

'I understand,' Hadden-Vane pressed on, 'that a departmental select committee cannot order a member of the House to appear before it as a witness under oath, but I nevertheless invite the member for Lambeth North to volunteer himself to do so now.' By the end of this sentence he had to raise his voice to an angry shout to make himself heard over the hubbub. 'Madam Chair,' he roared, 'Michael Grant's failure to respond amounts to a deliberate contempt of this committee and of the House!' He let the turmoil seethe around him for a while, until it looked as if the chair was about to act, then he cut in, 'Nevertheless, we are not entirely dependent on his cooperation.'

The noise died away as people registered this.

'I have here a piece of written evidence provided by another witness that may help us understand just how this was done.' He held a piece of paper dramatically aloft. 'This sworn testimony has been provided by a member of the Roach family. Given the public libel against her family by Mr Grant, she is reluctant to appear here in person, and asks that her name not be released. When you read what she has to say, you will appreciate why. She feels embarrassed and humiliated by the story she has to tell, but tell it she does, because she feels she must. Let us call her "Ms A". She describes how she, a recently divorced and emotionally vulnerable young woman, met a personable man at a nightclub. She met him again on a number of subsequent occasions, seemingly by accident, and he befriended her and gained her trust.

'Then, just last week, this charming fellow persuaded Ms A to take him home with her, to her parents' house where she was living, her parents being overseas at the time. The man had given her a great deal to drink during the evening, and she agreed. Once there he offered her drugs, which she declined. However, she believes he gave her something because she became disoriented and fell asleep. At some stage she woke up and went to the bathroom, and on the way she saw him in her father's office, using the photocopier. I have subsequently learned from her father, a director of Paramounts, that in his office he had a file of documents relating to that company's importation of Dragon Stout to the UK. Madam Chair, I table this statement, which has been witnessed by a lawyer, for consideration by the committee.'

He handed the letter to the clerk at his shoulder, and then, as if all this was costing him enormous personal effort, he snatched the blue handkerchief from his top pocket with a great flourish and dabbed at the pink dome of his head.

It was the second time he had reminded Kathy of Martin Connell's story, and as she watched him Kathy was struck by the sudden certain knowledge that this was the MP Martin had described, and that his tale had not been told at random, but had been a quite deliberate message to her. Martin Connell, the Roaches' lawyer, whose signature was no doubt on Magdalen's statement, had known two weeks ago that this scene was going to be played out, and had wanted Kathy to recognise it when it came. She swore softly, then tried to tell herself that this was impossible.

'Kathy?' Brock was looking at her curiously.

She was about to speak when Margaret Hart's voice cut through the noise in the committee room. 'I believe we should take a twenty-minute break—'

'If you please, Madam Chair, I believe that we should not!'

Hadden-Vane's extraordinary remark silenced everyone, including Hart, whose frown became angry. But he went on. 'The writer of the statement I have just tabled has identified the man who took advantage of her. He is here in this room. I do not think we should give him the opportunity to slip away during a break. I demand that he take the witness chair immediately and explain himself.'

'What a showman,' someone murmured.

Kathy felt sick, realising what was coming, and feeling as if it was on her rather than Tom Reeves that the blow was about to fall.

'You, sir!' Hadden-Vane pointed theatrically off-camera, and everyone turned and craned to see.

'No!' Michael Grant seemed suddenly to emerge from a torpor. 'I insist that we discuss . . .' But it was too late, the end of his sentence drowned out by the noise of voices and scraping chairs as the committee got to their feet. Slowly Tom came into view, Hadden-Vane triumphant at his side, as if displaying a prize. At the other end of the table, Margaret Hart, apparently dazed by the twists and turns of his melodramatic performance, was hurriedly consulting with the clerk. Finally, as Tom stood in front of the witness table, she said, 'Ladies and gentlemen, it is within our power to order a witness to appear and give evidence. Is it your wish that we do so in this case?'

The cry of assent was overwhelming, and everyone hurried back to their seats. For a brief moment, only Tom and Michael Grant remained standing, and as Brock watched the MP hesitate, he wondered if he was thinking that the slum boy from the Dungle had finally been caught red-handed among the gilt picture frames and Gothic wall panelling of the immortals.

TWENTY-SIX

'GIVE US YOUR FULL name, please.'

'Thomas Reeves.'

'What do you do for a living, Mr Reeves?'

'I'm a police officer.'

A groan went around the office at Queen Anne's Gate at that, but Kathy knew that Tom had no choice—Hadden-Vane already knew, and she saw that Brock realised that too.

'Of what rank?'

'Inspector.'

'And in what section?'

'I can't say.'

'Special Branch, perhaps?' Hadden-Vane suggested grimly. 'You do undercover work, don't you? Like befriending young women and persuading them to take you home with them?'

Tom didn't respond.

'Why did you befriend Ms A?'

Again Tom didn't answer, but this time a restive grumble came from several parts of the table and Hart spoke up. 'You must answer, Inspector Reeves.'

'I was seeking evidence in relation to an investigation.'

'Did you have a search warrant?' she asked.

'No.'

'And were you instructed by your superiors to befriend Ms A

or search her house?' Hadden-Vale said quickly, reluctant to let anyone else take over his role as interrogator.

'No.'

'And this investigation, it's been approved, has it? It is official?'

Tom hesitated, glanced at the chair, who peered back at him as if trying to place where she'd seen him before.

'Not at present.'

'So you inveigled your way into Ms A's house without authorisation on a case of your own invention, broke into her father's study, photocopied his private business papers, stole some letterheads that unfortunately happened to be out of date, and forged—'

'No!' Tom interrupted, but Hadden-Vane continued relentlessly.

'—forged additional documents to create an incriminating body of evidence.'

'Those documents were all exactly as I found them. I didn't manufacture any of them.'

The MP shook his head as if that wasn't worthy of a reply. 'I noticed you were sitting next to Mr Grant's research officer just now,' he said. 'How long have you known Mr Grant?'

'A . . . a couple of weeks, perhaps.'

'Have you visited his offices?'

Another image of Hadden-Vane came into Kathy's mind as she was listening to this, of the MP leaving the concert, and leaning in to give his little bow to Kerrie, Grant's office manager, and the woman's oddly vivacious response.

'Yes, once or twice.'

'In connection with what?'

'I think you should ask him, sir.'

'I'm asking you, and let me remind you that if you attempt to mislead the committee you will be in contempt of the House.'

'He felt I might be interested in some information he had been collecting, on crime in his constituency.'

'What kind of crime?'

'Drugs, violent crimes, Yardie gangs.'

'And also the business activities of the Roach family, am I right?'

'Yes.'

'Did he ask for access to police information?'

Tom hesitated, then said, 'Yes.'

'And you obliged.'

'No.'

'But you gave him the material you stole from Ms A's house?'

'That was the first time.'

'With the knowledge of your superiors?'

'No.'

Hadden-Vane gave a sigh of satisfaction, took a drink from the glass of water in front of him, sat back and mopped his brow with the blue handkerchief. 'Thank you.'

Now the others came in like a vengeful chorus. Was it commonplace for Special Branch officers to carry out investigations without the knowledge of their superiors? How many other innocent citizens' homes had he broken into? How many other documents had he forged? Tom answered in a stoic monotone, until finally they had exhausted the possibilities and seemed satisfied, at which point Margaret Hart declared a recess.

At Queen Anne's Gate the watchers sat back in stunned silence. Someone muttered 'Bastards,' as if to put on record the general outrage at what had been done to Tom, but it was said without much conviction, for they all felt contaminated by what Tom had apparently done, and failed to do.

'What got into him?' someone asked, and then Bren, shaking his head, said, 'And how did that smug bastard get all that stuff in just two days?'

He turned to Brock. 'It was the Roaches, yes? They must have fed it to him.'

Brock nodded.

'But why did they want to crucify Tom?'

'It's not Tom they're after, Bren. They're not finished yet.' Brock checked his watch and got stiffly to his feet. 'I'd better make some calls.'

'MADAM CHAIR,' MICHAEL GRANT said, sounding bereft of any real hope, 'I ask that we suspend this matter for a few days. My colleague's revelations this morning, if they're true, have been as disturbing to me as to the rest of the committee, and I need time to frame a response to his questions.'

'By all means,' Hadden-Vane responded, with a shark's smile. 'After you've heard all of my questions. We know the "What" and the "How." But we still have to consider the "Why." '

Grant tried to object, but it was clear that the committee was against him.

'I'm sorry, Michael,' Hart ruled. 'Nigel is right. We need to get all the issues out on the table.'

'Thank you. You see, the real mystery is why a member of Parliament, aided by a rogue police officer, would go to such lengths to malign a family of successful and respectable British businessmen. Now it is true that this family came from humble beginnings and that some of its members were involved in their youth in minor misdemeanours. They paid their debts, learned their lessons and devoted their talents to legitimate enterprises, but perhaps there are still members of the Metropolitan Police Service who resent that success and would like to settle old scores.'

A warning to Brock? Kathy wondered.

'Perhaps Inspector Reeves thought that he could score career points in some quarters by his actions, who knows? But why would the member for Lambeth North encourage such a thing? Indeed, why does he maintain a research office at taxpayers' expense that seems largely devoted to trying to find links between the Roach family businesses and the Yardies and drug dealers in his constituency?

'Mr Grant has never hidden the intensely personal nature of his campaigns against drugs and crime, and I think we're entitled to ask if there is perhaps some private reason for his attacks on the Roach family. After all, he knew them as a young immigrant in South London, living in the same area where they ran several small businesses. I asked myself if perhaps that was where the roots of this animosity lay, and so I took it upon myself to speak to one or two people who might be able to shed light on our dilemma. I wish to call one of them as my final witness. I believe the committee will find his testimony both credible and illuminating. His name is Father Terry Maguire.'

Margaret Hart looked puzzled. Kathy remembered seeing her talking to Father Maguire at the concert and thought she must be wondering, as Kathy herself was, why Hadden-Vane would want to call such an excellent character witness for his opponent.

'Do you have any objection, Mr Grant?' Hart asked.

Grant looked equally mystified. He shrugged and said no.

The priest was led into the room and shown to the witness seat. He looked somewhat overwhelmed by the setting, and beamed with relief at seeing the familiar faces of Margaret Hart and especially Michael Grant. As with each of the witnesses, the chair thanked him for attending and explained the circumstances.

'Oh, I'm very happy to speak on Michael's behalf,' Father Maguire said, 'although I'm sure he doesn't need any help from me. His works speak for themselves.'

'Indeed,' Hadden-Vale said, with ominous emphasis. 'You've known Mr Grant a long time, haven't you, Father?'

He prompted the priest to talk about Grant's youth and early career, which the old man did with such enthusiasm and at such length that the committee members began to become embarrassed and restless. When Hadden-Vane mentioned the Roach family, however, the priest's flow faltered. He said he knew of no particular reason for animosity between the young Grant and the Roaches, in fact he didn't think they'd had much contact.

'What about the local criminal types, Father, the so-called Yardies—did Michael have dealings with them?'

'No, no. He concentrated on his studies, kept his head down, an exemplary student.'

'So where does it come from, this single-minded crusade of his against those he imagines to be criminals in his community? Some might call it almost an obsession, rather like the excessive zeal of the reformed sinner. Yet you say he didn't get into trouble himself in those days?'

'Certainly not. His commitment comes from his experiences in Jamaica before he came to London. Those were terrible days, and he saw at firsthand what damage drugs and violence could do to poor folk.'

'Ah yes, in Jamaica. You've had a lot of experience with young people coming here from Jamaica, haven't you?'

'I've tried to help, mainly through support for the work of a colleague of mine, Father Guzowski, and his mission in Kingston. He helped many young people in trouble to leave and start a new life elsewhere.'

'What sort of trouble was Michael in, Father?'

'I didn't mean . . . I meant young people who were capable of bettering themselves,' he said, sounding flustered. 'Doing some-thing with their lives—'

Hadden-Vane narrowed his eyes at the priest. 'Come, come, Fa-ther Maguire. It's a very serious matter to mislead a Parliamentary committee.'

The old man's face turned deep red against the frame of white hair. 'I've no intention of misleading anyone, sir,' he protested.

'Good.' The MP beamed at him and suddenly reached for his pocket and produced the blue handkerchief with an exaggerated flourish. Father Maguire watched, bemused, as he mopped his face.

'Father Guzowski used to tell you about the background of the men he was sending you, didn't he? Their families, their circum-stances, things like that.'

'Ye-es, sometimes.' The old man nodded cautiously.

'What did he tell you about Michael Grant?'

'Madam Chair,' Grant interrupted. 'I object to this. I've made no secret of my background. This is offensive and irrelevant.'

'Yes, what is the point of this?' Hart agreed.

'It will only take a moment, if Father Maguire remembers his promise not to mislead us. Michael Grant arrived in this country with another man, Father, didn't he?'

'That's true. Joseph Kidd.'

'That's what he called himself, but you knew that wasn't his real name.'

'I'm not sure—'

'Father Guzowski told you his real name, didn't he? What was it?'

'I . . . I don't remember.'

'What about Michael Grant's real name?'

'I don't know . . .'

The priest's answer was almost drowned by a hubbub of voices and a shout of anger from Michael Grant.

'You knew they entered the country under false names, didn't you?' Hadden-Vale insisted, raising his voice above the din.

'They had to!' Father Maguire protested, and the noise was suddenly stilled. Even Michael Grant, half-risen out of his seat, was struck silent. 'They were in mortal danger.'

'From whom?'

'The police. The Jamaican police wanted them dead.'

'Because?'

'Because . . .' The old man looked at Michael with a stricken face, then back at Hadden-Vane. 'Because . . .' His voice faded and he seemed on the point of passing out.

'Because they'd murdered a police officer!' Hadden-Vane roared, and the priest bowed forward, his face in his hands.

Michael Grant was on his feet. He shouted something incoherent at his tormentor across the table and began to struggle towards him, knocking his chair over and pushing aside his neighbour, who got in his way. His face was transformed by anger, mouth open in a furious snarl, his movements wild and violent. All around him people began to move in confusion, some to block him and others to get out of his way. The clerk and a door attendant joined in, and Grant became locked in a tight scrum in the middle of the room. Beyond him, well out of range, Hadden-Vane was backed against the oak panelling, a look of elation on his face, dabbing at his mouth with his blue handkerchief.

TWENTY-SEVEN

FROM THE WINDOW OF the living room on the first floor Brock could see yellow and purple crocus tips pushing up through the last remaining crust of old snow against the fence of the garden below. If he listened carefully, he could hear the murmur of traffic on the high street, and the occasional muffled jangle of the bell on the front door of the antiques shop through the floor. He sat at the window, holding a mug of coffee, suspended.

Unlike Tom Reeves, whose suspension would become, after due process, an absolute rupture, his own, he'd been assured, was a temporary state designed to satisfy the ruffled sensibilities of the brass. All the same, it felt like being shouldered out of the way, out of the stream of life. Suicides were suspended, as were punch bags, victims in comas, and people holding their breath in fright. He wondered if that was how Suzanne's daughter had felt before she stretched herself out above the cliffs.

While he'd been waiting for the coffee to brew, he'd come across the pile of newspapers, tactfully stacked away beneath the kitchen table for disposal. It looked as if she'd bought every one, their headlines a study in sanctimonious outrage . . .

'Extraordinary scenes in Parliament'

'MP was a YARDIE GUNMAN.'

'PM condemns renegade MP'

'Tragedy of Boy from the Dungle'

Her voice on the phone had been tentative. She hadn't realised that he was involved, until Ginny had mentioned it, and was shocked when he told her he was suspended. What was he doing?

What he was doing was reading the papers and wondering at the speed with which they, as opposed to the police, had been able to uncover so much information in so little time. Here was a picture of a hovel beside a rubbish tip, where Michael Grant had grown up, and there an old lady, his grandmother, whose surname, Forrest, was the one that should have been on his passport. Here was Father Guzowski surrounded by small children, and there the sainted priest again, eyes closed, in a casket after his murder.

What he was also doing was imagining the research effort that must have gone into it, and the irony that, all the time Michael Grant had been beavering away gathering information on Spider Roach, Roach must have been doing exactly the same thing on Grant, saving up the juicy revelations, one by one, until the moment came to launch his devastating attack.

'Well,' Suzanne had suggested tentatively, 'if you'd like a break, a drive down to the country . . .'

He'd accepted readily, too readily he now thought. Maybe she'd intended it as a hypothetical option for some time in the future, instead of which he'd got straight in the car and motored down.

'We're here!' Suzanne's voice came from the foot of the stairs, accompanied by a chatter of children's voices, home from school. Miranda rushed in first, with the unself-conscious assumption that she would be found adorable, which she duly was. Brock knelt to give her a hug, then straightened as her older brother came in, holding out his hand stiffly, right shoulder tilted higher than the left as if expecting to have his arm twisted. Brock shook the hand, then gave him a hug too. He'd brought some presents, a Meccano set for Stewart, who had a practical bent, and a puppet theatre for Miranda, who was already something of a performance artist. They accepted them enthusiastically, but Brock thought he also sensed a wariness, as if perhaps they associated gifts with adult guilt, with being abandoned and returned to.

Stewart had homework to do before teatime, and while he got on with that Brock helped Miranda erect her theatre from the kit in the box. Later they ate together and talked about inconsequential things, TV shows and movies they'd seen, what they were going to do that weekend. Brock had the impression they were all being careful. When the children went to bed he stood to leave, but Suzanne said they hadn't had a chance to talk, and he agreed to stay for coffee.

They sat in armchairs on opposite sides of the fireplace and Brock remarked that the kids were looking happy. Suzanne spread her hand and rocked it like a bird caught in turbulence.

'You've been having problems?' he asked.

She sighed, then said, 'Look, if you insist on driving back tonight you won't be able to have a drink, and then I won't be able to have one, but I need one if we're going to talk about things—it's the Aussies' fault, they got me drinking more than I used to.'

'What do you suggest?'

'Well, there's a spare bed.'

He nodded. 'Suits me. I don't have a job to go to in the morning.'

'Right!' She got to her feet and fetched a bottle of wine and a corkscrew, which she handed to him while she went for glasses. On the way back she carefully shut the living-room door and when she spoke she kept her voice low.

'Cheers,' she said. 'No, they're doing pretty well, considering. Do you know, when they ran out of money Stewart started knocking on neighbours' doors, offering to wash their cars. In the snow. Nobody thought to ask what was going on. And I was 12,000 miles away. It's amazing Amber survived on the headland in that cold.'

'How's she doing now?'

'It's a terrible thing to say, but the stronger she gets the more trouble she becomes. She gets fretful, then abusive, then aggressive. What I'm most worried about is when she's completely recovered physically and starts demanding the children back.'

'Can she do that?'

'I'm getting advice.'

He refilled her glass, unable to express the sadness he felt for her. 'Would it help, do you think, if I came with you to see her in hospital?'

She looked surprised, then smiled. 'I don't know . . . Not now. Maybe later? Anyway, tell me about your disaster.'

So he did, and at the end of it she said, 'Poor you. And you still don't really know what happened to those two teenagers or the three men on the waste ground. You must be furious.'

'Am I? I don't know. When you peel away the hurt pride and the frustration, maybe I feel relieved. Coming on Roach again was like scratching at an old wound. Who needs it?'

'I'll drink to that.'

'The only thing is that I did have a theory about those men, and now I'll never know.'

'To do with the old files you were going through?'

'Yes. What I couldn't understand was how they'd been disposed of—three shallow trenches in open ground. It seemed unnecessarily exposed and risky, when the Roaches had a safe and discreet way of getting rid of their victims.'

'What was that?'

'They had their own funeral business. I knew that because I remembered we mounted a surveillance operation against it to try to find out what they were up to. But when I went back through the files I discovered that that came later. What happened was that one of the supergrasses we had at that time, a North London gang boss, started telling us about this perfect setup south of the river, that gangs all over the city were paying big money to make unwanted corpses disappear. We traced it to Cockpit Lane. The business was in the name of Cyrus Despinides, whose daughter Adonia was married to Spider Roach's son Ivor. But this didn't come out until late in the summer of 1981, at least four months after the three men on the railway land were buried. So the question was, if Ivor and his brothers killed those men, why didn't they use the family business to dispose of them, the same way everyone else did?'

'Hm, all right, why didn't they?'

'Perhaps they didn't want Cyrus to know what they'd done. Could the three Jamaicans have been friends of his or doing business with him? So I started investigating his background. We had quite a lot about him on old files, but nothing about any dealings with Jamaicans. In fact, from what I could gather, his attitudes were extremely racist. Then I had another thought. Perhaps it was his daughter Adonia, not Cyrus, who wasn't to know what the Roach boys had done.

'Tom Reeves had collected quite a bit on Adonia. Like her daughter Magdalen, who was used to trap Tom, she was fond of the Jamaican club scene. Before she married Ivor in '78 she'd had at least one Jamaican boyfriend, for whom she'd provided an alibi in a rape case.'

'You think she was involved with the three victims?'

'It's a thought, isn't it? With all or perhaps just one of them. A series of revenge killings, interrogating the victims, trying to find out which one of the Tosh Posse was playing around with Ivor's wife. Then there's the matter of her daughter Magdalen, born on the eighth of October 1981. Adonia was three months pregnant with Magdalen when the three victims were killed.'

'You think one of them might have been Magdalen's father? But . . . they were black. We'd know, surely?'

'Maybe, maybe not. She's darker than her mother. At thirty three weeks, Adonia and Ivor went to the US on family business, and Magdalen was born there, the only child they had. Maybe they wanted to see what colour she was before they brought her home.'

'You've just got a suspicious mind.'

'True, and even if one of them was Magdalen's father, I could hardly use it, could I? It doesn't prove that Ivor and his brothers killed them. But all the same . . .'

They sat in silence for a while, and then Suzanne murmured, 'The penitent—that's one of the meanings of the name Magdalen, isn't it?'

Later, they made their way upstairs. When they reached the landing Suzanne said, 'Oh damn, the spare bed isn't made up.'

'Ah,' he said. 'What shall we do?'

KATHY HAD PREPARED EXTREMELY carefully for their meeting. Though not herself suspended, she had been advised to keep out of the way while the review team was around, and she took the opportunity to buy some clothes and get her hair done. Martin had reacted with smug disingenuousness to her call, and had suggested Arnold's, an upmarket cocktail bar where he was apparently known.

She arrived a calculated fifteen minutes late and he was already there, looking at home in the deep green leather banquette, absorbed in a brief of evidence. He tossed it aside as she reached the table, and stood and kissed her on the cheek, giving her arm a squeeze.

'Mm, that smells nice. Is it new? I ordered you this. It's Arnold's trademark.' He pointed to a green drink on the table.

'Lovely.' She slid in at right angles to him.

He raised his glass. 'Great to see you. And you're looking so good! You've done your hair differently.'

'Well, I had to do something. Everyone's going around with such long faces.'

He gave a little smile. 'I wasn't sure you'd call.'

'Nor was I. It took a little courage.'

'Courage?'

'Well, you know . . . History.'

'Ah, history. But we're all different now, aren't we?'

'Are we? Sometimes I think so, but then something happens and I feel just as vulnerable as I ever did.' She guessed vulnerable was a word he'd like, a turn-on word.

'I know what you mean,' he nodded sagely. 'Something happens and suddenly you're back in short trousers, trying to hold back the tears.'

Tears? Martin? 'Your brother, you mean? Yes, of course. Are your parents still alive?'

'Mum is. She was devastated, of course. He was her favourite. Oh, I don't mean that in a resentful way. It was just a fact of life. Doted on him.'

'What did he do? I've forgotten.'

'Academic, earned a pittance, wrote incomprehensible books about philosophy that were reviewed at inordinate length in the *TLS* and sold about a dozen copies.'

'A philosopher?'

'Yuh. I told him, ages ago, he should get onto the popularising bandwagon, get on the box, write some bestsellers—*The Hegel Diet*, *Kiss me Kant*, that kind of thing.'

She smiled. 'He scorned your advice, then?'

'Of course, like always. But time has proved me right, hasn't it? They're all at it now. Daniel Connell could have been a household name. Never mind, what does it matter—money, fame—when you're gone?'

A moment's silence, then Kathy raised her glass. 'To Daniel.'

'Yeah, yeah. To Daniel. Poor old sod.'

'But it could have been confusing, having two household names in the one family.'

He gave his modestly roguish grin. 'Now you're being outrageously flattering, Kathy. I'm hardly that, hovering behind my notorious clients, a nameless legal functionary in the crowd.'

She laughed a little too much to show how absurd that idea was, and he ordered another round.

Finally he picked up the juicy little bait she'd offered at the start. 'So they're all going around with long faces, are they?'

'Oh God, yes! You should see the place. Brock's been suspended, and Tom Reeves, of course.'

'Mm, I had heard that. How do you feel?'

'Well, it always hurts to realise you've been beaten.'

'Sure.'

'But I suppose I wasn't altogether surprised. After we were so completely outmanoeuvred the first time, when we tried to arrest Ricky Roach, it just seemed too easy to snatch some incriminating documents from Ivor's study and hope to make it stick.'

'Did you try to tell them that?'

'Yes, but Tom was so desperate to believe in what he'd done, and Brock too, being obsessed with trapping Roach. It was psychologically perfect, wasn't it, offering something so completely over the top to people who couldn't stop themselves from swallowing it? I had seen the warning signs, but I still didn't see how they'd pull it off. They're rather brilliant, aren't they, in their way, the Roaches?'

'You're joking,' Martin snorted. 'They're a bunch of thugs. They've made it in business through stubborn bullying. They couldn't finesse a trick in a million years. It's not their style.'

'So they had great advice?'

'You could say that.' Martin was poker-faced, the playfulness gone from his manner. This was business, and Kathy sensed herself being led along a carefully selected route.

'But . . .' She looked thoughtful. 'You know, there was a moment, when I saw Nigel Hadden-Vane pull his handkerchief out of his pocket, that I remembered that funny story you told me about the MP, and I thought, Martin anticipated all this. But of course that was impossible.'

He gave an enigmatic little smile. 'Was it?'

'Well, yes. You told me the story days before Tom stole those papers, and long before Michael Grant and his committee got involved. You couldn't possibly have known that would happen.'

'Hm.' Still the mystery smile. 'You know what I think?'

'What?'

'I think we should have dinner.'

'Aren't you expected somewhere?'

'Nothing important. What about you?'

'Nothing special.'

'Good. I'll just make a couple of calls.'

'I'll powder my nose.' She got to her feet and left him to tell his lies.

In the taxi across the West End, and in the restaurant, Martin spoke of other things, things that touched upon their mutual lives but indirectly, like the increasingly erratic mental condition of his father-in-law, the former judge, and the state of the housing market in Finchley and Kathy's chances of getting a better place. Kathy suspected this was part of a test, and didn't attempt to steer things back to work.

Then, much later, ruminating over the last of the excellent red that had accompanied the main course, Martin returned to their earlier conversation.

'You know, I couldn't help noticing a subtle change in your way of talking about your boss,' he said.

'Really?' Kathy had always sensed Martin's antagonism towards her relationship with Brock. 'In what way?'

'More objective, more independent-minded. Am I right?'

He raised a challenging eyebrow, his grin suggesting the effects of drink, but Kathy remembered that ploy too, his way of luring people into confidences under the impression that he'd switched off. Martin never switched off.

'You may be right. Yes, I'm sure you are. I mean, it's been a long time. You get to know people's ways.'

'Do you remember that old Carly Simon song we were both crazy about, "You're So Vain"? And I was thinking about Brock, that he probably thinks this song was about him. Am I right?'

It took Kathy a moment to catch on. 'You mean the Dragon Stout business?'

Martin gave a sly nod.

'Well, yes, but it was a trap for him originally, wasn't it? Only he didn't fall for it, and Tom took it to Grant instead. I mean, the Roaches, or their very clever advisors, could hardly have antici-pated that, could they? But they recovered so quickly, that's what amazed me. All that information, all those witnesses lined up.' She leaned forward to stare into his eyes. 'It was amazing, Martin. You must have had a hair-raising weekend.'

He smiled expansively. 'Pretty relaxing, actually. Feet up, game of golf . . .'

'Well, how did you do it?'

'Couldn't tell you that now, could I? Like the magician, if he explains how he does it, nobody's interested any more.'

Kathy sat back, nodding, knowing not to push. 'You are a bit of a magician, aren't you, Martin?'

He narrowed his dark eyes and spoke more forcefully. 'You mentioned information. How right you are. That's what we're both about, information. It's our lifeblood. People have this odd picture of the cops, like anglers sitting around the edge of the water, keeping their feet dry, dipping their lines in and hoping to catch a big fish. But it isn't like that, is it? You have to go down into the dark water, both you and I, and swim with the sharks. It's the only way we get our information. Brock used to know that, in the old days. I think it's what you've come to understand now.'

Kathy wasn't sure she'd followed the switching metaphors. She smiled neutrally. 'Maybe so.'

'We all need allies, Kathy, friends. I thought we made pretty good allies at one time, before Brock took you under his wing. I'm not talking about betraying loyalties, just about having sources, for mutual advantage. It can get pretty cold out there, in the dark water. Tom found that out, didn't he?'

'Yes, maybe you're right.'

'Of course I am. You're going places, Kathy, no doubt about that. We should be friends.'

She frowned, as if needing time to think about this.

'Anyway.' Martin gave a dismissive flap of his hand. 'What about dessert?'

He had made his pitch, she felt, or at least half of it. The other half came later, after they got the taxi back to his office, where he picked up his car to drive her home. It was a cold night, and then the rain began as they reached Kentish Town. The beating of the

261

wipers and the dull glow of streetlights on drab buildings contrasted with the snugness of their capsule, dry, warm and smelling of new leather.

'You'll think about what I said, won't you?' he asked as his headlights swept across the forecourt of her block.

'Of course.'

He pulled in to a visitor's space, and as she detached her seatbelt he leaned over and cupped her cheek and kissed her mouth. She had to suppress a reaction of panic as she felt his tongue slide against her lips. Clammy, oppressive memories filled her head, of the claustrophobic intensity of treacherous love with him.

He pulled away at last. He was excited, breathing heavily. 'What about a nightcap then,' he said, not a question, reaching for the door handle.

'Not tonight, Martin.'

He turned back to her, lips pressed tight to contain his irritation. 'Don't be a tease, Kathy.'

'I think you're being the tease. You drop hints and mysterious pearls of wisdom all evening, but I'm really none the wiser. I still don't know what you did to us.'

He took a deep breath, exasperated. 'Got to sing for my supper, do I? Carly Simon, Kathy, remember? This wasn't about Brock.'

'Who then? Not Tom, surely. Michael Grant?'

He stared ahead through the running film of water on the windscreen for a moment, and when he looked at her again he was calm, in control. 'Not Brock, not Tom, not Grant. This was about Spider, Kathy. All about Spider. About keeping him safe, at all costs. Brock, Tom, Grant were collateral damage—most welcome to Spider, of course, vindictive old bastard that he is.'

She still didn't get it. Her incomprehension was written all over her face, and he frowned at her slowness. 'He's making amends, Kathy, coming in from the cold, spilling the beans, in return for amnesty, for him and his family. The last of the supergrasses. Your bodies under the snow threatened everything. He hadn't mentioned them. They weren't part of the package. The last thing they needed was Brock blundering around pinning a twenty-four-year-old murder rap on the old thug.'

Kathy felt herself press back against the soft leather as if by the force of his revelation. 'They? You said the last thing *they* needed?'

He raised his eyebrows. 'Come on, now you are being obtuse.'

'But . . . But the Roaches did murder those three men?'

' 'Course they did, but who now gives a monkey's fart? They were Jamaican illegals, for God's sake, drug dealers, scum. Okay? Mystery solved?'

And Dana and Dee-Ann, she wanted to say, were they scum too? But he had leaned forward and taken her in his arms again, nuzzling her cheek and neck as if trying to trace her new perfume to its source. His hand moved in under the lap of her coat, and she wondered how she could extricate herself without him thinking her an even bigger bitch than she felt.

Then another car turned into the car park, and Martin pulled away as its headlights caught them. For a moment the interior of his car was illuminated by the blinding beam, their faces brightly lit. Then the other car turned quickly and sped away. Kathy recognised the Subaru.

'That was Tom Reeves,' she said, and Martin swore.

'Does he know me?'

Kathy wasn't sure, but she said, 'Yes. You'd better go.'

He didn't argue, and as she ran through the rain to the front doors she heard his engine rev and drive quickly away.

When she reached her flat she dropped her coat and poured herself a big slug of Scotch and sat down to think. Then she got on the phone. She tried Tom first, without success, then rang Brock. He didn't answer his home phone, but she got him on his mobile.

TWENTY-EIGHT

THERE WAS NO ONE in when Kathy arrived at his house the next morning, although she was ten minutes later than the time they'd arranged for her to call. She listened to the bell echoing again inside, then turned at the rumble of tyres in the cobbled yard at the end of the lane. A car door slammed and Brock appeared, dressed in a windcheater and jeans.

He opened the front door, picking newspapers and mail off the mat, and followed her up the book-lined stairs to the living room on the first floor, where he took her coat and went into the kitchen to put on the kettle. There were no signs of breakfast, and Kathy wondered where he'd stayed overnight, but she didn't ask. He brought coffee and chocolate biscuits, fetched a pad of paper and they got to work.

She went over everything again, everything Martin had told her and then other things that had occurred to her since. She recalled Tom's comments about how he'd been encouraged by his boss to get involved with Brock's team, and they began to draw up a time-line of events. During the night she'd almost persuaded herself, with a sick sense of betrayal and self-recrimination, that Tom had known from the very beginning what he was doing, that he had groomed her from the moment he had reappeared in her life, on instructions from his boss. But Brock disagreed. It was Tom, he pointed out, who had given them the crucial lead to the Brown

Bread shootings, and it was that, Brock believed, which must have triggered alarms further up the line. She also told Brock what Tom had said about a friend in Special Branch pointing him in the direction of a 'weak link' in the Roach family whom he might target.

'He was steered every inch of the way,' Brock said. 'They knew their man, how desperate he was to make amends, even if it meant stepping outside the system and throwing his lot in with Michael Grant.'

'That was the phrase Martin Connell used about Spider Roach—making amends.'

'He must have plenty to trade if they were willing to give him this much protection, and sacrifice one of their own.'

'You think the Branch was behind this?'

'And the others. I wouldn't be surprised if MI5 already had that stuff on Grant's background in his security file. This would have been a JIC operation, Kathy, and only the people at the very top would know the full story.'

'So we should leave it alone.'

'Clearly . . . But.' He scratched his beard. 'I would still like to have a talk to Michael Grant.'

He gestured at the headlines on the newspapers: 'Yardie MP Vanishes' and 'Accused MP fails to face inquiry.'

'Aren't you angry?' Kathy asked him. 'You're one of their victims too. I'd be furious.'

'Yes, I suppose I am. But I'm also intrigued. I wonder if they really know what Spider's like to do business with. They must be worried that there may be other things he hasn't told them.'

Kathy looked at him curiously, sensing some hidden meaning. 'Did you find anything in the old files?'

'Probably not. A sniff of a possible motive for the three killings perhaps.' And he told her of his theory about Adonia and her daughter.

She thought about it, nodding. 'Yes, that makes sense. And poetic justice to use Magdalen as the bait to trap Tom and close down the Brown Bread inquiry.'

'That's what I thought.'

'Of course we could find out for sure.'

'With her DNA? Not much chance of getting that now.'

But Kathy was thinking of the handkerchief that Tom had left at her flat, smelling of J'Adore, and trying to remember if she'd thrown it out.

AFTER DRIVING ACROSS TOWN to Finchley, they made their way to Sundeep Mehta's pathology lab, where Brock explained the nature of the tests he wanted done.

'There are possibly three DNA sources here,' he said, giving him the handkerchief. 'Kathy's and two others. I want them tested against the DNA extracted from the three skeletons on the railway ground. A paternity test. Discreet, quick and in your name only, if you don't mind, Sundeep.'

The pathologist still hadn't forgiven Brock for failing to arrest Mr Teddy Vexx for Dana and Dee-Ann's murders, but he was addicted to mysteries and smiled conspiratorially at the odd procedure. 'I hear you've been having a spot of bother, old chap.'

'You could say that.'

'Twenty-four hours?'

'Make it four.'

'Four? My dear fellow, the processing lab is out at Abingdon.'

'That's one of the reasons I came to you.'

Sundeep pouted. 'Leave it with me. I'll give you a ring. Shall we take an elimination sample from Kathy, or is it her daddy we're looking for?'

He chuckled as he took a swab from Kathy's mouth before they left for Cockpit Lane.

FATHER MAGUIRE ANSWERED THEIR knock on the presbytery door with painful slowness. They saw the twitch of the curtain, heard the shuffle of his feet, and finally caught a narrow sighting of him through the barely opened door. He didn't remember them at first, and Brock had to introduce them. When the old man finally hauled the heavy door open his figure seemed more than ever diminished by the overscaled Victorian architecture that surrounded him. He was wearing an old grey cardigan and faded tartan slippers, and when he turned to lead them to the main room Kathy noticed that his clerical collar was yellowed and the seat of his black trousers was shiny with age.

'Sorry . . .' He'd caught Kathy looking at a tray with the remains of tea and a boiled egg. 'My housekeeper isn't with me at present. The siege, you know. It got too much for her. Gave her nervous palpitations. I had to tell her to go home.'

'Siege?'

'The press. They were out there for so long. I don't know what they expected to get from me. I had to disconnect the doorbell.' He sounded exhausted and defeated. 'The worst thing, of course, is knowing what Michael must think of me. I go over it all again and again, working out what I should have said. He's such a good man, has achieved so much, yet I betrayed him to his enemies. They snatched the words from out of my mouth and used them to destroy him. Now he must regard me as Judas incarnate.'

'I'm sure he doesn't,' Brock said gently. 'It was quite clear to everyone that you were trying to support and defend him. That's what made their choice of you so very effective. They were extremely cunning.'

'But were they telling the truth? Did Michael really commit a murder in Jamaica? I'm sure Father Guzowski never told me that, only that the police would kill him if they caught him. Some of them, you know, were as bad as the people they were up against.'

'I don't know what the truth is.'

'I've tried to find Father Guzowski's letter among my papers, but I can't. It's so long ago and everything's in such a mess. I haven't been very good with my paperwork, I'm afraid. Michael wanted me to write an account of our work here and did help me try to organise things a little, but of course he won't be interested in continuing now. It's like a terrible cloud, poisoning everything we've done, our whole lives and work.'

'He was helping organise your papers?'

'Well, not Michael himself. When he could spare her he sent over the girl who runs his constituency office.'

'Kerrie?'

'That's her. Very efficient young woman. Just what I needed.'

'So has Michael not been in touch with you?' Brock asked.

The priest shook his head sadly. 'I pray for him, but I've heard nothing.'

'Apparently he and his family haven't been seen at their home since Monday. Have you any idea where he might have gone? I really would like to talk to him.'

'To arrest him, do you mean?'

'No, no. I'd just like to talk to him about what happened on Monday.'

But he could see that the old man wasn't convinced. He had betrayed Michael Grant once and he wasn't about to do it again. 'Could be anywhere, I suppose,' he said vaguely. 'If I were him I'd probably take my family far away, to the Outer Hebrides perhaps, until things blow over. I'm sure if he'd felt he needed your help he would have asked for it.' This thought seemed to stiffen his resolve. 'I'll see you out now, if you don't mind. I have things to do, a funeral service to prepare . . .'

They buttoned up their coats and made their way down the path to the street. A few daffodils in the lee of the presbytery were bravely heralding the end of winter. There should have been more, Kathy realised, from the number of cut stalks around them. The rest were probably on sale in the market. As they reached the end of Cockpit Lane, where it divided each side of the churchyard, she looked down to the market and saw people gathering at its far end, and the pulsing lights of an ambulance.

Across the street, large pictures of Michael Grant's face still beamed with misplaced confidence from the windows of his constituency office. It was locked, but there was a light on at the back and eventually their persistent knocking brought Kerrie to the door. She mimed a message at them through the glass, pointing to the 'closed' sign, and Kathy responded by holding up her identification.

She opened the door a little and placed herself firmly in the gap.

'Sorry, didn't recognise you. Michael's not here.'

'Just a few words, Kerrie,' Kathy said, and moved forward. The woman reluctantly stood aside. While she locked the door behind them, they moved towards the single desk lamp lit at the back of the office. A computer was switched on there, and the letter that was lying in the printer tray caught Kathy's attention.

Dear Mr Grant, she read, *I regret that I have decided to resign my position . . .*

Kerrie appeared at her side and snatched the letter away. 'What is it you want?'

'We're looking for Michael, Kerrie.'

She snorted. 'So are a lot of people. Good luck.'

'You don't know where he is?'

'No idea. He's not been in touch since Monday and he's not answering his mobile.'

'You've decided to quit, have you?'

'None of your business, but yes, as a matter of fact. There's no point in staying here.'

'What will you do?'

'I'm moving to a staff position in Westminster, if you must know. It's a natural step up, after the experience I've had in the constituency.'

'But not with Michael? With another MP?'

'How long do you think he's going to have an office over there, do you reckon? He's not the only one allowed to have ambition, you know.'

Kerrie was angry as well as defensive, and Kathy felt she was catching sight of a drama she hadn't been aware of before. 'No, of course not. Did you resent being stuck here?'

'I've done my time here, that's all. It's a dead end, I have to move closer to the centre if I'm going to get on. That's the trouble, isn't it? If you're any good at what you do, the boss tries to keep you stuck.'

'Michael did that, did he?'

'There's a big gap between those who work in the constituencies and those who work in Westminster. He promised to help me move up, but in the end you've got to help yourself, haven't you?'

'Is that what you did when you went to sort out Father Maguire's papers? Help yourself?'

Kerrie gave an involuntary little jump, which she immediately tried to convert into a fussing gesture over her filing tray.

'Was that how you crossed the gap?' Kathy persisted. 'By offering things you'd found out about Michael to his political enemies?'

'Don't be stupid.' She turned away, shuffling papers.

'Who are you going to work for, Kerrie? Mr Hadden-Vane?'

She was close, Kathy realised, but not close enough, for Kerrie relaxed and turned to face her with a show of defiance.

'No. Now I'd like you to leave.'

As they stepped out into the street Brock murmured, 'You were on the right track, Kathy, but it would have been more indirect. Hadden-Vane probably fixed her up with a job with one of his mates.'

'Yes, I suppose so. So where do we go now?' She turned up the collar of her coat against the March wind, feeling its implacable cold like a verdict on their situation. The truth was, they'd pretty well explored every option, and discovered each to have been anticipated and blocked long before they got there.

Ahead of them she recognised Adam Nightingale emerging from the market. He was with his friend Jerry, both gesticulating wildly to their heads and ears, white teeth flashing.

'Hi, Adam,' Kathy called, and the boys stopped dead and stared at them. Then without a word they hunched into their parkas and turned and fled.

When they reached the car Kathy said she'd try Tom again, and called his home and mobile numbers without result. His voice on both answering services sounded painfully normal and buoyant, like Michael Grant's pictures in the shop window. She left more messages and rang off. Almost immediately her phone began to burble. The caller gave his name as McCulloch and Kathy recognised the gravelly voice.

'If you're still interested,' he said. 'The bloke you asked about, George Murray.'

'George, yes. What about him?'

'He was picked up by an ambulance not long ago, in Cockpit Lane. I'm going over to the hospital now.'

'He's been hurt?'

'Yeah. Somebody drove a nail into his head.'

'What?'

'That's what I've been told. They've taken him to St Thomas's.'

The same place they took Adam, Kathy thought, remembering the look of panic on the boy's face when she'd said hello.

Brock dropped her at the A&E entrance to the hospital on Lambeth Palace Road. The entrance to the hospital car park was jammed with a long queue, and he continued on to join Westminster Bridge Road and cross the Thames. Ahead of him Parliament brooded darkly.

Kathy found McCulloch sitting on a bench in a corridor talking to the stooped figure of a small dark woman, whom she recognised as Winnie Wellington when she turned her tear-streaked face towards her. Embarrassed, Winnie wiped the tears away with the back of her hand and sat a little straighter. Kathy sat beside her and put a hand on her arm. 'I'm sorry, Winnie.'

'I knew he'd get into trouble, dat boy. But he didn't deserve anything like this.'

McCulloch, impassive, raised an eyebrow at Kathy and nodded his head to one side. She got to her feet and followed him a little way away.

'What happened?' she murmured.

'Kids coming out of school for lunchbreak saw him stagger out of the side street opposite, clutching his head. He collapsed and they went and had a look. He had blood all over his face and someone called triple nine. When the ambulance men got there they discovered he had a six-inch nail rammed in his ear.'

Kathy screwed up her face in disgust.

'Yeah. Extremely lucky it didn't kill him. Punctured the eardrum of course. Very painful, apparently. They're trying to find out what other damage it's done inside his head. He hasn't spoken. Any ideas?'

'I visited him again at the girl's flat in Cove Street. Could it be punishment for talking to me?'

'That's what I wondered. "See and blind, hear and deaf," that's the Yardie code.'

Another horrible thought came to Kathy. 'Yes, that, and the fact that he's a musician.'

McCulloch grimaced. 'Some punishment. When did you visit him?'

Kathy checked her notebook. 'The eighth, over a week ago. The girl caught me in the flat talking to him. She could have told Vexx.'

'Long time to wait to teach him a lesson. Maybe it was something else.'

Kathy shook her head. 'No. You've been reading the papers? They waited till that was all over, then they cleaned up their own backyard.'

'Well, he certainly upset somebody.'

'It's Vexx. We should talk to him, and Carole, the girl.'

McCulloch raised an eyebrow.

'Sorry,' Kathy said. 'It's your case. Just a suggestion. Can I sit in?'

'Be my guest. We'll be waiting here for a while. Talk to Winnie while I fetch us all a cup of tea.'

ONE OF NATURE'S GREAT mysteries, Brock thought, along with migrating butterflies and holes in the ozone layer, was exactly what happened to fish and chips on the way home. Recalling the delicious package of hot crisp food he'd bought in the shop, he contemplated sadly the congealed mess that now lay before him on his plate. It seemed oddly personal, this transformation, like a deliberate insult. He also thought of the last plate of fish and chips he'd eaten, with Michael Grant in the Strangers' Dining Room, and imagined how he must be feeling now, the impostor, the boy from the Dungle, summarily crushed.

The Grant affair no longer made the six o'clock news. Brock poured himself a glass of the Dragon Stout he'd picked up at his local Paramounts. There had been a big run on it, he'd been told, and they had hardly any left. He poked around morosely in the ruined meal for the least soggy chips.

Kathy had rung him from the hospital to say that the doctors were cautiously optimistic about George's condition. The eardrum would probably be repairable, though the nail had penetrated the inner ear, damaging the cochlea. Time would tell whether a cochlear implant might be necessary, but things could have been a lot worse. George himself was sedated and saying nothing. Kathy was frustrated, both by the wait at the hospital and by McCulloch's cautious approach. She had the feeling that her possible involvement worried him and that he was dragging his feet.

Brock switched off the TV and tried to take the fish seriously. A slice of lemon might help. Or another beer.

He rang Suzanne. She sounded pleased to hear from him, but cautious, too. She had been to see Amber that afternoon and he gathered that the visit hadn't gone well.

'She gets things so out of proportion, deliberately misinterpreting everything I say to put it in the worst possible light. Anyway, one day at a time . . . How are you?'

He gave her a summary of his day and heard her sigh.

'It just gets worse, doesn't it?' she said. 'What they did to Michael Grant, and now this boy . . . I think you should let this go, David. Have a talk to your boss and then wash your hands of it. The past is over. You can't put it all to rights.'

He thought about that. Long after they hung up he pondered if that was really what he was trying to do. He remembered the Saturday lunchtime long ago, returning home to his abandoned flat, tweaking at that old wound, and of the conversations he had had that day with Joseph Kidd, whose remains had surfaced like an old nightmare so long after the event. But he wasn't convinced. It wasn't restitution he wanted so much as understanding. As startling as Hadden-Vane's disclosures had been, they hadn't explained what had happened on the eleventh of April 1981. In fact, thinking of the MP's performance now, it had the mesmerising quality of an illusionist show. He closed his eyes as he recalled each stage in the performance, and tried to rekindle a half-suppressed sense of something inconclusive, unexplained, behind the dazzling revelations.

He woke abruptly, two hours later, with the realisation of what had troubled him. In his presentation to the committee, Hadden-Vane had questioned whether Michael Grant had a personal reason for his campaign against Roach, a suggestion that Brock had found entirely plausible. This had been the basis on which he had called Father Maguire as a witness, yet the priest had thrown no light on that idea, and instead the MP had used him to expose Grant's past in Jamaica. Hadden-Vane hadn't answered his own question. Perhaps he didn't know the answer, or didn't want to know. Perhaps it lay in the relationship between Grant and his fellow immigrant, Joseph Kidd. Brock wondered who might know, and his thoughts returned as they had once before, to Abigail Lavender, who had taken Grant in when he first arrived in the UK, and whose influence had been so formative on his subsequent career. It seemed all the stranger now, after what Hadden-Vane had uncovered, that Grant hadn't put her on his list of people Kathy should speak to, nor invited her to his daughter's concert. And she was still alive, for he remembered her name cropping up in Kathy's last report, with an address in Roehampton.

He got stiffly to his feet, picked up the empty glass and the remnants of his fish supper and headed for the kitchen. As he reached the door the phone rang.

'Brock, my dear chap! Not woken you up, I hope?'

'Sundeep, you're working late.'

'Well, not exactly, but the lab is, and I asked them to phone me at home with their result. Bingo! You win the lottery.'

'Really?' Brock felt a tightening in his chest, of relief really, and excitement at an idea well-formed against all the odds. 'You've got a match?'

'That's right. Care to take a punt on which of the three was Daddy?'

'Number two, Bravo? Joseph Kidd?'

'Wrong! It was the mysterious number three, the man without a head. He was the father of the lady whose handkerchief you gave us.'

'Really?' The killers had worked through the other two to get to him. Robbie, surname unknown.

'Does the lady know?'

'That's a good question, Sundeep. A very good question.'

TWENTY-NINE

KATHY TOOK HER MORNING coffee into the monitor room and watched McCulloch on the screen. On the other side of the table Mr Teddy Vexx sat with his arms folded, motionless, eyes hooded as if in meditation. Martin Connell, next to him, seemed almost diminutive alongside his bulk.

'Resuming then, Mr Vexx, you insist that you haven't seen Mr Murray for the last two days?'

'We've been over this several times,' Martin objected smoothly.

'I have a witness who saw your car in the vicinity of Cockpit Lane shortly before Mr Murray was found.'

'What witness?' Martin asked sharply.

'A police officer,' McCulloch snapped back.

They both turned to look at Vexx, who slowly uncrossed his arms, put his right hand into his jacket pocket, then withdrew it and reached forward with his big fist across the table towards the detective, who, despite himself, drew back. For several seconds Vexx kept his hand cupped in front of McCulloch on the table, staring into his eyes. Then he lifted his hand away and leaned back. His chair creaked. A packet of chewing gum lay where his fist had been. He said, 'I went out to buy gum.'

Kathy sighed. This wasn't going well.

THE ALTON ESTATE AT Roehampton was one of the most heroic attempts by the London County Council architects to build the New Jerusalem in the 1950s. Overlooking the rolling green of Richmond Park, its towers and slabs ranged from Scandinavian modernism on the east to the tougher concrete Brutalism of Le Corbusier on the west. Between the two sides of this stylistic argument lay a convent and a Jesuit college, and Brock wondered, as he sat in Abigail Lavender's living room, eyeing the brightly decorated Virgins, crucifixes and papal photographs, whether this had been an attraction for her.

'Wonderful view,' he said.

'Oh yes.' She'd put on a lot of weight since he'd seen her in 1981, and she wobbled gently as she pointed out some of the sights in the park—the Royal Ballet School, the polo field, Prince Charles's Spinney—that he would have been able to see if it weren't for the mist.

'I'm so glad you came to see me, sir,' she said. She had a quiet, gentle voice that might, he imagined, turn into a powerful soprano given a decent hymn. 'I have been so distressed about what they been doin' to that poor boy. They lynched him, no two ways about it, as surely as if they'd hung him from a tree. I wanted to speak out, tell people what I know, but I waited to hear from Michael first. I s'pose he didn't need my help. Maybe it would make no difference anyway, since everybody thinks he's guilty.'

'What is it that you wanted to tell people, Abigail?'

'Why, the truth!'

'I'm very interested in that. Maybe I could help Michael if you told it to me.'

'I'll do that, on one condition, that you try my homemade cream sponge and chocolate macaroons.'

'I thought you'd never ask,' he said, and she went off chuckling to her little kitchen to prepare the feast.

'I grew up in Riverton City, same as Michael,' she said, when she finally settled herself in the armchair facing Brock, cups of tea balanced on their right chair arms and plates of confectionery on their left.

'My mother and his grandmother, Mrs Forrest, were close friends.'

'That was his name then, wasn't it?'

'That's right. He was called Billy Forrest. I remember when his mother brought him to live with his grandmother, the sweetest little pickney I ever saw, and I watched him grow up until I married Mr Lavender and came away to England. Billy was seven then, and already I could see that he was different. Well, he could read for a start, and he was quiet and you could tell from looking at him that there were things going on in his head that he wasn't telling you about. To tell the truth, I didn't know how long he'd survive in the Dungle. Do you know about the Dungle?'

'Michael mentioned it to me. A rubbish tip, yes?'

'The biggest filthiest rubbish tip you ever saw. Imagine the putrid stench under the hot sun, the smoke of fires, the seagulls wheeling overhead, the rats, the skinny dogs, the flies. And then imagine the garbage trucks roaring in and the bigger boys jumping on board so they can have the first pick of the rubbish before it gets tipped out and the smaller children and the women get to work, looking for cans and bottles, bits of material, anything you can sell or eat or make a shelter and clothes from.'

Abigail could clearly see it as she spoke, and when she paused to take a breath she blinked and looked around her at the spotless little flat as if still not quite able to believe that she'd escaped.

'And then, as if bein' poor wasn't bad enough, there was what people did to each other in that dreadful place, the guns, the beatin's, and what they did to the girls . . . It was bad enough then, when I was there, but it got worse, year by year, until by the time Billy left it had all got completely out of hand. The bad boys took handouts from the big politicians, Manley and Seaga's people, to terrorise the folk on the other side. They didn't stop at killing the men—little children and old women were murdered in their beds to teach the others what to expect. In May of that year they set fire to the Evening Tide Home for the elderly disabled, on Slipe Pen Road. A sister of my mother was living there, my Auntie May, who wasn't well in the head. It was a PNP area, but there was a rumour goin' round that over a hundred of the residents had voted for the JLP in the last election, so one night the PNP boys cut the phone lines and started fires. It was a big old wooden building, with seven hundred old folks inside, and it went up in an inferno. One hundred and fifty-three of the old people died that night, Auntie May among them. No one was ever arrested for that terrible deed, but the men who did it will surely face the Judgement of His Wrath. Will you have another slice of my cream sponge, Chief Inspector?'

'It is very good,' Brock conceded, handing her his empty plate with only a token show of resistance.

'You haven't been eatin' well lately, have you? I can see you're lookin' peaky. Another cuppa to go with it?'

'Thank you.'

'Anyway, what chance did a poor boy have of growing up straight in such a place? Some ran away to Bull Bay to become Rastas, reading the Scriptures and praising Jah and Selassie with the older dreads. Some were rescued by the likes of Father Guzowski or Monsignor Albert. Some joined the police force or the army. Some escaped overseas. But most joined the gangs and posses and got themselves a gun.'

'Which did Billy do?'

'Oh, he was one of Father Guzowski's boys, no mistake about that. That's what made it so unfair, what happened.

'There had been a spate of particularly violent murders in Jones Town during that August,' Abigail said, 'and on this particular night the police had finally been prodded into action, sending patrols out looking for the perpetrators. They were nervous, the police, grabbing anyone they didn't like the look of until they had a full quota to take back to the station. Billy was unlucky to be in the area that hot night, coming back from a visit to a relative in Kingston Public Hospital. He was arrested and taken in for questioning. It was chaotic at the police station, with young men being bundled into crowded cells to await their turn. Billy got talking to another prisoner, called Earl, a bit older than himself, who seemed to know the ropes and took Billy under his wing.

'The police officers who questioned Billy seemed uninterested in his story of visiting the hospital, and kept trying to get him to admit that he had been in Jones Town the previous night, which he had not. Their interrogation techniques were rough, and he was returned to his cell with two thick ears and a bloody nose. There Earl went over with him what had happened and explained where he'd gone wrong, arguing with his questioners. When they took him away for a second time he followed Earl's advice and came back without much further damage. Earl, on the other hand, returned from his session badly beaten, with a missing tooth and what later turned out to be two cracked ribs. He explained that someone in their cell had recognised him as a Shower Posse soldier and therefore a JLP supporter and had told the police, who were in the PNP camp.

'It was late in the night when Billy and Earl were finally released. By way of a final insult, the cops drove the two of them and a third prisoner into the heart of a Spangler-controlled area and kicked them out, confident that they would be identified as the enemy and treated accordingly. They were saved by an old woman, who, in an extraordinary act of charity, realised their danger and took them into her home.

'The next morning they set off together for the relative safety of Tivoli Gardens, where Earl lived, but on the way a car overtook them and stopped in the street ahead. Two men got out holding guns and began firing at them. Their companion was hit immediately in the head, clearly a fatal wound, while Billy and Earl jumped over a fence and ran, pursued by the gunmen. Trapped in a small yard, they grabbed whatever lay to hand and waited for the men to pass by. They heard one run past, but then the second stopped and came into their hiding place. Earl hit him with the stick he'd picked up, but it was rotten and snapped across the man's shoulder without doing any damage. The man turned to shoot and Billy, behind him, hit him on the head with the brick he'd found. The man fell, and Earl picked up his gun and fired it at the second gunman, who had heard the commotion. He ran back to his car and fled. The man on the ground was dead. When Earl emptied his wallet he found a police badge.

'They knew that they wouldn't be safe now in Tivoli Gardens, and Billy persuaded Earl to come with him to Riverton City. They caught a bus and went straight to Father Guzowski and told him their story. He hid them for several weeks until he was able to put them both on a plane to London.

'That's the truth,' she said with a sigh.

Brock didn't doubt it. Like everyone else, he had been tempted by the notion that Michael Grant's fall had been well deserved, that someone who had been just too good to be true had been exposed as a huge fraud. All of the newspapers had accepted this line, whether guardedly or with vicious relish, but it had never squared with Brock's own assessment of the man, despite the fact that Grant had lied to him about not knowing Joseph Kidd in Jamaica.

'I know that's how it happened because his grandmother got her friend to write to tell me the whole story, and to ask me to look out for him if he got to London. Then Father Maguire told me he was coming and I said we'd take him in, despite . . . well, despite experience.'

Brock gave her a quizzical smile over the rim of his teacup.

'We'd already had dealings with the Forrest family comin' over here that weren't so happy, but I thought I knew my little Billy, and I wasn't wrong.'

'There are other Forrests here?'

'Just the one, Billy's older brother, or half-brother you would say—same mother, but who knows who their fathers were? Sailors passing through. He was quite a bit older than Billy, closer to my age, and he came over a couple of years after we did.'

Abigail had become reluctant and subdued in telling this part of her story, and Brock said, 'Trouble, was he?'

She nodded. 'Good-looking boy, and a great one for the ladies. He even . . . well, I was an attractive woman in those days. Mr Lavender had to tell him to get out. But it wasn't just the flirting. He brought his bad ways over with him, the drugs, and got in with a bad crowd. It was on account of him that Mr Lavender got hurt. When he fell out with him, my husband threatened to go to the police about his drug dealing, and he told his friends, who came and beat Mr Lavender up bad.'

'The Roaches?'

'Mr Lavender never said a word, not even to me, but I'd seen Billy's brother hanging around with them. I didn't want to see Billy—Michael, as he now was—goin' the same way. It tells you what a good man my husband was that he agreed to take him in, God bless his soul.'

'What happened to this brother?'

'I don't know. He moved on, thank goodness, and Michael ful-filled all my hopes for him.'

'What was the brother's name?'

'Robbie, Robbie Forrest. He was a rascal, that one.' She shook her head, but the memory stirred something warmer than disap-proval, and she smiled to herself. 'He had one gold tooth.' She tapped one of her front teeth. 'Lost it in a fight back home, he said, and forced the man who'd knocked it out to give him a new one, in gold. The man with the golden kiss, he used to say. I sometimes wonder what ever became of him.'

'So where is Michael now, Abigail?'

'I really don't know.'

'I can understand your reluctance, but I may be able to help him.'

'But it's true, I don't know.' She hesitated. 'He did phone me on Monday evening. He said that things were impossible and he couldn't go home. He said that he and Jennifer were goin' away for a while, till things settled down. He didn't say where . . .'

Brock nodded patiently. 'But?'

'Well, they've been away before, when Michael said he couldn't stand London anymore and wanted to "go to ground"—that's

282

what he called it. A cottage that belongs to a friend of his. I don't know if that's where he's gone, but it's possible.'

'Whereabouts?'

'Somewhere in the country.'

'Didn't he mention where it was, or send you a postcard?'

'No.' She saw the frustration on Brock's face and added, 'The friend who owned it was someone he knew from his days in the building industry. A builder, I think.'

KATHY MET THEM IN the corridor as they were leaving the station. Martin started at seeing her, then recovered and gave a cautious smile. Vexx, at his shoulder, glowered.

'Do you have a moment, Mr Connell?' she asked.

He glanced at Vexx, then reached into his pocket for his keys. 'All right. Do you want to wait for me in the car, Teddy, while I have quick word with DS Kolla here?'

Vexx took the keys and shouldered past Kathy with a casual roll to his stride. Kathy showed Martin into an unoccupied interview room. They didn't sit down. Kathy folded her arms.

'You're very trusting,' she said, 'giving your keys to a bastard like that. He's probably driving your car back to your home right now, to steal your Georgian silver and rape your lovely wife.'

'Don't be like that, Kathy.'

'He drove a six-inch nail into a kid's head because I tried to talk to the lad, who never told me a thing. It's amazing the boy isn't dead.'

Seeing how angry she was, Connell replied carefully, trying to sound calm and reasonable. 'They can't prove that.'

'I know, I was watching. Interesting that you put it like that, Martin. Interesting that you don't say he's innocent, because of course you know he's not.'

'He's innocent until proven guilty.'

'I don't know how you can do it, how you can live with yourself.'

He seemed about to frame a response, then simply shook his head and said wearily, 'Is that all you wanted to say?'

'Not all, no. I wondered if Tom Reeves had been in touch with you.'

Martin looked alarmed. 'Christ, no. Has he spoken to you?'

'No. I just wondered, that's all.'

'Well, when you do see him make sure he understands that nothing happened between us and he must keep his trap shut. That's the last thing I . . . either of us needs right now.'

'Don't worry, Martin,' Kathy said softly. 'We're innocent, remember? Until proven guilty.' She walked out of the room.

As she paced down the corridor her phone rang. She opened it and heard Brock's voice.

'Kathy, what can you tell me about that builder friend of Michael Grant's?'

KATHY LED THE WAY across the mud towards the hut where she'd met Wayne Ferguson before. The site looked different now, with steel framing erected on the concrete slab. The site manager was standing talking to a man with a roll of drawings. He waved when he saw them and came over.

Kathy introduced Brock. 'Look, Mr Ferguson—'

'Wayne, please. You're lucky to catch me—it's St Patrick's Day. I should be down the pub.'

Kathy thought his joviality exaggerated. 'Wayne, we thought you could help us get in touch with Michael Grant.'

'Did you now? What gave you that idea, I wonder?'

'He's not staying at your cottage?'

His mouth dropped open, then he frowned and examined the toe of his boot while he thought. 'Michael needs a bit of peace and quiet right now. He wouldn't thank me for answering that question.'

'We're in much the same boat,' Brock said. 'I've been suspended, and Tom Reeves who was helping him will probably be kicked out of the force. We need to talk to each other, see what can be salvaged, if anything.'

'I felt pretty bad changing my story about seeing those two Roach boys in the Cat that night. I felt I'd let Michael down, and offering him the cottage was the least I could do.'

'Why not give him a ring and let me talk to him?'

'No, I can't do that.' He saw Brock about to argue and raised his hand. 'I mean, it's not possible. There's no phone.'

'Where is it?'

'North Wales, in the hills above the Vale of Clwyd. I don't even know if they got there okay. It's probably still snowbound.'

'Can you give me directions?'

Ferguson shrugged and reached for a pad of paper. 'Sure, I guess it's okay. It's not easy to find. I'll draw a map.'

He and Brock bent over the diagram for a while, discussing A and B road numbers, and Kathy picked up a few placenames—Mold, Ruthin and, more obscurely, Llanbedr Dyffryn Clwyd. It wasn't a part of the country she knew. 'When you get to the village you'll see the church spire on the right and the shop beyond it. Take the next turn on the left, it's easy to miss, and start to climb the hill, here . . .'

Beyond the window men were working on top of the frame, setting out the metal roof sheeting against a heavy sky.

'All right, I think I've got it, Wayne, thanks.' Brock straightened, pocketing the map. 'How long will it take to get there?'

'Four, five hours, depending on the traffic. I wouldn't try finding it in the dark, not if it's been snowing.'

They returned to the car and Brock checked his watch.

'You're not thinking of going today?' Kathy asked.

'No, I don't think so, and in any case, I think we know most of the story now.' He told her what Abigail had told him. 'Victim number three was Michael's brother, that's what made it so personal with Roach. But I'd like to hear what else Michael knows about the killing of those three men. There may be something that could still help us, which he couldn't talk about before without revealing his own story. Maybe at the weekend, I might take a trip up there.'

'Sounds nice, if the weather holds out.'

THIRTY

AT EIGHT THAT EVENING, Kathy was curled up on her sofa reading the book that Tom had given her. She was conscious of the rain spattering against the window and debating whether to put on a thicker jumper when her phone rang. It was the duty officer at Scotland Yard. A woman had rung wanting to speak to her. She had seemed distraught. She gave her name as Maureen Reeves.

Kathy rang the number and was answered straightaway. 'Yes?'

'Hello, is that Maureen?'

'Yes.'

'I'm Kathy Kolla, Maureen. I understand you were trying to reach me.'

'Oh, yes, thank you for ringing back.' She spoke in a hesitant rush, veering between panic and apology. 'I wondered . . . is Tom with you?'

'No.'

'Only, he was supposed to collect Amy over two hours ago, and he hasn't appeared. He's not answering his phone. It isn't like him, you see, to forget Amy. He'd have let me know. I was due to go out an hour ago . . .'

'I haven't seen him at all this week, Maureen, or even spoken to him.'

'Oh . . . I thought . . . He's been so down, you see. What happened, well, it was devastating, wasn't it? So public and humiliating.

I know things haven't been going well for him during the last couple of years, but I've never heard him sound so, well, shell-shocked. I've tried the obvious people, but nobody's heard from him. I'm worried.'

'Yes.' Kathy was becoming concerned as she listened. 'When did you last hear from him?'

'Yesterday lunchtime, on the phone. He sounded very flat, but he confirmed about tonight. I'd been worried that I couldn't reach him and he explained he wasn't answering the phone because the press had his numbers. He wanted to make sure they weren't hanging around my house. He said he was looking forward to seeing Amy. He'd called once before this week to speak to her. He was worried about what people might be saying to her at school.'

'All right. Something probably delayed him, Maureen, but I'll start looking. Tell me who you've contacted.' She jotted down the list of names—mutual friends, several workmates, a doctor. 'Okay, now I'll give you my mobile number so you can reach me as soon as you hear anything.'

She rang off, pushing down her anxiety, trying to clear her head. She began with the accident and emergency number, and while she waited for a result used her mobile to make calls to everyone she could think of—Nicole, Bren, Dot. By the time she rang Brock she'd had a negative result from A&E as well as all the others.

He listened in silence, then said, 'Do you know where he lives?'

'Kentish Town.' She told him the address.

'I think we'd better take a look.'

'Yes, that's what I thought.'

'See you there.'

She was the first to arrive, checking that there were no lights on in the basement flat before she rang the bells of the other flats above and on each side of Tom's. No one had seen him that day. Brock arrived and they went down into the well, knocked a pane of glass out of the front door and opened it. There was no sign of him, and they began a rapid search, quickly coming up with a string of negatives—the mail unopened, the bed unmade, breakfast plates unwashed, a message pad blank, the absence of a diary or note-book, the answering machine switched off, and no response to di-alling 1471 for the number of the last caller. There was no indication that anyone else had been in the flat recently. Then Kathy found the laptop.

She switched it on and checked his email, nothing but junk for two days. Then she tried Recent Applications, and found that the photo album was top of the list. She opened it, then called Brock over. The most recent picture had been taken at one thirty-five p.m. that day, of a smartly dressed young woman hailing a cab. She had jet-black hair and a warm tan complexion.

'Magdalen Roach,' Brock murmured.

Kathy clicked back through the album, pictures of Magdalen coming out of the office where she worked, in a bus queue, step-ping out of her aunt's red BMW.

'He's been stalking her,' Kathy said. She felt shocked, catching sight of something private and obsessive, and also sad. It was as if she were being allowed a glimpse into the depth of Tom's anger and despair at what had been done to him.

Brock asked, 'Do you think he wants to hurt her, pay her back?' Kathy found she couldn't give an answer.

Then she was staring at the next image on the screen, a stream disappearing into the mouth of a concrete tunnel set into a grassy bank. 'Oh no.'

'What is that?'

'I think it's the culvert that runs under the Roach place. Tom found some information on it.' She told him about the helicopter flight and their conversation afterwards. 'I told him it was a ridiculous idea, and he turned it into a joke.'

The picture had been taken two days earlier, the day after his mauling in the parliamentary committee meeting.

'Surely he wouldn't try to go back in there?' Kathy whispered.

'To justify himself,' Brock said. 'To prove he was right and everyone else was wrong. To make amends to Michael Grant. Yes, I think he would. But how is Magdalen involved?'

'Perhaps we should ask her,' Kathy said. She closed the photo album and opened his computer address book. Magdalen's email address and phone numbers were listed. Kathy raised her eyebrow at Brock and he nodded. She took out her phone and tapped in the mobile number. Brock watched her listen for a moment, then quickly switch off.

'Not there?'

'Yes, she answered, and I think I know where she is. There was the sound of a crowd in the background, and a heavy ragga number playing.'

'What's ragga?'

'Dancehall reggae. I think she's at the JOS club.'

THEY HEARD THE MUSIC from a block away. Kathy cruised slowly past the club entrance and parked on a double yellow line near the street corner. Brock stared at the old building, thinking of a night in April, twenty-four years before.

'I'd better do this,' she said.

'What if Vexx's in there? He knows you, doesn't he? I'll go.'

'He knows us both.'

'Then we'll both go. Come on.' Brock got out of the car and she followed. Clusters of people were standing around the entrance, smoking and appearing to be cooling off, sweat gleaming on their faces. They eyed them curiously as they walked up to two large men in suits and shaved heads at the door. Kathy was waved through but Brock was stopped with a hand on his chest.

'Hey!' Kathy laughed and slipped her arm around Brock and pressed herself against him. 'He's mine.'

Several watchers laughed and the men gave bleak smiles and stepped back. Brock handed over some money, and they climbed stairs towards the booming sound. At the top they were plunged into a dark space vibrating with dancing lights and figures and heat. It seemed impossible to identify anyone in here, let alone talk to them. They hesitated at the edge, trying to adjust their senses, then began to make their way slowly around the edge of the writhing crowd, Kathy half a dozen paces in front of Brock. Eventually he saw her stop and turn back to him, signalling to stay where he was. He watched her approach a couple against the wall, standing very close together, holding drinks, their faces almost touching so they could talk.

They separated when Kathy reached them, and after a moment the man moved away. Brock watched the two women trying to communicate, with hand and body gestures supplementing shouted words, but this seemed to prove impossible, and they began to thread their way through the crowd towards the entrance, Brock following them down the crowded stairway. They stepped through the doors and stopped as Magdalen fumbled in her bag for a cigarette. She was swaying slightly and seemed clumsy in her movements. Kathy was talking to her and trying to guide her away towards the car. Suddenly the girl's mood changed and she pulled away from Kathy and said something angry, flapping her hand in the air. Some of the people standing around were watching them now. Brock hurried forward and she tottered as she turned to him. He caught her arm.

'Easy now, Magdalen,' he murmured.

'Who are you?'

'He's another friend of Tom's,' Kathy said. 'It's okay.'

'Yeah, well don't hassle me. I just want a fag.' She fumbled with the lighter and got it going.

One of the bouncers at the door called out, 'You okay, Magda?'

'Yeah.' She waved to him. 'It's all right, Troy.'

'She saw Tom here last night,' Kathy said.

'That's right.' A gleam of perspiration lit Magdalen's face beneath the streetlights as she tilted her chin and blew out smoke. 'Look, I'm sorry about what happened to him, but he tried to use me too, right?'

Kathy nodded.

'Yeah. He told me he's goin' to lose his job, is that right?'

'Looks that way.'

'Well, who wants a job like that anyway?'

'Was he angry with you, last night?'

'No, no. He was sweet, really. Just kinda sad. He said he still liked me.'

'He does like you,' Kathy said, 'in spite of what he had to do. He likes you a lot.'

'Yeah?' She shivered suddenly and clutched her arms across her chest. In the cold wind of the street her short glittery dress looked like no protection at all.

'You'll catch a chill,' Kathy said. 'Let's talk in the car,' and before the girl could object they both steered her to the parked car and eased her in. Brock got behind the wheel and started the engine, turning up the heater.

'Did he say why he came to the club last night?'

'To see me, he said.'

'Did he talk about his plans?'

'No, I just assumed he'd be around. We talked about tonight, and I thought I might have seen him here again, but he never showed up.'

'How do you mean you talked about tonight?'

'Oh, about family and that. It's St Patrick's Day, right? The Roach family throws a big dinner-dance for all their friends. It's traditional, year after bloody year. I hate it. I told him I'd be the only one not there.'

'They hold this at home?'

'No, at a hotel on the river.'

'So there's no one at home tonight?'

She shook her head and Brock and Kathy exchanged a glance.

Magdalen caught their look. 'Hang on,' she said, 'you don't think—Oh, Christ, no. I can't believe—'

'Did you tell anyone else about your conversation with Tom?'

'No . . . Wait, yes. Teddy Vexx saw us together at the bar downstairs last night, and he asked me later what we were talking about.'

'Where's Vexx tonight?'

'I dunno. Troy said he had a job on. I'd better ring my dad. If that stupid bastard—'

'Better still,' Brock said, putting the car into gear, 'let's pay him a visit.'

As he drove, Kathy called for backup, and a patrol car joined them on Blackheath, leading them fast under lights and siren as far as the turnoff into Shooters Hill, where Brock overtook and led the way to the gates of The Glebe, which were open. They drove into the central courtyard where they saw a car parked askew outside Magdalen's parents' house, whose front door was standing open.

'That's Mum's car,' Magdalen said, and jumped out and ran to the house, the others following. Inside they found Magdalen's mother Adonia kneeling beside a chair on which Spider Roach was sprawled. She was holding a glass of water and a bottle of pills. Every light in the room was on, including the garish central chandelier, and the old man looked pale and sick in the dazzling illumination. Adonia rose to her feet as they ran in, saw the uniformed men and said, 'You took your time.'

As Magdalen ran to her mother, Brock said, 'What happened?'

'We had a robbery, that's what. Some bastard broke in here and started going through the place.' She gestured at a cabinet with drawers hanging open.

'Shut it,' Roach croaked from his seat.

Adonia misunderstood. 'I'll tidy up later, Dad.'

Kathy was sniffing the air. 'Someone's fired a gun in here.'

'I noticed a smell when I came in,' Adonia agreed. 'I know the man was hurt. Ivor got a call from his security men and came first, then Dad wasn't well and I brought him home.'

'So where are they now?' Brock said.

'Hospital, I suppose . . .'

'Shut it, you stupid cow!' Roach's voice lashed her like a slap, and she blinked in surprise. He had hauled himself upright and was beating the air with a claw-like hand. 'My daughter-in-law is confused. There was no burglar. Nobody's been hurt.'

'But Dad . . .' Her voice faded as he glared at her.

'You seemed to be expecting us,' Brock said. 'Did you ring for the police?'

'Well, no. I assumed Ivor would have . . .' The expression froze on Adonia's face as she finally understood what was going on. 'Dad's right. I must have got it all wrong.'

'Did you see him, Mum?' Magdalen cried. 'Did you see the man?'

Her mother frowned, shook her head. 'I got it wrong.'

'No you didn't,' Brock said. 'Where did they go, Spider? Where did they take him?'

Roach turned to Brock with a sneer on his mouth. Brock recognised the expression, the curl of the lip, full-blooded and terrifying once, still with the power to chill.

Brock turned to Adonia. 'What car was Ivor driving?'

She shrugged and turned away.

'Adonia, tell me. You have to stop this.' Getting no response, he hesitated then said, 'We found Robbie Forrest's body.'

She turned slowly back to him, her eyes huge with surprise. 'Robbie?'

'Yes. He was one of the three bodies we found recently, buried on the railway land behind Cockpit Lane. He died in 1981. Didn't you know?'

She shook her head in slow motion.

'No, well, Ivor didn't want you to know, of course.'

'Shut up!' Spider barked again. 'You keep your evil—'

'Where are they?' Brock repeated, and the old man's mouth snapped closed.

'What do you mean, about Ivor?' Adonia said.

'He murdered Robbie, shot him in the head, him and his two friends. I think you know why.'

'You're lying.' She turned away, her hand on the gold pendant at her throat.

'What car is Ivor driving?' he demanded, and when she still said nothing, he said, this time with a sigh of regret, 'Does Magdalen know, Adonia?'

'Know what?' Magdalen said. 'What is all this? Who's Robbie Forrest?'

'Nothing,' her mother said. 'Nobody.'

'Your father, Magdalen,' Brock said, and as Adonia shook her head and began to speak he went on, 'Six foot tall, left-handed, Jamaican. We believe he had a gold tooth.'

Adonia looked stunned. 'What do you mean, *believe*?'

'Part of his remains were missing. But we've done tests on his DNA and Magdalen's. He was her father.'

'Mum?' Magdalen was staring in horror at her mother, whose eyes were filling with tears.

Adonia turned to her father-in-law. 'You knew?'

Roach glared back at her defiantly. 'You stupid bitch. A nigger! A man as black as your sin. You Greek whore!'

'What are you saying?' Magdalen cried. She grabbed Brock's arm. 'What are you saying?'

'Ivor Roach murdered your father, who was having an affair with your mother, and now he's murdering your boyfriend Tom.'

Magdalen gazed at him, then whispered, 'A black guy?'

Brock nodded.

'I knew. I think I've always known.' She stared in horror at her mother, who was frantically turning over in her fingers the golden heart on its chain around her throat. 'You told me he gave it to you when I was born . . .' She blinked as if shaking herself awake from a dream. Then she turned to Brock and said, 'I think I know where they've taken Tom.'

'No!' Spider roared, his rage lifting him out of his chair, but he couldn't stop Magdalen, who went on.

'There's an old car yard . . . in Tallow Square.'

'I know it,' Kathy said. 'You've been inside, haven't you? You'd better come with us. You might be able to help.'

'I'm coming too,' Adonia said, and to her daughter, 'You'll need a coat, come on.'

Brock gave hurried instructions to the two patrol officers to secure the house and make sure Spider didn't use a phone, and to call for an armed response vehicle to meet them at Tallow Square. While he was talking, Kathy went after the two women. She heard them in a back room, voices raised, then they were hurrying out, pulling on their coats, and they ran to the car.

THERE WAS NO SIGN of the ARV when they turned into the mean little square. Magdalen pointed out Vexx's Peugeot, and described the layout of the place. 'The entrance is down the laneway there. There's a big old shed on this side, and beyond it what used to be the workshop. They . . .' she hesitated, 'store stuff there.'

'Drugs?'

'Yeah. There's a regular little laboratory at the back. And they have two bloody great pitbulls. Savage, they are.'

'We'll wait till help gets here,' Brock said.

'No,' Magdalen said. 'They're murdering Tom in there. I'm going in. They won't hurt me.' She pulled open the car door, ignoring their cries. Then Adonia, too, was tumbling out of the door and chasing after her daughter.

Kathy said, 'I'll stop them,' and followed, running towards the mouth of the lane. She heard the ARV skidding into the square behind her as the two women disappeared into the shadows.

There was a huge old battered metal sliding door with a small wicket-gate set into the side of the shed, and a speaker and keypad hidden inside an old fuse box bolted to the wall beside it. As Kathy caught up with them Magdalen pressed the button. From inside the building they heard the muffled scream of an electric motor, like a drill or a circular saw, which was abruptly cut as Magdalen began to speak.

'Dad? Dad, it's me, Magdalen. Open the door, will you? It's important. I need to talk to you.'

There was a moment's silence, then the small door clicked. Magdalen pushed and it swung open and she stepped inside, followed by her mother and Kathy. They waited, their eyes adjusting to the dim light reflected off the high cobwebby ceiling from striplights beyond a low partition.

Magdalen called out, 'Dad? Are you there?'

A door opened in the partition and Ivor Roach stood silhouetted against the light. 'Magdalen? What are you doing here? Who's that with you?'

He came towards them. He was in his shirtsleeves and wearing a bloodstained apron, a gun hanging in his right hand at his side. Behind him, Kathy made out the bulky figure of Teddy Vexx in the doorway, and beyond him, in a pool of brilliant light, a white foot on a table.

'It's me, Ivor,' Adonia said. 'And this is someone from the police. I brought her here.'

'You what?' Ivor Roach advanced closer, peering at them in disbelief. 'You brought a copper here? You stupid bitch . . .' He raised his gun to Kathy.

'It's all right. She's got something she wants to tell you.'

Kathy's mouth was dry. She swallowed, took a breath.

'Go on.' Adonia urged her. 'What your boss said to us. Tell him.'

Roach looked puzzled.

'I . . .' Kathy cleared her throat with a cough. 'We were telling them that we've been running tests on the three bodies we found buried behind Cockpit Lane. We've established that one of them was Magdalen's natural father. His name was Robbie Forrest.'

Roach's mouth opened, but he didn't speak.

Magdalen said, 'They say you killed my real dad. Is that true?'

Roach slowly shook his head, looking from his daughter to his wife. 'Of course not. How could she know that?'

'The bullets were fired by a pistol, a nine-millimetre Browning,' Kathy said. 'It was used again a couple of years later in a car hijack, fired by your brother Ricky.'

'It is true, isn't it?' Adonia said. 'Your dad confirmed it. He knew all about it.'

'Hey, darling . . .' Ivor began to step forward, lifting his free hand in a supplicating gesture.

Out of the corner of her eye Kathy saw Adonia pull something from her coat pocket and point it at her husband. It was a gun, she saw, swaying precariously in the woman's hands. Ivor saw it too, and an incredulous look came over his face. 'Adonia . . .' he said, and was abruptly silenced by a tremendous bang that reverberated through the metal shed, then a second. For a moment Ivor stared at Adonia in astonishment, then his knees buckled and he fell flat on his face.

Now there was the crash of boots and shouts as men burst in through the door behind them. Kathy took the pistol from Adonia's hand, and the woman reached to her throat, unfastened her pendant and threw it at her husband's body.

THIRTY-ONE

THEY SENT TWO PEOPLE to the meeting, the smooth and the rough. The smooth was MI5, Brock was fairly sure, and the rough a copper, a senior figure from Special Branch. They were there representing the Organised Crime Liaison Group. Facing them were Commander Sharpe and Brock, and the meeting was held in the Scotland Yard headquarters at 10 Broadway and chaired by an assistant commissioner.

Brock and Sharpe had been up all night, managing the aftermath of the Tallow Square incident. There had been the hunt across South London for Vexx and Crocker, who had escaped from the rear of the building while the three armed police were being tackled by the pitbulls. There had also been the first interviews with Adonia Roach, who appeared to have been liberated from years of intimidation and fear by her act of murder, and had begun talking about the activities of her husband and his brothers in an adrenaline rush. Like Magdalen, she was convinced that Ivor had had her pendant made from her lover's golden tooth, and had made her wear it all those years as a vindictive act of revenge. Then there was the forensic information coming in from the crime scenes, not to mention the search of Ivor and Adonia Roach's house and of the crack factory they found at Tallow Square. And there was Tom Reeves, on the critical list after three hours of emergency surgery.

Despite their lack of sleep, Sharpe was in good form, as if wading through murder scenes in the middle of the night had reawakened some long-dormant feeling for a life of action. Now he ignored the barbed inquiry from the pair from OCLG as to Brock's status and launched into a spirited description of the night's activities that left them momentarily speechless. Finally, Smooth conceded that there had been a JIC-sanctioned operation involving the Roach family, but refused to go into details. Sharpe responded that in that case he would feel free to instruct Brock to pursue his investigations which, in the light of Adonia Roach's revelations and material found in her home, would undoubtedly embroil the whole family. Rough broke his silence at that point, bursting with fury at what had happened.

'They were giving us everything,' he protested. 'Every drug lab in London, every dealer, every importer. They had it all, and they were giving it to us! This is a total disaster.'

'Then you shouldn't have tried to use us as puppets,' Sharpe said coldly. 'I've got one officer at death's door, another . . .' He indicated Brock. '. . . with his reputation in tatters, and a missing member of Parliament whose life has been ruined.'

'Oh, come now,' Smooth said with a pained air, 'nobody asked Reeves to try to burgle the Roach house, and I really don't think that anyone questions DCI Brock's reputation. As for Michael Grant, well, that was Roach's price, in the end. And let's face it, Grant was a troublemaker, out of control. He was regarded as a menace in the House, and he was never going to leave Roach alone. He was simply beyond reason.'

Brock spoke for the first time. 'They had murdered his brother,' he said quietly.

'So you say. But you have no proof, have you?'

'We'll see.'

The assistant commissioner stepped in. Perhaps, now that everything was out in the open, some way forward might be considered? Might it not still be possible to gain the information from the Roaches, who, after all, must be even more anxious than before to do a deal? Smooth thought this a constructive approach, although Rough was obviously still seething. After considerable discussion, it was agreed to share operational information daily and include Sharpe in the OCLG control group. The meeting broke up with handshakes and in a mood, at least to outward appearances, of conciliation and cooperation.

THE FOLLOWING MORNING, SATURDAY, Kathy was wrenched from sleep by the phone ringing. She stumbled through the dark and fumbled the receiver. It was Brock, calling from the hospital where he had been with Tom.

'Oh . . .' The curtains were drawn and she had no idea if it was night or day. It seemed only minutes since she had been there herself at Tom's bedside, and she could still smell the hospital. 'Any change?'

'Still critical but stable,' Brock said, 'and really as good as could be hoped for, given the terrible injuries compounded by loss of blood. Even if he survived the next few days, they still weren't sure if they could save his legs.'

Kathy groaned. They hadn't mentioned that to her. A wave of nausea rose inside her and she sat down heavily. She felt exhausted, unwilling to face it all again. Her eyes, adjusting to the gloom, made out pale light around the shape of the curtain. 'What time is it?'

'Eight-twenty. Sorry, did I wake you? The reason I'm ringing is to tell you that I'm going to drive up to see Michael Grant today, and tell him what's happened. So if there are any developments you'll phone me on my mobile, will you?'

'Yes, yes, of course. I'll come back over to the hospital soon.'

'Tom's daughter and her mother are here at the moment. They seem a little better today. The forecast is fair. Should be a nice day for a drive into the country. I expect I'll be home later tonight.'

'Right. Have a nice trip.'

'Thanks. Oh, one bit of news should appeal to you. I've just had the result of the tests on the gun Adonia used. It is Brown Bread.'

She opened the curtains and looked out on a dark morning sky, heavy with cloud. Ivor Roach, Brown Bread's last victim. Brock was implying that there was justice in that, a kind of resolution, but she couldn't really feel it. To her it just seemed as if all their digging around had brought some nasty dormant thing wriggling to the surface to create more pain and misery. What was the point of avenging those ancient deaths if it just caused more death, more anguish, more broken lives? She felt tired, so tired, and had to force herself under the shower to face the day.

She also didn't fancy meeting Tom's family at the hospital, and left her visit until mid-morning, by which time they'd gone. After an hour staring at his motionless, mummified form she felt restless and decided to get some fresh air with a walk along the river. She made her way down to the ground floor and had barely cleared the entrance doors when she was stopped by a cry.

'Kathy!'

She turned and saw Martin Connell running towards her, his coat flapping, hair flying in the wind. He looked pale, eyes pouchy, and she guessed he hadn't had much sleep either in the past forty-eight hours.

'Thank God,' he gasped. 'Where's Brock?'

His abruptness startled her. 'Hi, good morning to you too, Martin.'

'Sorry.' He took a deep breath, pulling himself up with a visible effort, and put on an unconvincing smile. He was agitated, blinking rapidly and she noticed a tremor in his cheek. 'Kathy, this is terribly important.' He took hold of her arm, gulping for air as if he were drowning. 'Do you know where he is? Is he inside? I haven't been able to find him.'

'No, he's not here. What on earth is wrong?'

'I have to see him, Kathy. It's very urgent!'

'Well, I'm afraid you can't, not until tonight anyway, or maybe tomorrow.'

Martin's face looked so racked that she added, 'He's gone to North Wales to speak to Michael Grant. But you can reach him on his mobile. Here's the number—'

'No, that's no good! I have to speak to him in person. North

Wales?' He shook his head as if this were impossible. 'Where? Do you know where?'

Kathy hesitated, thrown by Martin's obvious alarm. 'Grant's staying in a cottage out in the country somewhere, I don't know exactly where.'

'You must!'

'Martin,' she said, exasperated now, 'Brock got the directions himself from the friend of Michael's who owns the place. I wasn't really paying attention. Surely someone else can help?'

He shook his head desperately. 'How long ago did he leave?'

'Oh, three hours, but—'

'Maybe I can go after him. Who is this friend?'

'He's a builder. But why—'

'Can you get hold of him?'

'I do have his phone number, but—'

'Ring him, please. Get the directions from him.'

'Not until you tell me what this is all about. What's going on?'

'Kathy, please. I just have to get to Brock, now, today, as soon as possible. It's a matter of life and death. Believe me, please.'

She'd never seen him like this, panicky and wild, clutching his coat about him, looking more like a beggar or a mugging victim than a top criminal lawyer. She took out her phone and notebook, checked Wayne Ferguson's home number and made the call. His wife answered. There had been an emergency of some kind at the building site and Wayne had had to go in. She gave Kathy his mobile number, but when she tried it she got his message service.

'He's gone to a building site,' she said. 'A supermarket. There's been—'

She caught a look of alarm on Martin's face, his eyes on something over her shoulder, and when she turned she found herself staring into the faces of the two remaining Roach brothers, Mark and Ricky. Close up, in the flesh, they were nothing like the remote images on the walls at Queen Anne's Gate. Beefy men with heavy bodies and florid meaty faces, their father's thin gene had bypassed them or been gorged out of existence.

'You two having a cosy chat, or what?' Mark said menacingly. 'Who was she phoning, Martin?'

'It's all right,' Martin gabbled. 'I've found out where he is. She was trying to get directions . . .'

'Where is he then?'

Kathy stared at Martin. He forced his eyes away, to the two men. 'He's gone to North Wales, to see Grant. He's hiding up there.'

'Oh yeah?' The brothers exchanged a calculating look, then one glanced back over his shoulder at a group coming down the footpath towards them, and said, 'Let's go into the car park.' He took hold of Kathy's arm and gripped tight. She tried to wrench free and he said, 'Don't be stupid or we'll have to hurt you.' His brother took the other arm and they frogmarched her towards the parking building, Martin tagging along behind.

They walked up ramps and along aisles lined with deserted vehicles until they came to a black Mercedes luxury off-roader. Inside, Kathy made out the profile of Spider Roach, and saw him turn his cadaverous pale face towards them as they approached.

'Now,' Mark said as his brother pushed Kathy hard up against a concrete column. 'What's the story?'

Kathy said nothing, and Martin immediately responded. 'He left about three hours ago. The place is a cottage in the countryside. She doesn't know the address, so I got her to phone the owner, a friend of Grant's, but we couldn't get through. He's a builder and he's been called out to a site. A supermarket, right, Kathy?'

He looked at her, appealing with his eyes.

'What are you doing, Martin?' she said.

'They've got Lynne, Kathy, my wife. I spoke to her, she's hysterical. Vexx and Crocker have got her.'

'We're not too impressed with old Martin here at the moment,' Mark said, and gave the solicitor a playful punch on the upper arm that made him shudder. 'Sleeping with the enemy is what we hear.' He pointed an accusing finger at Kathy. 'That right, darling?'

Kathy just stared back. She wondered if it was Tom who'd planted that little seed in their minds.

'Tell them, Kathy!' Martin begged. 'Tell them it isn't true!'

'It isn't true.'

Mark gave a chuckle.

'What do you want?' Kathy asked.

'Dad wants to talk to Brock, about what happened to our brother. You too.'

'You didn't say anything about her,' Martin protested. 'You said it was Brock you wanted.'

'A supermarket, did you say?' Mark mused.

'That'll be Ferguson,' Ricky said. 'The one we spoke to before. In Walworth.'

Mark nodded and opened the vehicle door and got in beside his father. Kathy watched them talking, then turned back to Martin.

'When did this happen, with Lynne?'

'I was playing golf, not much more than an hour ago. I got this phone call. I had to drive over here. They . . .' He glanced at Ricky, still gripping Kathy's arm, so close to her that she could smell the fried onions on his breath and feel the hard lump of the gun under his jacket when he turned. '. . . they'd tried Brock's house, but he wasn't there. They wanted me to find him, and persuade him to come out to the car. They say they just want to talk . . .'

Kathy stared at him and the words died in his throat.

She turned to Ricky. 'What happened to Ivor wasn't Brock's doing. We just wanted Tom Reeves back.'

Ricky gave her a bleak look and said, 'If you say another word I'll smash your face in.'

Mark got out of the car and came over. He took Kathy's shoulder bag and searched her pockets, taking her mobile phone, which he switched off before throwing the lot into the boot of the Merc.

'Okay,' he said, 'get in.'

'Hey, Mark,' Martin protested, without much conviction. 'You don't need her. Let her go, eh?'

They shouldered past him without replying, pushing Kathy into the back alongside Spider, with Ricky close behind. Mark turned back to Martin and pointed at his chest. 'You—go home now and wait. Don't do anything stupid and maybe, just maybe, our black brothers won't be too rough with your missus, right?'

Kathy caught a glimpse of him as the car reversed out and roared away, standing in the roadway, clutching his coat around him as if he were freezing to death.

They drove through Saturday morning shopping streets, past mean brick terraces and concrete tower blocks. After a while, Spider spoke to Kathy for the first time. He didn't change his posture, staring stiffly ahead, but growled, 'Vexx told me what happened Thursday night. Now I want to hear your version.'

Kathy told him, briefly, without elaboration.

He nodded and said, 'Now tell me what Adonia's been telling you.'

She told him some of it, omitting things that they hadn't yet been able to follow up. The old man said no more.

An ambulance was leaving as they swung into the lane leading to the building site. They spotted Wayne Ferguson climbing the steps into his site hut and Mark parked the car and got out. Ricky followed, pulling Kathy out. As she straightened, she found the nose of a gun in her face, Mark's index finger curled around the trigger.

'Behave,' he said, 'or people will get hurt.' He pushed the gun hard into her side and together the two men steered her through the site gates and up to the foreman's hut. As she stepped inside Wayne Ferguson turned and began a smile that froze as he took in the others at her back.

'What do you want?'

Ricky stayed with Kathy while Mark advanced on Ferguson, pointing the gun at his chest.

'Jesus!' The builder's eyes widened.

'You're going to take us to your cottage, Wayne. Give me your mobile.'

As Wayne reached into his pocket, Kathy said, 'You don't need him. Just get him to draw you a map.'

'Don't be soft.' Mark kept his eyes on Wayne as he handed over the phone. 'We might take a wrong turning, and anyway, we don't want him talking to anybody once we're gone, do we?'

They made their way out of the hut, Mark taking up the rear. As they walked towards the gate a man in a hard hat and boots came hurrying up.

'Oh, Mick,' Wayne said, and Kathy felt herself and the two Roach brothers stiffen. 'Will you be all right now? I have to go.'

'That's fine, Wayne. Everything's sorted. See you tomorrow.'

The man marched away and they continued to the Merc. Wayne was prodded into the front with Mark, Kathy as before in the back between Spider and Ricky.

'So,' Mark said, 'M6 is it?'

'Yeah.' Wayne was chewing his lip, face taut.

'Just relax, Wayne,' Mark said soothingly. 'Put your seatbelt on and relax. Everything's going to be fine, as long as you two behave yourselves, okay?'

'Yeah, sure.'

'Lovely day for a trip to the country, eh?'

AS THEY CLEARED LONDON and headed north on the motorway, Mark switched on the radio, occasionally tapping his fingers on the wheel in time to the music. He showed no signs of being unduly distressed at having lost a brother, unlike Ricky, who seemed dangerously angry and morose. Mark made several calls on his mobile phone as he was driving, though Kathy couldn't hear much of what was said. From time to time he would light a cigarette, and Kathy was reminded of family outings when she was small. Her father was a heavy smoker, and as soon as he lit up she would feel the nausea rise in her throat, as automatically as if someone had thrown a switch.

Apart from Mark, hardly anyone spoke.

'So what's this place of yours like then, Wayne? Give us the picture.'

Wayne had sunk into himself, and took a moment to answer.

'It's small—living room, kitchen, two bedrooms. Stone walls, with a slate roof, couple of hundred years old.'

'Nice. Got a view, has it?'

'Yes. It looks out to Moel Fammau.'

'What's that then?'

'It's a mountain, the highest point in the Clwydian Range. From the top you can see Snowdon.'

'So it's wild country? Neighbours?'

'Not really. A couple of farms about a quarter mile in each direction along the lane. The village is half a mile away, down in the valley.'

'Much traffic on the lane?'

'None. It isn't made up and doesn't lead anywhere. It stops at the last farm, at the top of the hill.'

'Sounds ideal,' Mark said, but didn't say what for.

Wayne glanced back over his shoulder at Kathy and she understood the message in his eyes. She was the professional, wasn't she? This was what she had been trained for. Why didn't she do something? But she knew there was little she could do. The Roaches were watchful, and they had done this sort of thing before. Wayne and Kathy were following in the footsteps of the Brown Bread victims.

The traffic grew heavy around Birmingham, and several times the motorway came to a total stop. Mark began to drum his fingers impatiently, and Kathy recalled Wayne's comment to Brock about getting there before dark. With any luck, Brock would have left before they arrived.

'How long's this going to take?' Ricky said. It was the first time anyone had asked, and when Wayne said, 'Another two or three hours,' Ricky said, 'Fuck!' with disgusted surprise, as if he'd imagined the rest of the UK as a narrow fringe just beyond the London boundary. Maybe they flew everywhere.

'I'm hungry,' Ricky said. 'When are we getting lunch?'

Another echo of childhood, her final car journey doomed to be a dark reflection of her first.

'Let's stop at the next service station for a burger,' Ricky said.

Good idea, Kathy thought. She saw Wayne stir hopefully.

'No way. We keep going,' Mark said, but he was wrong, for his father made a rare sound. 'I'll need to pay a visit, son, and get a drink for my pills.'

Mark grunted reluctantly. 'Okay, Dad. There's a place coming up soon, if this fucking traffic would get a move on.'

They turned into the Birmingham North service area, and as soon as the car slowed to a crawl in the car park, Wayne Ferguson slipped his seatbelt, yanked at the door handle and threw himself against the door. Nothing happened. Mark laughed. He pulled to a stop.

'Child-proof locks, old chum.' He pulled the gun out of his pocket and pressed it into the other man's side. Ricky did the same with Kathy.

'Okay, Dad?' Mark said, and released the locks. The old man got out stiffly and hobbled off, and the locks clicked again.

'Actually, I need the toilet too,' Kathy said. 'Urgently.'

'Shut up,' Ricky hissed, as if he was desperate for an excuse to do something violent. Kathy shut up.

Spider returned, got back into the car and handed chocolate bars and bottles of juice to his sons. They set off again, and as they moved north of the Black Country they came upon the first dustings of white over the fields on either side. By Newcastle-under-Lyme it was thick all around, great banks of brown snow piled on the motorway verges, and in the fields beyond black tree skeletons stood stark against dazzling white beneath a dull grey shroud of sky. It looked as if the falls had been very recent, and slush and grit was sprayed over them by the traffic they overtook as they sped up the outside lane.

'When do we turn off?' Mark demanded, and Wayne said, 'Best to keep going until we reach the M56. That's the quickest way.'

Slowly, imperceptibly, the sky was getting darker, though whether this was due to bad weather ahead or the approach of evening was hard to tell. Everyone had headlights on.

They reached the complicated spaghetti of the M56 junction at last, and turned westward, across the lowlands of the Mersey and Dee estuaries, skirting Chester, and then leaving the dual highways for a quieter country of bilingual signs and odd-sounding places—Gwernymynydd, Nercwys and Pant-y-mwyn. An ambulance coming the other way carried the slogan AMBIWLANS, and Mark snorted, 'Can't they fucking spell up here?' Nobody laughed. He lit another cigarette, cracking his window open a fraction to let out the smoke.

Wayne directed them onto ever-narrower roads, until at last they saw the dark spike of a church spire up ahead, and beyond it a tiny pub and a corner store.

'This is the village,' he said. He was looking anxiously at the heavily laden white roofs and hedgerows. 'They've had fresh snow. Lots, by the look of it.'

They slowed to a crawl until Wayne pointed to a break in the bank on the left. 'That's the lane.'

'Blimey, just as well we got four-wheel drive.'

Which Brock didn't, Kathy thought in despair. In their head-lights the lane climbed steeply up the hillside, hard to make out among the rolling white mounds of undisturbed snow. Nothing had been up or down this way since the last snowfall. Mark was swearing as he pushed the pitching vehicle through the drifts, try-ing to keep the momentum, speeding up over a sheltered stretch in the lee of a tall bank, then plunging into deep snow on the far side. They came upon a car abandoned beneath a tree, roof cov-ered with snow, and Kathy recognised it as Brock's. The lane got steeper, the snow deeper, and finally the front of the Merc lurched alarmingly up into space and came crashing down into a deep drift and stalled. Ahead of them, through the frantically thump-ing wipers, they could see a cottage, snuggling into the white folds of the hillside, flickering orange lights glowing from its two front windows like eyes, a pale column of smoke rising from its chim-ney. Beyond it, a dark ridge of woods was almost indistinguishable in the gloom of twilight.

THIRTY-TWO

'THERE IT IS,' WAYNE said, in a flat voice.

'Right. In we go then. You two lead the way, and don't try anything 'cos we're right behind you. You want to stay here, Dad?'

'No way,' Spider growled. 'I've got to be there.'

The sudden shock of cold air stung their faces as they heaved the doors open against the snow. As she slid across the seat, Kathy reached into her pocket for her wallet, which she tucked into a corner of the upholstery. Then they were out in the snow, struggling in it up to their hips. Wayne, still in his site boots, was the only one remotely dressed for this, and they heaved and swore until they managed to clamber through to the shallower snow beyond the drift. The path to the front door gradually became easier, and they could make out signs of snow having been cleared around the cottage, and of human tracks leading to the back. There was some kind of outbuilding, and a mound of snow beneath which the wheel of another vehicle was visible.

They trudged forward, the smell of wood smoke in their lungs, their panting breath forming clouds. As they approached the door, solid braced timber with iron bolts, it swung open, and for a moment the scene froze in the light spilling out of the room as Michael Grant took in the group in front of him. Then Wayne started forward at a run, as if to get into the shelter of the cottage.

There was a sharp bang, and he staggered and fell forward into his friend's arms. Mark shoved his way in after them, pushing them aside, while Ricky jabbed Kathy forward into the doorway. Ahead of her she could see Mark peering through a door on the far side of the room, waving his gun.

'Where's Brock?' he was yelling. 'Where the fuck is Brock?'

Michael Grant was kneeling on the floor, Wayne prone in his arms, while Jennifer Grant sat stunned in an armchair beside the fire, eyes wide with fright. Mark marched across to her and pointed the gun at her head and bellowed at her husband.

'Pay attention! Where is Brock? Tell me or I'll blow her fucking head off!'

Michael looked confused. He seemed transfixed by the blood on his hands, oozing over his jeans. He blinked rapidly, looking up and seeing the terror in his wife's eyes.

Kathy spoke, trying to sound calm. 'Michael, is Brock not here?'

He gulped at her, then stared at the empty door beyond Mark Roach, and said, 'Er, no. He . . . went out.'

'Out?' Mark screamed. 'Where?'

'To . . . to the village. The electricity failed.'

Mark stared at him in disbelief, then turned to his father, who was shuffling towards the other armchair by the fire. The old man didn't look well after his struggle through the snow, with Ricky half-carrying him much of the way. He slumped into the seat and swore under his breath.

Mark pointed his gun at Kathy. 'Close the door. Now, sit on the floor, over there.' He pointed towards Michael and Wayne, who was feebly coughing up blood.

Kathy did as he said.

'Now,' Mark went on, turning to his brother. 'Have another look back there and make sure I didn't miss anything. And get Dad some water.'

Ricky nodded and went off, gun in hand.

'Wayne . . .' Michael said. 'He needs help.'

'Shut up!' Mark's scream, its message of violence barely contained, shocked Michael into silence. 'Brock can't have gone. We didn't see any tracks in the lane coming up here. Where is he?'

'There's a path across the fields. It's easier for walking, you don't get the drifts like you do in the lane.'

Mark narrowed his eyes at Michael, unsure whether to believe him. 'When did he leave?'

'About half an hour ago. He should be back soon.'

'With people?'

'No, alone. He went for more paraffin—for the lamps—and some wine for dinner.'

Kathy reached across to get a better look at Wayne, but Mark yelled at her to stay still. As she straightened, her eyes met Michael's, and for a moment his confused, frightened air was gone, and she thought she saw some message in the hard look he gave her.

Ricky returned with a glass of water. 'There's no sign of him.'

'Right. Then we wait. Which direction is the path?'

Michael pointed to the side.

'We'll need someone out there to watch for him,' Mark said. 'That's you, Ricky.'

'You're kidding. My feet are soaking wet.' He stared down at his trainers and the damp legs of his jeans below the knees. 'I'm freezing,' he muttered.

'Yeah, well, we're all like that. There's some boots by the back door, and you'll probably find dry socks in the bedroom. Get some for Dad and me as well.'

Ricky went out again, looking meaner and angrier with each passing minute.

'See if you can find something to tie them up with while you're at it,' Mark called after him.

BROCK WAS REGRETTING THE whole thing, the long drive up north, the skid into the ditch, and now this ridiculous expedition on foot down to the deserted village. He'd arrived at lunchtime, and after the accident in the lane had trudged up to the cottage carrying the bag of food he'd bought at the supermarket deli outside Chester. As soon as Michael opened the door he sensed the mood of dark gloom inside. The escape to the country clearly hadn't restored their spirits, and both Michael and Jennifer looked worn and deeply depressed, as if the isolation had only compressed and intensified their misery.

While Jennifer set about preparing lunch, Michael explained that they'd have to wait to ask one of the neighbouring farmers for a tractor to pull Brock's car out of the ditch. One was in Liverpool for the day, the other in Wrexham. Then the snow started again, light and picturesque at first, then unbelievably dense. Not long after, the electricity failed. This apparently was not uncommon. The truck with heating oil had been unable to negotiate the icebound lane earlier in the week, and the tank was empty, so they hauled logs in from the pile in the backyard and stoked up the fire and made themselves as comfortable as they could. The air of mild emergency actually seemed to lift their spirits a little.

Brock told them about the events in London, which they hadn't heard about. Michael confirmed Brock's suspicion, that his brother Robbie had warned him before he disappeared that the Roaches were after him, though he hadn't said why, and Michael had always believed they had killed him. Michael gave a bitter laugh at the idea that he and the Roaches could be said to be related, and that he was the uncle of Spider's granddaughter, and although he drew some grim satisfaction from the twist that had led to Ivor Roach's death, the story of violence, especially in relation to Tom Reeves, only deepened their despairing mood again. When Brock told him that he had seen Abigail Lavender, who had told him the truth about the killing of the policeman in Kingston, Michael shook his head sadly.

'That would be the authorised version,' he said, 'put about by my grandmother. I'm afraid the real truth was less palatable. The two cops came after us, as Abigail told you, and when the second one cornered us I was paralysed with fear. Earl's blow only made him stumble, but he did drop his gun. I picked it up and pointed it at him. He put up his hands in surrender. He was barely older than me, and now he was the terrified one. His fear changed me. Suddenly my hands, which had been shaking so violently that I could hardly hold the pistol, became steady. I shot him three times, quite deliberately, as if at a tree stump. It was cold-blooded murder, and I have relived that moment every day since. I have tried to atone for it, but nothing can.'

When the snow stopped, Brock had an overwhelming urge to get out into the fresh air and walk. Their stock of paraffin for the lamps was running low, and he suggested going down to the village for that and a bottle of wine, since it seemed he was going to have to spend the night there with them. Michael was reluctant to leave Jennifer alone without electricity, and described the easier trail down to the valley. At first, the walk across the pristine fields was exactly what Brock needed. He tried to phone Suzanne to describe the scene as he tramped through the snow, but there was no signal. Then the path moved into the woods, and the going became more uneven, and the route slower and harder to make out among the mounds of dead bracken and leaves, the fallen branches and the drifts of snow. The light filtering down through the tangle of branches overhead was becoming dimmer, and it occurred to him that he had left his walk rather late in the afternoon. By the time he finally emerged onto the road at the edge of the village, he was wondering if he would be able to find the route back up the way he'd come.

There seemed to be no one around. The lack of electric lights reinforced the impression of abandonment. The pub was closed and Brock had almost given up when he spied lamplight through the window of the general store. The door was locked, but his knock brought out Mrs Hughes. She told him apologetically that there had been a run on paraffin and all she had left was a single half-gallon can. He bought that, and some candles and matches. There was no wine.

As he made to return he happened to glance at the entrance to the lane further down across the road, and noticed what looked like wide vehicle tracks sweeping into it. When he went to investigate he saw two clear paths of hard-packed snow leading up the hill. With relief he began a quick march up one of them, hoping to get back before the darkness was total.

He came to his car but didn't stop, pressing on along the line cleared by the Roaches' two-tonne vehicle, which he assumed must have been made by one of the farmers. Then, as he approached the turn into the cottage yard, he saw it, lurched at an angle in the deepest drift, and his heart thumped as he remembered the same model in the shadows of the courtyard by his house, the night that Spider and Mark Roach came to call.

He carefully placed the rustling plastic bag with his purchases on the snow, and approached the car as silently as he could, ears straining for sounds. When he reached it, he brushed the snow from the back window and saw the name Roach Motors on a small sticker in the corner. He could see from the disturbed snow around it that all four doors had been opened. The two Roach sons, he thought, and Spider. Who else? Hired help? Vexx? He moved cautiously around, peering into the dim interior. Something, a small dark rectangle, was lying on the backseat. The driver's door wasn't shut properly, and its window was open half an inch. He gripped the door handle and began to pull, then stopped, realising the interior light would come on and alert anyone watching.

How had they found him? He tried to think of the possibilities, but could only come up with Wayne Ferguson. No one else knew both that he'd be here and how to find the place. Was Ferguson the fourth man? And willingly or not? He crouched and moved carefully forward into sight of the cottage, and was alarmed to see no lights at the windows. Perhaps they'd closed the shutters, or put out the lamps. He kept absolutely still, taking shallow breaths, and finally heard the crump of a boot on snow. To the left of the cottage, he thought, and stared into the darkness until his eyes seemed to see movement everywhere. He blinked, turned away then back, and made out the shape of a dark figure against the stone corner of the building.

He badly wanted to get up to the cottage to see what was going on, and tried to picture its layout. The back door was a possibility, but then an image came into his mind of Michael sliding a bolt after they'd brought in the last armful of wood for the fire. The direct route to the cottage, by way of the drive curving around on the right, provided no cover, and he doubted that he could reach it without being seen or heard by the man on the outside. He needed an edge, some help. He assumed they wouldn't have been stupid enough to leave any weapons in the car, but it was worth a look.

He noticed a hazel tree forming part of the hedge alongside the car. Its shoots grew long and straight from the stumps of earlier prunings, and he selected one and very slowly and carefully bent it until it split off with barely a whisper. At the driver's door he fed the thin branch through the window and manoeuvred its end to-wards the light switch. He knew he had to get it just right—too big a push and the switch would go to the on position and light up the car even with the door closed. He was sweating despite the cold, and when the trembling sapling stick failed for the third time to connect with its target he wondered whether this was going to be possible. Then there was a click. He froze, but nothing happened. He eased the door open. No light came on and he slid inside.

He reached to the back and his hand connected with the dark rectangle he'd spotted on the seat, and he held the wallet up to his face. Careless, he thought, then opened it and stiffened as he recognised the familiar outline of the Metropolitan Police card and, even in the dim light reflected from the snow, Kathy's picture.

He thought he understood now. Spider Roach had lost a son, and now he was going to wipe the slate clean. He only hoped that Kathy and Ferguson had made the journey alive.

Brock felt beneath the seats and in the side pockets, but came up with nothing. He reached for the glove compartment handle and opened it, then shut it sharply again as its light came on, but not before he'd seen a small box inside with the symbol of a bullet printed on it. He thought, then eased his coat off, draped it over the dash and glove box and opened the door, feeling inside. No gun, only books and the heavy little box, which he pulled out and pocketed.

He hauled his coat back on and tried his mobile again—still no signal. This was a time for cool, rational thought, but he didn't feel cool or rational. Perhaps the sensible thing would be to run back down the lane and rouse Mrs Hughes, and use her phone to call for help. But where would help come from—Chester? Ruthin? It might take an hour, more. And what might happen in the meantime? No, their help was here. He was it. He got out of the car and recovered the plastic bag, pulling out the can of paraffin and the matches. He took them back to the car and began sprinkling the fluid over the beautiful leather seats, the dashboard, the thick carpets, ending with a trickle over the door ledge. He lit a match in his cupped hands and touched it to the sill, and a blue flame caught, then rippled brightly across the floor. Brock turned and started plunging through the thick snow to the left, partly screened from the cottage by the mounds of snow-covered bushes that surrounded a wide circular patch of clear flat snow, like a lawn, lying directly before the front door. His heart was pounding from the exertion as he strained to hear the reaction.

It didn't take long. There was a shout—'Hey, who's there?'— and then a muffled exclamation and a hammering at the front door. Another yell: 'Mark, the car, the fucking car's on fire!' Brock dropped to his knees behind a snow-mound.

The front door was thrown open, and he saw that the lights inside the cottage had been doused, although there was still the flicker of firelight. Mark said something in an angry rush and started running down the drive to the right, towards the car, gun in hand, leaving Ricky hovering around the open front door. Brock waited a moment, then rose to his feet and stepped though a patch of bracken with a loud crunch. Ricky saw him, and stepped forward, peering at his shape in the gloom.

'You—stay where you are!' Ricky was hurrying forward, brandishing his pistol at Brock who stood quite still. About a third of the way across the clear space between them there was a dull splintering sound as Ricky's boot crunched down into the snow. His next step produced a louder crack, and then he abruptly dropped, disappearing up to his chest through the snow. He gave a loud shriek as freezing water hit his skin. Ricky had discovered the pond.

Brock turned and plunged on around the perimeter of the pond towards the open front door while the Roach brothers bellowed at each other behind him. He reached it and was inside as the first shot banged into the stone wall beside his shoulder. He slammed the heavy door shut and a second shot thumped into it, but didn't penetrate through. He slid the bolts home on the door and turned, gasping for breath, to scan the room. He saw four figures huddled on the floor to the left, a fifth rising out of a chair by the fire to the right. He recognised Spider, angular and gaunt, waving a fist at him and spluttering, 'You! . . . You!' but apparently unarmed.

He ran across to the other group, against the wall in the shadow of the sideboard, and felt a jolt of relief to see movement and hear muffled sounds. He recognised Kathy's blonde hair and as he bent closer saw a patch of brown adhesive bandage across her mouth. He stripped it off and she gulped air.

'Spider . . .' she gasped, and he turned to see the old man at the door, struggling to release the bolts. He ran back and tussled with him, dragging him bodily back to the other group.

Ricky had had trouble finding anything to tie up their prisoners with, and had made do with a length of electrical cable and some bandages and tape from a first-aid kit. Kathy and Michael were already untangling themselves and helping Jennifer. Brock was feeling for a pulse at Wayne Ferguson's throat. He shook his head. 'Dead.'

'That's what you'll be, Brock!' Spider rasped, chest heaving.

Brock got up from Wayne's body and went to search Spider's pockets. He found nothing of use. 'Kathy, see if you can tie him up before he does any more mischief.' He started searching through the drawers of the sideboard, pulling out a carving set, some glasses, a wooden breadboard.

'What else have we got in here?' he urged Michael Grant.

'There are more knives in the kitchen, and some tools. Not much else. The axe is in the shed. There's no gun.'

'All I have is what I found in their car.' Brock pulled out the box of ammunition.

Kathy had taken Spider to a chair and tied his hands behind him, then gone to one of the shuttered windows. 'Ricky's on his hands and knees. Mark's with him. What's wrong with him?'

'Soaking wet and frozen,' Brock replied from the kitchen, where he and Michael were frantically searching cupboards. 'He went through the ice on the pond, like I almost did this afternoon. It won't be long before they come for us.'

He and Michael returned from the kitchen, carrying a box of tools.

'They won't save you,' Spider said.

Kathy slammed the shutter closed. 'Mark and Ricky are coming.'

There was a hammering at the door, a shout to open up.

'Better do as they say,' Spider went on. 'It's you we came for, Brock. You can save your friends. Do what the boys tell you.'

'The way you saved Wayne Ferguson?'

'You'll burn in hell for what you did to my Ivor,' Spider spat at him furiously. 'I should have done for you years ago, when I chased that wife of yours away.'

Brock broke off his search of the toolbox and turned to stare at the old man.

'That's right,' Spider sneered at him, 'chased her out of town I did. Scared the living daylights out of her.' He put on a pathetic whimper, ' "Don't touch me. You mustn't hurt my baby." Did you know she was pregnant, Brock? Eh? Eh?'

Michael Grant broke in, 'Perhaps I can negotiate with them. After all, we've got a stalemate here.'

Spider cackled. 'Not for long. You can't keep my boys out of here. Open the door now and beg for mercy. I'll put in a good word for you . . . For some of you.'

Brock turned to Michael. 'I think right now we need less of the MP and more of the boy from the Dungle.'

Michael stared at him, then nodded. 'You're right.' His eyes dropped to the open toolbox. 'I remember a story my brother told me when I was a kid, about the boy who didn't have a gun.'

There was renewed hammering on the door and angry shouts.

Kathy, peering through the crack in the window shutter to the left, said, 'I can see headlights. Someone else is coming.'

Brock hurried over to Kathy's side and peered out. 'You're right. There's another vehicle out there, turning into the drive.'

'It'll be the farmer up the hill,' Michael said. He had pulled a cordless drill out of the toolbox and was groping through a case of drill bits, his fingers fumbling in his haste.

'What's he like?'

'Almost seventy, about five foot six.'

'Will he have a shotgun?'

'They've just been to Liverpool, shopping,' Michael said.

Brock groaned. 'My God, it'll be a massacre.'

He heard the whine of the electric motor and turned to see Michael drilling a hole in the wooden breadboard, cursing under his breath about the battery not being charged. Brock hadn't the faintest idea what he was trying to do, and the image was so bizarre that he called out, 'Michael, for God's sake, this is no time for woodwork.'

Grant glanced at him with a tight smile, withdrew the drill, and reached for one of the bullets from the box. He lifted the board onto its edge and slid the bullet into the nine-millimetre hole he'd drilled.

'Ah.' Brock looked doubtful. 'Was it a true story?'

Michael met his eye and said, 'I have no idea.'

Just then there was an explosion of shattering glass and splintering timber. They must have found tools, Brock thought—a tyre lever, the axe, a length of wood—whatever it was, they were using

320

it to demolish the other window. Its wooden shutters were shivering and bulging as they worked outside. Brock and Kathy grabbed knives and a monkey wrench and stood each side of it, while Michael called his wife over to hold the breadboard upright on the table while he selected a hammer and a screwdriver from the toolbox.

The shutters burst open with a crash, and the figure of Mark Roach reared up into the void where the window had been. His feet were on the sill, one hand groping the side frame and the other waving his silver pistol. Behind him his brother was pushing him forward, screaming furiously. Brock and Kathy had been forced back by the swinging shutters, and Mark's blazing eyes focused on Michael Grant and his wife directly in front of him. He gave a roar and lifted his gun. Brock watched helplessly as Michael held the point of the screwdriver against the back of the bullet in the board and smacked it with the hammer, like the firing pin of a gun. There was a loud explosion, but not from Mark Roach's gun, which wavered for moment, then dropped as Mark toppled forward into the room. Michael gave a loud whoop, scrambled over him and launched himself through the window at Ricky, the hammer still in his hand.

Brock threw himself at the front door, heaved back the bolts, and ran outside. Michael and Ricky were struggling on the ground, and Brock jumped on Roach, pinning down his right arm while Michael held his left. Ricky squirmed under them, twisting his head from side to side. Then he suddenly stopped struggling. 'Teddy,' he said.

Brock and Michael both looked up to the figure standing silhouetted in the headlights of the newly arrived car, the bulky outline unmistakably that of Mr Teddy Vexx. From his right hand dangled the strap of the machine pistol he was carrying.

'About bloody time,' Ricky gasped. 'Kill these bastards for me, will you, please?'

'My pleasure, Ricky,' Vexx growled. He stepped forward and raised the gun.

There was a single loud report, and Vexx hesitated, then slowly turned. He looked blankly around him for a moment, then toppled backwards into the snow.

In the open doorway of the cottage Kathy lay prone upon the floor, Mark Roach's silver pistol gripped in her hands. She got slowly to her feet, keeping the gun trained on the motionless figure of Vexx. As she came close, she saw his startled expression, eyes open, but moving not a muscle. She thought of the final scene of *Breathless*, Jean-Paul Belmondo lying just like that, flat out on his back in the street after being shot by the cops. Jean Seberg looks down at him and he opens his mouth and a curl of cigarette smoke rises into the air and he says . . .

'Bitch,' Vexx murmured.

Startled, Kathy stared down at him. Had he seen the movie too?

She put her mouth closer to his ear and said, 'That's for Dana and Dee-Ann.'

Vexx's glazed eyes focused momentarily on Kathy and he whispered, '. . . still don't get it.' Then he closed his eyes and died.

THIRTY-THREE

IT HAD BEEN INTENDED as a very low-key affair, a quiet home-coming for Michael Grant to mark his return to normal life and, perhaps, the start of his rehabilitation as a public figure, but it had turned into a great party. As Kathy squeezed through the crowd crammed into his constituency office in Cockpit Lane, she saw that his popularity had only been enhanced by what had happened, and his supporters (more women than men, it had to be said) were there in force. Not that his rehabilitation was being delayed, from what she'd heard. The Jamaican police had confirmed that they had no outstanding warrants or interest in either Michael Grant or Billy Forrest, while the British government had an amnesty on passport irregularities over twenty years old. Although Michael's resignation had been accepted and he had said he would begin a new career in journalism, the strength of support among his constituents was so great that the party machine was urging a rethink.

A jolly woman thrust a plate of food under Kathy's nose. She realised it was codfish fritters—stamp and go—and she felt a stab of regret as she thought of Tom. He wasn't there, although he had been invited. As soon as the hospital had discharged him, legs more or less intact, he'd taken off on his crutches to stay with old friends in Scotland. On her last visit to his bedside they had both felt the sad inevitability of their final parting.

Almost everyone else seemed to be there, though: Bren and Brock, McCulloch and Savage, Winnie Wellington and Abigail Lavender, and from the far end of the room came the sound of music played by Elizabeth Grant together with George Murray, tilting his one good ear to his keyboard.

The noise level was rising steadily. Everyone seemed so happy, Kathy thought, catching a glimpse of Andrea waving her hand to make a point to Brock. He was subtly different since Suzanne had come back, she realised, more open and expansive, and she was glad. She, too, had reason to feel content, since her promotion to inspector had finally been confirmed. She knew that Brock had forced the issue, taking advantage of the hiatus after the business in North Wales to get it through. So, like him, she had come to Cockpit Lane a sergeant and left an inspector. But then, history had done a lot of repeating and echoing over the past weeks, and her pleasure in the evening was spoilt by the uneasy suspicion— no, more than that, a haunting certainty—that it wasn't finished with them yet.

Teddy Vexx's dying words had never left her. She had repeated them over and over in her mind, trying to squeeze every trace of meaning out of them. What had he really meant? That he still didn't get it? Or that she didn't? Neither seemed to make sense. And who was the 'bitch' he'd referred to in his Belmondo moment? She'd assumed it was herself, yet she vividly recalled the look of surprise in his eyes when he'd then focused on her. But how rational was a human brain in terminal shock? How much meaning could one expect to find in those last whispers really, especially by her—traumatised, according to the staff counsellor, by feelings of guilt towards her victim?

The more she'd worried at it, the more convinced she'd become that things were not right. That was the phrase that kept forming in her mind: things weren't right. She'd tried to talk it through with Brock, and he had been enormously patient and supportive, but she could sense his underlying conviction that it was she that wasn't quite right. 'It's a terrible thing to kill someone, Kathy,' he'd said, very gently, 'even when it's unavoidable and necessary, as it was in this case. I know, I understand. You must go through the process. Let them help you.'

She'd become obsessed by Vexx's dying words, she realised that, and accepted that this might be a coping mechanism, concentrating on one little detail to avoid thinking about the big fact that she'd shot and killed a man. But obsession brought other things to the surface: she'd be driving along, noticing the mess in her car, when some thought would strike her and she would have to pull in to the kerb to pester someone over the phone. Or she would wake up in the middle of the night with a forensic image vivid in her mind, and phone Sundeep at his home over breakfast for an explanation. If it had been anyone else, he said, he'd have created merry hell, spoiling his boiled egg like a Bombay telemarketer, but for her he was happy to oblige. Afterwards, he would phone Brock to say he was worried about her.

And this party was more than a welcome home to Michael Grant, she realised. It was also the end of the story, the end of Dee-Ann and Dana's story. She felt suddenly unbearably hot and breathless, and turned towards the shopfront facing out to the Lane. A small boy was standing outside, face pressed so close to the glass that his spectacles were tipped up on his nose. For a moment they stared at each other. Then, as she made towards the door, Adam jumped away and began to run, leaving the marks of his nose and hands on the window. He had been the snowball, she thought, that started an avalanche. If he hadn't made his mad expedition across the railway line, none of this might have happened. As she watched him scampering away she imagined herself returning, like Brock, in twenty-four years' time, and wondered what he would have become. Another Michael Grant? Or the next Spider Roach?

'You look sad.'

Kathy turned to find George standing at her side.

'I'm sad about what happened to you, George,' she said.

He shrugged. 'I'll be all right. Anyway, you took care of Teddy Vexx.'

'Yes.' She looked away.

'You should feel good about that. I wanted to tell you what I saw that night the girls died, but I couldn't. Nobody's that brave or stupid, leastwise, I'm not.'

'What did you see?'

'About one o'clock, I was coming back to Winnie's after practising with the group. I saw his Peugeot standing outside the school and I wondered what it was doing there.'

'Ah.'

'You're mad at me, yeah?'

'No. What else did you see?'

'Mm?' George looked at his feet.

'The other car.'

He shrugged, keeping mum.

Kathy said, 'It's all right, George. I'd worked it out.' It was why they had been unable to connect Ivor Roach to the crime scene. They'd been looking for the wrong car on the CCTV footage.

'I'd better get back to do our next number,' George said.

'Sure.' Kathy watched him shuffle back into the crowd, then retrieved her coat from the pegs behind the door and left.

SHE PULLED HER CAR in at the gates and spoke into the intercom. Magdalen answered.

'What do you want?'

'Is your mother with you, Magdalen?' Adonia was on bail, Kathy knew, while the CPS negotiated with the family lawyers (no longer Martin Connell, of course) over questions of murder and voluntary manslaughter.

'Yes.'

'I'd like to see you both, if I may.'

'Mum can't speak to anyone without her lawyers present.'

'I appreciate that, but this isn't about Ivor's death. I'm on leave at the moment, not on duty. There's something I need to clear up

for my own peace of mind. I know it's an imposition, but it shouldn't take long.'

There was silence, and Kathy was on the point of turning away, but then at last the gates clicked and swung open. She drove to the house and saw Magdalen waiting at the front door. The young woman looked fragile and weightless as she led her silently into the living room, where her mother sat beneath the chandelier. Even before they spoke Kathy saw a marked difference in them both. Adonia sat upright, pale but alert and determined, and all signs of her earlier assault, the bruises and bandages, were gone. Her daughter, on the other hand, seemed utterly exhausted and diminished by what they'd been through.

Adonia spoke first, her voice firm. 'I don't think we should be talking to you. We're both very tired. I think you should come back another day.'

For the second time, Kathy almost left. She really did want to leave, and she felt an awful hollowness in the pit of her stomach, not unlike that she had felt lying on the floor of the cottage, training the pistol on Teddy Vexx.

'Well?'

'I'm sorry. This is a terrible time for both of you. But I have to ask you this.'

Again she hesitated, and again Adonia said impatiently, 'Well?'

'When your car was stolen, Mrs Roach, you told me that your pendant was also taken, and you later found it on the floor of the car. Is that right?'

Adonia looked astonished by the question. The mention of the pendant threw her for a moment. 'Yes. Why?'

'Where exactly did you find it?'

'I can't remember. What is this?'

'You see,' Kathy went on, 'we checked with the people who examined your car when it was recovered. They said they searched it very thoroughly. It would be impossible for them to have missed something like that.'

Adonia stared at her, then said, 'No, you're right of course. It was Ivor who returned it to me. He told me to say I'd found it in the car, but I don't need to lie for him anymore.' Then she added, 'You said you're no longer on duty. Is it because you killed that man?'

'Yes.'

'So we're both the same, you and I. Why are you asking these questions?'

Kathy hesitated, gazing helplessly at one woman, then the other. 'I'm sorry. I have to know. You see we couldn't connect Ivor to Teddy Vexx or Cockpit Lane that night. That was because we were checking the wrong phone records, looking for the wrong car. It wasn't Ivor that got the pendant back, was it, Magdalen? It was you.'

The young woman shuddered suddenly, hugging her arms around herself as if against the cold. 'That bloody pendant,' she said, and began to sob, big tears running down her cheeks.

'Stop it!' her mother said sharply. 'Don't say another word.'

'You got it from Dee-Ann's neck. You pulled it off so hard it left a small lesion.'

'Yes.' Magdalen bowed her head, her whole body rocking back and forth. 'Yes, yes, yes.'

Adonia turned on Kathy. 'Get out! Get out this minute!'

'Vexx phoned Magdalen that night,' Kathy said. 'I've traced the call. And there are CCTV pictures.'

Adonia fell silent, staring in horror at Kathy.

And there would be other evidence, Kathy guessed. It had been so cold the night the girls died, and Magdalen would have worn gloves, which now would carry microscopic traces of barium, lead and antimony from the firing of Brown Bread.

'I asked Teddy Vexx to find out who'd hurt Mum and stolen her pendant.' Magdalen spoke in a gulping rush, as if wanting to bring up something unpleasant she'd swallowed. 'The pendant that meant so much to her.' She gave a bitter shake of her head. 'He phoned me late Thursday night to say he and Jay had found them. I drove to the place they said, next to the school on Cockpit Lane. I took a gun I got from Grandpa's cabinet. I didn't even know if it was loaded, but I wanted to frighten them. I was very angry at what they'd done to Mum. I wanted to scare them to death. Teddy and Vexx had them on their knees. I was shocked when I saw they were girls, but still . . .'

Adonia moved to her daughter's side and put an arm around her. It was the same protective gesture that Magdalen had made to comfort her mother, Kathy remembered, that first time she had spoken to them in this room. 'That's enough, darling,' Adonia said, but Magdalen continued.

'Teddy had found Mum's bag there in the squat, but not the pendant, and the girls refused to say where it was. I screamed at them, but they just sort of laughed, even when Teddy smacked them. So I took out the gun. I had no idea how to cock it and Teddy had to show me what to do. I pointed it to the head of the bigger one. My hand was shaking. But she wouldn't tell me where it was.' Magdalen stared at Kathy as if she still couldn't quite believe it. 'They didn't care, you see. They really didn't care what I did. My finger pressed on the trigger, and then suddenly there was this huge bang and the girl fell over. The other one started screaming, and Teddy took the gun out of my hand. He said he'd have to finish her off too. It was only later that he found the pendant under the scarf around her neck, and he pulled it off for me.'

'Did you tell Ivor?'

'Teddy did. He said he'd contact Da—Ivor the next day and explain what had happened. He said I had to get rid of the gun, and told me a place in Deptford, on the way home, to throw it in the river. But I was so shaken up I forgot, and when I got home I hid it in my cupboard. The next day Ivor went berserk when he heard from Teddy. I was scared and told him I'd got rid of the gun, and he calmed down a bit. Then you started digging up the bodies on the railway land and he started on at me again. I didn't understand why. Later he told me I had to do that stuff with Tom to put things right. That's the truth.'

Kathy didn't doubt it. It had always seemed so implausible for Ivor or his brothers to have risked so much, at that stage in their negotiations with the authorities, by becoming involved in the girls' murders, far less to have failed afterwards to dispose of the gun and then to have left it lying around where Adonia could find it.

'You knew all this, Adonia?' Kathy asked.

The woman nodded. 'I heard Ivor shouting at Magdalen the day after it happened. Of course, I didn't understand all the implications that he saw. It was a judgement on him, a judgement on us all . . . But it was an accident, what Magdalen did. You heard her . . .'

Magdalen had turned into her mother's arms. 'I can't think anymore,' she mumbled. 'I just want to sleep.'

'You will,' Kathy said. 'It'll be much easier when all this is out in the open.'

It was the only lie she'd told that evening, Kathy thought. They sat there in silence for a while, the three of them under the chandelier, weighed down by the burden that the past had placed on them. Finally, Kathy roused herself. She cautioned Magdalen and led the two women out to her car.